THE VIRGIN AND THE GIPSY

and Other Stories

D1125602

THE VIRGIN AND THE GIPSY

and Other Stories

◆

D. H. Lawrence

With an Introduction and Notes by
JEFF WALLACE
University of Glamorgan

WORDSWORTH CLASSICS

In loving memory of
MICHAEL TRAYLER
the founder of Wordsworth Editions

3

Readers who are interested in other titles from
Wordsworth Editions are invited to visit our website at
www.wordsworth-editions.com

For our latest list and a full mail-order service contact
Bibliophile Books, 5 Thomas Road, London E14 7BN
TEL: +44 (0)20 7515 9222 FAX: +44 (0)20 7538 4115
E-MAIL: orders@bibliophilebooks.com

This edition published 1999 by Wordsworth Editions Limited
8B East Street, Ware, Hertfordshire SG12 9HJ
Reset with Introduction and Notes 2004

ISBN 978-1-85326-195-4

Text © Wordsworth Editions Limited 2004
Introduction and Notes © Jeff Wallace 2004

Wordsworth® is a registered trade mark of
Wordsworth Editions Limited

All rights reserved. This publication may not be
reproduced, stored in a retrieval system or
transmitted, in any form or by any means, electronic,
mechanical, photocopying, recording or otherwise,
without the prior permission of the publishers.

Typeset in Great Britain by Antony Gray
Printed and bound by Clays Ltd, St Ives plc

CONTENTS

GENERAL INTRODUCTION

Wordsworth Classics are inexpensive editions designed to appeal to the general reader and students. We commissioned teachers and specialists to write wide ranging, jargon-free introductions and to provide notes that would assist the understanding of our readers rather than interpret the stories for them. In the same spirit, because the pleasures of reading are inseparable from the surprises, secrets and revelations that all narratives contain, we strongly advise you to enjoy this book before turning to the Introduction.

General Adviser
KEITH CARABINE
Rutherford College, University of Kent at Canterbury

INTRODUCTION

David Herbert Lawrence (1885–1930) occupies a secure position in that tradition of early-twentieth-century innovation and experiment in literature and the arts which we now, retrospectively, call modernism. Like British contemporaries such as Virginia Woolf and James Joyce, Lawrence took the forms of realist fiction and made of them something radically new. Yet certain characteristic features of Lawrence's work insist on the need to distinguish it from the modernist aesthetic as it is found in Woolf and Joyce. We associate modernism with a turn towards what T. S. Eliot called 'impersonality', towards highly symbolic languages of abstraction and difficulty designed to represent the new complexities of experience in a world of rapid, bewildering change.[1] With, perhaps,

1 For a vivid account of modernism and modernity in this light, see Berman. For full details of this and other references turn to the Bibliography at the end of this Introduction.

Joseph Conrad's magnificent and troubling novella *Heart of Darkness* (1899) as a starting point, modernist literature seems often to be founded on a conviction of its own inadequacy in the face of such complexities, drawing attention to our imprisonment within the limits of expression and representation.

To read Lawrence, on the other hand, is to become aware of a strong, personal authorial presence, and of a didactic, even prophetic tone which his art seems powerless to disguise. Against all the dictates of modernist impersonality, Lawrence persisted in wanting to *tell* his readers things: 'I do write,' he insisted in a letter to A. W. McLeod in 1913, 'because I want folk – English folk – to alter, and have more sense' (Boulton [ed.], p. 544). To remedy a condition of 'atrophy' in the England of his birth, Lawrence proposed a 'readjustment between men and women', a 'making free and healthy' of the sexual relation, which he was to pursue in the symbolic forms of his fiction. Here, in other words, we have the D. H. Lawrence of popular cultural mythology – a 'Priest of Love', whose answer to the discontents of civilisation was a rediscovery of authentic, uncontaminated sexuality. This image of Lawrence gained ground in the 'swinging' 1960s, an era for which the lifting of the censor's ban on *Lady Chatterley's Lover* in 1960 was an inaugural event.

The essentially oppositional nature of Lawrence's writing may be explained by a life in which he appeared forever caught between worlds. While Woolf, the daughter of Leslie Stephen, was effectively born into the English literary establishment, and Joyce was of respectable Dublin middle-class stock, Lawrence was the son of a Nottinghamshire collier, and grew up in the East Midlands mining village of Eastwood. His mother was of genteel origins, and in his early life he saw played out in his parents' relationship the tensions between bourgeois aspirations and the patterns of working-class culture. Lawrence was stimulated into intellectual life by non-conformist religion and by the advanced literary and political ideas of his Eastwood circle. But, in a classic paradox, the intellectuality which he derived from a vibrant working-class culture became the very means of his flight from it. After scholarship, university and a taste of schoolteaching, in the spring of 1912 Lawrence scandal-ously fled abroad with Frieda Weekley, the wife of his university languages tutor and a member of a famous German aristocratic family, the von Richthofens. His commitment to a life of writing became entwined with a nomadic existence with Frieda, confirming a distance both from established, bourgeois literary culture and from the close-knit communities of his origins. It is true that Lawrence quickly became well connected in the literary world, the distinctiveness of his writing and of his working-class origins giving him a unique position; but the question of belonging remained forever open and unsettled.

All of the stories in the present collection were published between the mid-1920s and 1930, towards the end of a life tragically cut short by tuberculosis. Whilst they therefore highlight some characteristic features of Lawrence's later fictional writing, belonging essentially to the period in which his last great novel, *Lady Chatterley's Lover*, was being drafted and redrafted, one story provides an unusual opportunity to view a continuity of concerns across the early and later periods of his work. 'Love Among the Haystacks' was first drafted in 1911, but the story was revised and published in 1930, the year of Lawrence's death.

'Love Among the Haystacks' typifies the meticulous realism of Lawrence's early fiction, whether in the vivid and detailed evocation of the agricultural landscape in which the Wookey brothers are working, or in the carefully observed East Midlands vernacular spoken by the brothers. The reader only has to note a pattern in the opening sentences of some of the later stories – 'There was a woman who was beautiful . . . ', 'There was a man who loved islands . . . ', 'There was a peasant near Jerusalem . . . ' – to sense a marked contrast between the painstaking descriptive rendering of the early mode and the blithe, almost offhand, fairytale sketching of the later. However, it is soon plain that there is more at stake in the early story than the faithful reflection of a rural way of life. A sense of dangerous rivalry and antagonism between Maurice and Geoffrey is quickly established. Maurice, a year younger, has upstaged Geoffrey in the affections of Paula, the vicar's young *au pair*, and his taunts prompt a barely suppressed impulse in Geoffrey, 'flushed with hate', to stamp on his brother's mouth. The story's analysis of the conflict then moves equally swiftly from the immediate circumstances of mood or temper into a diagnosis of a whole condition of being: Geoffrey's 'inflamed self-consciousness was a disease in him', and there was 'a danger of his sinking into a morbid state, from sheer lack of living, lack of self-interest' (pp. 76–7).

Two features of this analysis are both distinctively Lawrentian and noticeably modernist, and we will soon encounter them again in the other stories in the volume. First, life histories are delineated with brushstrokes of striking economy, as if the equivalent in writing of the Cubist techniques of the great French modernist painter Paul

Cézanne, for whom Lawrence had such admiration. In the space of a short paragraph, we learn that Maurice and Geoffrey had been brought up by 'a proud mother, a stranger in the country', placing barriers both of class and of sexuality between them and all other women, so that they had grown up 'virgin but tormented' (p. 77). Second, there is an unmistakable preoccupation with the unconscious motivations behind conscious behaviour. While Lawrence was to express reservations about the theories of Sigmund Freud, he shared with Freudian psychoanalysis a sense of the intimate relation between psychological repression and physical expression. States of being thus appear as bodily habits and gestures: Geoffrey's blue eyes are 'unsteady', his mouth 'morbidly sensitive', his whole face 'sullen', his hand 'slack with brooding'. Maurice's face, that of 'a young man roused for the first time in passion', reflects the unanticipated sexual success which prepares the ground for subsequent dramatic events to unfold.

In Geoffrey Wookey we find an emblematic figure whose significance resonates through the later stories of this volume. Geoffrey's life is thwarted, arrested by a lack of fulfilment through human contact. Overcoming this impasse becomes, both literally and metaphorically, a matter of life or death. The damned-up forces of Geoffrey's suppressed life-impulse are momentarily expressed in the struggle on the haystack, when Maurice's fall threatens both of them with oblivion. Geoffrey briefly contemplates suicide, for at least in death there would be an absolute certainty and finality; were he to live and Maurice to die, his would henceforth be a death-in-life, a 'shrinking', 'coiling up in himself like a tortoise with no shell' (p. 82). Yet neither brother is to die; rather, each is to be delivered into life by the discovery of human warmth. Both of the women concerned, Paula and Lydia, are outsiders, on the cultural or social margins of the narrow world of the Wookeys. The foreignness of the tempestuous Paula (the narrative seems unable to decide whether she is a Pole or a German), with her restless search for 'life', is a challenge to the confined Englishness of the vicar, 'a rather pale, cold man', who expresses relief that this 'wild thing – disobedient and insolent', has only three weeks of her tenure left. She and Maurice are soon engaged, though not before her passionate anger at the suspicion that Maurice had tricked her into spending the night with him on the haystack has run its course. Acting as a corrective to Maurice's earlier gloating, this device underlines the fact that the real revelation of the story is Geoffrey's encounter with the vagrant's wife, Lydia. In a scene of delicate intensity, which anticipates the ending of *The Virgin and the Gipsy*, Geoffrey warms Lydia's freezing feet, the prelude to 'his first love kiss' and the night in each other's arms.

Readers may be surprised, again, at the swiftness of events, and at the lack of the conventional romantic trappings of courtship in the story. Geoffrey feels profound 'tenderness' as he wakes to gaze upon Lydia's face, and the attachment is already decisive: 'With her to complete him, to form the core of him, he was firm and whole. Needing her so much, he loved her fervently' (p. 103). Within minutes, he is asking her to marry him and emigrate to Canada with him. This, however, is only partly explicable in the historical context of a time when a night of passion might oblige the participants to marriage and a lifetime's commitment. Again and again in Lawrence's fiction, the value of genuine human contact and communication can change a life; this is embodied in a vocabulary of touch and warmth, the 'tenderness' which is felt at last by the 'man who died' in this volume, and which Lawrence was to propose as an alternative title for *Lady Chatterley's Lover*. By contrast, the trappings of romantic love and fine feeling were for Lawrence more likely to obstruct than to facilitate this flow of human connection.

To turn from this early story to a later one, 'The Lovely Lady' (1927), is to find the model of Geoffrey's thwarted, repressed life echoed both in Robert Attenborough and in his cousin Cecilia. The two share a curious *ménage* with the overweening 'lovely lady', Pauline Attenborough, mother to Robert and aunt to Cecilia, in a 'quite exquisite though rather small Queen Anne house some twenty-five miles out of town'. The fact that this is 'an ideal place and an ideal life for Aunt Pauline' will immediately place experienced readers of Lawrence on the alert. Far from being something to strive for, the 'ideal' characterises the tendency, which Lawrence found on a grander historical scale in Christian doctrine and in post-Enlightenment democratic modernity, to substitute ideas of perfection for the messy physical realities and contradictions of life itself.[2] Sure enough, the ideal is literally embodied in the figure of Pauline herself, in the form of an indomitable egotism which effectively represses her own ageing and enables her to 'wonderfully preserve' the appearance of a thirty-year-old.

2   See, for example, Lawrence, 'Democracy', in *Phoenix*, pp. 699–718.

The motif of this story is the museum, a symbol of Western imperial modernity which wrests things, often forcibly, out of their contexts and turns them into objects of contemplation in pristine, artificial settings. Pauline has turned herself into just such a fetish, and the enormous energy expended upon the preservation of exquisite objects is at the expense of the lives of her sons. 'Ciss' knows that Henry, the elder son who died at the age of twenty-two, was killed by his mother's 'poisonous' opposition to his passionate attachment to the actress Claudia; she also knows that the lovely lady is in the process of killing her younger son, 'convulsed with shyness', whose life is a 'negative affair' (p. 118). Ciss suspects that Pauline wishes she and Robert to marry, but only after her death, by which time Robert will be 'the shell of a man who had never lived'. The issue is posed with the characteristically dramatic clarity and intensity of Lawrence's stories: can Pauline's egotism be allowed to sap the lives of her young people? Who is to live, she or they? When the grotesque comic bathos of the sun-bathing scenario begins, Ciss realises that 'one of them would surely have to die' (Lawrence was writing 'The Lovely Lady' for a book of murder stories collected by Cynthia Asquith). When Ciss strikes through Pauline's psychological armour, the lovely lady begins to crumple and shrivel, in a process of transformation worthy of a low-budget horror movie. Lawrence deftly uses Gothic conventions for the purposes of his own critique: Pauline dies having had her mirrors taken away from her and having been condemned as the vampire who 'put a sucker into one's soul and sucked up one's essential life' (p. 124). The open ending allows the reader to assume that Ciss and Robert can live happily ever after, but not without the warning that idealism is so powerful and difficult to root out, it can endure beyond the grave, in the form of the 'Pauline Attenborough Museum'.

The vengeful, murderous impulses at work in such stories can be disconcerting for readers of Lawrence. We are reminded of the infamous judgement of the philosopher Bertrand Russell, who after a brief but finally acrimonious collaboration with Lawrence in 1915 declared that his theories of 'blood knowledge', of the primary powers of the instincts over and above the rational, intellectual faculty, led straight to Auschwitz.[3] If Lawrence wanted folk to overcome the 'atrophy' of their instincts, what kind of dangerous everyday advice might his writings imply? It is, however, perhaps timely to reflect here upon the symbolic function of all fictions. Are the deathly actions in the stories really practical recommendations for everyday life, or are they a kind of narrative language, which allowed Lawrence to articulate the very existence of those unconscious forces or motives most threatening to civilised society? At their best, the stories demonstrate how far such psychological forces are *themselves* the complex products of a whole social order, and not simply reactions to it. The most eloquent example of this is the long title story or novella of this volume, *The Virgin and the Gypsy*. Here, the familiar pattern of repression extends to the Saywell family as a whole, with Granny or 'the Mater' eternally prolonging her life at the expense of those existing within her shadow: Aunt Cissie, 'gnawed by an inward worm'; Uncle Fred, who 'just lived dingily for himself', and the rector, Arthur, an 'utter unbeliever' at heart. Yvette and Lucille look set to be the victims of this pattern in the next generation. Scandalously forsaken by their mother Cynthia, whom they remember bringing a 'great glow, a flow of life' into their previous home, 'like a swift and dangerous sun', the young women can only seek distraction in aimless motor excursions with their well-heeled friends, finding there the predictable reproduction of the rituals of courtship and marriage.

How can their lives be resolved? Where might a life-belief be found, to set against the unbelievers? In Yvette's encounter with the alluring gipsy, the story seems to flirt dangerously with cliché. Foreigner and social outcast combine in the figure of Joe, 'one of the black, loose-bodied, handsome sort'. Yvette's heart jumps at the first sight of him, and something 'took fire in her breast' when their eyes meet: 'She thought: "He is stronger than I am! He doesn't care!"' (p. 18). Prim English rose finds love at first sight with dark, handsome stranger? Lawrence, however, cannot leave the story stranded at this level of romantic convention. First, Yvette encounters another alternative to the established order of things, in the form of the Eastwoods. As John Turner has noted in a fine essay on the story, the timing of their arrival – Yvette is about to step, entranced, into the gipsy's caravan – wrenches the story out of the familiar ballad tradition of 'Wraggle Taggle Gypsies', in which 'a woman throws over all the advantages of class, education and wealth in order to roam the wildness of nature with her chosen gipsy' (Turner, p. 143). Instead, the site of seduction is dangerously relocated, from the caravan to the rectory, from a position beyond the pale to a position at the heart of Christian bourgeois society. Second, the extraordinary resolution of the story suggests how deeply problematic is the task of challenging and successfully breaking free from social convention – so problematic that it can only be represented in mythical form, in precisely that mode of the imaginative expression of desire which is unavailable to the rational, materialistic Saywells. Joe, himself a 'resurrected man' after his brush with pneumonia during the war, appears bounding around the bend of the road with the flood close behind him, an image of dammed-up forces finally released: 'a shaggy, tawny wave-front of water advancing like a wall of lions' (p. 66). Yvette was 'barely conscious: as if the flood was in her soul'. Only in this dreamlike, semiconscious state can the two come together in a mutually warming sleep, Yvette waking to find the sun 'shining in heaven'. However, the gipsy has subsided, like the dream figure he always was, and is replaced in Yvette's suspended bedroom, as a reminder of the dogged persistence of conscious, conventional life, by the hapless figure of the policeman.

The flood is necessary, then, not just for the purposes of Yvette's personal and sexual transfiguration. It strikes precisely at the source of a wider malaise: the house, and the Mater with it. Lawrence reserves some of his most mischievous invective for the domestic situation in this story, with Granny slobbering her food and rifting in 'gross physical complacency' as she presides over crossword puzzles 'invented by Satan himself' (p. 11). There seems little doubt that Lawrence, like our contemporary Alan Bennett, had first-hand experience of the deadening rituals of lower-middle-class life – 'the eternal and everlasting piece of bought cake' (p. 13) – though in Lawrence it surely forms the basis of a more searching critique of a taboo-ridden bourgeois culture. Here again Lawrence is typically modernist, as he homes in on the fraught issues of food and cleanliness, thus sharing with Gertrude Stein and Franz Kafka a capacity to expose the inner, psychic neuroses behind bourgeois respectability.[4] The counterpart to Granny's voracious, indiscriminate appetite is Cissie's anorexic hatred of food, both expressing a denial of healthy bodily life and the production of the waste that necessarily accompanies it. Dirt, whether literal or metaphorical, cannot be acknowledged; hence the elaborate sanitation systems of the twentieth-century house. But to stigmatise dirt and the body is, precisely, to sully life itself through a false idealisation of it, just as

4 See Stein, *Three Lives*, and Kafka, *Metamorphosis*.

Lawrence argued that pornography was created, as a concept, by the very people who sought to repress it.[5] Like the museum of 'The Lovely Lady', then, the modern house is the literal embodiment of a repressive social structure, just as the Saywells must 'say well', at whatever cost to the truth. Yvette's thoughts are a summation worth pausing upon:

> Only she lay and wished she were a gipsy. To live in a camp, in a caravan, and never set foot in a house, not know the existence of a parish, never look at a church. Her heart was hard with repugnance against the rectory. She loathed these houses with their indoor sanitation and their bathrooms, and their extraordinary repulsiveness. She hated the rectory, and everything it implied. The whole stagnant, sewerage sort of life, where sewerage is never mentioned, but where it seems to smell from the centre to every two-legged inmate, from Granny to the servants, was foul. If gipsies had no bathrooms, at least they had no sewerage. There was fresh air. In the rectory there was *never* fresh air. And in the souls of the people, the air was stale till it stank (p. 27).

Joe is, then, far more than a means of romantic deliverance for Yvette. As a gipsy, he represents a long-established oppositional culture (always stigmatised as dirty by the middle-classes, yet scrupulously clean in Lawrence's story), committed to alternative forms of labour and livelihood, property-owning and family relations (Turner, p. 158). The house, and Granny with it, must go, the apparent solidity of the bourgeois world undermined by an earlier (though equally social, perhaps Roman) structure, a tunnel 'unsuspected, undreamed of'.

This critique of the bourgeois-capitalist order of things is even more pointed in 'The Rocking-Horse Winner', ostensibly a tale of the power of psychic forces. The story was a contribution to another Cynthia Asquith anthology, this time of ghost stories. The house is again the key motif, and Paul's house is indeed 'haunted'. But the whispered phrase *'There must be more money!'* is scarcely an other-worldly phenomenon: more evidently, it is the actual crystallisation of a pervasive materialism, a sign of how deeply greed can embed itself in the human consciousness. The whisper – 'nobody ever said it aloud' – recalls the repressive model of the 'say wells',

5 See, for example, Lawrence, 'Pornography and Obscenity', in *Phoenix*, pp. 170–87.

compounding two forms of artificial or idealised appearance. First, Paul's mother cannot love her children, and covers her coldness by being 'all the more gentle and anxious' for them, 'as if she loved them very much'. Second, entangled with this dissembling is the need to 'keep up' a prosperous middle-class social position or image without the resources to do so. 'Luck' is the form of mystification or self-deception by which the mother justifies her dissatisfaction, and it becomes the central ironic device of the story. Luck for Paul, we feel, would be love and warmth from his mother, and thereby an exorcising of the spirit of cold, hungry materialism with which he and his sisters must live. In desperation to gain his mother's approval, however, Paul discovers that 'luck' is simply 'what causes you to have money' (p. 136). Lawrence here uses the potent fictional device of the innocent perspective of the child to devastating effect. Paul's uncanny ability to pick winning horses is not so much a form of supernatural mediation as an extension of the Romantic conception of the child as a highly impressionable, sensitive and receptive instrument. Through a supreme exertion of will, Paul can see into the future, but only at the expense of his fragile life. His mother ironically misreads his nervous condition, attributing the 'damage' to the vice of gambling rather than to the money-system to which she is enslaved, and which turns all human activities towards the principles of mechanism and calculation.

' "It seems to me, men and women have really hurt one another so much, nowadays, that they had better stay apart till they have learned to be gentle with one another again . . . Now, it's only each one fighting for his own – or her own – underneath the cover of tenderness" ' (*St Mawr and Other Stories*, p. 122), reflects Lou Witt, the central character in Lawrence's novella *St Mawr*. Lawrence's writing consistently reapproaches this view that the exploitative nature of an industrial-capitalist society finds expression in the most intimate areas of human experience. A materialistic individualism interposes itself between people, making relationship itself impossible – relationship being, as the critic Raymond Williams puts it, 'precisely an alternative to the use of others as raw material' (Raymond Williams, p. 213). Lawrence's stories thus exhort their readers to a kind of critical vigilance, ever on the alert for the ways in which exploitation can work by stealth, masking its damage beneath the *appearance* of tenderness. The stories show us individuals who are particularly adept at inculcating a false consciousness, deceiving themselves, if not others, as to their motives: Paul's mother, who seems to know but cannot act on the true nature of her son's degeneration; Granny Saywell, who is able to believe her own lie about 'half-depraved stock'; Pauline Attenborough, whose monologues with her dead son maintain a state of self-delusion.

In this light, and despite Lawrence's reputation for popularising a version of free love, the last thing his fictions endorse is relationship at any cost. On the contrary, an equally strong tendency, especially in his later work, is towards the proud disavowal of human contact. The two other substantial stories in this volume, 'The Man Who Loved Islands' and 'The Man Who Died', demonstrate this tendency towards singleness and isolation. At this time a sense of disillusionment, born out of what Lawrence once referred to as the frustration of his 'instinct' of community, seems to become transferred to the act of writing itself. Thus in February 1926, in between the completion of *The Virgin and the Gipsy* and the composition of 'The Rocking-Horse Winner', Lawrence declared himself 'really awful sick of writing', much preferring to paint; in the spring of 1927, whilst revising 'The Lovely Lady', he continually alludes to the attractions of a hermit life: 'I feel like turning hermit and hiding away the rest of my days from everybody' (Sagar, pp. 149, 162).

This is not quite the decision of the islander in Lawrence's story, for he wants an island 'not necessarily to be alone on it', but to be Master, in a world of his own making. The story, however, satirises the contradictions within a Utopian impulse which is also an act of egotism by demonstrating that he needs three attempts at his plan, each time becoming rather more desolate and drifting further towards an open but ominous conclusion. Again the money system cannot be evaded, the first island having the ability to make a hole in his capital 'as if it were an octopus with invisible arms stealing from you in every direction' (p. 158). Neither, it seems, can he escape from debased human relationship, despite the second island being no longer a 'world' but simply a refuge. In 'falling' into an affair with the widow's daughter, Flora (an ironical reference to his safer passion for the earnest cataloguing of the wild flowers of the islands), the islander soon finds himself faced with the prospect of family responsibility and domesticity – 'They might have been a young couple in Golders Green' (p. 164). This, apparently, has been the wrong kind of sex: automatic, mechanical, 'driven by the will' on Flora's part, even though she too, 'in her true self', hadn't wanted it. Having failed to meet on that 'third rare place' where the true 'crocus-flame' of desire between man and woman might burn, the islander is already arranging his own third place, edging towards obliteration through a state of withdrawal from organic life whereby even the 'lumps of sheep' appear to him hideous and gross. The encroaching snow is a familiar Lawrentian ending (see, for example, the fate of Gerald Crich in *Women in Love*), connoting the tragic decline of Western 'man' into the wastes of frozen rationality and materialism.

If, however, for a moment we strip away this grand metaphysical scheme from Lawrence's stories, an alternative pattern or interpretation can begin to emerge. According to this interpretation, the islander's action becomes a rather more familiar form of desertion, in which the man escapes the impending 'millstone' by going off to seek his own destiny, leaving the woman, Flora, with the responsibility of the child. Woman, in a version of the biblical myth, is the temptress threatening to expel man from paradise, and from motives which are more worldly than transcendent. Flora might weep when the islander announces that 'he had to go away for a time', but Lawrence has her revive noticeably when the islander hands over his chequebook. At the beginning of the 1970s, after a decade in which Lawrence's reputation had enjoyed some revival in the post-Chatterley era of sexual emancipation, feminist critics like Kate Millett began to question the sexual politics of his fictions, arguing that the terms of liberation were for and on behalf of men, leaving women in a familiar subordinate position. In recalling her adolescent response to the 1922 novel *Aaron's Rod*, which clearly bears some structural similarity to 'The Man Who Loved Islands', Sheila Macleod gives a classic illustration of how a gendered perspective can help us to read against the grain of Lawrence's fictions:

> The beginning of *Aaron's Rod*, where Aaron walks out on his wife and children just before Christmas, enraged and frightened me to an extent I would not have been able to admit. I didn't want to know what happened to Aaron. I wanted to know what happened to Lottie Sisson without her husband and to Millicent and Marjory without their father. It was as if Lawrence had wiped them out, relegated them to some sub-world not worth writing about. But this world of women and children was the only world I knew.[6]

This critical angle can profitably inform our reading of 'The Man Who Died', a beautiful and melancholy tale whose overtly mythic structure clearly summarises many of the Lawrentian

6 MacLeod, p. 2

preoccupations found elsewhere in this volume. It is, of course, *the* Resurrection story, of a man restored to life, prefigured by the cockerel which, though eventually re-tethered (the original title of the story, based on its first half, was 'The Escaped Cock'), continues to cry out the 'triumph of life'. But Lawrence's rewriting of the Christian myth contains a number of further distinctive turns. First, this Christ experiences the rebirth of an actual life of the body, not simply a prelude to heavenly ascension. Despite the vibrant example of the cock, there is nothing ideal about this experience: after the peace of desirelessness, life hurts, and Christ is filled with nausea and disillusion. He thus rejects the importunities of Madeleine (or Magdalene, another worldly-woman figure whose eyes flicker with 'the greed of giving'), not because he is about to ascend but on the contrary because he has now 'outlived' his mission, and must devote himself to his own withdrawal into the phenomenal world: ' "I can learn to be alone." ' Lawrence's Christ acts, then, as a vehicle for the critique of Christian doctrine: the 'compulsion' to love is a form of idealist tyranny, warping the true feelings and shielding us from an authentic experience of the world in its 'vast complexity of entanglements and allurements' (p. 190).

The 'phallic' second half of the tale decisively completes the act of revision. Here Lawrence merges the Christian myth with another myth of resurrection, that of Osiris, this time from pagan mythology. Modernist writers, notably T. S. Eliot, had become interested in the rehabilitation of ancient knowledges and cultural forms as alternatives to a sceptical and exhausted modernity, and a widely influential source of ideas was J. G. Frazer's *The Golden Bough*, published in twelve volumes between 1890 and 1915. Lawrence's reading in anthropology included Frazer, and he would have found there the components of the Isis and Osiris myth. In ancient Egypt, Osiris was worshipped as a god of fertility who, when alive as a king, advocated techniques of early agriculture which took him travelling around the world. Osiris suffered a violent death, his body dismembered into fourteen parts, but after much searching they were recovered by his wife Isis, save for his genitals, which had been eaten by a fish. In a sacred rite aided by her sister and a messenger of the sun-god Ra, Isis succeeds in reviving Osiris, who then reigns as king of the dead in the other world. Combined thus in the episode of Osiris are the ideas of bodily resurrection and, in his image as 'corn-god', the seasonal growth and decay of the vegetable world.

The encounter between Christ and the priestess of Isis in

Lawrence's story is thus an almost programmatic fusion of two religious tendencies, the Christian and the pagan. As in Eliot's *The Waste Land*, the possibility of a renewed sense of the sacred in the modern is seen to lie in an imaginative – or imagined – transaction between theologies. The priestess has remained pure, finding in the military men of Rome and Egypt – even Antony himself – an 'inward meanness' and 'inadequacy'. Instead, heeding the words of an old philosopher – ' "rare women wait for the reborn man" ' – she waits for 'the lotus to stir'. Like Yvette and the gipsy, the effect of transfiguration is swift when it happens: 'For the first time, she was touched on the quick at the sight of a man, as if the tip of a fine flame of living had touched her' (p. 197). Likewise the Christ-figure finds in her the tenderness and warmth which will complete his 'destiny of splendour': she is 'sunshine', 'a tender flame of healing'. Their lovemaking gives a scandalously physical twist to the resurrection theme: 'I am risen!' (p. 209).

Kate Millett has noted that behind Lawrence's 'resurrection of the body' narratives there usually lurked 'the transformation of masculine ascendancy into a mystical religion' (Millett, p. 238). Certainly, beneath the lyricism of 'The Man Who Died' there could be said to be a weary predictability to the course of events – not only the phallic supremacy of the man, for which alone the priestess has been waiting, but the subsequent desertion of the pregnant woman after he has 'sowed the seeds' of his life. The mythic dimensions of the tale cannot obscure its sexual politics; it was, we remember, written in the late nineteen-twenties. Yet the critical debates around Lawrence's work go on, testifying in the end to a slipperiness and open-endedness which perhaps belies the image of the hectoring counsellor and preacher. Readers will decide for themselves how far his stories are 'hymns to the phallus', or how far they dramatise a sexual mutuality, women such as Yvette, Cecilia or the priestess showing a resolute independence which often involves a rejection of conventional models of masculinity. Even in as slight and unsatisfactory a story as 'Rawdon's Roof' – the only real evidence in this volume that Lawrence might have been weary of writing – a pervasive satirising of men's inability to form healthy and open relationships with women seems to be at issue. From the perspectives of gender studies today, Lawrence's analysis of sexual morality and relationship could be said to encompass the trials and tribulations of the constructed categories of femininity *and* masculinity in equal measure; some critics have already begun to suggest that Lawrence's significance is to be far less 'straightforwardly sexist' than was once thought.[7]

Thus, at the outset of the twenty-first century, with gender boundaries and modes of human relationship constantly open to new challenges and redefinition, the re-publication of these stories of resurrection might represent a cultural moment at which Lawrence's writing undergoes its own, periodic resurrection – not just for its continuing critical exploration of the constraining and liberating potential of our ideas of ourselves, but also for its enduring, intrinsic power and subtlety as literary expression.

JEFF WALLACE
University of Glamorgan

7   See Carter, 'Lorenzo as Closet-queen', and Linda Ruth Williams, *Sex in the Head*.

BIBLIOGRAPHY

Marshall Berman, *All That is Solid Melts into Air: The Experience of Modernity*, Verso, London 1983

James T. Boulton (ed.), *The Letters of D. H. Lawrence, Vol. I (September 1901–May 1913)*, Cambridge University Press, Cambridge 1979

Robert Burden, *Radicalizing Lawrence: Critical Interventions in the Reading and Reception of D. H. Lawrence's Narrative Fiction*, Editions Rodopi, Amsterdam–Atlanta 2000 – a new study of Lawrence from the perspectives of critical theory, with two substantial chapters on 'Deconstructing Masculinity' in the 1920s fictions

Angela Carter, 'Lorenzo as Closet-queen', in *Nothing Sacred*, Virago, London 1982 – playful and irreverent analysis of Lawrence's writing-as-cross-dressing, as in, for example, the preoccupation with women's clothing in *Women in Love*

David Ellis, *D. H. Lawrence: Dying Game 1922–1930*, Cambridge University Press, Cambridge 1998 – final volume of the new exhaustive CUP biography of Lawrence, covering the later phase of his life and writing

Anne Fernihough (ed.), *The Cambridge Companion to D. H. Lawrence*, Cambridge University Press, Cambridge 2001 – scholarly essays providing an excellent introduction to Lawrence

J. G. Frazer, *The Golden Bough: A Study in Magic and Religion* (Abridged Edition), 1922, Macmillan, London and Basingstoke 1976

Virginia Hyde, *The Risen Adam: D. H. Lawrence's Revisionist Typology*, Pennsylvania, Pennsylvania State University Press 1992 – on ecclesiastical images in Lawrence's work, including a chapter on the theme of resurrection in 'The Man Who Died'

Franz Kafka, *Metamorphosis and Other Stories*, Penguin, Harmondsworth 1983

D. H. Lawrence, *Phoenix: The Posthumous Papers, 1936*, ed. Edward D. McDonald, Penguin, Harmondsworth 1978

D. H. Lawrence, *St Mawr and Other Stories*, ed. Brian Finney, Cambridge University Press, Cambridge 1983

Sheila MacLeod, *Lawrence's Men and Women*, Heinemann, London 1985

Kate Millett, *Sexual Politics*, 1971, Abacus, London 1972 – the chapter on Lawrence was a seminal early feminist study, preceded only by Simone de Beauvoir's *The Second Sex* (1949)

Edward Nehls, *D. H. Lawrence: A Composite Biography*, 3 vols., University of Wisconsin Press, Madison 1957, 1958, 1959 – substantial compilation of biographical and autobiographical material

Keith Sagar, *D. H. Lawrence: A Calendar of His Works*, Manchester University Press, Manchester 1979 – an invaluable month-by-month summary of Lawrence's writing life

Hilary Simpson, *D. H. Lawrence and Feminism*, Croom Helm, London 1982 – important historical study of Lawrence's encounter with feminism

Gertrude Stein, *Three Lives*, Penguin, Harmondsworth 1990

John Turner, 'Purity and Danger in D. H. Lawrence's *The Virgin and the Gipsy*', in Mara Kalnins (ed.), *D. H. Lawrence: Centenary Essays*, Bristol Classical Press, Bristol 1986

Linda Ruth Williams, *D. H. Lawrence*, Northcote House in association with the British Council (Writers and Their Work series), Plymouth 1997 – a stimulating contemporary introduction to Lawrence

Linda Ruth Williams, *Sex in the Head: Visions of Femininity and Film in D. H. Lawrence*, Harvester Wheatsheaf, Hemel Hempstead 1993 – develops Carter's suggestions on sexual ambiguity in Lawrence by focusing on the themes of sight and blindness, light and dark

Raymond Williams, *Towards 2000*, Pelican, Harmondsworth 1985

THE VIRGIN AND THE GIPSY

and Other Stories

The Virgin and the Gipsy
is dedicated
TO FRIEDA

The Virgin and the Gipsy

CHAPTER ONE

WHEN THE VICAR'S WIFE went off with a young and penniless man the scandal knew no bounds. Her two little girls were only seven and nine years old respectively. And the vicar was such a good husband. True, his hair was grey. But his moustache was dark, he was handsome, and still full of furtive passion for his unrestrained and beautiful wife.

Why did she go? Why did she burst away with such an *éclat*[1] of revulsion, like a touch of madness?

Nobody gave any answer. Only the pious said she was a bad woman. While some of the good women kept silent. They knew.

The two little girls never knew. Wounded, they decided that it was because their mother found them negligible.

The ill wind that blows nobody any good swept away the vicarage family on its blast. Then lo and behold! the vicar, who was somewhat distinguished as an essayist and a controversialist, and whose case had aroused sympathy among the bookish men, received the living of Papplewick. The Lord had tempered the wind of misfortune with a rectorate in the north country.

The rectory was a rather ugly stone house down by the river Papple, before you come into the village. Further on, beyond where the road crosses the stream, were the big old stone cotton-mills, once driven by water. The road curved uphill, into the bleak stone streets of the village.

The vicarage family received decided modification, upon its transference into the rectory. The vicar, now the rector, fetched up his old mother and his sister, and a brother from the city. The two little girls had a very different milieu from the old home.

The rector was now forty-seven years old; he had displayed an intense and not very dignified grief after the flight of his wife. Sympathetic ladies had stayed him from suicide. His hair was almost white, and he had a wild-eyed, tragic look. You had only to look at him, to know how dreadful it all was, and how he had been wronged.

Yet somewhere there was a false note. And some of the ladies, who had sympathised most profoundly with the vicar, secretly rather disliked the rector. There was a certain furtive self-righteousness about him, when all was said and done.

The little girls, of course, in the vague way of children, accepted the family verdict. Granny, who was over seventy and whose sight was failing, became the central figure in the house. Aunt Cissie, who was over forty, pale, pious, and gnawed by an inward worm, kept house. Uncle Fred, a stingy and grey-faced man of forty, who just lived dingily for himself, went into town every day. And the rector, of course, was the most important person, after Granny.

They called her the Mater. She was one of those physically vulgar, clever old bodies who had got her own way all her life by buttering the weaknesses of her menfolk. Very quickly she took her cue. The rector still 'loved' his delinquent wife, and would 'love her' till he died. Therefore hush! The rector's feeling was sacred. In his heart was enshrined the pure girl he had wedded and worshipped.

Out in the evil world, at the same time, there wandered a disreputable woman who had betrayed the rector and abandoned his little children. She was now yoked to a young and despicable man, who no doubt would bring her the degradation she deserved. Let this be clearly understood, and then hush! For in the pure loftiness of the rector's heart still bloomed the pure white snow-flower of his young bride. This white snow-flower did not wither. That other creature, who had gone off with that despicable young man, was none of his affair.

The Mater, who had been somewhat diminished and insignificant as a widow in a small house, now climbed into the chief armchair in the rectory, and planted her old bulk firmly again. She was not going to be dethroned. Astutely she gave a sigh of homage to the rector's fidelity to the pure white snow-flower, while she pretended to disapprove. In sly reverence for her son's great love, she spoke no word against that nettle which flourished in the evil world, and which had once been called Mrs Arthur Saywell. Now, thank heaven, having married again, she was no more Mrs Arthur Saywell. No woman bore the rector's name. The pure white snow-flower bloomed *in perpetuum*,[2] without nomenclature. The family even thought of her as She-who-was-Cynthia.

All this was water on the Mater's mill. It secured her against Arthur's ever marrying again. She had him by his feeblest weakness, his skulking self-love. He had married an imperishable white snow-flower. Lucky man! He had been injured. Unhappy man! He had suffered. Ah, what a heart of love! And he had – forgiven! Yes, the white snow-flower was forgiven. He even had made provision in his will for her, when that other scoundrel – But hush! Don't even *think* too near to that horrid nettle in the rank outer world! She-who-was-Cynthia. Let the white snow-flower bloom inaccessible on the heights of the past. The present is another story.

The children were brought up in this atmosphere of cunning self-sanctification and of unmentionability. They, too, saw the snow-flower on inaccessible heights. They too knew that it was throned in lone splendour aloft their lives, never to be touched.

At the same time, out of the squalid world sometimes would come a rank, evil smell of selfishness and degraded lust, the smell of that awful nettle, She-who-was-Cynthia. This nettle actually contrived at intervals, to get a little note through to the girls, her children. And at this the silver-haired Mater shook inwardly with hate. For if She-who-was-Cynthia ever came back, there wouldn't be much left of the Mater. A secret gust of hate went from the old granny to the girls, children of that foul nettle of lust, that Cynthia who had had such an affectionate contempt for the Mater.

Mingled with all this, was the children's perfectly distinct recollection of their real home – the vicarage in the south – and their glamorous but not very dependable mother, Cynthia. She had made a great glow, a flow of life, like a swift and dangerous sun in the home, forever coming and going. They always associated her presence with brightness, but also with danger; with glamour, but with fearful selfishness.

Now the glamour was gone, and the white snow-flower, like a porcelain wreath, froze on its grave. The danger of instability, the peculiarly *dangerous* sort of selfishness, like lions and tigers, was also gone. There was now a complete stability, in which one could perish safely.

But they were growing up. And as they grew, they became more definitely confused, more actively puzzled. The Mater, as she grew older, grew blinder. Somebody had to lead her about. She did not get up till towards midday. Yet blind or bed-ridden, she held the house.

Besides, she wasn't bed-ridden. Whenever the *men* were present, the Mater was in her throne. She was too cunning to court neglect. Especially as she had rivals.

Her great rival was the younger girl, Yvette. Yvette had some of the vague, careless blitheness of She-who-was-Cynthia. But this one was more docile. Granny perhaps had caught her in time. Perhaps!

The rector adored Yvette, and spoiled her with a doting fondness;

as much as to say: am I not a soft-hearted, indulgent old boy! He liked to have this opinion of himself, and the Mater knew his weaknesses to a hair's-breadth. She knew them, and she traded on them by turning them into decorations for him, for his character. He wanted, in his own eyes, to have a fascinating character, as women want to have fascinating dresses. And the Mater cunningly put beauty-spots over his defects and deficiencies. Her mother-love gave her the clue to his weaknesses, and she hid them for him with decorations. Whereas She-who-was-Cynthia – ! But don't mention *her*, in this connection. In her eyes, the rector was almost hump-backed and an idiot.

The funny thing was, Granny secretly hated Lucille, the elder girl, more than the pampered Yvette. Lucille, the uneasy and irritable, was more conscious of being under Granny's power, than was the spoilt and vague Yvette.

On the other hand, Aunt Cissie hated Yvette. She hated her very name. Aunt Cissie's life had been sacrificed to the Mater, and Aunt Cissie knew it, and the Mater knew she knew it. Yet as the years went on, it became a convention. The convention of Aunt Cissie's sacrifice was accepted by everybody, including the selfsame Cissie. She prayed a good deal about it. Which also showed that she had her own private feelings somewhere, poor thing. She had ceased to be Cissie, she had lost her life and her sex. And now, she was creeping towards fifty, strange green flares of rage would come up in her, and at such times, she was insane.

But Granny held her in her power. Aunt Cissie's one object in life was to look after the Mater.

Aunt Cissie's green flares of hellish hate would go up against all young things, sometimes. Poor thing, she prayed and tried to obtain forgiveness from heaven. But what had been done to her, *she* could not forgive, and the vitriol would spurt in her veins sometimes.

It was not as if the Mater were a warm, kindly soul. She wasn't. She only seemed it, cunningly. And the fact dawned gradually on the girls. Under her old-fashioned lace cap, under her silver hair, under the black silk of her stout, short, forward-bulging body, this old woman had a cunning heart, seeking forever her own female power. And through the weakness of the unfresh, stagnant men she had bred, she kept her power, as her years rolled on, from seventy to eighty, and from eighty on the new lap, towards ninety.

For in the family there was a whole tradition of 'loyalty'; loyalty to one another, and especially to the Mater. The Mater, of course, was the pivot of the family. The family was her own extended ego.

Naturally she covered it with her power. And her sons and daughters, being weak and disintegrated, naturally were loyal. Outside the family, what was there for them but danger and insult and ignominy? Had not the rector experienced it, in his marriage? So now, caution! Caution and loyalty, fronting the world! Let there be as much hate and friction *inside* the family, as you like. To the outer world, a stubborn fence of unison.

CHAPTER TWO

BUT IT WAS NOT until the girls finally came home from school that they felt the full weight of Granny's dead old hand on their lives. Lucille was now nearly twenty-one, and Yvette nineteen. They had been to a good girls' school, and had had a finishing year in Lausanne, and were quite the usual thing, tall young creatures with fresh, sensitive faces and bobbed hair and young-manly, deuce-take-it manners.

'What's so awfully *boring* about Papplewick,' said Yvette, as they stood on the Channel boat watching the grey, grey cliffs of Dover draw near, 'is that there are no *men* about. Why doesn't Daddy have some good old sports for friends? As for Uncle Fred, he's the limit!'

'Oh, you never know what will turn up,' said Lucille, more philosophic.

'You jolly well know what to expect,' said Yvette. 'Choir on Sundays, and I hate mixed choirs. Boys' voices are *lovely*, when there are no women. And Sunday School and Girls' Friendly, and socials, all the dear old souls that enquire after Granny! Not a decent young fellow for miles.'

'Oh I don't know!' said Lucille. 'There's always the Framleys. And you know Gerry Somercotes *adores* you.'

'Oh but I *hate* fellows who adore me!' cried Yvette, turning up her sensitive nose. 'They *bore* me. They hang on like lead.'

'Well what *do* you want, if you can't stand being adored? *I* think it's perfectly all right to be adored. You know you'll never marry them, so why not let them go on adoring, if it amuses them.'

'Oh but I *want* to get married,' cried Yvette.

'Well in that case, let them go on adoring you till you find one that you can *possibly* marry.'

'I never should, that way. Nothing puts me off like an adoring fellow. They *bore* me so! They make me feel beastly.'

'Oh, so they do me, if they get pressing. But at a distance, I think they're rather nice.'

'I should like to fall *violently* in love.'

'Oh, very likely! I shouldn't! I should hate it. Probably so would you, if it actually happened. After all, we've got to settle down a bit, before we know what we want.'

'But don't you *hate* going back to Papplewick?' cried Yvette, turning up her young, sensitive nose.

'No, not particularly. I suppose we shall be rather bored. I wish Daddy would get a car. I suppose we shall have to drag the old bikes out. Wouldn't you like to get up to Tansy Moor?'

'Oh, *love* it! Though it's an awful *strain*, shoving an old push-bike up those hills.'

The ship was nearing the grey cliffs. It was summer, but a grey day. The two girls wore their coats with fur collars turned up, and little *chic* hats pulled down over their ears. Tall, slender, fresh-faced, naïve, yet confident, too confident, in their school-girlish arrogance, they were so terribly English. They seemed so free, and were as a matter of fact so tangled and tied up, inside themselves. They seemed so dashing and unconventional, and were really so conventional, so, as it were, shut up indoors inside themselves. They looked like bold, tall young sloops, just slipping from the harbour into the wide seas of life. And they were, as a matter of fact, two poor young rudderless lives, moving from one chain anchorage to another.

The rectory struck a chill into their hearts as they entered. It seemed ugly, and almost sordid, with the dank air of that middle-class, degenerated comfort which has ceased to be comfortable and has turned stuffy, unclean. The hard, stone house struck the girls as being unclean, they could not have said why. The shabby furniture seemed somehow sordid, nothing was fresh. Even the food at meals had that awful dreary sordidness which is so repulsive to a young thing coming from abroad. Roast beef and wet cabbage, cold mutton and mashed potatoes, sour pickles, inexcusable puddings.

Granny, who 'loved a bit of pork', also had special dishes, beef-tea and rusks, or a small savoury custard. The grey-faced Aunt Cissie ate nothing at all. She would sit at table, and take a single lonely and naked boiled potato on to her plate. She never ate meat. So she sat in sordid durance, while the meal went on, and Granny quickly slobbered her portion – lucky if she spilled nothing on her protuberant stomach. The food was not appetising in itself: how could it be, when Aunt Cissie hated food herself, hated the fact of eating, and never could keep a maidservant for three months? The girls ate with repulsion,

Lucille bravely bearing up, Yvette's tender nose showing her disgust. Only the rector, white-haired, wiped his long grey moustache with his serviette, and cracked jokes. He too was getting heavy and inert, sitting in his study all day, never taking exercise. But he cracked sarcastic little jokes all the time, sitting there under the shelter of the Mater.

The country, with its steep hills and its deep, narrow valleys, was dark and gloomy, yet had a certain powerful strength of its own. Twenty miles away was the black industrialism of the north. Yet the village of Papplewick was comparatively lonely, almost lost, the life in it stony and dour. Everything was stone, with a hardness that was almost poetic, it was so unrelenting.

It was as the girls had known: they went back into the choir, they helped in the parish. But Yvette struck absolutely against Sunday School, the Band of Hope, the Girls' Friendlies – indeed against all those functions that were conducted by determined old maids and obstinate, stupid elderly men. She avoided church duties as much as possible, and got away from the rectory whenever she could. The Framleys, a big, untidy, jolly family up at the Grange, were an enormous stand-by. And if anybody asked her out to a meal, even if a woman in one of the workmen's houses asked her to stay to tea, she accepted at once. In fact, she was rather thrilled. She liked talking to the working men, they had often such fine, hard heads. But of course they were in another world.

So the months went by. Gerry Somercotes was still an adorer. There were others, too, sons of farmers or mill-owners. Yvette really ought to have had a good time. She was always out to parties and dances, friends came for her in their motor-cars, and off she went to the city, to the afternoon dance in the chief hotel, or in the gorgeous new Palais de Danse, called the Pally.

Yet she always seemed like a creature mesmerised. She was never free to be quite jolly. Deep inside her worked an intolerable irritation, which she thought she *ought* not to feel, and which she hated feeling, thereby making it worse. She never understood at all whence it arose.

At home, she truly was irritable, and outrageously rude to Aunt Cissie. In fact, Yvette's awful temper became one of the family by-words.

Lucille, always more practical, got a job in the city as private secretary to a man who needed somebody with fluent French and shorthand. She went back and forth every day, by the same train as Uncle Fred. But she never travelled with him, and wet or fine, bicycled to the station, while he went on foot.

The two girls were both determined that what they wanted was a really jolly social life. And they resented with fury that the rectory was, for their friends, impossible. There were only four rooms downstairs: the kitchen, where lived the two discontented maid-servants: the dark dining-room: the rector's study: and the big, 'homely', dreary living-room or drawing-room. In the dining-room there was a gas fire. Only in the living-room was a good hot fire kept going. Because, of course, here Granny reigned.

In this room the family was assembled. At evening, after dinner, Uncle Fred and the rector invariably played crossword puzzles with Granny.

'Now, Mater, are you ready? N blank blank blank blank W: a Siamese functionary.'

'Eh? Eh? M blank blank blank blank W?'

Granny was hard of hearing.

'No Mater. Not M! N blank blank blank blank W: a Siamese functionary.'

'N blank blank blank blank W: a Chinese functionary.'

'SIAMESE.'

'Eh?'

'SIAMESE! SIAM!'

'A Siamese functionary! Now what can that be?' said the old lady profoundly, folding her hands on her round stomach. Her two sons proceeded to make suggestions, at which she said Ah! Ah! The rector was amazingly clever at crossword puzzles. But Fred had a certain technical vocabulary.

'This certainly is a hard nut to crack,' said the old lady, when they were all stuck.

Meanwhile Lucille sat in a corner with her hands over her ears, pretending to read, and Yvette irritably made drawings, or hummed loud and exasperating tunes, to add to the family concert. Aunt Cissie continually reached for a chocolate, and her jaws worked ceaselessly. She literally lived on chocolates. Sitting in the distance, she put another into her mouth, then looked again at the parish magazine. Then she lifted her head, and saw it was time to fetch Granny's cup of Horlicks.

While she was gone, in nervous exasperation Yvette would open the window. The room was never fresh, she imagined it smelt: smelt of Granny. And Granny, who was hard of hearing, heard like a weasel when she wasn't wanted to.

'Did you open the window, Yvette? I think you might remember there are older people than yourself in the room,' she said.

'It's stifling! It's unbearable! No wonder we've all of us always got colds.'

'I'm sure the room is large enough, and a good fire burning.' The old lady gave a little shudder. 'A draught to give us all our death.'

'Not a draught at all,' roared Yvette. 'A breath of fresh air.'

The old lady shuddered again, and said: 'Indeed!'

The rector, in silence, marched to the window and firmly closed it. He did not look at his daughter meanwhile. He hated thwarting her. But she must know what's what!

The crossword puzzles, invented by Satan himself, continued till Granny had had her Horlicks, and was to go to bed. Then came the ceremony of Goodnight! Everybody stood up. The girls went to be kissed by the blind old woman, the rector gave his arm, and Aunt Cissie followed with a candle.

But this was already nine o'clock, although Granny was really getting old, and should have been in bed sooner. But when she was in bed, she could not sleep, till Aunt Cissie came.

'You see,' said Granny, 'I have *never* slept alone. For fifty-four years I never slept a night without the Pater's arm round me. And when he was gone I tried to sleep alone. But as sure as my eyes closed to sleep, my heart nearly jumped out of my body, and I lay in a palpitation. Oh, you may think what you will, but it was a fearful experience, after fifty-four years of perfect married life! I would have prayed to be taken first, but the Pater, well, no I don't think he would have been able to bear up.'

So Aunt Cissie slept with Granny. And she hated it. She said *she* could never sleep. And she grew greyer and greyer, and the food in the house got worse, and Aunt Cissie had to have an operation.

But the Mater rose as ever, towards noon, and at the midday meal, she presided from her armchair, with her stomach protruding; her reddish, pendulous face, that had a sort of horrible majesty, dropping soft under the wall of her high brow, and her blue eyes peering unseeing. Her white hair was getting scanty, it was altogether a little indecent. But the rector jovially cracked his jokes to her, and she pretended to disapprove. But she was perfectly complacent, sitting in her ancient obesity, and after meals, getting the wind from her stomach, pressing her bosom with her hand as she 'rifted' in gross physical complacency.

What the girls minded most was that, when they brought their young friends to the house, Granny always was there, like some awful idol of old flesh, consuming all the attention. There was only the one room for everybody. And there sat the old lady, with Aunt Cissie keeping an acrid guard over her. Everybody must be presented first to Granny: she was ready to be genial, she liked company. She had to know who everybody was, where they came from, every circumstance of their lives. And then, when she was *au fait*, she could get hold of the conversation.

Nothing could be more exasperating to the girls. 'Isn't old Mrs Saywell wonderful! She takes *such* an interest in life, at nearly ninety!'

'She does take an interest in people's affairs, if that's life,' said Yvette.

Then she would immediately feel guilty. After all, it *was* wonderful to be nearly ninety, and have such a clear mind! And Granny never *actually* did anybody any harm. It was more that she was in the way. And perhaps it was rather awful to hate somebody because they were old and in the way.

Yvette immediately repented, and was nice. Granny blossomed forth into reminiscences of when she was a girl, in the little town in Buckinghamshire. She talked and talked away, and was so entertaining. She really *was* rather wonderful.

Then in the afternoon Lottie and Ella and Bob Framley came, with Leo Wetherell.

'Oh, come in!' – and in they all trooped to the sitting-room, where Granny, in her white cap, sat by the fire.

'Granny, this is Mr Wetherell.'

'Mr What-did-you-say? You must excuse me, I'm a little deaf!'

Granny gave her hand to the uncomfortable young man, and gazed silently at him, sightlessly.

'You are not from our parish?' she asked him.

'Dinnington!' he shouted.

'We want to go on a picnic tomorrow, to Bonsall Head, in Leo's car. We can all squeeze in,' said Ella, in a low voice.

'Did you say Bonsall Head?' asked Granny.

'Yes!'

There was a blank silence.

'Did you say you were going in a car?'

'Yes! In Mr Wetherell's.'

'I hope he's a good driver. It's a very dangerous road.'

'He's a *very* good driver.'

'Not a very good driver?'

'Yes! He *is* a very good driver.'

'If you go to Bonsall Head, I think I must send a message to Lady Louth.'

Granny always dragged in this miserable Lady Louth, when there was company.

'Oh, we shan't go that way,' cried Yvette.

'Which way?' said Granny. 'You must go by Heanor.'

The whole party sat, as Bob expressed it, like stuffed ducks, fidgeting on their chairs.

Aunt Cissie came in – and then the maid with the tea. There was the eternal and everlasting piece of bought cake. Then appeared a plate of little fresh cakes. Aunt Cissie had actually sent to the baker's.

'Tea, Mater!'

The old lady gripped the arms of her chair. Everybody rose and stood, while she waded slowly across, on Aunt Cissie's arm, to her place at table.

During tea Lucille came in from town, from her job. She was simply worn out, with black marks under her eyes. She gave a cry, seeing all the company.

As soon as the noise had subsided, and the awkwardness was resumed, Granny said: 'You have never mentioned Mr Wetherell to me, have you, Lucille?'

'I don't remember,' said Lucille.

'You can't have done. The name is strange to me.'

Yvette absently grabbed another cake, from the now almost empty plate. Aunt Cissie, who was driven almost crazy by Yvette's vague and inconsiderate ways, felt the green rage fuse in her heart. She picked up her own plate, on which was the one cake she allowed herself, and said with vitriolic politeness, offering it to Yvette: 'Won't you have mine?'

'Oh thanks!' said Yvette, starting in her angry vagueness. And with an appearance of the same insouciance, she helped herself to Aunt Cissie's cake also, adding as an afterthought: 'If you're sure you don't want it.'

She now had two cakes on her plate. Lucille had gone white as a ghost, bending to her tea. Aunt Cissie sat with a green look of poisonous resignation. The awkwardness was an agony.

But Granny, bulkily enthroned and unaware, only said, in the centre of the cyclone: 'If you are motoring to Bonsall Head tomorrow, Lucille, I wish you would take a message from me to Lady Louth.'

'Oh!' said Lucille, giving a queer look across the table at the sightless old woman. Lady Louth was the King Charles's Head[3] of the family, invariably produced by Granny for the benefit of visitors. 'Very well!'

'She was so very kind last week. She sent her chauffeur over with a crossword puzzle book for me.'

'But you thanked her then,' cried Yvette.

'I should like to send her a note.'

'We can post it,' cried Lucille.

'Oh no! I should like you to take it. When Lady Louth called last time . . . '

The young ones sat like a shoal of young fishes dumbly mouthing at the surface of the water, while Granny went on about Lady Louth. Aunt Cissie, the two girls knew, was still helpless, almost unconscious in a paroxysm of rage about the cake. Perhaps, poor thing, she was praying.

It was a mercy when the friends departed. But by that time the two girls were both haggard-eyed. And it was then that Yvette, looking round, suddenly saw the stony, implacable will-to-power in the old and motherly-seeming Granny. She sat there bulging backwards in her chair, impassive, her reddish, pendulous old face rather mottled, almost unconscious, but implacable, her face like a mask that hid something stony, relentless. It was the static inertia of her unsavoury power. Yet in a minute she would open her ancient mouth to find out every detail about Leo Wetherell. For the moment she was hibernating in her oldness, her agedness. But in a minute her mouth would open, her mind would flicker awake and with her insatiable greed for life, other people's life, she would start on her quest for every detail. She was like the old toad which Yvette had watched, fascinated, as it sat on the ledge of the beehive, immediately in front of the little entrance by which the bees emerged, and which, with a demonish lightning-like snap of its pursed jaws, caught every bee as it came out to launch into the air, swallowed them one after the other, as if it could consume the whole hive-full, into its aged, bulging, purse-like wrinkledness. It had been swallowing bees as they launched into the air of spring, year after year, year after year, for generations.

But the gardener, called by Yvette, was in a rage, and killed the creature with a stone.

' 'Appen tha *art* good for th' snails,' he said, as he came down with the stone. 'But tha 'rt none goin' ter emp'y th' bee-'ive into thy guts.'

CHAPTER THREE

THE NEXT DAY WAS DULL AND LOW, and the roads were awful, for it had been raining for weeks, yet the young ones set off on their trip, without taking Granny's message either. They just slipped out while she was making her slow trip upstairs after lunch. Not for anything would they have called at Lady Louth's house. That widow of a knighted doctor, a harmless person indeed, had become an obnoxity in their lives.

Six young rebels, they sat very perkily in the car as they swished through the mud. Yet they had a peaked look too. After all, they had nothing really to rebel against, any of them. They were left so very free in their movements. Their parents let them do almost entirely as they liked. There wasn't really a fetter to break, nor a prison-bar to file through, nor a bolt to shatter. The keys of their lives were in their own hands. And there they dangled inert.

It is very much easier to shatter prison bars than to open undiscovered doors to life. As the younger generation finds out somewhat to its chagrin. True, there was Granny. But poor old Granny, you couldn't actually say to her: 'Lie down and die, you old woman!' She might be an old nuisance, but she never really *did* anything. It wasn't fair to hate her.

So the young people set off on their jaunt, trying to be very full of beans. They could really do as they liked. And so, of course, there was nothing to do but sit in the car and talk a lot of criticism of other people, and silly flirty gallantry that was really rather a bore. If there had only been a few 'strict orders' to be disobeyed! But nothing: beyond the refusal to carry the message to Lady Louth, of which the rector would approve because he didn't encourage King Charles' Head either.

They sang, rather scrappily, the latest would-be comic songs, as they went through the grim villages. In the great park the deer were in groups near the road, roe deer and fallow, nestling in the gloom of the afternoon under the oaks by the road, as if for the stimulus of human company.

Yvette insisted on stopping and getting out to talk to them. The girls, in their Russian boots, tramped through the damp grass, while the deer watched them with big, unfrightened eyes. The hart trotted away mildly, holding back his head, because of the weight of the horns. But the doe, balancing her big ears, did not rise from under the tree, with her half-grown young ones, till the girls were almost in touch. Then she walked light-foot away, lifting her tail from her spotted flanks, while the young ones nimbly trotted.

'Aren't they awfully dainty and nice!' cried Yvette. 'You'd wonder they could lie so cosily in this horrid wet grass.'

'Well I suppose they've got to lie down *sometime*,' said Lucille. 'And it's *fairly* dry under the tree.' She looked at the crushed grass, where the deer had lain.

Yvette went and put her hand down, to feel how it felt.

'Yes!' she said doubtfully, 'I believe it's a bit warm.'

The deer had bunched again a few yards away, and were standing motionless in the gloom of the afternoon. Away below the slopes of grass and trees, beyond the swift river with its balustraded bridge, sat the huge ducal house, one or two chimneys smoking bluely. Behind it rose purplish woods.

The girls, pushing their fur collars up to their ears, dangling one long arm, stood watching in silence, their wide Russian boots protecting them from the wet grass. The great house squatted square and creamy-grey below. The deer, in little groups, were scattered under the old trees close by. It all seemed so still, so unpretentious, and so sad.

'I wonder where the Duke is now,' said Ella.

'Not here, wherever he is,' said Lucille. 'I expect he's abroad where the sun shines.'

The motor horn called from the road, and they heard Leo's voice: 'Come on, boys! If we're going to get to the Head and down to Amberdale for tea, we'd better move.'

They crowded into the car again, with chilled feet, and set off through the park, past the silent spire of the church, out through the great gates and over the bridge, on into the wide, damp, stony village of Woodlinkin, where the river ran. And thence, for a long time, they stayed in the mud and dark and dampness of the valley, often with sheer rock above them; the water brawling on one hand, the steep rock or dark trees on the other.

Till, through the darkness of overhanging trees, they began to climb, and Leo changed the gear. Slowly the car toiled up through the whitey-grey mud, into the stony village of Bolehill, that hung on the slope, round the old cross, with its steps, that stood where the road branched, on past the cottages whence came a wonderful smell of hot tea-cakes, and beyond, still upwards, under dripping trees and past broken slopes of bracken, always climbing. Until the cleft became shallower, and the trees finished, and the slopes on either side were bare, gloomy grass, with low dry-stone walls. They were emerging on to the Head.

The party had been silent for some time. On either side the road was grass, then a low stone fence, and the swelling curve of the hill-summit, traced with the low, dry-stone walls. Above this, the low sky.

The car ran out, under the low, grey sky, on the naked tops.

'Shall we stay a moment?' called Leo.

'Oh yes!' cried the girls.

And they scrambled out once more, to look around. They knew the place quite well. But still, if one came to the Head, one got out to look.

The hills were like the knuckles of a hand, the dales were below, between the fingers, narrow, steep, and dark. In the deeps a train was steaming, slowly pulling north: a small thing of the underworld. The noise of the engine re-echoed curiously upwards. Then came the dull, familiar sound of blasting in a quarry.

Leo, always on the go, moved quickly.

'Shall we be going?' he said. 'Do we *want* to get down to Amberdale for tea? Or shall we try somewhere nearer?'

They all voted for Amberdale, for the Marquis of Grantham.

'Well, which way shall we go back? Shall we go by Codnor and over Crosshill, or shall we go by Ashbourne?'

There was the usual dilemma. Then they finally decided on the Codnor top road. Off went the car, gallantly.

They were on the top of the world, now, on the back of the fist. It was naked, too, as the back of your fist, high under heaven, and dull, heavy green. Only it was veined with a network of old stone walls, dividing the fields, and broken here and there with ruins of old lead-mines and works. A sparse stone farm bristled with six naked sharp trees. In the distance was a patch of smoky grey stone, a hamlet. In some fields grey, dark sheep fed silently, sombrely. But there was not a sound nor a movement. It was the roof of England, stony and arid as any roof. Beyond, below, were the shires.

' "And see the coloured counties," '⁴ said Yvette to herself. Here anyhow they were not coloured. A stream of rooks trailed out from nowhere. They had been walking, pecking, on a naked field that had been manured. The car ran on between the grass and the stone walls of the upland lane, and the young people were silent, looking out over the far network of stone fences, under the sky, looking for the curves downward that indicated a drop to one of the underneath, hidden dales.

Ahead was a light cart, driven by a man, and trudging along at the side was a woman, sturdy and elderly, with a pack on her back. The man in the cart had caught her up, and now was keeping pace.

The road was narrow. Leo sounded the horn sharply. The man on the cart looked round, but the woman on foot only trudged steadily, rapidly forward, without turning her head.

Yvette's heart gave a jump. The man on the cart was a gipsy, one of the black, loose-bodied, handsome sort. He remained seated on his cart, turning round and gazing at the occupants of the motor-car, from under the brim of his cap. And his pose was loose, his gaze insolent in its indifference. He had a thin black moustache under his thin, straight nose, and a big silk handkerchief of red and yellow tied round his neck. He spoke a word to the woman. She stood a second, solid, to turn round and look at the occupants of the car, which had now drawn quite close. Leo honked the horn again, imperiously. The woman, who had a grey-and-white kerchief tied round her head, turned sharply, to keep pace with the cart, whose driver also had settled back, and was lifting the reins, moving his loose, light shoulders. But still he did not pull aside.

Leo made the horn scream, as he put the brakes on and the car slowed up near the back of the cart. The gipsy turned round at the din, laughing in his dark face under his dark-green cap, and said something which they did not hear, showing white teeth under the line of black moustache, and making a gesture with his dark, loose hand.

'Get out o' the way then!' yelled Leo. For answer, the man delicately pulled the horse to a standstill, as it curved to the side of the road. It was a good roan horse and a good, natty, dark-green cart.

Leo, in a rage, had to jam on the brake and pull up too.

'Don't the pretty young ladies want to hear their fortunes?' said the gipsy on the cart, laughing except for his dark, watchful eyes, which went from face to face, and lingered on Yvette's young, tender face.

She met his dark eyes for a second, their level search, their insolence, their complete indifference to people like Bob and Leo, and something took fire in her breast. She thought: 'He is stronger than I am! He doesn't care!'

'Oh yes! let's!' cried Lucille at once.

'Oh yes!' chorused the girls.

'I say! What about the time?' cried Leo.

'Oh bother the old time! Somebody's always dragging in time by the forelock,' cried Lucille.

'Well, if you don't mind *when* we get back, *I* don't!' said Leo heroically.

The gipsy man had been sitting loosely on the side of his cart, watching the faces. He now jumped softly down from the shaft, his knees a bit stiff. He was apparently a man something over thirty, and a beau in his way. He wore a sort of shooting-jacket, double-breasted, coming only to the hips, of dark green-and-black frieze; rather tight black trousers, black boots, and a dark-green cap; with the big yellow-and-red bandanna handkerchief round his neck. His appearance was curiously elegant, and quite expensive in its gipsy style. He was handsome, too, pressing in his chin with the old, gipsy conceit, and now apparently not heeding the strangers any more, as he led his good roan horse off the road, preparing to back his cart.

The girls saw for the first time a deep recess in the side of the road, and two caravans smoking. Yvette got quickly down. They had suddenly come upon a disused quarry, cut into the slope of the road-side, and in this sudden lair, almost like a cave, were three caravans, dismantled for the winter. There was also deep at the back, a shelter built of boughs, as a stable for the horse. The grey, crude rock rose high above the caravans, and curved round towards the road. The floor was heaped chips of stone, with grasses growing among. It was a hidden, snug winter camp.

The elderly woman with the pack had gone into one of the caravans, leaving the door open. Two children were peeping out, showing black heads. The gipsy man gave a little call, as he backed his cart into the quarry, and an elderly man came out to help him untackle.

The gipsy himself went up the steps into the newest caravan, that had its door closed. Underneath, a tied-up dog ranged forth. It was a white hound spotted liver-coloured. It gave a low growl as Leo and Bob approached.

At the same moment, a dark-faced gipsy-woman with a pink shawl or kerchief round her head and big gold earrings in her ears, came down the steps of the newest caravan, swinging her flounced, voluminous green skirt. She was handsome in a bold, dark, long-faced way, just a bit wolfish. She looked like one of the bold, loping Spanish gipsies.

'Good morning, my ladies and gentlemen,' she said, eyeing the girls from her bold, predative eyes. She spoke with a certain foreign stiffness.

'Good afternoon!' said the girls.

'Which beautiful little lady like to hear her fortune? Give me her little hand?'

She was a tall woman, with a frightening way of reaching forward her neck like a menace. Her eyes went from face to face, very active, heartlessly searching out what she wanted. Meanwhile the man, apparently her husband, appeared at the top of the caravan steps smoking a pipe, and with a small, black-haired child in his arms. He stood on his limber legs, casually looking down on the group, as if from a distance, his long black lashes lifted from his full, conceited, impudent black eyes. There was something peculiarly transfusing in his stare. Yvette felt it, felt it in her knees. She pretended to be interested in the white-and-liver-coloured hound.

'How much do you want, if we all have our fortunes told?' asked Lottie Framley, as the six fresh-faced young Christians hung back rather reluctantly from this pagan pariah woman.

'All of you? ladies and gentlemen, all?' said the woman shrewdly.

'I don't want mine told! You go ahead!' cried Leo.

'Neither do I,' said Bob. 'You four girls.'

'The four ladies?' said the gipsy woman, eyeing them shrewdly, after having looked at the boys. And she fixed her price. 'Each one give me a sheeling, and a little bit more for luck? a little bit!' She smiled in a way that was more wolfish than cajoling, and the force of her will was felt, heavy as iron beneath the velvet of her words.

'All right,' said Leo. 'Make it a shilling a head. Don't spin it out too long.'

'Oh, *you*!' cried Lucille at him. 'We want to hear it *all*.'

The woman took two wooden stools, from under a caravan, and placed them near the wheel. Then she took the tall, dark Lottie Framley by the hand, and bade her sit down.

'You don't care if everybody hear?' she said, looking up curiously into Lottie's face.

Lottie blushed dark with nervousness, as the gipsy woman held her hand, and stroked her palm with hard, cruel-seeming fingers.

'Oh, I don't mind,' she said.

The gipsy woman peered into the palm tracing the lines of the hand with a hard, dark forefinger. But she seemed clean.

And slowly she told the fortune, while the others, standing listening, kept on crying out: 'Oh, that's Jim Baggaley! Oh, I don't believe it! Oh, that's not true! A fair woman who lives beneath a tree! Why, whoever's that?' until Leo stopped them with a manly warning: 'Oh, hold on, girls! You give everything away.'

Lottie retired blushing and confused, and it was Ella's turn. She was much more calm and shrewd, trying to read the oracular words. Lucille kept breaking out with: 'Oh, I say!' The gipsy man at the top of the steps stood imperturbable, without any expression at all. But his bold eyes kept staring at Yvette, she could feel them on her cheek, on her neck, and she dared not look up. But Framley would some-times look up at him, and got a level stare back from the handsome face of the male gipsy, from the dark conceited proud eyes. It was a peculiar look, in the eyes that belonged to the tribe of the humble: the pride of the pariah, the half-sneering challenge of the outcast, who sneered at law-abiding men, and went his own way. All the time, the gipsy man stood there, holding his child in his arms, looking on without being concerned.

Lucille was having her hand read – 'You have been across the sea, and there you met a man – a brown-haired man – but he was too old – '

'Oh, I *say*!' cried Lucille, looking round at Yvette.

But Yvette was abstracted, agitated, hardly heeding: in one of her mesmerised states.

'You will marry in a few years – not now, but a few years – perhaps four – and you will not be rich, but you will have plenty – enough – and you will go away, a long journey.'

'With my husband, or without?' cried Lucille.

'With him – '

When it came to Yvette's turn, and the woman looked up boldly, cruelly, searching for a long time in her face, Yvette said nervously: 'I don't think I want mine told. No, I won't have mine told! No I won't, really!'

'You are afraid of something?' said the gipsy woman cruelly.

'No, it's not that – ' Yvette fidgeted.

'You have some secret? You are afraid I shall say it? Come, would you like to go in the caravan, where nobody hears?'

The woman was curiously insinuating; while Yvette was always wayward, perverse. The look of perversity was on her soft, frail young face now, giving her a queer hardness.

'Yes!' she said suddenly. 'Yes! I might do that!'

'Oh, I say!' cried the others. 'Be a sport!'

'I don't think you'd *better*!' cried Lucille.

'Yes!' said Yvette, with that hard little way of hers. 'I'll do that. I'll go in the caravan.'

The gipsy woman called something to the man on the steps. He went into the caravan for a moment or two, then reappeared, and came down the steps, setting the small child on its uncertain feet, and holding it by the hand. A dandy, in his polished black boots, tight black trousers and tight dark-green jersey, he walked slowly across with the toddling child to where the elderly gipsy was giving the roan horse a feed of oats, in the bough shelter between pits of grey rock, with dry bracken upon the stone chip floor. He looked at Yvette as he passed, staring her full in the eyes, with his pariah's bold yet dishonest stare. Something hard inside her met his stare. But the surface of her body seemed to turn to water. Nevertheless, something hard in her registered the peculiar pure lines of his face, of his straight, pure nose, of his cheeks and temples. The curious dark, suave purity of all his body, outlined in the green jersey: a purity like a living sneer.

And as he loped slowly past her, on his flexible hips, it seemed to her still that he was stronger than she was. Of all the men she had ever seen, this one was the only one who was stronger than she was, in her own kind of strength, her own kind of understanding.

So, with curiosity, she followed the woman up the steps of the caravan, the skirts of her well-cut tan coat swinging and almost showing her knees, under the pale-green cloth dress. She had long, long-striding, fine legs, too slim rather than too thick, and she wore curiously-patterned pale-and-fawn stockings of fine wool, suggesting the legs of some delicate animal.

At the top of the steps she paused and turned, debonair, to the others, saying in her naïve, lordly way, so off-hand: 'I won't let her be long.'

Her grey fur collar was open, showing her soft throat and pale green dress, her little plaited tan-coloured hat came down to her ears, round her soft, fresh face. There was something soft and yet overbearing, unscrupulous, about her. She knew the gipsy man had turned to look at her. She was aware of the pure dark nape of his neck, the black hair groomed away. He watched as she entered his house.

What the gipsy told her, no one ever knew. It was a long time to wait, the others felt. Twilight was deepening on the gloom, and it was turning raw and cold. From the chimney on the second caravan came smoke and a smell of rich food. The horse was fed, a yellow blanket strapped round him, and two gipsy men talked together in the distance, in low tones. There was a peculiar feeling of silence and secrecy in that lonely, hidden quarry.

At last the caravan door opened, and Yvette emerged, bending forward and stepping with long, witch-like slim legs down the steps. There was a stooping, witch-like silence about her as she emerged on the twilight.

'Did it seem long?' she said vaguely, not looking at anybody and keeping her own counsel hard within her soft, vague waywardness. 'I hope you weren't bored! Wouldn't tea be nice! Shall we go?'

'You get in!' said Bob. 'I'll pay.'

The gipsy-woman's full, metallic skirts of jade-green alpaca came swinging down the steps. She rose to her height, a big, triumphant-looking woman with a dark-wolf face. The pink cashmere kerchief stamped with red roses, was slipping to one side over her black and crimped hair. She gazed at the young people in the twilight with bold arrogance.

Bob put two half-crowns in her hand.

'A little bit more, for luck, for your young lady's luck,' she wheedled, like a wheedling wolf. 'Another bit of silver, to bring you luck.'

'You've got a shilling for luck, that's enough,' said Bob calmly and quietly, as they moved away to the car.

'A little bit of silver! Just a little bit, for your luck in love!'

Yvette, with the sudden long, startling gestures of her long limbs, swung round as she was entering the car, and with long arm outstretched, strode and put something into the gipsy's hand, then stepped, bending her height, into the car.

'Prosperity to the beautiful young lady, and the gipsy's blessing on her,' came the suggestive, half-sneering voice of the woman.

The engine *birred!* then *birred!* again more fiercely, and started. Leo switched on the lights, and immediately the quarry with the gipsies fell back into the blackness of night.

'Goodnight!' called Yvette's voice, as the car started. But hers was the only voice that piped up, chirpy and impudent in its nonchalance. The headlights glared down the stone lane.

'Yvette, you've got to tell us what she said to you,' cried Lucille, in the teeth of Yvette's silent will *not* to be asked.

'Oh, nothing at *all* thrilling,' said Yvette, with false warmth. 'Just the usual old thing: a dark man who means good luck, and a fair one who means bad: and a death in the family, which if it means Granny, won't be so *very* awful: and I shall marry when I'm twenty-three, and have heaps of money and heaps of love, and two children. All sounds very nice, but it's a bit too much of a good thing, you know.'

'Oh, but why did you give her more money?'

'Oh well, I wanted to! You *have* to be a bit lordly with people like that – '

CHAPTER FOUR

THERE WAS A TERRIFIC RUMPUS down at the rectory, on account of
Yvette and the Window Fund. After the war, Aunt Cissie had set her
heart on a stained-glass window in the church, as a memorial for the
men of the parish who had fallen. But the bulk of the fallen had been
nonconformists, so the memorial took the form of an ugly little
monument in front of the Wesleyan chapel.

This did not vanquish Aunt Cissie. She canvassed, she had bazaars,
she made the girls get up amateur theatrical shows, for her precious
window. Yvette, who quite liked the acting and showing-off part of it,
took charge of the farce called *Mary in the Mirror*, and gathered in the
proceeds, which were to be paid to the Window Fund when accounts
were settled. Each of the girls was supposed to have a money-box for
the Fund.

Aunt Cissie, feeling that the united sums must now almost suffice,
suddenly called in Yvette's box. It contained fifteen shillings. There
was a moment of green horror.

'Where is all the rest?'

'Oh!' said Yvette casually. 'I just borrowed it. It wasn't so awfully
much.'

'What about the three pounds thirteen for *Mary in the Mirror*?'
asked Aunt Cissie, as if the jaws of hell were yawning.

'Oh quite! I just borrowed it. I can pay it back.'

Poor Aunt Cissie! The green tumour of hate burst inside her, and
there was a ghastly, abnormal scene, which left Yvette shivering with
fear and nervous loathing.

Even the rector was rather severe.

'If you needed money, why didn't you tell me?' he said coldly.
'Have you ever been refused anything in reason?'

'I – I thought it didn't matter,' stammered Yvette.

'And what have you done with the money?'

'I suppose I've spent it,' said Yvette, with wide distraught eyes and
a peaked face.

'Spent it, on what?'

'I can't remember everything: stockings and things, and I gave
some of it away.'

Poor Yvette! Her lordly airs and ways were already hitting back at
her, on the reflex. The rector was angry: his face had a snarling,

doggish look, a sort of sneer. He was afraid his daughter was developing some of the rank, tainted qualities of She-who-was-Cynthia.

'You *would* do the large with somebody else's money, wouldn't you?' he said, with a cold, mongrel sort of sneer, which showed what an utter unbeliever he was, at the heart. The inferiority of a heart which has no core of warm belief in it, no pride in life. He had utterly no belief in her.

Yvette went pale, and very distant. Her pride, that frail, precious flame which everybody tried to quench, recoiled like a flame blown far away, on a cold wind, as if blown out, and her face, white now and still like a snowdrop, the white snow-flower of his conceit, seemed to have no life in it, only this pure, strange abstraction.

'He has no belief in me!' she thought in her soul. 'I am really nothing to him. I am nothing, only a shameful thing. Everything is shameful, everything is shameful!'

A flame of passion or rage, while it might have overwhelmed or infuriated her, would not have degraded her as did her father's unbelief, his final attitude of a sneer against her.

He became a little afraid, in the silence of sterile thought. After all, he needed the *appearance* of love and belief and bright life, he would never dare to face the fat worm of his own unbelief, that stirred in his heart.

'What have you to say for yourself?' he asked.

She only looked at him from that senseless snowdrop face which haunted him with fear, and gave him a helpless sense of guilt. That other one, She-who-was Cynthia, she had looked back at him with the same numb, white fear, the fear of his degrading unbelief, the worm which was his heart's core. He *knew* his heart's core was a fat, awful worm. His dread was lest anyone else should know. His anguish of hate was against anyone who knew, and recoiled.

He saw Yvette recoiling, and immediately his manner changed to the worldly old good-humoured cynic which he affected.

'Ah well!' he said. 'You have to pay it back, my girl, that's all. I will advance you the money out of your allowance. But I shall charge you four per cent a month's interest. Even the devil himself must pay a percentage on his debts. Another time, if you can't trust yourself, don't handle money which isn't your own. Dishonesty isn't pretty.'

Yvette remained crushed, and deflowered and humiliated. She crept about, trailing the rays of her pride. She had a revulsion even from herself. Oh, why had she ever touched the leprous money! Her whole flesh shrank as if it were defiled. Why was that? Why, why was that?

She admitted herself wrong in having spent the money. 'Of course I shouldn't have done it. They are quite right to be angry,' she said to herself.

But where did the horrible wincing of her flesh come from? Why did she feel she had caught some physical contagion?

'Where you're so *silly*, Yvette,' Lucille lectured her: poor Lucille was in great distress – 'is that you give yourself away to them all. You might *know* they'd find out. I could have raised the money for you, and saved all this bother. It's perfectly awful! But you never will think beforehand where your actions are going to land you! Fancy Aunt Cissie saying all those things to you! How *awful*! Whatever would Mamma have said, if she'd heard it?'

When things went very wrong, they thought of their mother, and despised their father and all the low brood of the Saywells. Their mother, of course, had belonged to a higher, if more dangerous and 'immoral' world. More selfish, decidedly. But with a showier gesture. More unscrupulous and more easily moved to contempt: but not so humiliating.

Yvette always considered that she got her fine, delicate flesh from her mother. The Saywells were all a bit leathery, and grubby somewhere inside. But then the Saywells never let you down. Whereas the fine She-who-was-Cynthia had let the rector down with a bang, and his little children along with him. Her little children! They could not quite forgive her.

Only dimly, after the row, Yvette began to realise the other sanctity of herself, the sanctity of her sensitive, clean flesh and blood, which the Saywells with their so-called morality succeeded in defiling. They always wanted to defile it. They were the life unbelievers. Whereas, perhaps She-who-was-Cynthia had only been a moral unbeliever.

Yvette went about dazed and peaked and confused. The rector paid in the money to Aunt Cissie, much to that lady's rage. The helpless tumour of her rage was still running. She would have liked to announce her niece's delinquency in the parish magazine. It was anguish to the destroyed woman that she could not publish the news to all the world. The selfishness! The selfishness! The selfishness!

Then the rector handed his daughter a little account with himself: her debt to him, interest thereon, the amount deducted from her small allowance. But to her credit he had placed a guinea, which was the fee he had to pay for complicity.

'As father of the culprit,' he said humorously, 'I am fined one guinea. And with that I wash the ashes out of my hair.'

He was always generous about money. But somehow, he seemed to think that by being free about money he could absolutely call himself a generous man. Whereas he used money, even generosity, as a hold over her.

But he let the affair drop entirely. He was by this time more amused than anything, to judge from appearances. He thought still he was safe.

Aunt Cissie, however, could not get over her convulsion. One night when Yvette had gone rather early, miserably, to bed, when Lucille was away at a party, and she was lying with soft, peaked limbs aching with a sort of numbness and defilement, the door softly opened, and there stood Aunt Cissie, pushing her grey-green face through the opening of the door. Yvette started up in terror.

'Liar! Thief! Selfish little beast!' hissed the maniacal face of Aunt Cissie. 'You little hypocrite! You liar! You selfish beast! You greedy little beast!'

There was such extraordinary impersonal hatred in that grey-green mask, and those frantic words, that Yvette opened her mouth to scream with hysterics. But Aunt Cissie shut the door as suddenly as she had opened it, and disappeared. Yvette leaped from her bed and turned the key. Then she crept back, half demented with fear of the squalid abnormal, half numbed with paralysis of damaged pride. And amid it all, up came a bubble of distracted laughter. It *was* so filthily ridiculous!

Aunt Cissie's behaviour did not hurt the girl so very much. It was after all somewhat fantastic. Yet hurt she was: in her limbs, in her body, in her sex, hurt. Hurt, numbed, and half destroyed, with only her nerves vibrating and jangled. And still so young, she could not conceive what was happening.

Only she lay and wished she were a gipsy. To live in a camp, in a caravan, and never set foot in a house, not know the existence of a parish, never look at a church. Her heart was hard with repugnance against the rectory. She loathed these houses with their indoor sanitation and their bathrooms, and their extraordinary repulsiveness. She hated the rectory, and everything it implied. The whole stagnant, sewerage sort of life, where sewerage is never mentioned, but where it seems to smell from the centre to every two-legged inmate, from Granny to the servants, was foul. If gipsies had no bathrooms, at least they had no sewerage. There was fresh air. In the rectory there was *never* fresh air. And in the souls of the people, the air was stale till it stank.

Hate kindled her heart, as she lay with numbed limbs. And she thought of the words of the gipsy woman: 'There is a dark man who never lived in a house. He loves you. The other people are treading on your heart. They will tread on your heart till you think it is dead. But the dark man will blow the one spark up into fire again, good fire. You will see what good fire.'

Even as the woman was saying it, Yvette felt there was some duplicity somewhere. But she didn't mind. She hated with the cold, acrid hatred of a child the rectory interior, the sort of putridity in the life. She liked that big, swarthy, wolf-like gipsy-woman, with the big gold rings in her ears, the pink scarf over her wavy black hair, the tight bodice of brown velvet, the green, fan-like skirt. She liked her dusky, strong, relentless hands, that had pressed so firm, like wolf's paws, in Yvette's own soft palm. She liked her. She liked the danger and the covert fearlessness of her. She liked her covert, unyielding sex, that was immoral, but with a hard, defiant pride of its own. Nothing would ever get that woman under. She would despise the rectory and the rectory morality, utterly! She would strangle Granny with one hand. And she would have the same contempt for Daddy and for Uncle Fred, as men, as she would have for fat old slobbery Rover, the Newfoundland dog. A great, sardonic female contempt, for such domesticated dogs, calling themselves men.

And the gipsy man himself! Yvette quivered suddenly, as if she had seen his big, bold eyes upon her, with the naked insinuation of desire in them. The absolutely naked insinuation of desire made her lie prone and powerless in the bed, as if a drug had cast her in a new, molten mould.

She never confessed to anybody that two of the ill-starred Window Fund pounds had gone to the gipsy woman. What if Daddy and Aunt Cissie knew *that*! Yvette stirred luxuriously in the bed. The thought of the gipsy had released the life of her limbs, and crystallised in her heart the hate of the rectory: so that now she felt potent, instead of impotent.

When, later, Yvette told Lucille about Aunt Cissie's dramatic interlude in the bedroom doorway, Lucille was indignant.

'Oh, hang it all!' cried she. 'She might let it drop now. I should think we've heard enough about it by now! Good heavens, you'd think Aunt Cissie was a perfect bird of paradise! Daddy's dropped it, and after all, it's his business if it's anybody's. Let Aunt Cissie shut up!'

It was the very fact that the rector had dropped it, and that he again treated the vague and inconsiderate Yvette as if she were some specially-licensed being, that kept Aunt Cissie's bile flowing. The fact that Yvette really was most of the time unaware of other people's feelings, and being unaware, couldn't care about them, nearly sent Aunt Cissie mad. Why should that young creature, with a delinquent mother, go through life as a privileged being, even unaware of other people's existence, though they were under her nose?

Lucille at this time was very irritable. She seemed as if she simply went a little unbalanced, when she entered the rectory. Poor Lucille, she was so thoughtful and responsible. She did all the extra troubling, thought about doctors, medicines, servants, and all that sort of thing. She slaved conscientiously at her job all day in town, working in a room with artificial light from ten till five. And she came home to have her nerves rubbed almost to frenzy by Granny's horrible and persistent inquisitiveness and parasitic agedness.

The affair of the Window Fund had apparently blown over, but there remained a stuffy tension in the atmosphere. The weather continued bad. Lucille stayed at home on the afternoon of her half holiday, and did herself no good by it. The rector was in his study, she and Yvette were making a dress for the latter young woman, Granny was resting on the couch.

The dress was of blue silk velours, French material, and was going to be very becoming. Lucille made Yvette try it on again: she was nervously uneasy about the hang, under the arms.

'Oh bother!' cried Yvette, stretching her long, tender, childish arms, that tended to go bluish with the cold. 'Don't be so frightfully *fussy*, Lucille! It's quite all right.'

'If that's all the thanks I get, slaving my half-day away making dresses for you, I might as well do something for myself!'

'Well, Lucille! You know I never *asked* you! You know you can't bear it unless you *do* supervise,' said Yvette, with that irritating blandness of hers, as she raised her naked elbows and peered over her shoulder into the long mirror.

'Oh yes! you never *asked* me!' cried Lucille. 'As if I didn't know what you meant, when you started sighing and flouncing about.'

'I!' said Yvette, with vague surprise. 'Why, when did I start sighing and flouncing about?'

'Of course you know you did.'

'Did I? No, I didn't know! When was it?' Yvette could put a peculiar annoyance into her mild, straying questions.

'I shan't do another thing to this frock, if you don't stand still and *stop* it,' said Lucille, in her rather sonorous, burning voice.

'You know you are most awfully nagging and irritable, Lucille,' said Yvette, standing as if on hot bricks.

'Now Yvette!' cried Lucille, her eyes suddenly flashing in her sister's face, with wild flashes. 'Stop it at once! Why should everybody put up with your abominable and overbearing temper?'

'Well, I don't know about *my* temper,' said Yvette, writhing slowly out of the half-made frock, and slipping into her dress again.

Then, with an obstinate little look on her face, she sat down again at the table, in the gloomy afternoon, and began to sew at the blue stuff. The room was littered with blue clippings, the scissors were lying on the floor, the workbasket was spilled in chaos all over the table, and a second mirror was perched perilously on the piano.

Granny, who had been in a semi-coma, called a doze, roused herself on the big, soft couch and put her cap straight.

'I don't get much peace for my nap,' she said, slowly feeling her thin white hair, to see that it was in order. She had heard vague noises.

Aunt Cissie came in, fumbling in a bag for a chocolate.

'I never saw such a mess!' she said. 'You'd better clear some of that litter away, Yvette.'

'All right,' said Yvette. 'I will in a minute.'

'Which means never!' sneered Aunt Cissie, suddenly darting and picking up the scissors.

There was silence for a few moments, and Lucille slowly pushed her hands in her hair, as she read a book.

'You'd better clear away, Yvette,' persisted Aunt Cissie.

'I will, before tea,' replied Yvette, rising once more and pulling the blue dress over her head, flourishing her long, naked arms through the sleeveless armholes. Then she went between the mirrors, to look at herself once more.

As she did so, she sent the second mirror, that she had perched carelessly on the piano, sliding with a rattle to the floor. Luckily it did not break. But everybody started badly.

'She's smashed the mirror!' cried Aunt Cissie.

'Smashed a mirror! Which mirror! Who's smashed it?' came Granny's sharp voice.

'I haven't smashed anything,' came the calm voice of Yvette. 'It's quite all right.'

'You'd better not perch it up there again,' said Lucille.

Yvette, with a little impatient shrug at all the fuss, tried making the mirror stand in another place. She was not successful.

'If one had a fire in one's own room,' she said crossly, 'one needn't have a lot of people fussing when one wants to sew.'

'Which mirror are you moving about?' asked Granny.

'One of our own that came from the vicarage,' said Yvette rudely.

'Don't break it in *this* house, wherever it came from,' said Granny. There was a sort of family dislike for the furniture that had belonged to She-who-was-Cynthia. It was most of it shoved into the kitchen, and the servants' bedrooms.

'Oh, *I'm* not superstitious,' said Yvette, 'about mirrors or any of that sort of thing.'

'Perhaps you're not,' said Granny. 'People who never take the responsibility for their own actions usually don't care what happens.'

'After all,' said Yvette, 'I may say it's my own looking-glass, even if I did break it.'

'And I say,' said Granny, 'that there shall be no mirrors broken in *this* house, if we can help it; no matter who they belong to, or did belong to. Cissie, have I got my cap straight?'

Aunt Cissie went over and straightened the old lady. Yvette loudly and irritatingly trilled a tuneless tune.

'And now, Yvette, will you please clear away?' said Aunt Cissie.

'Oh bother!' cried Yvette angrily. 'It's simply *awful* to live with a lot of people who are always nagging and fussing over trifles.'

'What people, may I ask?' said Aunt Cissie ominously.

Another row was imminent. Lucille looked up with a queer cast in her eyes. In the two girls, the blood of She-who-was-Cynthia was roused.

'Of course you may ask! You know quite well I mean the people in this beastly house,' said the outrageous Yvette.

'At least,' said Granny, 'we don't come of half-depraved stock.'

There was a second's electric pause. Then Lucille sprang from her low seat, with sparks flying from her.

'You shut up!' she shouted, in a blast full upon the mottled majesty of the old lady.

The old woman's breast began to heave with heaven knows what emotions. The pause this time, as after the thunderbolt, was icy.

Then Aunt Cissie, livid, sprang upon Lucille, pushing her like a Fury.

'Go to your room!' she cried hoarsely. 'Go to your room!'

And she proceeded to push the white but fiery-eyed Lucille from the room. Lucille let herself be pushed, while Aunt Cissie vociferated: 'Stay in your room till you've apologised for this! – till you've apologised to the Mater for this!'

'I shan't apologise!' came the clear voice of Lucille, from the passage, while Aunt Cissie shoved her.

Aunt Cissie drove her more wildly upstairs.

Yvette stood tall and bemused in the sitting-room, with the air of offended dignity, at the same time bemused, which was so odd on her. She still was bare-armed, in the half-made blue dress. And even *she* was half-aghast at Lucille's attack on the majesty of age. But also, she was coldly indignant against Granny's aspersion of the maternal blood in their veins.

'Of course I meant no offence,' said Granny.

'Didn't you?' said Yvette coolly.

'Of course not. I only said we're not depraved, just because we happen to be superstitious about breaking mirrors.'

Yvette could hardly believe her ears. Had she heard right? Was it possible! Or was Granny, at her age, just telling a barefaced lie?

Yvette knew that the old woman was telling a cool, barefaced lie. But already, so quickly, Granny believed her own statement.

The rector appeared, having left time for a lull.

'What's wrong?' he asked cautiously, genially.

'Oh nothing!' drawled Yvette. 'Lucille told Granny to shut up, when she was saying something. And Aunt Cissie drove her up to her room. *Tant de bruit pour une omelette!*[5] Though Lucille was a bit over the mark, that time.'

The old lady couldn't quite catch what Yvette said.

'Lucille really will have to learn to control her nerves,' said the old woman. 'The mirror fell down, and it worried me. I said so to Yvette, and she said something about superstitions and the people in the beastly house. I told her the people in the house were not depraved, if they happened to mind when a mirror was broken. And at that Lucille flew at me and told me to shut up. It really is disgraceful how these children give way to their nerves. I know it's nothing but nerves.'

Aunt Cissie had come in during this speech. At first even she was dumb. Then it seemed to her, it was as Granny had said.

'I have forbidden her to come down until she comes to apologise to the Mater,' she said.

'I doubt if she'll apologise,' said the calm, queenly Yvette, holding her bare arms.

'And I don't want any apology,' said the old lady. 'It is merely nerves. I don't know what they'll come to, if they have nerves like that, at their age! She must take Vibrofat. – I am sure Arthur would like his tea, Cissie.'

Yvette swept her sewing together, to go upstairs. And again she trilled her tune, rather shrill and tuneless. She was trembling inwardly.

'More glad rags!' said her father to her, genially.

'More glad rags!' she reiterated sagely, as she sauntered upstairs, with her day dress over one arm. She wanted to console Lucille, and ask her how the blue stuff hung now.

At the first landing she stood as she nearly always did, to gaze through the window that looked to the road and the bridge. Like the Lady of Shalott,[6] she seemed always to imagine that someone would come along singing *Tirra-lirra!* or something equally intelligent, by the river.

CHAPTER FIVE

IT WAS NEARLY TEA-TIME. The snowdrops were out by the short drive going to the gate from the side of the house, and the gardener was pottering at the round, damp flower-beds, on the wet grass that sloped to the stream. Past the gate went the whitish muddy road, crossing the stone bridge almost immediately, and winding in a curve up to the steep, clustering, stony, smoking northern village, that perched over the grim stone mills which Yvette could see ahead down the narrow valley, their tall chimneys long and erect.

The rectory was on one side the Papple, in the rather steep valley, the village was beyond and above, further down, on the other side the swift stream. At the back of the rectory the hill went up steep, with a grove of dark, bare larches, through which the road disappeared. And immediately across stream from the rectory, facing the house, the river-bank rose steep and bushy, up to the sloping, dreary meadows, that sloped up again to dark hillsides of trees, with grey rock cropping out.

But from the end of the house, Yvette could only see the road curving round past the wall with its laurel hedge, down to the bridge, then up again round the shoulder to that first hard cluster of houses in Papplewick village, beyond the dry-stone walls of the steep fields.

She always expected *something* to come down the slant of the road from Papplewick, and she always lingered at the landing window. Often a cart came, or a motor-car, or a lorry with stone, or a labourer, or one of the servants. But never anybody who sang *Tirra-lirra!* by the river. The tirralirraing days seem to have gone by.

This day, however, round the corner on the white-grey road, between the grass and the low stone walls, a roan horse came stepping bravely and briskly downhill, driven by a man in a cap, perched on the front of his light cart. The man swayed loosely to the swing of the cart, as the horse stepped downhill, in the silent sombreness of the afternoon. At the back of the cart, long duster-brooms of reed and feather stuck out, nodding on their stalks of cane.

Yvette stood close to the window, and put the casement-cloth curtains behind her, clutching her bare upper arms with her hands.

At the foot of the slope the horse started into a brisk trot to the bridge. The cart rattled on the stone bridge, the brooms bobbed and flustered, the driver sat as if in a kind of dream, swinging along. It was like something seen in a sleep.

But as he crossed the end of the bridge, and was passing along the rectory wall, he looked up at the grim stone house that seemed to have backed away from the gate, under the hill. Yvette moved her hands quickly on her arms. And as quickly, from under the peak of his cap, he had seen her, his swarthy predative face was alert.

He pulled up suddenly at the white gate, still gazing upwards at the landing window; while Yvette, always clasping her cold and mottled arms, still gazed abstractedly down at him, from the window.

His head gave a little, quick jerk of signal, and he led his horse well aside, on to the grass. Then, limber and alert, he turned back the tarpaulin of the cart, fetched out various articles, pulled forth two or three of the long brooms of reed or turkey-feathers, covered the cart, and turned towards the house, looking up at Yvette as he opened the white gate.

She nodded to him, and flew to the bathroom to put on her dress, hoping she had disguised her nod so that he wouldn't be sure she had nodded. Meanwhile she heard the hoarse deep roaring of that old fool, Rover, punctuated by the yapping of that young idiot, Trixie.

She and the housemaid arrived at the same moment at the sitting-room door.

'Was it the man selling brooms?' said Yvette to the maid. 'All right!' and she opened the door. 'Aunt Cissie, there's a man selling brooms. Shall I go?'

'What sort of a man?' said Aunt Cissie, who was sitting at tea with the rector and the Mater: the girls having been excluded for once from the meal.

'A man with a cart,' said Yvette.

'A gipsy,' said the maid.

Of course Aunt Cissie rose at once. She had to look at him.

The gipsy stood at the back door, under the steep dark bank where the larches grew. The long brooms flourished from one hand, and from the other hung various objects of shining copper and brass: a saucepan, a candlestick, plates of beaten copper. The man himself was neat and dapper, almost rakish, in his dark-green cap and double-breasted green check coat. But his manner was subdued, very quiet: and at the same time proud, with a touch of condescension and aloofness.

'Anything today, lady?' he said, looking at Aunt Cissie with dark, shrewd, searching eyes, but putting a very quiet tenderness into his voice.

Aunt Cissie saw how handsome he was, saw the flexible curve of his lips under the line of black moustache, and she was fluttered. The merest hint of roughness or aggression on the man's part would have made her shut the door contemptuously in his face. But he managed to insinuate such a subtle suggestion of submission into his male bearing, that she began to hesitate.

'The candlestick is lovely!' said Yvette. 'Did you make it?'

And she looked up at the man with her naïve, childlike eyes, that were as capable of double meanings as his own.

'Yes, lady!' He looked back into her eyes for a second, with that naked suggestion of desire which acted on her like a spell, and robbed her of her will. Her tender face seemed to go into a sleep.

'It's awfully nice!' she murmured vaguely.

Aunt Cissie began to bargain for the candlestick: which was a low, thick stem of copper, rising from a double bowl. With patient aloofness the man attended to her, without ever looking at Yvette, who leaned against the doorway and watched in a muse.

'How is your wife?' she asked him suddenly, when Aunt Cissie had gone indoors to show the candlestick to the rector, and ask him if he thought it was worth it.

The man looked fully at Yvette, and a scarcely discernible smile curled his lips. His eyes did not smile: the insinuation in them only hardened to a glare.

'She's all right. When are you coming that way again?' he murmured, in a low, caressive, intimate voice.

'Oh, I don't know,' said Yvette vaguely.

'You come Fridays, when I'm there,' he said.

Yvette gazed over his shoulder as if she had not heard him. Aunt Cissie returned, with the candlestick and the money to pay for it. Yvette turned nonchalant away, trilling one of her broken tunes, abandoning the whole affair with a certain rudeness.

Nevertheless, hiding this time at the landing window, she stood to watch the man go. What she wanted to know was whether he really had any power over her. She did not intend him to see her this time.

She saw him go down to the gate, with his brooms and pans, and out to the cart. He carefully stowed away his pans and his brooms, and fixed down the tarpaulin over the cart. Then with a slow, effortless spring of his flexible loins, he was on the cart again, and touching the horse with the reins. The roan horse was away at once, the cart-wheels grinding uphill, and soon the man was gone, without looking round. Gone like a dream which was only a dream, yet which she could not shake off.

'No, he hasn't any power over me!' she said to herself: rather disappointed really, because she wanted somebody, or something, to have power over her.

She went up to reason with the pale and overwrought Lucille, scolding her for getting into a state over nothing.

'What does it *matter*,' she expostulated, 'if you told Granny to shut up! Why, everybody ought to be told to shut up, when they're being beastly. But she didn't mean it, you know. No, she didn't mean it. And she's quite sorry she said it. There's absolutely no reason to make a fuss. Come on, let's dress ourselves up and sail down to dinner like duchesses. Let's have our own back that way. Come on, Lucille!'

There was something strange and mazy, like having cobwebs over one's face, about Yvette's vague blitheness; her queer, misty side-stepping from an unpleasantness. It was cheering too. But it was like walking in one of those autumn mists, when gossamer strands blow over your face. You don't quite know where you are.

She succeeded, however, in persuading Lucille, and the girls got out their best party frocks: Lucille in green and silver, Yvette in a pale lilac colour with turquoise chenille threading. A little rouge and powder, and their best slippers, and the gardens of paradise began to blossom. Yvette hummed and looked at herself, and put on her most *dégagé*[7] airs of one of the young marchionesses. She had an odd way of slanting her eyebrows and pursing her lips, and to all appearances detaching herself from every earthly consideration, and floating through the cloud of her own pearl-coloured reserves. It was amusing, and not quite convincing.

'Of course I am beautiful, Lucille,' she said blandly. 'And you're perfectly lovely, now you look a bit reproachful. Of course you're the most aristocratic of the two of us, with your nose! And now your eyes look reproachful, that adds an appealing look, and you're perfect, perfectly lovely. But I'm more *winning*, in a way – Don't you agree?' She turned with arch, complicated simplicity to Lucille.

She was truly simple in what she said. It was just what she thought. But it gave no hint of the very different *feeling* that also preoccupied her: the feeling that she had been looked upon, not from the outside, but from the inside, from her secret female self. She was dressing herself up and looking her most dazzling, just to counteract the effect that the gipsy had had on her, when he had looked at her, and seen none of her pretty face and her pretty ways, but just the dark, tremulous potent secret of her virginity.

The two girls started downstairs in state when the dinner-gong rang: but they waited till they heard the voices of the men. Then they sailed down and into the sitting-room, Yvette preening herself in her vague, debonair way, always a little bit absent; and Lucille shy, ready to burst into tears.

'My goodness gracious!' exclaimed Aunt Cissie, who was still wearing her dark-brown knitted sports coat. 'What an apparition! Wherever do you think you're going?'

'We're dining with the family,' said Yvette naïvely, 'and we've put on our best gewgaws in honour of the occasion.'

The rector laughed aloud, and Uncle Fred said: 'The family feels itself highly honoured.'

Both the elderly men were quite gallant, which was what Yvette wanted.

'Come and let me feel your dresses, do!' said Granny. 'Are they your best? It *is* a shame I can't see them.'

'Tonight, Mater,' said Uncle Fred, 'we shall have to take the young ladies in to dinner, and live up to the honour. Will you go with Cissie?'

'I certainly will,' said Granny. 'Youth and beauty must come first.'

'Well, tonight, Mater!' said the rector, pleased.

And he offered his arm to Lucille, while Uncle Fred escorted Yvette.

But it was a draggled, dull meal, all the same. Lucille tried to be bright and sociable, and Yvette really was most amiable, in her vague, cobwebby way. Dimly, at the back of her mind, she was thinking: Why are we all only like mortal pieces of furniture? Why is nothing *important*?

That was her constant refrain to herself: Why is nothing important? Whether she was in church, or at a party of young people, or dancing in the hotel in the city, the same little bubble of a question rose repeatedly on her consciousness: Why is nothing important?

There were plenty of young men to make love to her: even devotedly. But with impatience she had to shake them off. Why were they so unimportant? – so irritating!

She never even thought of the gipsy. He was a perfectly negligible incident. Yet the approach of Friday loomed strangely significant. 'What are we doing on Friday?' she said to Lucille. To which Lucille replied that they were doing nothing. And Yvette was vexed.

Friday came, and in spite of herself she thought all day of the quarry off the road up high Bonsall Head. She wanted to be there. That was all she was conscious of. She wanted to be there. She had not even a dawning idea of going there. Besides, it was raining again. But as she sewed the blue dress, finishing it for the party up at Lambley Close tomorrow, she just felt that her soul was up there, at the quarry, among the caravans, with the gipsies. Like one lost, or whose soul was stolen, she was not present in her body, the shell of her body. Her intrinsic body was away at the quarry, among the caravans.

The next day, at the party, she had no idea that she was being sweet to Leo. She had no idea that she was snatching him away from the tortured Ella Framley. Not until, when she was eating her pistachio ice, he said to her: 'Why don't you and me get engaged, Yvette? I'm absolutely sure it's the right thing for us both.'

Leo was a bit common, but good-natured and well-off. Yvette quite liked him. But engaged! How perfectly silly! She felt like offering him a set of her silk underwear to get engaged to.

'But I thought it was Ella!' she said, in wonder.

'Well! It might ha' been, but for you. It's your doings, you know! Ever since those gipsies told your fortune, I felt it was me or nobody, for you, and you or nobody, for me.'

'Really!' said Yvette, simply lost in amazement. 'Really!'

'Didn't you feel a bit the same?' he asked.

'Really!' Yvette kept on gasping softly, like a fish.

'You felt a bit the same, didn't you?' he said.

'What? About what?' she asked, coming to.

'About me, as I feel about you.'

'Why? What? Getting engaged, you mean? I? no! Why how *could* I? I could never have dreamed of such an impossible thing.'

She spoke with her usual heedless candour, utterly unoccupied with his feelings.

'What was to prevent you?' he said, a bit nettled. 'I thought you did.'

'Did you *really now*?' she breathed in amazement, with that soft, virgin, heedless candour which made her her admirers and her enemies.

She was so completely amazed, there was nothing for him to do but twiddle his thumbs in annoyance.

The music began, and he looked at her.

'No! I won't dance any more,' she said, drawing herself up and gazing away rather loftily over the assembly, as if he did not exist. There was a touch of puzzled wonder on her brow, and her soft, dim virgin face did indeed suggest the snowdrop of her father's pathetic imagery.

'But of course *you* will dance,' she said, turning to him with young condescension. 'Do ask somebody to have this with you.'

He rose, angry, and went down the room.

She remained soft and remote in her amazement. Expect Leo to propose to her! She might as well have expected old Rover the Newfoundland dog to propose to her. Get engaged, to any man on earth? No, good heavens, nothing more ridiculous could be imagined!

It was then, in a fleeting side-thought, that she realised that the gipsy existed. Instantly, she was indignant. Him, of all things! Him! Never!

'Now why?' she asked herself, again in hushed amazement. 'Why? It's *absolutely* impossible: absolutely! So why is it?'

This was a nut to crack. She looked at the young men dancing, elbows out, hips prominent, waists elegantly in. They gave her no clue to her problem. Yet she did particularly dislike the forced elegance of the waists and the prominent hips, over which the well-tailored coats hung with such effeminate discretion.

'There is something about me which they don't see and never would see,' she said angrily to herself. And at the same time, she was relieved that they didn't and couldn't. It made life so very much simpler.

And again, since she was one of the people who are conscious in visual images, she saw the dark-green jersey rolled on the black trousers of the gipsy, his fine, quick hips, alert as eyes. They were elegant. The elegance of these dancers seemed so stuffed, hips merely wadded with flesh. Leo the same, thinking himself such a fine dancer! and a fine figure of a fellow!

Then she saw the gipsy's face; the straight nose, the slender mobile lips, and the level, significant stare of the black eyes, which seemed to shoot her in some vital, undiscovered place, unerring.

She drew herself up angrily. How dared he look at her like that? So she gazed glaringly at the insipid beaux on the dancing floor. And she despised them. Just as the raggle-taggle gipsy women despise men who are not gipsies, despise their dog-like walk down the streets, she found herself despising this crowd. Where among them was the subtle, lonely, insinuating challenge that could reach her?

She did not want to mate with a housedog.

Her sensitive nose turned up, her soft brown hair fell like a soft sheath round her tender, flower-like face, as she sat musing. She seemed so virginal. At the same time, there was a touch of the tall young virgin *witch* about her, that made the housedog men shy off. She might metamorphose into something uncanny before you knew where you were.

This made her lonely, in spite of all the courting. Perhaps the courting only made her lonelier.

Leo, who was a sort of mastiff among the housedogs, returned after his dance, with fresh cheery-o! courage.

'You've had a little think about it, haven't you?' he said, sitting down beside her: a comfortable, well-nourished, determined sort of fellow. She did not know why it irritated her so unreasonably, when he hitched up his trousers at the knee, over his good-sized but very distinguished legs, and lowered himself assuredly on to a chair.

'Have I?' she said vaguely. 'About what?'

'You know what about,' he said. 'Did you make up your mind?'

'Make up my mind about what?' she asked, innocently.

In her upper consciousness, she truly had forgotten.

'Oh!' said Leo, settling his trousers again. 'About me and you getting engaged, you know.' He was almost as off-hand as she.

'Oh that's *absolutely* impossible,' she said, with mild amiability, as if it were some stray question among the rest. 'Why I never even thought of it again. Oh, don't talk about that sort of nonsense! That sort of thing is *absolutely* impossible,' she reiterated like a child.

'That sort of thing is, is it?' he said, with an odd smile at her calm, distant assertion. 'Well what sort of thing is possible, then? You don't want to die an old maid, do you?'

'Oh I don't mind,' she said absently.

'I do,' he said.

She turned round and looked at him in wonder.

'Why?' she said. 'Why should you mind if I was an old maid?'

'Every reason in the world,' he said, looking up at her with a bold, meaningful smile, that wanted to make its meaning blatant, if not patent.

But instead of penetrating into some deep, secret place, and shooting her there, Leo's bold and patent smile only hit her on the outside of the body, like a tennis ball, and caused the same kind of sudden irritated reaction.

'I think this sort of thing is awfully silly,' she said, with minx-like spite. 'Why, you're practically engaged to – to – ' she pulled herself up in time – 'probably half a dozen other girls. I'm not flattered by what you've said. I should hate it if anybody knew! – Hate it! – I shan't breathe a word of it, and I hope you'll have the sense not to. There's Ella!'

And keeping her face averted from him, she sailed away like a tall, soft flower, to join poor Ella Framley.

Leo flapped his white gloves.

'Catty little bitch!' he said to himself. But he was of the mastiff type, he rather liked the kitten to fly in his face. He began definitely to single her out.

CHAPTER SIX

THE NEXT WEEK it poured again with rain. And this irritated Yvette with strange anger. She had intended it should be fine. Especially she insisted it should be fine towards the weekend. Why, she did not ask herself.

Thursday, the half-holiday, came with a hard frost, and sun. Leo arrived with his car, the usual bunch. Yvette disagreeably and unaccountably refused to go.

'No thanks, I don't feel like it,' she said.

She rather enjoyed being Mary-Mary-quite-contrary.

Then she went for a walk by herself, up the frozen hills, to the Black Rocks.

The next day also came sunny and frosty. It was February, but in the north country the ground did not thaw in the sun. Yvette announced that she was going for a ride on her bicycle, and taking her lunch as she might not be back till afternoon.

She set off, not hurrying. In spite of the frost, the sun had a touch of spring. In the park, the deer were standing in the distance, in the sunlight, to be warm. One doe, white spotted, walked slowly across the motionless landscape.

Cycling, Yvette found it difficult to keep her hands warm, even when bodily she was quite hot. Only when she had to walk up the long hill, to the top, and there was no wind.

The upland was very bare and clear, like another world. She had climbed on to another level. She cycled slowly, a little afraid of taking the wrong lane, in the vast maze of stone fences. As she passed along the lane she thought was the right one, she heard a faint tapping noise, with a slight metallic resonance.

The gipsy man was seated on the ground with his back to the

cart-shaft, hammering a copper bowl. He was in the sun, bare-headed, but wearing his green jersey. Three small children were moving quietly round, playing in the horse's shelter: the horse and cart were gone. An old woman, bent, with a kerchief round her head, was cooking over a fire of sticks. The only sound was the rapid, ringing tap-tap-tap! of the small hammer on the dull copper.

The man looked up at once, as Yvette stepped from her bicycle, but he did not move, though he ceased hammering. A delicate, barely discernible smile of triumph was on his face. The old woman looked round, keenly, from under her dirty grey hair. The man spoke a half-audible word to her, and she turned again to her fire. He looked up at Yvette.

'How are you all getting on?' she asked politely.

'All right, eh! You sit down a minute?' He turned as he sat, and pulled a stool from under the caravan for Yvette. Then, as she wheeled her bicycle to the side of the quarry, he started hammering again, with that bird-like, rapid light stroke.

Yvette went to the fire to warm her hands.

'Is this the dinner cooking?' she asked childishly, of the old gipsy, as she spread her long tender hands, mottled red with the cold, to the embers.

'Dinner, yes!' said the old woman. 'For him! And for the children.'

She pointed with the long fork at the three black-eyed, staring children, who were staring at her from under their black fringes. But they were clean. Only the old woman was not clean. The quarry itself they had kept perfectly clean.

Yvette crouched in silence, warming her hands. The man rapidly hammered away with intervals of silence. The old hag slowly climbed the steps to the third, oldest caravan. The children began to play again, like little wild animals, quiet and busy.

'Are they your children?' asked Yvette, rising from the fire and turning to the man.

He looked her in the eyes, and nodded.

'But where's your wife?'

'She's gone out with the basket. They've all gone out, cart and all, selling things. I don't go selling things. I make them, but I don't go selling them. Not often. I don't often.'

'You make all the copper and brass things?' she said.

He nodded, and again offered her the stool. She sat down.

'You said you'd be here on Fridays,' she said. 'So I came this way, as it was so fine.'

'Very fine day!' said the gipsy, looking at her cheek, that was still a bit blanched by the cold, and the soft hair over her reddened ear, and the long, still mottled hands on her knee.

'You get cold, riding a bicycle?' he asked.

'My hands!' she said, clasping them nervously.

'You didn't wear gloves?'

'I did, but they weren't much good.'

'Cold comes through,' he said.

'Yes!' she replied.

The old woman came slowly, grotesquely down the steps of the caravan, with some enamel plates.

'The dinner cooked, eh?' he called softly.

The old woman muttered something, as she spread the plates near the fire. Two pots hung from a long iron horizontal bar, over the embers of the fire. A little pan seethed on a small iron tripod. In the sunshine, heat and vapour wavered together.

He put down his tools and the pot, and rose from the ground.

'You eat something along of us?' he asked Yvette, not looking at her.

'Oh, I brought my lunch,' said Yvette.

'You eat some stew?' he said. And again he called quietly, secretly to the old woman, who muttered in answer, as she slid the iron pot towards the end of the bar.

'Some beans, and some mutton in it,' he said.

'Oh thanks awfully!' said Yvette. Then, suddenly taking courage, added: 'Well yes, just a very little, if I may.'

She went across to untie her lunch from her bicycle, and he went up the steps to his own caravan. After a minute, he emerged, wiping his hands on a towel.

'You want to come up and wash your hands?' he said.

'No, I think not,' she said. 'They are clean.'

He threw away his wash-water, and set off down the road with a high brass jug, to fetch clean water from the spring that trickled into a small pool, taking a cup to dip it with.

When he returned, he set the jug and the cup by the fire, and fetched himself a short log, to sit on. The children sat on the floor, by the fire, in a cluster, eating beans and bits of meat with spoon or fingers. The man on the log ate in silence, absorbedly. The woman made coffee in the black pot on the tripod, hobbling upstairs for the cups. There was silence in the camp. Yvette sat on her stool, having taken off her hat and shaken her hair in the sun.

'How many children have you?' Yvette asked suddenly.

'Say five,' he replied slowly, as he looked up into her eyes.

And again the bird of her heart sank down and seemed to die. Vaguely, as in a dream, she received from him the cup of coffee. She was aware only of his silent figure, sitting like a shadow there on the log, with an enamel cup in his hand, drinking his coffee in silence. Her will had departed from her limbs, he had power over her: his shadow was on her.

And he, as he blew his hot coffee, was aware of one thing only, the mysterious fruit of her virginity, her perfect tenderness in the body.

At length he put down his coffee-cup by the fire, then looked round at her. Her hair fell across her face, as she tried to sip from the hot cup. On her face was that tender look of sleep, which a nodding flower has when it is full out. Like a mysterious early flower, she was full out, like a snowdrop which spreads its three white wings in a flight into the waking sleep of its brief blossoming. The waking sleep of her full-opened virginity, entranced like a snowdrop in the sunshine, was upon her.

The gipsy, supremely aware of her, waited for her like the substance of shadow, as shadow waits and is there.

At length his voice said, without breaking the spell: 'You want to go in my caravan now, and wash your hands?'

The childlike, sleep-waking eyes of her moment of perfect virginity looked into his, unseeing. She was only aware of the dark strange effluence of him bathing her limbs, washing her at last purely will-less. She was aware of *him*, as a dark, complete power.

'I think I might,' she said.

He rose silently, then turned to speak, in a low command, to the old woman. And then again he looked at Yvette, and putting his power over her, so that she had no burden of herself, or of action.

'Come!' he said.

She followed simply, followed the silent, secret, overpowering motion of his body in front of her. It cost her nothing. She was gone in his will.

He was at the top of the steps, and she at the foot, when she became aware of an intruding sound. She stood still, at the foot of the steps. A motor-car was coming. He stood at the top of the steps, looking round strangely. The old woman harshly called something, as with rapidly increasing sound, a car rushed near. It was passing.

Then they heard the cry of a woman's voice, and the brakes on the car. It had pulled up, just beyond the quarry.

The gipsy came down the steps, having closed the door of the caravan.

'You want to put your hat on,' he said to her.

Obediently she went to the stool by the fire, and took up her hat. He sat down by the cart-wheel, darkly, and took up his tools. The rapid tap-tap-tap of his hammer, rapid and angry now like the sound of a tiny machine-gun, broke out just as the voice of the woman was heard crying: 'May we warm our hands at the camp fire?'

She advanced, dressed in a sleek but bulky coat of sable fur. A man followed, in a blue great-coat; pulling off his fur gloves and pulling out a pipe.

'It looked so tempting,' said the woman in the coat of many dead little animals, smiling a broad, half-condescending, half-hesitant simper, around the company.

No one said a word.

She advanced to the fire, shuddering a little inside her coat, with the cold. They had been driving in an open car.

She was a very small woman, with a rather large nose: probably a Jewess. Tiny almost as a child, in that sable coat she looked much more bulky than she should, and her wide, rather resentful brown eyes of a spoilt Jewess gazed oddly out of her expensive get-up.

She crouched over the low fire, spreading her little hands, on which diamonds and emeralds glittered.

'Ugh!' she shuddered. 'Of course we ought not to have come in an open car! But my husband won't even let me say I'm cold!' She looked round at him with her large, childish, reproachful eyes, that had still the canny shrewdness of a bourgeois Jewess: a rich one, probably.

Apparently she was in love, in a Jewess's curious way, with the big, blond man. He looked back at her with his abstracted blue eyes, that seemed to have no lashes, and a small smile creased his smooth, curiously naked cheeks. The smile didn't mean anything at all.

He was a man one connects instantly with winter sports, skiing and skating. Athletic, unconnected with life, he slowly filled his pipe, pressing in the tobacco with long, powerful, reddened finger.

The Jewess looked at him to see if she got any response from him. Nothing at all, but that odd, blank smile. She turned again to the fire, tilting her eyebrows and looking at her small, white, spread hands.

He slipped off his heavily-lined coat, and appeared in one of the handsome, sharp-patterned knitted jerseys, in yellow and grey and black, over well-cut trousers, rather wide. Yes, they were both expensive! And he had a magnificent figure, an athletic, prominent chest. Like an experienced camper, he began building the fire together, quietly: like a soldier on campaign.

'D'you think they'd mind if we put some fir-cones on, to make a

blaze?' he asked of Yvette, with a silent glance at the hammering
gipsy.

'Love it, I should think,' said Yvette, in a daze, as the spell of the
gipsy slowly left her, feeling stranded and blank.

The man went to the car, and returned with a little sack of cones,
from which he drew a handful.

'Mind if we make a blaze?' he called to the gipsy.

'Eh?'

'Mind if we make a blaze with a few cones!'

'You go ahead!' said the gipsy.

The man began placing the cones lightly, carefully on the red
embers. And soon, one by one, they caught fire, and burned like roses
of flame, with a sweet scent.

'Ah lovely! lovely!' cried the little Jewess, looking up at her man
again. He looked down at her quite kindly, like the sun on ice. 'Don't
you love fire? Oh, I love it!' the little Jewess cried to Yvette, across
the hammering.

The hammering annoyed her. She looked round with a slight
frown on her fine little brows, as if she would bid the man stop.
Yvette looked round too. The gipsy was bent over his copper bowl,
legs apart, head down, lithe arm lifted. Already he seemed so far
from her.

The man who accompanied the little Jewess strolled over to the
gipsy, and stood in silence looking down on him, holding his pipe to
his mouth. Now they were two men, like two strange male dogs,
having to sniff one another.

'We're on our honeymoon,' said the little Jewess, with an arch,
resentful look at Yvette. She spoke in a rather high, defiant voice, like
some bird, a jay, or a rook, calling.

'Are you really?' said Yvette.

'Yes! Before we're married! Have you heard of Simon Fawcett?' –
she named a wealthy and well-known engineer of the north country.
'Well, I'm Mrs Fawcett, and he's just divorcing me!' She looked at
Yvette with curious defiance and wistfulness.

'Are you really!' said Yvette.

She understood now the look of resentment and defiance in the
little Jewess's big, childlike brown eyes. She was an honest little
thing, but perhaps her honesty was *too* rational. Perhaps it partly
explained the notorious unscrupulousness of the well-known Simon
Fawcett.

'Yes! As soon as we get the divorce, I'm going to marry Major
Eastwood.'

Her cards were now all on the table. She was not going to deceive anybody.

Behind her, the two men were talking briefly. She glanced round, and fixed the gipsy with her big brown eyes.

He was looking up, as if shyly, at the big fellow in the sparkling jersey, who was standing pipe in mouth, man to man, looking down.

'With the horses back of Arras,'[8] said the gipsy, in a low voice.

They were talking war. The gipsy had served with the artillery teams, in the Major's own regiment.

'Ein schöner Mensch!' said the Jewess. 'A handsome man, eh?'

For her, too, the gipsy was one of the common men, the Tommies.

'Quite handsome!' said Yvette.

'You are cycling?' asked the Jewess in a tone of surprise.

'Yes! Down to Papplewick. My father is rector of Papplewick: Mr Saywell!'

'Oh!' said the Jewess. 'I know! A clever writer! Very clever! I have read him.'

The fir-cones were all consumed already, the fire was a tall pile now of crumbling, shattering fire-roses. The sky was clouding over for afternoon. Perhaps towards evening it would snow.

The Major came back, and slung himself into his coat.

'I thought I remembered his face!' he said. 'One of our grooms, AI man with horses.'

'Look!' cried the Jewess to Yvette. 'Why don't you let us motor you down to Normanton. We live in Scoresby. We can tie the bicycle on behind.'

'I think I will,' said Yvette.

'Come!' called the Jewess to the peeping children, as the blond man wheeled away the bicycle. 'Come! Come here!' and taking out her little purse, she held out a shilling.

'Come!' she cried. 'Come and take it!'

The gipsy had laid down his work, and gone into his caravan. The old woman called hoarsely to the children, from her enclosure. The two elder children came stealing forward. The Jewess gave them the two bits of silver, a shilling and a florin, which she had in her purse, and again the hoarse voice of the unseen old woman was heard.

The gipsy descended from his caravan and strolled to the fire. The Jewess searched his face with the peculiar bourgeois boldness of her race.

'You were in the war, in Major Eastwood's regiment?' she said.

'Yes, lady!'

'Imagine you both being here now! – It's going to snow.' She looked up at the sky.

'Later on,' said the man, looking at the sky.

He too had gone inaccessible. His race was very old, in its peculiar battle with established society, and had no conception of winning. Only now and then it could score.

But since the war, even the old sporting chance of scoring now and then, was pretty well quenched. There was no question of yielding. The gipsy's eyes still had their bold look: but it was hardened and directed far away, the touch of insolent intimacy was gone. He had been through the war.

He looked at Yvette.

'You're going back in the motor-car?' he said.

'Yes!' she replied, with a rather mincing mannerism. 'The weather is so treacherous!'

'Treacherous weather!' he repeated, looking at the sky.

She could not tell in the least what his feelings were. In truth, she wasn't very much interested. She was rather fascinated, now, by the little Jewess, mother of two children, who was taking her wealth away from the well-known engineer and transferring it to the penniless, sporting young Major Eastwood, who must be five or six years younger than she. Rather intriguing!

The blond man returned.

'A cigarette, Charles!' cried the little Jewess, plaintively.

He took out his case, slowly, with his slow, athletic movement. Something sensitive in him made him slow, cautious, as if he had hurt himself against people. He gave a cigarette to his wife, then one to Yvette, then offered the case, quite simply, to the gipsy. The gipsy took one.

'Thank you, sir!'

And he went quietly to the fire, and stooping, lit it at the red embers. Both women watched him.

'Well goodbye!' said the Jewess, with her old bourgeois freemasonry. 'Thank you for the warm fire.'

'Fire is everybody's,' said the gipsy.

The young child came toddling to him.

'Goodbye!' said Yvette. 'I hope it won't snow for you.'

'We don't mind a bit of snow,' said the gipsy.

'Don't you?' said Yvette. 'I should have thought you would!'

'No!' said the gipsy.

She flung her scarf royally over her shoulder, and followed the fur coat of the Jewess, which seemed to walk on little legs of its own.

CHAPTER SEVEN

YVETTE WAS RATHER THRILLED by the Eastwoods, as she called them. The little Jewess had only to wait three months now, for the final decree. She had boldly rented a small summer cottage, by the moors up at Scoresby, not far from the hills. Now it was dead winter, and she and the Major lived in comparative isolation, without any maid-ervant. He had already resigned his commission in the regular army, and called himself Mr Eastwood. In fact, they were already Mr and Mrs Eastwood, to the common world.

The little Jewess was thirty-six, and her two children were both over twelve years of age. The husband had agreed that she should have the custody, as soon as she was married to Eastwood.

So there they were, this queer couple, the tiny, finely-formed little Jewess with her big, resentful reproachful eyes, and her mop of carefully-barbered black, curly hair, an elegant little thing in her way; and the big, pale-eyed young man, powerful and wintry, the remnant, surely of some old uncanny Danish stock: living together in a small modern house near the moors and the hills, and doing their own housework.

It was a funny household. The cottage was hired furnished, but the little Jewess had brought along her dearest pieces of furniture. She had an odd little taste for the rococo,[9] strange curving cupboards inlaid with mother of pearl, tortoiseshell, ebony, heaven knows what; strange tall flamboyant chairs, from Italy, with sea-green brocade: astonishing saints with wind-blown, richly-coloured carven garments and pink faces: shelves of weird old Saxe and Capo di Monte figurines:[10] and finally, a strange assortment of astonishing pictures painted on the back of glass, done probably in the early years of the nineteenth century, or in the late eighteenth.

In this crowded and extraordinary interior she received Yvette, when the latter made a stolen visit. A whole system of stoves had been installed into the cottage, every corner was warm, almost hot. And there was the tiny rococo figurine of the Jewess herself, in a perfect little frock, and an apron, putting slices of ham on the dish, while the great snow-bird of a major, in a white sweater and grey trousers, cut bread, mixed mustard, prepared coffee, and did all the rest. He had even made the dish of jugged hare which followed the cold meats and caviare.

The silver and the china were really valuable, part of the bride's trousseau. The Major drank beer from a silver mug, the little Jewess and Yvette had champagne in lovely glasses, the Major brought in coffee. They talked away. The little Jewess had a burning indignation against her first husband. She was intensely moral, so moral, that she was a divorcée. The Major too, strange wintry bird, so powerful, handsome, too, in his way, but pale round the eyes as if he had no eyelashes, like a bird, he too had a curious indignation against life, because of the false morality. That powerful, athletic chest hid a strange, snowy sort of anger. And his tenderness for the little Jewess was based on his sense of outraged justice, the abstract morality of the north blowing him, like a strange wind, into isolation.

As the afternoon drew on, they went to the kitchen, the Major pushed back his sleeves, showing his powerful athletic white arms, and carefully, deftly washed the dishes, while the women wiped. It was not for nothing his muscles were trained. Then he went round attending to the stoves of the small house, which only needed a moment or two of care each day. And after this, he brought out the small, closed car and drove Yvette home, in the rain, depositing her at the back gate, a little wicket among the larches, through which the earthen steps sloped downwards to the house.

She was really amazed by this couple.

'Really, Lucille!' she said. 'I do meet the most extraordinary people!' And she gave a detailed description.

'I think they sound rather nice!' said Lucille. 'I like the Major doing the housework, and looking so frightfully Bond Streety with it all. I should think, *when they're married*, it would be rather fun knowing them.'

'Yes!' said Yvette vaguely. 'Yes! Yes, it would!'

The very strangeness of the connection between the tiny Jewess and that pale-eyed, athletic young officer made her think again of her gipsy, who had been utterly absent from her consciousness, but who now returned with sudden painful force.

'What is it, Lucille,' she asked, 'that brings people together? People like the Eastwoods, for instance? and Daddy and Mamma, so frightfully unsuitable? – and that gipsy woman who told my fortune, like a great horse, and the gipsy man, so fine and delicately cut? What is it?'

'I suppose it's sex, whatever that is,' said Lucille.

'Yes, what is it? It's not really anything common, like *common* sensuality, you know, Lucille. It really isn't.'

'No, I suppose not,' said Lucille. 'Anyhow I suppose it needn't be.'

'Because, you see, the *common* fellows, you know, who make a girl feel *low*: nobody cares much about them. Nobody feels any connection with them. Yet they're supposed to be the sexual sort.'

'I suppose,' said Lucille, 'there's the low sort of sex, and there's the other sort, that isn't low. It's frightfully complicated, really! I *loathe* common fellows. And I never feel anything *sexual* – ' she laid a rather disgusted stress on the word – 'for fellows who aren't common. Perhaps I haven't got any sex.'

'That's just it!' said Yvette. 'Perhaps neither of us has. Perhaps we haven't really got any sex, to connect us with men.'

'How horrible it sounds: *connect us with men*!' cried Lucille, with revulsion. 'Wouldn't you hate to be connected with men that way? Oh I think it's an awful pity there has to *be* sex! It would be so much better if we could still be men and women, without that sort of thing.'

Yvette pondered. Far in the background was the image of the gipsy as he had looked round at her, when she had said: 'The weather is so treacherous.' She felt rather like Peter when the cock crew,[11] as she denied him. Or rather, she did not deny the gipsy; she didn't care about his part in the show, anyhow. It was some hidden part of herself which she denied: that part which mysteriously and unconfessedly responded to him. And it was a strange, lustrous black cock which crew in mockery of her.

'Yes!' she said vaguely. 'Yes! Sex is an awful bore, you know, Lucille. When you haven't got it, you feel you *ought* to have it, somehow. And when you've got it – or *if* you have it – ' she lifted her head and wrinkled her nose disdainfully – 'you hate it.'

'Oh, I don't know!' cried Lucille. 'I think I should *like* to be awfully in love with a man.'

'You think so!' said Yvette, again wrinkling her nose. 'But if you were you wouldn't.'

'How do you know?' asked Lucille.

'Well, I don't really,' said Yvette. 'But I think so! Yes I think so!'

'Oh, it's very likely!' said Lucille disgustedly. 'And anyhow one would be sure to get out of love again, and it would be merely disgusting.'

'Yes,' said Yvette. 'It's a problem.' She hummed a little tune.

'Oh hang it all, it's not a problem for us two yet. We're neither of us really in love, and we probably never shall be, so the problem is settled that way.'

'I'm not so sure!' said Yvette sagely. 'I'm not so sure. I believe, one day, I shall fall *awfully* in love.'

'Probably you never will,' said Lucille brutally. 'That's what most old maids are thinking all the time.'

Yvette looked at her sister from pensive but apparently insouciant eyes.

'Is it?' she said. 'Do you really think so, Lucille? How perfectly awful for them, poor things! Why ever do they *care*?'

'Why do they?' said Lucille. 'Perhaps they don't, really – Probably it's all because people say: *Poor old girl, she couldn't catch a man.*'

'I suppose it is!' said Yvette. 'They get to mind the beastly things people always do say about old maids. What a shame!'

'Anyhow we have a good time, and we do have lots of boys who make a fuss of us,' said Lucille.

'Yes!' said Yvette. 'Yes! But I couldn't possibly marry any of them.'

'Neither could I,' said Lucille. 'But why shouldn't we? Why should we bother about marrying, when we have a perfectly good time with the boys, who are awfully good sorts, and you must say, Yvette, awfully sporting and *decent* to us.'

'Oh, they are!' said Yvette absently.

'I think it's time to think of marrying somebody,' said Lucille, 'when you feel you're *not* having a good time any more. Then marry, and just settle down.'

'Quite!' said Yvette.

But now, under all her bland, soft amiability, she was annoyed with Lucille. Suddenly she wanted to turn her back on Lucille.

Besides, look at the shadows under poor Lucille's eyes, and the wistfulness in the beautiful eyes themselves. Oh, if some awfully nice, kind, protective sort of man would but marry her! And if the sporting Lucille would let him!

Yvette did not tell the rector, nor Granny about the Eastwoods. It would only have started a lot of talk which she detested. The rector wouldn't have minded, for himself, privately. But he too knew the necessity of keeping as clear as possible from that poisonous, many-headed serpent, the tongue of the people.

'But I don't *want* you to come if your father doesn't know,' cried the little Jewess.

'I suppose I'll have to tell him,' said Yvette. 'I'm sure he doesn't mind, really. But if he knew, he'd have to, I suppose.'

The young officer looked at her with an odd amusement, bird-like and unemotional, in his keen eyes. He too was by way of falling in love with Yvette. It was her peculiar virgin tenderness, and her straying, absent-minded detachment from things, which attracted him.

She was aware of what was happening, and she rather preened

herself. Eastwood piqued her fancy. Such a smart young officer, awfully good class, so calm and amazing with a motor-car, and quite a champion swimmer, it was intriguing to see him quietly, calmly washing dishes, smoking his pipe, doing his job so alert and skilful. Or, with the same interested care with which he made his investigation into the mysterious inside of an automobile, concocting jugged hare in the cottage kitchen. Then going out in the icy weather and cleaning his car till it looked like a live thing, like a cat when she has licked herself. Then coming in to talk so unassumingly and responsively, if briefly, with the little Jewess. And apparently, never bored. Sitting at the window with his pipe in bad weather, silent for hours, abstracted, musing, yet with his athletic body alert in its stillness.

Yvette did not flirt with him. But she *did* like him.

'But what about your future?' she asked him.

'What about it?' he said, taking his pipe from his mouth, the unemotional point of a smile in his bird's eyes.

'A career! Doesn't every man have to carve out a career? – like some huge goose with gravy?' She gazed with odd *naïveté* into his eyes.

'I'm perfectly all right today, and I shall be all right tomorrow,' he said, with a cold, decided look. 'Why shouldn't my future be continuous todays and tomorrows?'

He looked at her with unmoved searching.

'Quite!' she said. 'I hate jobs, and all that side of life.' But she was thinking of the Jewess's money.

To which he did not answer. His anger was of the soft, snowy sort, which comfortably muffles the soul.

They had come to the point of talking philosophically together. The little Jewess looked a bit wan. She was curiously naïve, and not possessive in her attitude to the man. Nor was she at all catty with Yvette. Only rather wan, and dumb.

Yvette, on a sudden impulse, thought she had better clear herself.

'I think life's *awfully* difficult,' she said.

'Life is!' cried the Jewess.

'What's so beastly, is that one is supposed to *fall in love*, and get married!' said Yvette, curling up her nose.

'Don't you *want* to fall in love and get married?' cried the Jewess, with great glaring eyes of astounded reproach.

'No, not particularly!' said Yvette. 'Especially as one feels there's nothing else to do. It's an awful chicken-coop one has to run into.'

'But you don't know what love is?' cried the Jewess.

'No!' said Yvette. 'Do you?'

'I!' bawled the tiny Jewess. 'I! My goodness, don't I!' She looked with reflective gloom at Eastwood, who was smoking his pipe, the dimples of his disconnected amusement showing on his smooth, scrupulous face. He had a very fine, smooth skin, which yet did not suffer from the weather, so that his face looked naked as a baby's. But it was not a round face: it was characteristic enough, and took queer ironical dimples, like a mask which is comic but frozen.

'Do you mean to say you don't know what love is?' insisted the Jewess.

'No!' said Yvette, with insouciant candour. 'I don't believe I do! Is it awful of me, at my age?'

'Is there never any man that makes you feel quite, quite different?' said the Jewess, with another big-eyed look at Eastwood. He smoked, utterly unimplicated.

'I don't think there is,' said Yvette. 'Unless – yes! – unless it is that gipsy' – she had put her head pensively sideways.

'Which gipsy?' bawled the little Jewess.

'The one who was a Tommy and looked after horses in Major Eastwood's regiment in the war,' said Yvette coolly.

The little Jewess gazed at Yvette with great eyes of stupor.

'You're not in love with that *gipsy*!' she said.

'Well!' said Yvette. 'I don't know. He's the only one that makes me feel – different! He really is!'

'But how? How? Has he ever *said* anything to you?'

'No! No!'

'Then how? What has he done?'

'Oh, just looked at me!'

'How?'

'Well you see, I don't know. But different! Yes, different! Different, quite different from the way any man ever looked at me.'

'But *how* did he look at you?' insisted the Jewess.

'Why – as if he really, but *really*, *desired* me,' said Yvette, her meditative face looking like the bud of a flower.

'What a vile fellow! What *right* had he to look at you like that?' cried the indignant Jewess.

'A cat may look at a king,' calmly interposed the Major, and now his face had the smiles of a cat's face.

'You think he oughtn't to?' asked Yvette, turning to him.

'Certainly not! A gipsy fellow, with half a dozen dirty women trailing after him! Certainly not!' cried the tiny Jewess.

'I wondered!' said Yvette. 'Because it *was* rather wonderful, really! And it *was* something quite different in my life.'

'I think,' said the Major, taking his pipe from his mouth, 'that desire is the most wonderful thing in life. Anybody who can really feel it, is a king, and I envy nobody else!' He put back his pipe.

The Jewess looked at him stupefied.

'But Charles!' she cried. 'Every common low man in Halifax feels nothing else!'

He again took his pipe from his mouth.

'That's merely appetite,' he said.

And he put back his pipe.

'You think the gipsy is the real thing?' Yvette asked him.

He lifted his shoulders.

'It's not for me to say,' he replied. 'If I were you, I should know, I shouldn't be asking other people.'

'Yes – but – ' Yvette trailed out.

'Charles! You're wrong! How *could* it be a real thing! As if she could possibly marry him and go round in a caravan!'

'I didn't say marry him,' said Charles.

'Or a love affair! Why it's monstrous! What would she think of herself! – That's not love! That's – that's prostitution!'

Charles smoked for some moments.

'That gipsy was the best man we had, with horses. Nearly died of pneumonia. I thought he *was* dead. He's a resurrected man to me. I'm a resurrected man myself, as far as that goes.' He looked at Yvette. 'I was buried for twenty hours under snow,' he said. 'And not much the worse for it, when they dug me out.'

There was a frozen pause in the conversation.

'Life's awful!' said Yvette.

'They dug me out by accident,' he said.

'Oh! – ' Yvette trailed slowly. 'It might be destiny, you know.'

To which he did not answer.

CHAPTER EIGHT

THE RECTOR HEARD ABOUT Yvette's intimacy with the Eastwoods, and she was somewhat startled by the result. She had thought he wouldn't care. Verbally, in his would-be humorous fashion, he was so entirely unconventional, such a frightfully good sport. As he said himself, he was a conservative anarchist;[12] which meant, he was like a great many more people, a mere unbeliever. The anarchy extended to his humorous talk, and his secret thinking. The conservatism, based on a mongrel fear of the anarchy, controlled every action. His thoughts, secretly, were something to be scared of. Therefore, in his life, he was fanatically afraid of the unconventional.

When his conservatism and his abject sort of fear were uppermost, he always lifted his lip and bared his teeth a little, in a dog-like sneer.

'I hear your latest friends are the half-divorced Mrs Fawcett and the *maquereau*[13] Eastwood,' he said to Yvette.

She didn't know what a *maquereau* was, but she felt the poison in the rector's fangs.

'I just know them,' she said. 'They're awfully nice, really. And they'll be married in about a month's time.'

The rector looked at her insouciant face with hatred. Somewhere inside him, he was cowed, he had been born cowed. And those who are born cowed are natural slaves, and deep instinct makes them fear with poisonous fear those who might suddenly snap the slave's collar round their necks.

It was for this reason the rector had so abjectly curled up, still so abjectly curled up before She-who-was-Cynthia: because of his slave's fear of her contempt, the contempt of a born-free nature for a base-born nature.

Yvette too had a free-born quality. She too, one day, would know him, and clap the slave's collar of her contempt round his neck.

But should she? He would fight to the death, this time, first. The slave in him was cornered this time, like a cornered rat, and with the courage of a cornered rat.

'I suppose they're your sort!' he sneered.

'Well, they are, really,' she said, with that blithe vagueness. 'I do like them awfully. They seem so solid, you know, so honest.'

'You've got a peculiar notion of honesty!' he sneered. 'A young sponge going off with a woman older than himself, so that he can live on her money! The woman leaving her home and her children! I don't know where you get your idea of honesty. Not from me, I hope. – And you seem to be very well acquainted with them, considering you say you just know them. Where did you meet them?'

'When I was out bicycling. They came along in their car, and we happened to talk. She told me at once who she was, so that I shouldn't make a mistake. She *is* honest.'

Poor Yvette was struggling to bear up.

'And how often have you seen them since?'

'Oh, I've just been over twice.'

'Over where?'

'To their cottage in Scoresby.'

He looked at her in hate, as if he could kill her. And he backed away from her, against the window-curtains of his study, like a rat at bay. Somewhere in his mind he was thinking unspeakable depravities about his daughter, as he had thought them of She-who-was-Cynthia. He was powerless against the lowest insinuations of his own mind. And these depravities which he attributed to the still-uncowed but frightened girl in front of him, made him recoil, showing all his fangs in his handsome face.

'So you just know them, do you?' he said. 'Lying is in your blood, I see. I don't believe you get it from me.'

Yvette half averted her mute face, and thought of Granny's bare-faced prevarication. She did not answer.

'What takes you creeping round such couples?' he sneered. 'Aren't there enough decent people in the world for you to know? Anyone would think you were a stray dog, having to run round indecent couples, because the decent ones wouldn't have you. Have you got something worse than lying in your blood?'

'What have I got worse than lying in my blood?' she asked. A cold deadness was coming over her. Was she abnormal, one of the semi-criminal abnormals? It made her feel cold and dead.

In his eyes, she was just brazening out the depravity that underlay her virgin, tender, bird-like face. She-who-was-Cynthia had been like this: a snow-flower. And he had convulsions of sadistic horror, thinking what might be the *actual* depravity of She-who-was-Cynthia. Even his *own* love for her, which had been the lust-love of the born cowed, had been a depravity, in secret, to him. So what must an illegal love be?

'You know best yourself, what you have got,' he sneered. 'But it is something you had best curb, and quickly, if you don't intend to finish in a criminal-lunacy asylum.'

'Why?' she said, pale and muted, numbed with frozen fear. 'Why criminal lunacy? What have I done?'

'That is between you and your Maker,' he jeered. 'I shall never ask. But certain tendencies end in criminal lunacy, unless they are curbed in time.'

'Do you mean like knowing the Eastwoods?' asked Yvette, after a pause of numb fear.

'Do I mean like nosing round such people as Mrs Fawcett, a Jewess, and ex-Major Eastwood, a man who goes off with an older woman for the sake of her money? Why yes, I do!'

'But you *can't* say that,' cried Yvette. 'He's an awfully simple, straightforward man.'

'He is apparently one of your sort.'

'Well. – In a way, I thought he was. I thought you'd like him too,' she said simply, hardly knowing what she said.

The rector backed into the curtains, as if the girl menaced him with something fearful.

'Don't say any more,' he snarled, abject. 'Don't say any more. You've said too much, to implicate you. I don't want to learn any more horrors.'

'But what horrors?' she persisted.

The very naïveté of her unscrupulous innocence repelled him, cowed him still more.

'Say no more!' he said, in a low, hissing voice. 'But I will kill you before you shall go the way of your mother.'

She looked at him, as he stood there backed against the velvet curtains of his study, his face yellow, his eyes distraught like a rat's with fear and rage and hate, and a numb, frozen loneliness came over her. For her too, the meaning had gone out of everything.

It was hard to break the frozen, sterile silence that ensued. At last, however, she looked at him. And in spite of herself, beyond her own knowledge, the contempt for him was in her young, clear, baffled eyes. It fell like the slave's collar over his neck, finally.

'Do you mean I mustn't know the Eastwoods?' she said.

'You can know them if you wish,' he sneered. 'But you must not expect to associate with your Granny, and your Aunt Cissie, and Lucille, if you do. I cannot have *them* contaminated. Your Granny was a faithful wife and a faithful mother, if ever one existed. She has already had one shock of shame and abomination to endure. She shall never be exposed to another.'

Yvette heard it all dimly, half hearing.

'I can send a note and say you disapprove,' she said dimly.

'You follow your own course of action. But remember, you have to choose between clean people, and reverence for your Granny's blameless old age, and people who are unclean in their minds and their bodies.'

Again there was a silence. Then she looked at him, and her face was more puzzled than anything. But somewhere at the back of her perplexity was that peculiar calm, virgin contempt of the free-born for the base-born. He, and all the Saywells, were base-born.

'All right,' she said. 'I'll write and say you disapprove.'

He did not answer. He was partly flattered, secretly triumphant, but abjectly.

'I have tried to keep this from your Granny and Aunt Cissie,' he said. 'It need not be public property, since you choose to make your friendship clandestine.'

There was a dreary silence.

'All right,' she said. 'I'll go and write.'

And she crept out of the room.

She addressed her little note to Mrs Eastwood. 'Dear Mrs Eastwood, Daddy doesn't approve of my coming to see you. So you will understand if we have to break it off. I'm awfully sorry – ' That was all.

Yet she felt a dreary blank when she had posted her letter. She was now even afraid of her own thoughts. She wanted, now, to be held against the slender, fine-shaped breast of the gipsy. She wanted him to hold her in his arms, if only for once, for once, and comfort and confirm her. She wanted to be confirmed by him, against her father, who had only a repulsive fear of her.

And at the same time she cringed and winced, so that she could hardly walk, for fear the thought was obscene, a criminal lunacy. It seemed to wound her heels as she walked, the fear. The fear, the great cold fear of the base-born, her father, everything human and swarming. Like a great bog humanity swamped her, and she sank in, weak at the knees, filled with repulsion and fear of every person she met.

She adjusted herself, however, quite rapidly to her new conception of people. She had to live. It is useless to quarrel with one's bread and butter. And to expect a great deal out of life is puerile. So, with the rapid adaptability of the post-war generation, she adjusted herself to the new facts. Her father was what he was. He would always play up to appearances. She would do the same. She too would play up to appearances.

So, underneath the blithe, gossamer-straying insouciance, a certain hardness formed, like rock crystallising in her heart. She lost her illusions in the collapse of her sympathies. Outwardly, she seemed the same. Inwardly she was hard and detached, and, unknown to herself, revengeful.

Outwardly she remained the same. It was part of her game. While circumstances remained as they were, she must remain, at least in appearance, true to what was expected of her.

But the revengefulness came out in her new vision of people. Under the rector's apparently gallant handsomeness, she saw the weak, feeble nullity. And she despised him. Yet still, in a way, she liked him too. Feelings are so complicated.

It was Granny whom she came to detest with all her soul. That obese old woman, sitting there in her blindness like some great red-blotched fungus, her neck swallowed between her heaped-up shoulders and her rolling, ancient chins, so that she was neckless as a double potato, her Yvette really hated, with that pure, sheer hatred which is almost a joy. Her hate was so clear, that while she was feeling strong, she enjoyed it.

The old woman sat with her big, reddened face pressed a little back, her lace cap perched on her thin white hair, her stub nose still assertive, and her old mouth shut like a trap. This motherly old soul, her mouth gave her away. It always had been one of the compressed sort. But in her great age, it had gone like a toad's, lipless, the jaw pressing up like the lower jaw of a trap. The look Yvette most hated was the look of that lower jaw pressing relentlessly up, with an ancient prognathous thrust, so that the snub nose in turn was forced to press upwards, and the whole face was pressed a little back, beneath the big, wall-like forehead. The will, the ancient, toad-like, obscene *will* in the old woman, was fearful, once you saw it: a toad-like self-will that was godless, and less than human! It belonged to the old, enduring race of toads, or tortoises. And it made one feel that Granny would never die. She would live on like these higher reptiles, in a state of semi-coma, for ever.

Yvette dared not even suggest to her father that Granny was not perfect. He would have threatened his daughter with the lunatic asylum. That was the threat he always seemed to have up his sleeve: the lunatic asylum. Exactly as if a distaste for Granny and for that horrible house of relatives was in itself a proof of lunacy, dangerous lunacy.

Yet in one of her moods of irritable depression, she did once fling out: 'How perfectly beastly this house is! Aunt Lucy comes, and Aunt Nell, and Aunt Alice, and they make a ring like a ring of crows, with Granny and Aunt Cissie, all lifting their skirts up and warming their legs at the fire, and shutting Lucille and me out. We're nothing but outsiders in this beastly house!'

Her father glanced at her curiously. But she managed to put a petulance into her speech, and a mere cross rudeness into her look, so that he could laugh, as at a childish tantrum. Somewhere, though, he knew that she coldly, venomously meant what she said, and he was wary of her.

Her life seemed now nothing but an irritable friction against the unsavoury household of the Saywells, in which she was immersed. She loathed the rectory with a loathing that consumed her life, a loathing so strong that she could not really go away from the place. While it endured, she was spell-bound to it, in revulsion.

She forgot the Eastwoods again. After all, what was the revolt of the little Jewess, compared to Granny and the Saywell bunch! A husband was never more than a semi-casual thing! But a family! – an awful, smelly family that would never disperse, stuck half dead round the base of a fungoid old woman! How was one to cope with that?

She did not forget the gipsy entirely. But she had no time for him. She, who was bored almost to agony, and who had nothing at all to do, she had not time to think even, seriously, of anything. Time being, after all, only the current of the soul in its flow.

She saw the gipsy twice. Once he came to the house, with things to sell. And she, watching him from the landing window, refused to go down. He saw her too, as he was putting his things back into his cart. But he too gave no sign. Being of a race that exists only to be harrying the outskirts of our society, forever hostile and living only by spoil, he was too much master of himself, and too wary, to expose himself openly to the vast and gruesome clutch of our law. He had been through the war. He had been enslaved against his will, that time.

So now, he showed himself at the rectory, and slowly, quietly busied himself at his cart outside the white gate, with that air of silent and forever-unyielding outsideness which gave him his lonely, predative grace. He knew she saw him. And she should see him unyielding, quietly hawking his copper vessels, on an old, old war-path against such as herself.

Such as herself? Perhaps he was mistaken. Her heart, in its stroke, now rang hard as his hammer upon his copper, beating against circumstances. But he struck stealthily on the outside, and she still more secretly on the inside of the establishment. She liked him. She liked the quiet, noiseless clean-cut presence of him. She liked that mysterious endurance in him, which endures in opposition, without any idea of victory. And she liked that peculiar added relentlessness, the disillusion in hostility, which belongs to after the war. Yes, if she belonged to any side, and to any clan, it was to his. Almost she could have found it in her heart to go with him, and be a pariah gipsy-woman.

But she was born inside the pale. And she liked comfort, and a certain prestige. Even as a mere rector's daughter, one did have a certain prestige. And she liked that. Also she liked to chip against the pillars of the temple, from the inside. She wanted to be safe under the temple roof. Yet she enjoyed chipping fragments off the supporting pillars. Doubtless many fragments had been whittled away from the pillars of the Philistine, before Samson pulled the temple down.[14]

'I'm not sure one shouldn't have one's fling till one is twenty-six, and then give in, and marry!'

This was Lucille's philosophy, learned from older women. Yvette was twenty-one. It meant she had five more years in which to have this precious fling. And the fling meant, at the moment, the gipsy. The marriage, at the age of twenty-six, meant Leo or Gerry.

So, a woman could eat her cake and have her bread and butter.

Yvette, pitched in gruesome, deadlocked hostility to the Saywell household, was very old and very wise: with the agedness and the wisdom of the young, which always overleaps the agedness and the wisdom of the old, or the elderly.

The second time she met the gipsy by accident. It was March, and sunny weather, after unheard-of rains. Celandines were yellow in the hedges, and primroses among the rocks. But still there came a smell of sulphur from far-away steel-works, out of the steel-blue sky.

And yet it was spring!

Yvette was cycling slowly along by Codnor Gate, past the lime quarries, when she saw the gipsy coming away from the door of a stone cottage. His cart stood there in the road. He was returning with his brooms and copper things, to the cart.

She got down from her bicycle. As she saw him, she loved with curious tenderness the slim lines of his body in the green jersey, the turn of his silent face. She felt she knew him better than she knew anybody on earth, even Lucille, and belonged to him, in some way, for ever.

'Have you made anything new and nice?' she asked innocently, looking at his copper things.

'I don't think,' he said, glancing back at her.

The desire was still there, still curious and naked, in his eyes. But it was more remote, the boldness was diminished. There was a tiny glint, as if he might dislike her. But this dissolved again, as he saw her looking among his bits of copper and brass-work. She searched them diligently.

There was a little oval brass plate, with a queer figure like a palm tree beaten upon it.

'I like that,' she said. 'How much is it?'

'What you like,' he said.

This made her nervous: he seemed offhand, almost mocking.

'I'd rather you said,' she told him, looking up at him.

'You give me what you like,' he said.

'No!' she said, suddenly. 'If you won't tell me I won't have it.'

'All right,' he said. 'Two shilling.'

She found half a crown, and he drew from his pocket a handful of silver, from which he gave her her sixpence.

'The old gipsy dreamed something about you,' he said, looking at her with curious, searching eyes.

'Did she!' cried Yvette, at once interested. 'What was it?'

'She said: Be braver in your heart, or you lose your game. She said it this way: "Be braver in your body, or your luck will leave you." And she said as well: "Listen for the voice of water." '

Yvette was very much impressed.

'And what does it mean?' she asked.

'I asked her,' he said. 'She says she don't know.'

'Tell me again what it was,' said Yvette.

' "Be braver in your body, or your luck will go." And: "Listen for the voice of water." '

He looked in silence at her soft, pondering face. Something almost like a perfume seemed to flow from her young bosom direct to him, in a grateful connection.

'I'm to be braver in my body, and I'm to listen for the voice of water! All right!' she said. 'I don't understand, but perhaps I shall.'

She looked at him with clear eyes. Man or woman is made up of many selves. With one self, she loved this gipsy man. With many selves, she ignored him or had a distaste for him.

'You're not coming up to the Head no more?' he asked.

Again she looked at him absently.

'Perhaps I will,' she said, 'sometime. Sometime.'

'Spring weather!' he said, smiling faintly and glancing round at the sun. 'We're going to break camp soon, and go away.'

'When?' she said.

'Perhaps next week.'

'Where to?'

Again he made a move with his head.

'Perhaps up north,' he said.

She looked at him.

'All right!' she said. 'Perhaps I *will* come up before you go, and say goodbye to your wife and to the old woman who sent me the message.'

CHAPTER NINE

YVETTE DID NOT keep her promise. The few March days were
lovely, and she let them slip. She had a curious reluctance, always,
towards taking action, or making any real move of her own. She
always wanted someone else to make a move for her, as if she did not
want to play her own game of life.

She lived as usual, went out to her friends, to parties, and danced
with the undiminished Leo. She wanted to go up and say goodbye to
the gipsies. She wanted to. And nothing prevented her.

On the Friday afternoon especially she wanted to go. It was sunny,
and the last yellow crocuses down the drive were in full blaze, wide
open, the first bees rolling in them. The Papple rushed under the
stone bridge, uncannily full, nearly filling the arches. There was the
scent of a mezereon tree.

And she felt too lazy, too lazy, too lazy. She strayed in the garden
by the river, half dreamy, expecting something. While the gleam of
spring sun lasted, she would be out of doors. Indoors Granny, sitting
back like some awful old prelate, in her bulk of black silk and her
white lace cap, was warming her feet by the fire, and hearing
everything that Aunt Nell had to say. Friday was Aunt Nell's day. She
usually came for lunch, and left after an early tea. So the mother and
the large, rather common daughter, who was a widow at the age of
forty, sat gossiping by the fire, while Aunt Cissie prowled in and out.
Friday was the rector's day for going to town: it was also the
housemaid's half-day.

Yvette sat on a wooden seat in the garden, only a few feet above the
bank of the swollen river, which rolled a strange, uncanny mass of
water. The crocuses were passing in the ornamental beds, the grass
was dark green where it was mown, the laurels looked a little
brighter. Aunt Cissie appeared at the top of the porch steps, and
called to ask if Yvette wanted that early cup of tea. Because of the
river just below, Yvette could not hear what Aunt Cissie said, but she
guessed, and shook her head. An early cup of tea, indoors, when the
sun actually shone? No thanks!

She was conscious of her gipsy, as she sat there musing in the sun.
Her soul had the half painful, half easing knack of leaving her, and
straying away to some place, to somebody that had caught her
imagination. Some days she would be at the Framleys', even though

she did not go near them. Some days, she was all the time in spirit with the Eastwoods. And today it was the gipsies. She was up at their encampment in the quarry. She saw the man hammering his copper, lifting his head to look at the road; and the children playing in the horse-shelter: and the women, the gipsy's wife and the strong, elderly woman, coming home with their packs, along with the elderly man. For this afternoon, she felt intensely that *that* was home for her: the gipsy camp, the fire, the stool, the man with the hammer, the old crone.

It was part of her nature, to get these fits of yearning for some place she knew; to be in a certain place; with somebody who meant home to her. This afternoon it was the gipsy camp. And the man in the green jersey made it home to her. Just to be where he was, that was to be at home. The caravans, the brats, the other women: everything was natural to her, her home, as if she had been born there. She wondered if the gipsy was aware of her: if he could see her sitting on the stool by the fire; if he would lift his head and see her as she rose, looking at him slowly and significantly, turning towards the steps of his caravan. Did he know? Did he know?

Vaguely she looked up the steep of dark larch trees north of the house, where unseen the road climbed, going towards the Head. There was nothing, and her glance strayed down again. At the foot of the slope the river turned, thrown back harshly, ominously, against the low rocks across stream, then pouring past the garden to the bridge. It was unnaturally full, and whitey-muddy, and ponderous, 'Listen for the voice of water,' she said to herself. 'No need to listen for it, if the voice means the noise!'

And again she looked at the swollen river breaking angrily as it came round the bend. Above it the black-looking kitchen garden hung, and the hard-natured fruit trees. Everything was on the tilt, facing south and south-west, for the sun. Behind, above the house and the kitchen garden hung the steep little wood of withered-seeming larches. The gardener was working in the kitchen garden, high up there, by the edge of the larch-wood.

She heard a call. It was Aunt Cissie and Aunt Nell. They were on the drive, waving Goodbye! Yvette waved back. Then Aunt Cissie, pitching her voice against the waters, called: 'I shan't be long. Don't forget Granny is alone!'

'All right!' screamed Yvette rather ineffectually.

And she sat on her bench and watched the two undignified, long-coated women walk slowly over the bridge and begin the curving climb on the opposite slope, Aunt Nell carrying a sort of suitcase in which she brought a few goods for Granny and took back vegetables or whatever the rectory garden or cupboard was yielding. Slowly the two figures diminished, on the whitish, up-curving road, labouring slowly up towards Papplewick village. Aunt Cissie was going as far as the village for something.

The sun was yellowing to decline. What a pity! Oh what a pity the sunny day was going, and she would have to turn indoors, to those hateful rooms, and Granny! Aunt Cissie would be back directly: it was past five. And all the others would be arriving from town, rather irritable and tired, soon after six.

As she looked uneasily round, she heard, across the running of water, the sharp noise of a horse and cart rattling on the road hidden in the larch trees. The gardener was looking up too. Yvette turned away again, lingering, strolling by the full river a few paces, unwilling to go in; glancing up the road to see if Aunt Cissie were coming. If she saw her, she would go indoors.

She heard somebody shouting, and looked round. Down the path through the larch trees the gipsy was bounding. The gardener, away beyond, was also running. Simultaneously she became aware of a great roar, which, before she could move, accumulated to a vast deafening snarl. The gipsy was gesticulating. She looked round, behind her.

And to her horror and amazement, round the bend of the river she saw a shaggy, tawny wave-front of water advancing like a wall of lions. The roaring sound wiped out everything. She was powerless, too amazed and wonder-struck, she wanted to see it.

Before she could think twice, it was near, a roaring cliff of water. She almost fainted with horror. She heard the scream of the gipsy, and looked up to see him bounding upon her, his black eyes starting out of his head.

'Run!' he screamed, seizing her arm.

And in the instant the first wave was washing her feet from under her, swirling, in the insane noise, which suddenly for some reason seemed like stillness, with a devouring flood over the garden. The horrible mowing of water!

The gipsy dragged her heavily, lurching, plunging, but still keeping foothold for both of them, towards the house. She was barely conscious: as if the flood was in her soul.

There was one grass-banked terrace of the garden, near the path round the house. The gipsy clawed his way up this terrace to the dry level of the path, dragging her after him, and sprang with her past the windows to the porch steps. Before they got there, a new great surge of water came mowing, mowing trees down even, and mowed them down too.

Yvette felt herself gone in an agonising mill-race of icy water, whirled, with only the fearful grip of the gipsy's hand on her wrist. They were both down and gone. She felt a dull but stunning bruise somewhere.

Then he pulled her up. He was up, streaming forth water, clinging to the stem of the great wisteria that grew against the wall, crushed against the wall by the water. Her head was above water, he held her arm till it seemed dislocated: but she could not get her footing. With a ghastly sickness like a dream, she struggled and struggled, and could not get her feet. Only his hand was locked on her wrist.

He dragged her nearer till her one hand caught his leg. He nearly went down again. But the wisteria held him, and he pulled her up to him. She clawed at him, horribly; and got to her feet, he hanging on like a man torn in two, to the wisteria trunk.

The water was above her knees. The man and she looked into each other's ghastly streaming faces.

'Get to the steps!' he screamed.

It was only just round the corner: four strides! She looked at him: she could not go. His eyes glared on her like a tiger's, and he pushed her from him. She clung to the wall, and the water seemed to abate a little. Round the corner she staggered, but staggering, reeled and was pitched up against the cornice of the balustrade of the porch steps, the man after her.

They got on to the steps, when another roar was heard amid the roar, and the wall of the house shook. Up heaved the water round their legs again, but the gipsy had opened the hall door. In they poured with the water, reeling to the stairs. And as they did so, they saw the short but strange bulk of Granny emerge in the hall, away down from the dining-room door. She had her hands lifted and clawing, as the first water swirled round her legs, and her coffin-like mouth was opened in a hoarse scream.

Yvette was blind to everything but the stairs. Blind, unconscious of everything save the steps rising beyond the water, she clambered up like a wet, shuddering cat, in a state of unconsciousness. It was not till she was on the landing, dripping and shuddering till she could not stand erect, clinging to the banisters, while the house shook and the water raved below, that she was aware of the sodden gipsy, in paroxysms of coughing at the head of the stairs, his cap gone, his black hair over his eyes, peering between his washed-down hair at the sickening heave of water below, in the hall. Yvette, fainting, looked too and saw Granny bob up, like a strange float, her face purple, her blind blue eyes bolting, spume hissing from her mouth. One old purple hand clawed at a banister rail, and held for a moment, showing the glint of a wedding ring.

The gipsy, who had coughed himself free and pushed back his hair, said to that awful float-like face below: 'Not good enough! Not good enough!'

With a low thud like thunder, the house was struck again, and shuddered, and a strange cracking, rattling, spitting noise began. Up heaved the water like a sea. The hand was gone, all sign of anything was gone, but upheaving water.

Yvette turned in blind unconscious frenzy, staggering like a wet cat to the upper staircase, and climbing swiftly. It was not till she was at the door of her room that she stopped, paralysed by the sound of a sickening, tearing crash, while the house swayed.

'The house is coming down!' yelled the green-white face of the gipsy, in her face.

He glared into her crazed face.

'Where is the chimney? the back chimney? – which room? The chimney will stand – '

He glared with strange ferocity into her face, forcing her to understand. And she nodded with a strange, crazed poise, nodded quite serenely, saying: 'In here! In here! It's all right.'

They entered her room, which had a narrow fireplace. It was a back room with two windows, one on each side the great chimney-flue. The gipsy, coughing bitterly and trembling in every limb, went to the window to look out.

Below, between the house and the steep rise of the hill, was a wild mill-race of water rushing with refuse, including Rover's green dog-kennel. The gipsy coughed and coughed, and gazed down blankly. Tree after tree went down, mown by the water, which must have been ten feet deep.

Shuddering and pressing his sodden arms on his sodden breast, a look of resignation on his livid face, he turned to Yvette. A fearful tearing noise tore the house, then there was a deep, watery explosion. Something had gone down, some part of the house, the floor heaved and wavered beneath them. For some moments both were suspended, stupefied. Then he roused.

'Not good enough! Not good enough! This will stand. This here will stand. See that chimney! like a tower. Yes! All right! All right! You take your clothes off and go to bed. You'll die of the cold.'

'It's all right! It's quite all right!' she said to him, sitting on a chair and looking up into his face with her white, insane little face, round which the hair was plastered.

'No!' he cried. 'No! Take your things off and I rub you with this towel. I rub myself. If the house falls then die warm. If it don't fall, then live, not die of pneumonia.'

Coughing, shuddering violently, he pulled up his jersey hem and wrestled with all his shuddering, cold-racked might, to get off his wet, tight jersey.

'Help me!' he cried, his face muffled.

She seized the edge of the jersey, obediently, and pulled with all her might. The garment came over his head, and he stood in his braces.

'Take your things off! Rub with this towel!' he commanded ferociously, the savageness of the war on him. And like a thing obsessed, he pushed himself out of his trousers, and got out of his wet, clinging shirt, emerging slim and livid, shuddering in every fibre with cold and shock.

He seized a towel, and began quickly to rub his body, his teeth chattering like plates rattling together. Yvette dimly saw it was wise. She tried to get out of her dress. He pulled the horrible wet death-gripping thing off her, then, resuming his rubbing, went to the door, tiptoeing on the wet floor.

There he stood, naked, towel in hand, petrified. He looked west, towards where the upper landing window had been, and was looking into the sunset, over an insane sea of waters, bristling with uptorn trees and refuse. The end corner of the house where the porch had been, and the stairs, had gone. The wall had fallen, leaving the floors sticking out. The stairs had gone.

Motionless, he watched the water. A cold wind blew in upon him. He clenched his rattling teeth with a great effort of will, and turned into the room again, closing the door.

Yvette, naked, shuddering so much that she was sick, was trying to wipe herself dry.

'All right!' he cried. 'All right! The water don't rise no more! All right!'

With his towel he began to rub her, himself shaking all over, but holding her gripped by the shoulder, and slowly, numbedly rubbing her tender body, even trying to rub up into some dryness the pitiful hair of her small head.

Suddenly he left off.

'Better lie in the bed,' he commanded, 'I want to rub myself.'

His teeth went snap-snap-snap-snap, in great snaps, cutting off his words. Yvette crept shaking and semi-conscious into her bed. He, making strained efforts to hold himself still and rub himself warm, went again to the north window, to look out.

The water had risen a little. The sun had gone down, and there was a reddish glow. He rubbed his hair into a black, wet tangle, then paused for breath, in a sudden access of shuddering, then looked out again, then rubbed again on his breast, and began to cough afresh, because of the water he had swallowed. His towel was red: he had hurt himself somewhere: but he felt nothing.

There was still the strange huge noise of water, and the horrible bump of things bumping against the walls. The wind was rising with sundown, cold and hard. The house shook with explosive thuds, and weird, weird frightening noises came up.

A terror creeping over his soul, he went again to the door. The wind, roaring with the waters, blew in as he opened it. Through the awesome gap in the house he saw the world, the waters, the chaos of horrible waters, the twilight, the perfect new moon high above the sunset, a faint thing, and clouds pushing dark into the sky, on the cold, blustery wind.

Clenching his teeth again, fear mingling with resignation, or fatalism, in his soul, he went into the room and closed the door, picking up her towel to see if it were drier than his own, and less blood-stained, again rubbing his head, and going to the window.

He turned away, unable to control his spasms of shivering. Yvette had disappeared right under the bedclothes, and nothing of her was visible but a shivering mound under the white quilt. He laid his hand on this shivering mound, as if for company. It did not stop shivering.

'All right!' he said. 'All right! Water's going down!'

She suddenly uncovered her head and peered out at him from a white face. She peered into his greenish, curiously calm face, semi-conscious. His teeth were chattering unheeded, as he gazed down at her, his black eyes still full of the fire of life and a certain vagabond calm of fatalistic resignation.

'Warm me!' she moaned, with chattering teeth. 'Warm me! I shall die of shivering.'

A terrible convulsion went through her curled-up white body, enough indeed to rupture her and cause her to die.

The gipsy nodded, and took her in his arms, and held her in a clasp like a vice, to still his own shuddering. He himself was shuddering fearfully, and only semiconscious. It was the shock.

The vice-like grip of his arms round her seemed to her the only stable point in her consciousness. It was a fearful relief to her heart, which was strained to bursting. And though his body, wrapped round her strange and lithe and powerful, like tentacles, rippled with shuddering as an electric current, still the rigid tension of the muscles that held her clenched steadied them both, and gradually the sickening violence of the shuddering, caused by shock, abated, in his body first, then in hers, and the warmth revived between them. And as it roused, their tortured, semiconscious minds became unconscious, they passed away into sleep.

CHAPTER TEN

THE SUN WAS SHINING in heaven before men were able to get across the Papple with ladders. The bridge was gone. But the flood had abated, and the house, that leaned forwards as if it were making a stiff bow to the stream, stood now in mud and wreckage, with a great heap of fallen masonry and debris at the south-west corner. Awful were the gaping mouths of rooms!

Inside, there was no sign of life. But across-stream the gardener had come to reconnoitre, and the cook appeared, thrilled with curiosity. She had escaped from the back door and up through the larches to the high-road, when she saw the gipsy bound past the house: thinking he was coming to murder somebody. At the little top gate she had found his cart standing. The gardener had led the horse away to the Red Lion up at Darley, when night had fallen.

This the men from Papplewick learned when at last they got across the stream with ladders, and to the back of the house. They were nervous, fearing a collapse of the building, whose front was all undermined and whose back was choked up. They gazed with horror at the silent shelves of the rector's rows of books, in his torn-open study; at the big brass bedstead of Granny's room, the bed so deep and comfortably made, but one brass leg of the bedstead perching tentatively over the torn void; at the wreckage of the maid's room upstairs. The housemaid and the cook wept. Then a man climbed in cautiously through a smashed kitchen window, into the jungle and morass of the ground floor. He found the body of the old woman: or at least he saw her foot, in its flat black slipper, muddily protruding from a mud-heap of debris. And he fled.

The gardener said he was sure that Miss Yvette was not in the house. He had seen her and the gipsy swept away. But the policeman insisted on a search, and the Framley boys rushing up at last, the ladders were roped together. Then the whole party set up a loud yell. But without result. No answer from within.

A ladder was up, Bob Framley climbed, smashed a window, and clambered into Aunt Cissie's room. The perfect homely familiarity of everything terrified him like ghosts. The house might go down any minute.

They had just got the ladder up to the top floor, when men came running from Darley, saying the old gipsy had been to the Red Lion for the horse and cart, leaving word that his son had seen Yvette at the top of the house. But by that time the policeman was smashing the window of Yvette's room.

Yvette, fast asleep, started from under the bedclothes with a scream as the glass flew. She clutched the sheets round her nakedness. The policeman uttered a startled yell, which he converted into a cry of: 'Miss Yvette! Miss Yvette!'

He turned round on the ladder and shouted to the faces below: 'Miss Yvette's in bed! – in bed!'

And he perched there on the ladder, an unmarried man, clutching the window in peril, not knowing what to do.

Yvette sat up in bed, her hair in a matted tangle, and stared with wild eyes, clutching up the sheets at her naked breast. She had been so very fast asleep that she was still not there.

The policeman, terrified at the flabby ladder, climbed into the room, saying: 'Don't be frightened, miss! Don't you worry any more about it. You're safe now.'

And Yvette, so dazed, thought he meant the gipsy. Where was the gipsy? This was the first thing in her mind. Where was her gipsy of this world's-end night?

He was gone! He was gone! And a policeman was in the room! A policeman!

She rubbed her hand over her dazed brow.

'If you'll get dressed, miss, we can get you down to safe ground. The house is likely to fall. I suppose there's nobody in the other rooms?'

He stepped gingerly into the passage and gazed in terror through the torn-out end of the house, and far-off saw the rector coming down in a motor-car, on the sunlit hill.

Yvette, her face gone numb and disappointed, got up quickly, closing the bedclothes, and looked at herself a moment, then opened her drawers for clothing. She dressed herself, then looked in a mirror, and saw her matted hair with horror. Yet she did not care. The gipsy was gone, anyhow.

Her own clothes lay in a sodden heap. There was a great sodden place on the carpet where his had been, and two bloodstained filthy towels. Otherwise there was no sign of him.

She was tugging at her hair when the policeman tapped at her door. She called him to come in. He saw with relief that she was dressed and in her right senses.

'We'd better get out of the house as soon as possible, miss,' he reiterated. 'It might fall any minute.'

'Really!' said Yvette calmly. 'Is it as bad as that?'

There were great shouts. She had to go to the window. There, below, was the rector, his arms wide open, tears streaming down his face.

'I'm perfectly all right, Daddy!' she said, with the calmness of her contradictory feelings. She would keep the gipsy a secret from him. At the same time, tears ran down her face.

'Don't you cry, miss, don't you cry! The rector's lost his mother, but he's thanking his stars to have his daughter. We all thought you were gone as well, we did that!'

'Is Granny drowned?' said Yvette.

'I'm afraid she is, poor lady!' said the policeman, with a grave face.

Yvette wept away into her hanky, which she had had to fetch from a drawer.

'Dare you go down that ladder, miss?' said the policeman.

Yvette looked at the sagging depth of it, and said promptly to herself: 'No! Not for anything!' – But then she remembered the gipsy's saying: 'Be braver in the body.'

'Have you been in all the other rooms?' she said, in her weeping, turning to the policeman.

'Yes, miss! But you was the only person in the house, you know, save the old lady. Cook got away in time, and Lizzie was up at her mother's. It was only you and the poor old lady we was fretting about. Do you think you dare go down that ladder?'

'Oh yes!' said Yvette, with indifference. The gipsy was gone anyway.

And now the rector in torment watched his tall, slender daughter slowly stepping backwards down the sagging ladder, the policeman, peering heroically from the smashed window, holding the ladder's top end.

At the foot of the ladder Yvette appropriately fainted in her father's arms, and was borne away with him, in the car, by Bob, to the

Framley home. There the poor Lucille, a ghost of ghosts, wept with relief till she had hysterics, and even Aunt Cissie cried out among her tears: 'Let the old be taken and the young spared! Oh I *can't* cry for the Mater, now Yvette is spared!'

And she wept gallons.

The flood was caused by the sudden bursting of the great reservoir, up in Papple Highdale, five miles from the rectory. It was found out later that an ancient, perhaps even a Roman mine tunnel, unsuspected, undreamed of, beneath the reservoir dam, had collapsed, undermining the whole dam. That was why the Papple had been, for that last day, so uncannily full. And then the dam had burst.

The rector and the two girls stayed on at the Framleys', till a new home could be found. Yvette did not attend Granny's funeral. She stayed in bed.

Telling her tale, she only told how the gipsy had got her inside the porch, and she had crawled to the stairs out of the water. It was known that he had escaped: the old gipsy had said so, when he fetched the horse and cart from the Red Lion.

Yvette could tell little. She was vague, confused, she seemed hardly to remember anything. But that was just like her.

It was Bob Framley who said: 'You know, I think that gipsy deserves a medal.'

The whole family suddenly was struck.

'Oh, we *ought* to thank him!' cried Lucille.

The rector himself went with Bob in the car. But the quarry was deserted. The gipsies had lifted camp and gone, no one knew whither.

And Yvette, lying in bed, moaned in her heart: Oh, I love him! I love him! I love him! The grief over him kept her prostrate. Yet practically, she too was acquiescent in the fact of his disappearance. Her young soul knew the wisdom of it.

But after Granny's funeral, she received a little letter, dated from some unknown place.

> DEAR MISS, I see in the paper you are all right after your ducking, as is the same with me. I hope I see you again one day, maybe at Tideswell cattle fair, or maybe we come that way again. I come that day to say goodbye! and I never said it, well, the water give no time, but I live in hopes. Your obedient servant Joe Boswell.

And only then she realised that he had a name.

Love Among the Haystacks

CHAPTER ONE

THE TWO LARGE FIELDS lay on a hillside facing south. Being newly cleared of hay, they were golden green, and they shone almost blindingly in the sunlight. Across the hill, half-way up, ran a high hedge, that flung its black shadow finely across the molten glow of the sward. The stack was being built just above the hedge. It was of great size, massive, but so silvery and delicately bright in tone that it seemed not to have weight. It rose dishevelled and radiant among the steady, golden-green glare of the field. A little farther back was another, finished stack.

The empty wagon was just passing through the gap in the hedge. From the far-off corner of the bottom field, where the sward was still striped grey with winrows,[15] the loaded wagon launched forward to climb the hill to the stack. The white dots of the haymakers showed distinctly among the hay.

The two brothers were having a moment's rest, waiting for the load to come up. They stood wiping their brows with their arms, sighing from the heat and the labour of placing the last load. The stack they rode was high, lifting them up above the hedge-tops, and very broad, a great slightly-hollowed vessel into which the sunlight poured, in which the hot, sweet scent of hay was suffocating. Small and inefficacious the brothers looked, half-submerged in the loose, great trough, lifted high up as if on an altar reared to the sun.

Maurice, the younger brother, was a handsome young fellow of twenty-one, careless and debonair, and full of vigour. His grey eyes, as he taunted his brother, were bright and baffled with a strong emotion. His swarthy face had the same peculiar smile, expectant and glad and nervous, of a young man roused for the first time in passion.

'Tha sees,' he said, as he leaned on the pommel of his fork, 'tha thowt as tha'd done me one, didna ter?' He smiled as he spoke, then fell again into his pleasant torment of musing.

'I thought nowt – tha knows so much,' retorted Geoffrey, with the touch of a sneer. His brother had the better of him. Geoffrey was a very heavy, hulking fellow, a year older than Maurice. His blue eyes were unsteady, they glanced away quickly; his mouth was morbidly sensitive. One felt him wince away, through the whole of his great body. His inflamed self-consciousness was a disease in him.

'Ah, but though, I know tha did,' mocked Maurice. 'Tha went slinkin' off' – Geoffrey winced convulsively – 'thinking as that wor the last night as any of us'ud ha'e ter stop here, an' so tha'd leave me to sleep out, though it wor thy turn – '

He smiled to himself, thinking of the result of Geoffrey's ruse.

'I didna go slinkin' off neither,' retorted Geoffrey, in his heavy, clumsy manner, wincing at the phrase. 'Didna my feyther send me to fetch some coal – '

'Oh yes, oh yes – we know all about it. But tha sees what tha missed, my lad.'

Maurice, chuckling, threw himself on his back in the bed of hay. There was absolutely nothing in his world, then, except the shallow ramparts of the stack, and the blazing sky. He clenched his fists tight, threw his arms across his face, and braced his muscles again. He was evidently very much moved, so acutely that it was hardly pleasant, though he still smiled. Geoffrey, standing behind him, could just see his red mouth, with the young moustache like black fur, curling back and showing the teeth in a smile. The elder brother leaned his chin on the pommel of his fork, looking out across the country.

Far away was the faint blue heap of Nottingham. Between, the country lay under a haze of heat, with here and there a flag of colliery smoke waving. But near at hand, at the foot of the hill, across the deep-hedged high road, was only the silence of the old church and the castle farm, among their trees. The large view only made Geoffrey more sick. He looked away, to the wagons crossing the field below him, the empty cart like a big insect moving downhill, the load coming up, rocking like a ship, the brown head of the horse ducking, the brown knees lifted and planted strenuously. Geoffrey wished it would be quick.

'Tha didna think – '

Geoffrey started, coiled within himself, and looked down at the handsome lips moving in speech below the brown arms of his brother.

'Tha didna think 'er'd be thur wi' me – or tha wouldna ha' left me to it,' Maurice said, ending with a little laugh of excited memory. Geoffrey flushed with hate, and had an impulse to set his foot on that moving, taunting mouth which was there below him. There was silence for a time then, in a peculiar tone of delight, Maurice's voice came again, spelling out the words, as it were:

> *'Ich bin klein, mein Herz ist rein,*
> *Ist niemand d'rin als Christ allein.'*[16]

Maurice chuckled, then, convulsed at a twinge of recollection, keen as pain, he twisted over, pressed himself into the hay.

'Can thee say thy prayers in German?' came his muffled voice.

'I non want,' growled Geoffrey.

Maurice chuckled. His face was quite hidden, and in the dark he was going over again his last night's experiences.

'What about kissing 'er under th' ear, Sonny,' he said, in a curious, uneasy tone. He writhed, still startled and inflamed by his first contact with love.

Geoffrey's heart swelled within him, and things went dark. He could not see the landscape.

'An' there's just a nice two-handful of her bosom,' came the low, provocative tones of Maurice, who seemed to be talking to himself.

The two brothers were both fiercely shy of women, and until this hay harvest, the whole feminine sex had been represented by their mother and in presence of any other women they were dumb louts. Moreover, brought up by a proud mother, a stranger in the country, they held the common girls as beneath them, because beneath their mother, who spoke pure English, and was very quiet. Loud-mouthed and broad-tongued the common girls were. So these two young men had grown up virgin but tormented.

Now again Maurice had the start of Geoffrey, and the elder brother was deeply mortified. There was a danger of his sinking into a morbid state, from sheer lack of living, lack of interest. The foreign governess at the vicarage, whose garden lay beside the top field, had talked to the lads through the hedge, and had fascinated them. There was a great elder bush, with its broad creamy flowers crumbling on to the garden path, and into the field. Geoffrey never smelled elder-flower without starting and wincing, thinking of the strange foreign voice that had so startled him as he mowed out with the scythe in the hedge bottom. A baby had run through the gap, and the Fräulein, calling in German, had come brushing down the flowers in pursuit. She had started so on seeing a man standing there in the shade, that for a moment she could not move: and then she had blundered into the rake which was lying by his side. Geoffrey, forgetting she was a woman when he saw her pitch forward, had picked her up carefully, asking: 'Have you hurt you?'

Then she had broken into a laugh, and answered in German, showing him her arms, and knitting her brows. She was nettled rather badly.

'You want a dock leaf,' he said.

She frowned in a puzzled fashion.

'A dock leaf?' she repeated.

He had rubbed her arms with the green leaf.

And now, she had taken to Maurice. She had seemed to prefer himself at first. Now she had sat with Maurice in the moonlight, and had let him kiss her. Geoffrey sullenly suffered, making no fight.

Unconsciously, he was looking at the vicarage garden. There she was, in a golden-brown dress. He took off his hat, and held up his right hand in greeting to her. She, a small, golden figure, waved her hand negligently from among the potato rows. He remained, arrested, in the same posture, his hat in his left hand, his right arm upraised, thinking. He could tell by the negligence of her greeting that she was waiting for Maurice. What did she think of himself? Why wouldn't she have him?

Hearing the voice of the wagoner leading the load, Maurice rose. Geoffrey still stood in the same way, but his face was sullen, and his upraised hand was slack with brooding. Maurice faced uphill. His eyes lit up and he laughed. Geoffrey dropped his own arm, watching.

'Lad!' chuckled Maurice. 'I non knowed 'er wor there.' He waved his hand clumsily. In these matters Geoffrey did better. The elder brother watched the girl. She ran to the end of the path, behind the bushes, so that she was screened from the house. Then she waved her handkerchief wildly. Maurice did not notice the manoeuvre. There was the cry of a child. The girl's figure vanished, reappeared holding up a white childish bundle, and came down the path. There she put down her charge, sped uphill to a great ash tree, climbed quickly to a large horizontal bar that formed the fence there and, standing poised, blew kisses with both her hands, in a foreign fashion that excited the brothers. Maurice laughed aloud, as he waved his red handkerchief.

'Well, what's the danger?' shouted a mocking voice from below. Maurice collapsed, blushing furiously.

'Nowt!' he called.

There was a hearty laugh from below.

The load rode up, sheered with a hiss against the stack, then sank back again upon the scotches. The brothers ploughed across the mass of hay, taking the forks. Presently a big burly man, red and glistening, climbed to the top of the load. Then he turned round, scrutinised the hillside from under his shaggy brows. He caught sight of the girl under the ash tree.

'Oh, that's who it is,' he laughed. 'I thought it was some such bird, but I couldn't see her.'

The father laughed in a hearty, chaffing way, then began to teem the load. Geoffrey, on the stack above, received his great forkfuls, and swung them over to Maurice, who took them, placed them, building the stack. In the intense sunlight, the three worked in silence, knit together in a brief passion of work. The father stirred slowly for a moment, getting the hay from under his feet. Geoffrey waited, the blue tines of his fork glittering in expectation: the mass rose, his fork swung beneath it, there was a light clash of blades, then the hay was swept on to the stack, caught by Maurice, who placed it judiciously. One after another, the shoulders of the three men bowed and braced themselves. All wore light blue, bleached shirts that stuck close to their backs. The father moved mechanically, his thick, rounded shoulders bending and lifting dully: he worked monotonously. Geoffrey flung away his strength. His massive shoulders swept and flung the hay extravagantly.

'Dost want to knock me ower?' asked Maurice angrily. He had to brace himself against the impact. The three men worked intensely, as if some will urged them. Maurice was light and swift at the work, but he had to use his judgement. Also, when he had to place the hay along the far ends, he had some distance to carry it. So he was too slow for Geoffrey. Ordinarily, the elder would have placed the hay as far as possible where his brother wanted it. Now, however, he pitched his forkfuls into the middle of the stack. Maurice strode swiftly and handsomely across the bed, but the work was too much for him. The other two men, clenched in their receive and deliver, kept up a high pitch of labour. Geoffrey still flung the hay at random. Maurice was perspiring heavily with heat and exertion, and was getting worried. Now and again, Geoffrey wiped his arm across his brow, mechanically, like an animal. Then he glanced with satisfaction at Maurice's moiled condition, and caught the next forkful.

'Wheer dost think thou'rt hollin' it, fool!' panted Maurice, as his brother flung a forkful out of reach.

'Wheer I've a mind,' answered Geoffrey.

Maurice toiled on, now very angry. He felt the sweat trickling down his body: drops fell into his long black lashes, blinding him, so that he had to stop and angrily dash his eyes clear. The veins stood out in his swarthy neck. He felt he would burst, or drop, if the work did not soon slacken off. He heard his father's fork dully scrape the cart bottom.

'There, the last,' the father panted. Geoffrey tossed the last light lot at random, took off his hat, and, steaming in the sunshine as he wiped himself, stood complacently watching Maurice struggle with clearing the bed.

'Don't you think you've got your bottom corner a bit far out?' came the father's voice from below. 'You'd better be drawing in now, hadn't you?'

'I thought you said next load,' Maurice called sulkily.

'Aye! All right. But isn't this bottom corner – ?'

Maurice, impatient, took no notice.

Geoffrey strode over the stack, and stuck his fork in the offending corner. 'What – here?' he bawled in his great voice.

'Aye – isn't it a bit loose?' came the irritating voice.

Geoffrey pushed his fork in the jutting corner, and, leaning his weight on the handle, shoved. He thought it shook. He thrust again with all his power. The mass swayed.

'What art up to, tha fool!' cried Maurice, in a high voice.

'Mind who tha'rt callin' a fool,' said Geoffrey, and he prepared to push again. Maurice sprang across, and elbowed his brother aside. On the yielding, swaying bed of hay, Geoffrey lost his foothold and fell grovelling. Maurice tried the corner.

'It's solid enough,' he shouted angrily.

'Aye – all right,' came the conciliatory voice of the father; 'you do get a bit of rest now there's such a long way to cart it,' he added reflectively.

Geoffrey had got to his feet.

'Tha'll mind who tha'rt nudging, I can tell thee,' he threatened heavily; adding, as Maurice continued to work, 'an' tha non ca's him a fool again, dost hear?'

'Not till next time,' sneered Maurice.

As he worked silently round the stack, he neared where his brother stood like a sullen statue, leaning on his fork-handle, looking out over the countryside. Maurice's heart quickened in its beat. He worked forward, until a point of his fork caught in the leather of Geoffrey's boot, and the metal rang sharply.

'Are ter going ta shift thysen?' asked Maurice threateningly. There was no reply from the great block. Maurice lifted his upper lip like a dog. Then he put out his elbow and tried to push his brother into the stack, clear of his way.

'Who are ter shovin'?' came the deep, dangerous voice.

'Thaïgh,' replied Maurice, with a sneer, and straightway the two brothers set themselves against each other, like opposing bulls, Maurice trying his hardest to shift Geoffrey from his footing, Geoffrey leaning all his weight in resistance. Maurice, insecure in his footing, staggered a little, and Geoffrey's weight followed him. He went slithering over the edge of the stack.

Geoffrey turned white to the lips, and remained standing, listening. He heard the fall. Then a flush of darkness came over him, and he remained standing only because he was planted. He had not strength to move. He could hear no sound from below, was only faintly aware of a sharp shriek from a long way off. He listened again. Then he filled with sudden panic.

'Feyther!' he roared, in his tremendous voice: 'Feyther! Feyther!'

The valley re-echoed with the sound. Small cattle on the hillside looked up. Men's figures came running from the bottom field, and much nearer a woman's figure was racing across the upper field. Geoffrey waited in terrible suspense.

'Ah–h!' he heard the strange, wild voice of the girl cry out. 'Ah–h!' – and then some foreign wailing speech. Then: 'Ah–h! Are you dea–ed!'

He stood sullenly erect on the stack, not daring to go down, longing to hide in the hay, but too sullen to stoop out of sight. He heard his eldest brother come up, panting: 'Whatever's amiss!' and then the labourer, and then his father.

'Whatever have you been doing?' he heard his father ask, while yet he had not come round the corner of the stack. And then, in a low, bitter tone: 'Eh, he's done for! I'd no business to ha' put it all on that stack.'

There was a moment or two of silence, then the voice of Henry, the eldest brother, said crisply: 'He's not dead – he's coming round.'

Geoffrey heard, but was not glad. He had as lief Maurice were dead. At least that would be final: better than meeting his brother's charges, and of seeing his mother pass to the sickroom. If Maurice was killed, he himself would not explain, no, not a word, and they could hang him if they liked. If Maurice were only hurt, then everybody would know, and Geoffrey could never lift his face again. What added torture, to pass along, everybody knowing. He wanted something that he could stand back to, something definite, if it were only the knowledge that he had killed his brother. He *must* have something firm to back up to, or he would go mad. He was so lonely, he who above all needed the support of sympathy.

'No, he's commin' to; I tell you he is,' said the labourer.

'He's not dea–ed, he's not dea–ed,' came the passionate, strange sing-song of the foreign girl. 'He's not dead – no–o.'

'He wants some brandy – look at the colour of his lips,' said the crisp, cold voice of Henry. 'Can you fetch some?'

'Wha–at? Fetch?' Fräulein did not understand.

'Brandy,' said Henry, very distinct.

'Brrandy!' she re-echoed.

'You go, Bill,' groaned the father.

'Aye, I'll go,' replied Bill, and he ran across the field.

Maurice was not dead, nor going to die. This Geoffrey now realised. He was glad after all that the extreme penalty was revoked. But he hated to think of himself going on. He would always shrink now. He had hoped and hoped for the time when he would be careless, bold as Maurice, when he would not wince and shrink. Now he would always be the same, coiling up in himself like a tortoise with no shell.

'Ah-h! He's getting better!' came the wild voice of the Fräulein, and she began to cry, a strange sound, that startled the men, made the animal bristle within them. Geoffrey shuddered as he heard, between her sobbing, the impatient moaning of his brother as the breath came back.

The labourer returned at a run, followed by the vicar. After the brandy, Maurice made more moaning, hiccuping noise. Geoffrey listened in torture. He heard the vicar asking for explanations. All the united, anxious voices replied in brief phrases.

'It was that other,' cried the Fräulein. 'He knocked him over – Ha!' She was shrill and vindictive.

'I don't think so,' said the father to the vicar, in a quite audible but private tone, speaking as if the Fräulein did not understand his English.

The vicar addressed his children's governess in bad German. She replied in a torrent which he would not confess was too much for him. Maurice was making little moaning, sighing noises.

'Where's your pain, boy, eh?' the father asked pathetically.

'Leave him alone a bit,' came the cool voice of Henry. 'He's winded, if no more.'

'You'd better see that no bones are broken,' said the anxious vicar.

'It wor a blessing as he should a dropped on that heap of hay just there,' said the labourer. 'If he'd happened to ha' catched hisself on this nog o' wood 'e wouldna ha' stood much chance.'

Geoffrey wondered when he would have courage to venture down. He had wild notions of pitching himself head foremost from the stack: if he could only extinguish himself, he would be safe.

Quite frantically, he longed not to be. The idea of going through life thus coiled up within himself in morbid self-consciousness, always lonely, surly, and a misery, was enough to make him cry out. What would they all think when they knew he had knocked Maurice off that high stack?

They were talking to Maurice down below. The lad had recovered in great measure, and was able to answer faintly.

'Whatever was you doin'?' the father asked gently. 'Was you playing about with our Geoffrey? – Aye, and where is he?'

Geoffrey's heart stood still.

'I dunno,' said Henry, in a curious, ironic tone.

'Go an' have a look,' pleaded the father, infinitely relieved over one son, anxious now concerning the other. Geoffrey could not bear that his eldest brother should climb up and question him in his high-pitched drawl of curiosity. The culprit doggedly set his feet on the ladder. His nailed boots slipped a rung.

'Mind yourself,' shouted the over-wrought father.

Geoffrey stood like a criminal at the foot of the ladder, glancing furtively at the group. Maurice was lying, pale and slightly convulsed, upon a heap of hay. The Fräulein was kneeling beside his head. The vicar had the lad's shirt full open down the breast, and was feeling for broken ribs. The father kneeled on the other side, the labourer and Henry stood aside.

'I can't find anything broken,' said the vicar, and he sounded slightly disappointed.

'There's nowt broken to find,' murmured Maurice, smiling.

The father started. 'Eh?' he said. 'Eh?' and he bent over the invalid.

'I say it's not hurt me,' repeated Maurice.

'What were you doing?' asked the cold, ironic voice of Henry. Geoffrey turned his head away: he had not yet raised his face.

'Nowt as I know on,' he muttered in a surly tone.

'Why!' cried Fräulein in a reproachful tone. 'I see him knock him over!' She made a fierce gesture with her elbow. Henry curled his long moustache sardonically.

'Nay lass, niver,' smiled the wan Maurice. 'He was fur enough away from me when I slipped.'

'Oh, ah!' cried the Fräulein, not understanding.

'Yi,' smiled Maurice indulgently.

'I think you're mistaken,' said the father, rather pathetically, smiling at the girl as if she were 'wanting'.

'Oh no,' she cried 'I *see* him.'

'Nay, lass,' smiled Maurice quietly.

She was a Pole, named Paula Jablonowsky: young, only twenty years old, swift and light as a wild cat, with a strange, wild-cat way of grinning. Her hair was blonde and full of life, all crisped into many tendrils with vitality, shaking round her face. Her fine blue eyes were peculiarly lidded, and she seemed to look piercingly, then languorously, like a wild cat. She had somewhat Slavonic cheek-bones, and was very much freckled. It was evident that the vicar, a pale, rather cold man, hated her.

Maurice lay pale and smiling in her lap, whilst she cleaved to him like a mate. One felt instinctively that they were mated. She was ready at any minute to fight with ferocity in his defence, now he was hurt. Her looks at Geoffrey were full of fierceness. She bowed over Maurice and caressed him with her foreign-sounding English.

'You say what you lai–ike,' she laughed, giving him lordship over her.

'Hadn't you better be going and looking what has become of Margery?' asked the vicar in tones of reprimand.

'She is with her mother – I heared her. I will go in a whai–ile,' smiled the girl coolly.

'Do you feel as if you could stand?' asked the father, still anxiously.

'Aye, in a bit,' smiled Maurice.

'You want to get up?' caressed the girl, bowing over him, till her face was not far from his.

'I'm in no hurry,' he replied, smiling brilliantly.

This accident had given him quite a strange new ease, an authority. He felt extraordinarily glad. New power had come to him all at once.

'You in no hurry,' she repeated, gathering his meaning. She smiled tenderly: she was in his service.

'She leaves us in another month – Mrs Inwood could stand no more of her,' apologised the vicar quietly to the father.

'Why, is she – '

'Like a wild thing – disobedient and insolent.'

'Ha!'

The father sounded abstract.

'No more foreign governesses for me.'

Maurice stirred, and looked up at the girl.

'You stand up?' she asked brightly. 'You well?'

He laughed again, showing his teeth winsomely. She lifted his head, sprang to her feet, her hands still holding his head, then she took him under the armpits and had him on his feet before anyone could help. He was much taller than she. He grasped her strong shoulders heavily, leaned against her, and, feeling her round, firm breast doubled up against his side, he smiled, catching his breath.

'You see, I'm all right,' he gasped. 'I was only winded.'

'You all raïght?' she cried, in great glee.

'Yes, I am.'

He walked a few steps after a moment.

'There's nowt ails me, father,' he laughed.

'Quite well, you?' she cried in a pleading tone. He laughed outright, looked down at her, touching her cheek with his fingers.

'That's it – if tha likes.'

'If I lai–ike!' she repeated, radiant.

'She's going at the end of three weeks,' said the vicar consolingly to the farmer.

CHAPTER TWO

WHILE THEY WERE TALKING, they heard the far-off hooting of a pit.

'There goes th' loose 'a,' said Henry coldly. 'We're *not* going to get that corner up today.'

The father looked round anxiously.

'Now, Maurice, are you sure you're all right?' he asked.

'Yes, I'm all right. Haven't I told you?'

'Then you sit down there, and in a bit you can be getting dinner out. Henry, you go on the stack. Wheer's Jim? Oh, he's minding the hosses. Bill, and you, Geoffrey, you can pick while Jim loads.'

Maurice sat down under the wych elm to recover. The Fräulein had fled back. He made up his mind to ask her to marry him. He had got fifty pounds of his own, and his mother would help him. For a long time he sat musing, thinking what he would do. Then, from the float he fetched a big basket covered with a cloth, and spread the dinner. There was an immense rabbit-pie, a dish of cold potatoes, much bread, a great piece of cheese, and a solid rice pudding.

These two fields were four miles from the home farm. But they had been in the hands of the Wookeys for several generations, therefore the father kept them on, and everyone looked forward to the hay harvest at Greasley: it was a kind of picnic. They brought dinner and tea in the milk-float, which the father drove over in the morning. The lads and the labourers cycled. Off and on, the harvest lasted a fortnight. As the high road from Alfreton to Nottingham ran at the foot of the fields, someone usually slept in the hay under the shed to guard the tools. The sons took it in turns. They did not care for it much, and were for that reason anxious to finish the harvest on this day. But work went slack and disjointed after Maurice's accident.

When the load was teemed, they gathered round the white cloth, which was spread under a tree between the hedge and the stack, and, sitting on the ground, ate their meal. Mrs Wookey sent always a clean cloth, and knives and forks and plates for everybody. Mr Wookey was always rather proud of this spread: everything was so proper.

'There now,' he said, sitting down jovially. 'Doesn't this look nice now – eh?'

They all sat round the white spread, in the shadow of the tree and the stack, and looked out up the fields as they ate. From their shady coolness, the gold sward seemed liquid, molten with heat. The horse with the empty wagon wandered a few yards, then stood feeding. Everything was still as a trance. Now and again, the horse between the shafts of the load that stood propped beside the stack, jingled his loose bit as he ate. The men ate and drank in silence, the father reading the newspaper, Maurice leaning back on a saddle, Henry reading the *Nation*,[17] the others eating busily.

Presently 'Helloa! 'Er's 'ere again!' exclaimed Bill. All looked up. Paula was coming across the field carrying a plate.

'She's bringing something to tempt your appetite, Maurice,' said the eldest brother ironically. Maurice was midway through a large wedge of rabbit-pie and some cold potatoes.

'Aye, bless me if she's not,' laughed the father. 'Put that away, Maurice, it's a shame to disappoint her.'

Maurice looked round very shamefaced, not knowing what to do with his plate.

'Give it over here,' said Bill. 'I'll polish him off.'

'Bringing something for the invalid?' laughed the father to the Fräulein. 'He's looking up nicely.'

'I bring him some chicken, him!' She nodded her head at Maurice childishly. He flushed and smiled.

'Tha doesna mean ter bust 'im,' said Bill.

Everybody laughed aloud. The girl did not understand, so she laughed also. Maurice ate his portion very sheepishly.

The father pitied his son's shyness.

'Come here and sit by me,' he said. 'Eh, Fräulein! Is that what they call you?'

'I sit by you, father,' she said innocently.

Henry threw his head back and laughed long and noiselessly.

She settled near to the big, handsome man.

'My name,' she said, 'is Paula Jablonowsky.'

'Is what?' said the father, and the other men went into roars of laughter.

'Tell me again,' said the father. 'Your name – '

'Paula.'

'Paula? Oh – well, it's a rum sort of name, eh? His name – ' he nodded at his son.

'Maurice – I know.' She pronounced it sweetly, then laughed into the father's eyes. Maurice blushed to the roots of his hair.

They questioned her concerning her history, and made out that she came from Hanover, that her father was a shopkeeper, and that she had run away from home because she did not like her father. She had gone to Paris.

'Oh,' said the father, now dubious. 'And what did you do there?'

'In school – in a young ladies' school.'

'Did you like it?'

'Oh no – no laïfe – no life!'

'What?'

'When we go out – two and two – all together – no more. Ah, no life, no life.'

'Well, that's a winder!' exclaimed the father. 'No life in Paris! And have you found much life in England?'

'No – ah no. I don't like it.' She made a grimace at the vicarage.

'How long have you been in England?'

'Chreestmas – so.'

'And what will you do?'

'I will go to London, or to Paris. Ah, Paris! – Or get married!' She laughed into the father's eyes.

The father laughed heartily.

'Get married, eh? And who to?'

'I don't know. I am going away.'

'The country's too quiet for you?' asked the father.

'Too quiet – hm!' she nodded in assent.

'You wouldn't care for making butter and cheese?'

'Making butter – hm!' She turned to him with a glad, bright gesture. 'I like it.'

'Oh,' laughed the father. 'You would, would you?'

She nodded vehemently, with glowing eyes.

'She'd like anything in the shape of a change,' said Henry judicially.

'I think she would,' agreed the father. It did not occur to them that she fully understood what they said. She looked at them closely, then thought with bowed head.

'Hullo!' exclaimed Henry, the alert. A tramp was slouching towards them through the gap. He was a very seedy, slinking fellow, with a tang of horsey braggadocio about him. Small, thin, and ferrety, with a week's red beard bristling on his pointed chin, he came slouching forward.

'Have yer got a bit of a job goin'?' he asked.

'A bit of a job,' repeated the father. 'Why, can't you see as we've a'most done?'

'Aye – but I noticed you was a hand short, an' I thowt as 'appen you'd gie me half a day.'

'What, are *you* any good in a hay close?' asked Henry, with a sneer.

The man stood slouching against the haystack. All the others were seated on the floor. He had an advantage.

'I could work aside any on yer,' he bragged.

'Tha looks it,' laughed Bill.

'And what's your regular trade?' asked the father.

'I'm a jockey by rights. But I did a bit o' dirty work for a boss o' mine, an' I was landed. '*E* got the benefit, *I* got kicked out. '*E* axed me – an' then 'e looked as if 'e'd never seed me.'

'Did he, though!' exclaimed the father sympathetically.

' 'E did that!' asserted the man.

'But we've got nothing for you,' said Henry coldly.

'What does the boss say?' asked the man, impudent.

'No, we've no work you can do,' said the father. 'You can have a bit o' something to eat, if you like.'

'I should be glad of it,' said the man.

He was given the chunk of rabbit-pie that remained. This he ate greedily. There was something debased, parasitic, about him, which disgusted Henry. The others regarded him as a curiosity.

'That was nice and tasty,' said the tramp, with gusto.

'Do you want a piece of bread 'n' cheese?' asked the father.

'It'll help to fill up,' was the reply.

The man ate this more slowly. The company was embarrassed by his presence, and could not talk. All the men lit their pipes, the meal over.

'So you dunna want any help?' said the tramp at last.

'No – we can manage what bit there is to do.'

'You don't happen to have a fill of bacca to spare, do you?'

The father gave him a good pinch.

'You're all right here,' he said, looking round. They resented this familiarity. However, he filled his clay pipe and smoked with the rest.

As they were sitting silent, another figure came through the gap in the hedge, and noiselessly approached. It was a woman. She was rather small and finely made. Her face was small, very ruddy, and comely, save for the look of bitterness and aloofness that it wore. Her hair was drawn tightly back under a sailor hat. She gave an impression of cleanness, of precision and directness.

'Have you got some work?' she asked of her man. She ignored the rest. He tucked his tail between his legs.

'No, they haven't got no work for me. They've just gave me a draw of bacca.'

He was a mean crawl of a man.

'An' am I goin' to wait for you out there on the lane all day?'

'You needn't if you don't like. You could go on.'

'Well, are you coming?' she asked contemptuously. He rose to his feet in a rickety fashion.

'You needn't be in such a mighty hurry,' he said. 'If you'd wait a bit you might get summat.'

She glanced for the first time over the men. She was quite young, and would have been pretty, were she not so hard and callous-looking.

'Have you had your dinner?' asked the father.

She looked at him with a kind of anger and turned away. Her face was so childish in its contours, contrasting strangely with her expression.

'Are you coming?' she said to the man.

'He's had his tuck-in. Have a bit, if you want it,' coaxed the father.

'What have you had?' she flashed to the man.

'He's had all what was left o' th' rabbit-pie,' said Geoffrey, in an indignant, mocking tone, 'and a great hunk o' bread an' cheese.'

'Well, it was gave me,' said the man.

The young woman looked at Geoffrey, and he at her. There was a sort of kinship between them. Both were at odds with the world. Geoffrey smiled satirically. She was too grave, too deeply incensed even to smile.

'There's a cake here, though – you can have a bit o' that,' said Maurice blithely.

She eyed him with scorn.

Again she looked at Geoffrey. He seemed to understand her. She turned, and in silence departed. The man remained obstinately sucking at his pipe. Everybody looked at him with hostility.

'We'll be getting to work,' said Henry, rising, pulling off his coat. Paula got to her feet. She was a little bit confused by the presence of the tramp.

'I go,' she said, smiling brilliantly. Maurice rose and followed her sheepishly.

'A good grind, eh?' said the tramp, nodding after the Fräulein. The men only half understood him, but they hated him.

'Hadn't you better be getting off?' said Henry.

The man rose obediently. He was all slouching, parasitic insolence. Geoffrey loathed him, longed to exterminate him. He was exactly the worst foe of the hypersensitive: insolence without sensibility, preying on sensibility.

'Aren't you goin' to give me summat for her? It's nowt she's had all day, to my knowin'. She'll 'appen eat it if I take it 'er – though she gets more than I've any knowledge of' – this with a lewd wink of jealous spite. 'And then tries to keep a tight hand on me,' he sneered, taking the bread and cheese, and stuffing it in his pocket.

CHAPTER THREE

GEOFFREY worked sullenly all the afternoon, and Maurice did the horse-raking. It was exceedingly hot. So the day wore on, the atmosphere thickened, and the sunlight grew blurred. Geoffrey was picking with Bill – helping to load the wagons from the winrows. He was sulky, though extraordinarily relieved: Maurice would not tell. Since the quarrel neither brother had spoken to the other. But their silence was entirely amicable, almost affectionate. They had both been deeply moved, so much so that their ordinary intercourse was interrupted: but underneath, each felt a strong regard for the other. Maurice was peculiarly happy, his feeling of affection swimming over everything. But Geoffrey was still sullenly hostile to the most part of the world. He felt isolated. The free and easy inter-communication between the other workers left him distinctly alone. And he was a man who could not bear to stand alone, he was too much afraid of the vast confusion of life surrounding him, in which he was helpless. Geoffrey mistrusted himself with everybody.

The work went on slowly. It was unbearably hot, and everyone was disheartened.

'We s'll have getting-on-for another day of it,' said the father at tea-time, as they sat under the tree.

'Quite a day,' said Henry.

'Somebody'll have to stop, then,' said Geoffrey. 'It 'ud better be me.'

'Nay, lad, I'll stop,' said Maurice, and he hid his head in confusion.

'Stop again tonight!' exclaimed the father. 'I'd rather you went home.'

'Nay, I'm stoppin',' protested Maurice.

'He wants to do his courting,' Henry enlightened them.

The father thought seriously about it.

'I don't know . . . ' he mused, rather perturbed.

But Maurice stayed. Towards eight o'clock, after sundown, the men mounted their bicycles, the father put the horse in the float, and all departed. Maurice stood in the gap of the hedge and watched them go, the cart rolling and swinging downhill, over the grass stubble, the cyclists dipping swiftly like shadows in front. All passed through the gate, there was a quick clatter of hoofs on the roadway under the lime trees, and they were gone. The young man was very much excited, almost afraid, at finding himself alone.

Darkness was rising from the valley. Already, up the steep hill the cart-lamps crept indecisively, and the cottage windows were lit. Everything looked strange to Maurice, as if he had not seen it before. Down the hedge a large lime tree teemed with scent that seemed almost like a voice speaking. It startled him. He caught a breath of the over-sweet fragrance, then stood still, listening expectantly.

Uphill, a horse whinneyed. It was the young mare. The heavy horses went thundering across to the far hedge.

Maurice wondered what to do. He wandered round the deserted stacks restlessly. Heat came in wafts, in thick strands. The evening was a long time cooling. He thought he would go and wash himself. There was a trough of pure water in the hedge bottom. It was filled by a tiny spring that filtered over the brim of the trough down the lush hedge bottom of the lower held. All round the trough, in the upper field, the land was marshy, and there the meadow-sweet stood like clots of mist, very sickly-smelling in the twilight. The night did not darken, for the moon was in the sky, so that as the tawny colour drew off the heavens they remained pallid with a dimmed moon. The purple bell-flowers in the hedge went black, the ragged robin turned its pink to a faded white, the meadow-sweet gathered light as if it were phosphorescent, and it made the air ache with scent.

Maurice kneeled on the slab of stone bathing his hands and arms, then his face. The water was deliciously cool. He had still an hour before Paula would come: she was not due till nine. So he decided to take his bath at night instead of waiting till morning. Was he not sticky, and was not Paula coming to talk to him? He was delighted the thought had occurred to him. As he soused his head in the trough, he wondered what the little creatures that lived in the velvety silt at the bottom would think of the taste of soap. Laughing to himself, he squeezed his cloth into the water. He washed himself from head to foot, standing in the fresh, forsaken corner of the field, where no one could see him by daylight, so that now, in the veiled grey tinge of moonlight, he was no more noticeable than the crowded flowers. The night had on a new look: he never remembered to have seen the lustrous grey sheen of it before, nor to have noticed how vital the lights looked, like live folk inhabiting the silvery spaces. And the tall trees, wrapped obscurely in their mantles, would not have surprised him had they begun to move in converse. As he dried himself, he discovered little wanderings in the air, felt on his sides soft touches and caresses that were peculiarly delicious: sometimes they startled him, and he laughed as if he were not alone. The flowers, the meadow-sweet particularly, haunted him. He reached to put his hand over their fleeciness. They touched his thighs. Laughing, he gathered them and dusted himself all over with their cream dust and fragrance. For a moment he hesitated in wonder at himself: but the subtle glow in the hoary and black night reassured him. Things never had looked so personal and full of beauty, he had never known the wonder in himself before.

At nine o'clock he was waiting under the elder bush, in a state of high trepidation, but feeling that he was worthy, having a sense of his own wonder. She was late. At a quarter-past nine she came, flitting swiftly, in her own eager way.

'No, she would *not* go to sleep,' said Paula, with a world of wrath in her tone. He laughed bashfully. They wandered out into the dim, hillside field.

'I have sat – in that bedroom – for an hour, for hours,' she cried indignantly. She took a deep breath: 'Ah, breathe!' she smiled.

She was very intense, and full of energy.

'I want' – she was clumsy with the language – 'I want – I should laike – to run – there!' She pointed across the field.

'Let's run, then,' he said curiously.

'Yes!'

And in an instant she was gone. He raced after her. For all he was so young and limber, he had difficulty in catching her. At first he could scarcely see her, though he could hear the rustle of her dress. She sped with astonishing fleetness. He overtook her, caught her by the arm, and they stood panting, facing one another with laughter.

'I could win,' she asserted blithely.

'Tha couldna,' he replied, with a peculiar, excited laugh. They walked on, rather breathless. In front of them suddenly appeared the dark shapes of the three feeding horses.

'We ride a horse?' she said.

'What, bareback?' he asked.

'You say?' She did not understand.

'With no saddle?'

'No saddle – yes – no saddle.'

'Coop, lass!' he said to the mare, and in a minute he had her by the forelock, and was leading her down to the stacks, where he put a halter on her. She was a big, strong mare. Maurice seated the Fräulein, clambered himself in front of the girl, using the wheel of the wagon as a mount, and together they trotted uphill, she holding lightly round his waist. From the crest of the hill they looked round.

The sky was darkening with an awning of cloud. On the left the hill rose black and wooded, made cosy by a few lights from cottages along the highway. The hill spread to the right, and tufts of trees shut round. But in front was a great vista of night, a sprinkle of cottage candles, a twinkling cluster of lights, like an elfish fair in full swing, at the colliery an encampment of light at a village, a red flare on the sky far off, above an iron-foundry, and in the farthest distance the dim breathing of town lights. As they watched the night stretch far out, her arms tightened round his waist, and he pressed his elbows to his side, pressing her arms closer still. The horse moved restlessly. They clung to each other.

'Tha daesna want to go right away?' he asked the girl behind him.

'I stay with you,' she answered softly, and he felt her crouching close against him. He laughed curiously. He was afraid to kiss her, though he was urged to do so. They remained still, on the restless horse, watching the small lights lead deep into the night, in infinite distance.

'I don't want to go,' he said, in a tone half pleading.

She did not answer. The horse stirred restlessly.

'Let him run,' cried Paula, 'fast!'

She broke the spell, startled him into a little fury. He kicked the mare, hit her, and away she plunged downhill. The girl clung tightly to the young man. They were riding bareback down a rough, steep hill. Maurice clung hard with hands and knees. Paula held him fast round the waist, leaning her head on his shoulders, and thrilling with excitement.

'We shall be off, we shall be off,' he cried, laughing with excitement; but she only crouched behind and pressed tight to him. The mare tore across the field. Maurice expected every moment to be flung on to the grass. He gripped with all the strength of his knees. Paula tucked herself behind him, and often wrenched him almost from his hold. Man and girl were taut with effort.

At last the mare came to a standstill, blowing. Paula slid off, and in an instant Maurice was beside her. They were both highly excited. Before he knew what he was doing, he had her in his arms, fast, and was kissing her, and laughing. They did not move for some time. Then, in silence, they walked towards the stacks.

It had grown quite dark, the night was thick with cloud. He walked with his arm round Paula's waist, she with her arm round him. They were near the stacks when Maurice felt a spot of rain.

'It's going to rain,' he said.

'Rain!' she echoed, as if it were trivial.

'I s'll have to put the stack-cloth on,' he said gravely. She did not understand.

When they got to the stacks, he went round to the shed, to return staggering in the darkness under the burden of the immense and heavy cloth. It had not been used once during the hay harvest.

'What are you going to do?' asked Paula, coming close to him in the darkness.

'Cover the top of the stack with it,' he replied. 'Put it over the stack, to keep the rain out.'

'Ah!' she cried, 'up there!'

He dropped his burden. 'Yes,' he answered.

Fumbling he reared the long ladder up the side of the stack. He could not see the top.

'I hope it's solid,' he said softly.

A few smart drops of rain sounded drumming on the cloth. They seemed like another presence. It was very dark indeed between the great buildings of hay. She looked up the black wall and shrank to him.

'You carry it up there?' she asked.

'Yes,' he answered.

'I help you?' she said.

And she did. They opened the cloth. He clambered first up the steep ladder, bearing the upper part, she followed closely, carrying her full share. They mounted the shaky ladder in silence, stealthily.

CHAPTER FOUR

As they climbed the stacks a light stopped at the gate on the high road. It was Geoffrey, come to help his brother with the cloth. Afraid of his own intrusion, he wheeled his bicycle silently towards the shed. This was a corrugated- iron erection, on the opposite side of the hedge from the stacks. Geoffrey let his light go in front of him, but there was no sign from the lovers. He thought he saw a shadow slinking away. The light of the bicycle lamp sheered yellowly across the dark, catching a glint of raindrops, a mist of darkness, shadow of leaves, and strokes of long grass. Geoffrey entered the shed – no one was there. He walked slowly and doggedly round to the stacks. He had passed the wagon, when he heard something sheering down upon him. Starting back under the wall of hay, he saw the long ladder slither across the side of the stack, and fall with a bruising ring.

'What wor that?' he heard Maurice, aloft, ask cautiously.

'Something fall,' came the curious, almost pleased voice of the Fräulein.

'It wor niver th' ladder,' said Maurice. He peered over the side of the stack. He lay down, looking.

'It is an' a'!' he exclaimed. 'We knocked it down with the cloth, dragging it over.'

'We fast up here?' she exclaimed with a thrill.

'We are that – without I shout and make 'em hear at the vicarage.'

'Oh no,' she said quickly.

'I don't want to,' he replied, with a short laugh. There came a swift clatter of raindrops on the cloth. Geoffrey crouched under the wall of the other stack.

'Mind where you tread – here, let me straighten this end,' said Maurice, with a peculiar intimate tone – a command and an embrace. 'We s'll have to sit under it. At any rate, we shan't get wet.'

'Not get wet!' echoed the girl, pleased, but agitated.

Geoffrey heard the slide and rustle of the cloth over the top of the stack, heard Maurice telling her to 'Mind!'

'Mind!' she repeated. 'Mind! you say "Mind!"'

'Well, what if I do?' he laughed. 'I don't want you to fall over th' side, do I?' His tone was masterful, but he was not quite sure of himself.

There was silence a moment or two.

'Maurice!' she said plaintively.

'I'm here,' he answered tenderly, his voice shaky with excitement that was near to distress. 'There, I've done. Now should we – we'll sit under this corner.'

'Maurice!' she was rather pitiful.

'What? You'll be all right,' he remonstrated, tenderly indignant.

'I be all raïght,' she repeated, 'I be all raïght, Maurice?'

'Tha knows tha will – I canna ca' thee Powla. Should I ca' thee Minnie?'

It was the name of a dead sister.

'Minnie?' she exclaimed in surprise.

'Aye, should I?'

She answered in full-throated German. He laughed shakily.

'Come on – come on under. But do yer wish you was safe in th' vicarage? Should I shout for somebody?' he asked.

'I don't wish, no!' She was vehement.

'Art sure?' he insisted, almost indignantly.

'Sure – I quite sure.' She laughed.

Geoffrey turned away at the last words. Then the rain beat heavily. The lonely brother slouched miserably to the hut, where the rain played a mad tattoo. He felt very miserable, and jealous of Maurice.

His bicycle lamp, downcast, shone a yellow light on the stark floor of the shed or hut with one wall open. It lit up the trodden earth, the shafts of tools lying piled under the beam, beside the dreary grey metal of the building. He took off the lamp, shone it round the hut. There were piles of harness, tools, a big sugar-box, a deep bed of hay – then the beams across the corrugated iron, all very dreary and stark. He shone the lamp into the night: nothing but the furtive glitter of raindrops through the mist of darkness, and black shapes hovering round.

Geoffrey blew out the light and flung himself on to the hay. He would put the ladder up for them in a while, when they would be wanting it. Meanwhile he sat and gloated over Maurice's felicity. He was imaginative, and now he had something concrete to work upon. Nothing in the whole of life stirred him so profoundly, and so utterly, as the thought of this woman. For Paula was strange, foreign, different from the ordinary girls: the rousing, feminine quality seemed in her concentrated, brighter, more fascinating than in anyone he had known, so that he felt most like a moth near a candle. He would have loved her wildly – but Maurice had got her. His thoughts beat the same course, round and round. What was it like when you kissed her, when she held you tight round the waist, how did she feel towards Maurice, did she love to touch him, was he fine and attractive to her; what did she think of himself – she merely disregarded him, as she would disregard a horse in a field; why would she do so, why couldn't he make her regard himself, instead of Maurice: he would never command a woman's regard like that, he always gave in to her too soon; if only some woman would come and take him for what he was worth, though he was such a stumbler and showed to such disadvantage, ah, what a grand thing it would be; how he would kiss her. Then round he went again in the same course, brooding almost like a madman. Meanwhile the rain drummed deep on the shed, then grew lighter and softer. There came the drip, drip of the drops falling outside.

Geoffrey's heart leaped up his chest, and he clenched himself, as a black shape crept round the post of the shed and, bowing, entered silently. The young man's heart beat so heavily in plunges, he could not get his breath to speak. It was shock, rather than fear. The form felt towards him. He sprang up, gripped it with his great hand's panting 'Now, then!'

There was no resistance, only a little whimper of despair.

'Let me go,' said a woman's voice.

'What are you after?' he asked, in deep, gruff tones.

'I thought 'e was 'ere,' she wept despairingly, with little, stubborn sobs.

'An' you've found what you didn't expect, have you?'

At the sound of his bullying she tried to get away from him.

'Let me go,' she said.

'Who did you expect to find here?' he asked, but more his natural self.

'I expected my husband – him as you saw at dinner. Let me go.'

'Why, is it you?' exclaimed Geoffrey. 'Has he left you?'

'Let me go,' said the women sullenly, trying to draw away. He realised that the sleeve was very wet, her arm slender under his grasp. Suddenly he grew ashamed of himself: he had no doubt hurt her, gripping her so hard. He relaxed, but did not let her go.

'An' are you searching round after that snipe as was here at dinner?' he asked. She did not answer.

'Where did he leave you?'

'I left him – here. I've seen nothing of him since.'

'I s'd think it's good riddance,' he said. She did not answer. He gave a short laugh, saying: 'I should ha' thought you wouldn't ha' wanted to clap eyes on him again.'

'He's my husband – an' he's not goin' to run off if I can stop him.'

Geoffrey was silent, not knowing what to say.

'Have you got a jacket on?' he asked at last.

'What do you think? You've got hold of it.'

'You're wet through, aren't you?'

'I shouldn't be dry, comin' through that teemin' rain. But 'e's not here, so I'll go.'

'I mean,' he said humbly, 'are you wet through?'

She did not answer. He felt her shiver.

'Are you cold?' he asked, in surprise and concern.

She did not answer. He did not know what to say.

'Stop a minute,' he said, and he fumbled in his pocket for his matches. He struck a light, holding it in the hollow of his large, hard palm. He was a big man, and he looked anxious. Shedding the light on her, he saw she was rather pale, and very weary looking. Her old sailor hat was sodden and drooping with rain. She wore a fawn-coloured jacket of smooth cloth. This jacket was black-wet where the rain had beaten, her skirt hung sodden, and dripped on to her boots. The match went out.

'Why, you're wet through!' he said.

She did not answer.

'Shall you stop in here while it gives over?' he asked. She did not answer.

' 'Cause if you will, you'd better take your things off, an' have th' rug. There's a horse-rug in the box.'

He waited, but she would not answer. So he lit his bicycle lamp, and rummaged in the box, pulling out a large brown blanket, striped with scarlet and yellow. She stood stock still. He shone the light on her. She was very pale, and trembling fitfully.

'Are you that cold?' he asked in concern. 'Take your jacket off, and your hat, and put this right over you.'

Mechanically, she undid the enormous fawn-coloured buttons, and unpinned her hat. With her black hair drawn back from her low, honest brow, she looked little more than a girl, like a girl driven hard with womanhood by stress of life. She was small, and natty, with neat little features. But she shivered convulsively.

'Is something a-matter with you?' he asked.

'I've walked to Bulwell and back,' she quivered, 'looking for him – an' I've not touched a thing since this morning.' She did not weep – she was too dreary-hardened to cry. He looked at her in dismay, his mouth half open: 'Gormin' as Maurice would have said.

' 'Aven't you had nothing to eat?' he said.

Then he turned aside to the box. There, the bread remaining was kept, and the great piece of cheese, and such things as sugar and salt, with all table utensils: there was some butter.

She sat down drearily on the bed of hay. He cut her a piece of bread and butter, and a piece of cheese. This she took, but ate listlessly.

'I want a drink,' she said.

'We 'aven't got no beer,' he answered. 'My father doesn't have it.'

'I want water,' she said.

He took a can and plunged through the wet darkness, under the great black hedge, down to the trough. As he came back he saw her in the half-lit little cave sitting bunched together. The soaked grass wet his feet – he thought of her. When he gave her a cup of water, her hand touched his and he felt her fingers hot and glossy. She trembled so she spilled the water.

'Do you feel badly?' he asked.

'I can't keep myself still – but it's only with being tired and having nothing to eat.'

He scratched his head contemplatively, waited while she ate her piece of bread and butter. Then he offered her another piece.

'I don't want it just now,' she said.

'You'll have to eat summat,' he said.

'I couldn't eat any more just now.'

He put the piece down undecidedly on the box. Then there was another long pause. He stood up with bent head. The bicycle, like a restful animal, glittered behind him, turning towards the wall. The woman sat hunched on the hay, shivering.

'Can't you get warm?' he asked.

'I shall by an' by – don't you bother. I'm taking your seat – are you stopping here all night?'

'Yes.'

'I'll be goin' in a bit,' she said.

'Nay, I non want you to go. I'm thinkin' how you could get warm.'

'Don't you bother about me,' she remonstrated, almost irritably.

'I just want to see as the stacks is all right. You take your shoes an' stockin's an' all your wet things off: you can easy wrap yourself all over in that rug, there's not so much of you.'

'It's raining – I s'll be all right – I s'll be going in a minute.'

'I've got to see as the stacks is safe. Take your wet things off.'

'Are you coming back?' she asked.

'I mightn't, not till morning.'

'Well, I s'll be gone in ten minutes, then. I've no rights to be here, an I s'll not let anybody be turned out for me.'

'You won't be turning me out.'

'Whether or no, I shan't stop.'

'Well, shall you if I come back?' he asked. She did not answer.

He went. In a few moments, she blew the light out. The rain was falling steadily, and the night was a black gulf. All was intensely still. Geoffrey listened everywhere: no sound save the rain. He stood between the stacks, but only heard the trickle of water, and the light swish of rain. Everything was lost in blackness. He imagined death was like that, many things dissolved in silence and darkness, blotted out, but existing. In the dense blackness he felt himself almost extinguished. He was afraid he might not find things the same. Almost frantically, he stumbled, feeling his way, till his hand touched the wet metal. He had been looking for a gleam of light.

'Did you blow the lamp out?' he asked, fearful lest the silence should answer him.

'Yes,' she answered humbly. He was glad to hear her voice. Groping into the pitch-dark shed, he knocked against the box, part of whose cover served as table. There was a clatter and a fall.

'That's the lamp, an' the knife, an' the cup,' he said. He struck a match.

'Th' cup's not broke.' He put it into the box.

'But th' oil's spilled out o' th' lamp. It always was a rotten old thing.' He hastily blew out his match, which was burning his fingers. Then he struck another light.

'You don't want a lamp, you know you don't, and I s'll be going directly, so you come an' lie down an' get your night's rest. I'm not taking any of your place.'

He looked at her by the light of another match. She was a queer little bundle, all brown, with gaudy border folding in and out, and her little face peering at him. As the match went out she saw him beginning to smile.

'I can sit right at this end,' she said. 'You lie down.'

He came and sat on the hay, at some distance from her. After a spell of silence: 'Is he really your husband?' he asked.

'He is!' she answered grimly.

'Hm!' Then there was silence again.

After a while: 'Are you warm now?'

'Why do you bother yourself?'

'I don't bother myself – do you follow him because you like him?' He put it very timidly. He wanted to know.

'I don't – I wish he was dead,' this with bitter contempt. Then doggedly: 'But he's my husband.'

He gave a short laugh.

'By Gad!' he said.

Again, after a while: 'Have you been married long?'

'Four years.'

'Four years – why, how old are you?'

'Twenty-three.'

'Are you turned twenty-three?'

'Last May.'

'Then you're four month older than me.' He mused over it. They were only two voices in the pitch-black night. It was eerie silence again.

'And do you just tramp about?' he asked.

'He reckons he's looking for a job. But he doesn't like work in any shape or form. He was a stableman when I married him, at Greenhalgh's, the horse-dealers, at Chesterfield, where I was house-maid. He left that job when the baby was only two months, and I've been badgered about from pillar to post ever sin'. They say a rolling stone gathers no moss . . . '

'An' where's the baby?'

'It died when it was ten months old.'

Now the silence was clinched between them. It was quite a long time before Geoffrey ventured to say sympathetically: 'You haven't much to look forward to.'

'I've wished many a score time when I've started shiverin' an' shakin' at nights, as I was taken bad for death. But we're not that handy at dying.'

He was silent. 'But whatever shall you do?' he faltered.

'I s'll find him, if I drop by th' road.'

'Why?' he asked, wondering, looking her way, though he saw nothing but solid darkness.

'Because I shall. He's not going to have it all his own road.'

'But why don't you leave him?'

'Because he's *not goin' to have it all his own road.*'

She sounded very determined, even vindictive. He sat in wonder, feeling uneasy, and vaguely miserable on her behalf. She sat extraordinarily still. She seemed like a voice only, a presence.

'Are you warm now?' he asked, half afraid.

'A bit warmer – but my feet!' She sounded pitiful.

'Let me warm them with my hands,' he asked her. 'I'm hot enough.'

'No, thank you,' she said coldly.

Then, in the darkness, she felt she had wounded him. He was writhing under her rebuff, for his offer had been pure kindness.

'They're 'appen dirty,' she said, half mocking.

'Well – mine is – an' I have a bath a'most every day,' he answered.

'I don't know when they'll get warm,' she moaned to herself.

'Well, then, put them in my hands.'

She heard him faintly rattling the matchbox, and then a phosphorescent glare began to fume in his direction. Presently he was holding two smoking, blue-green blotches of light towards her feet. She was afraid. But her feet ached so, and the impulse drove her on, so she placed her soles lightly on the two blotches of smoke. His large hands clasped over her instep, warm and hard.

'They're like ice!' he said, in deep concern.

He warmed her feet as best he could, putting them close against him. Now and again convulsive tremors ran over her. She felt his warm breath on the balls of her toes, that were bunched up in his hands. Leaning forward, she touched his hair delicately with her fingers. He thrilled. She fell to gently stroking his hair, with timid, pleading fingertips.

'Do they feel any better?' he asked, in a low voice, suddenly lifting his face to her. This sent her hand sliding softly over his face, and her fingertips caught on his mouth. She drew quickly away. He put his hand out to find hers, in his other palm holding both her feet. His wandering hand met her face. He touched it curiously. It was wet. He put his big fingers cautiously on her eyes, into two little pools of tears.

'What's a matter?' he asked in a low, choked voice.

She leaned down to him and gripped him tightly round the neck, pressing him to her bosom in a little frenzy of pain. Her bitter disillusionment with life, her unalleviated shame and degradation during the last four years, had driven her into loneliness, and hardened her till a large part of her nature was caked and sterile. Now she softened again, and her spring might be beautiful. She had been in a fair way to make an ugly old woman.

She clasped the head of Geoffrey to her breast, which heaved and fell, and heaved again. He was bewildered, full of wonder. He allowed the woman to do as she would with him. Her tears fell on his hair, as she wept noiselessly; and he breathed deep as she did. At last she let go her clasp. He put his arms round her.

'Come and let me warm you,' he said, folding up on his knee and lapping her with his heavy arms against himself. She was small and *câline*.[18] He held her very warm and close. Presently she stole her arms round him.

'You *are* big,' she whispered.

He gripped her hard, started, put his mouth down wanderingly, seeking her out. His lips met her temple. She slowly, deliberately turned her mouth to his, and with opened lips, met him in a kiss, his first love kiss.

CHAPTER FIVE

IT WAS BREAKING cold dawn when Geoffrey woke. The woman was still sleeping in his arms. Her face in sleep moved all his tenderness: the tight shutting of her mouth, as if in resolution to bear what was very hard to bear, contrasted so pitifully with the small mould of her features. Geoffrey pressed her to his bosom: having her, he felt he could bruise the lips of the scornful, and pass on erect, unabateable. With her to complete him, to form the core of him, he was firm and whole. Needing her so much, he loved her fervently.

Meanwhile the dawn came like death, one of those slow, livid mornings that seem to come in a cold sweat. Slowly, and painfully, the air began to whiten. Geoffrey saw it was not raining. As he was watching the ghastly transformation outside, he felt aware of something. He glanced down: she was open-eyed, watching him; she had golden-brown, calm eyes, that immediately smiled into his. He also smiled, bowed softly down and kissed her. They did not speak for some time.

Then: 'What's thy name?' he asked curiously.

'Lydia,' she said.

'Lydia!' he repeated wonderingly. He felt rather shy.

'Mine's Geoffrey Wookey,' he said.

She merely smiled at him.

They were silent for a considerate time. By morning light, things look small. The huge trees of the evening were dwindled to hoary, small, uncertain things, trespassing in the sick pallor of the atmosphere. There was a dense mist, so that the light could scarcely breathe. Everything seemed to quiver with cold and sickliness.

'Have you often slept out?' he asked her.

'Not so very,' she answered.

'You won't go after *him*?' he asked.

'I s'll have to,' she replied, but she nestled in to Geoffrey. He felt a sudden panic.

'You mustn't,' he exclaimed, and she saw he was afraid for himself. She let it be, was silent.

'We couldn't get married?' he asked thoughtfully.

'No.'

He brooded deeply over this. At length: 'Would you go to Canada with me?'

'We'll see what you think in two months' time,' she replied quietly, without bitterness.

'I s'll think the same,' he protested, hurt.

She did not answer, only watched him steadily. She was there for him to do as he liked with; but she would not injure his fortunes; no, not to save his soul.

'Haven't you got no relations?' he asked.

'A married sister at Crick.'

'On a farm?'

'No – married a farm labourer – but she's very comfortable. I'll go there, if you want me to, just till I can get another place in service.'

He considered this.

'Could you get on a farm?' he asked wistfully.

'Greenhalgh's was a farm.'

He saw the future brighten: she would be a help to him. She agreed to go to her sister, and to get a place of service until spring, he said, when they would sail for Canada. He waited for the assent.

'You will come with me, then?' he asked.

'When the time comes,' she said.

Her want of faith made him bow his head: she had reason for it.

'Shall you walk to Crick, or go from Langley Mill to Ambergate? But it's only ten mile to walk. So we can go together up Hunt's Hill – you'd have to go past our lane-end, then I could easy nip down an' fetch you some money,' he said humbly.

'I've got half a sovereign by me – it's more than I s'll want.'

'Let's see it,' he said.

After a while, fumbling under the blanket, she brought out the piece of money. He felt she was independent of him. Brooding rather bitterly, he told himself she'd forsake him. His anger gave him courage to ask: 'Shall you go in service in your maiden name?'

'No.'

He was bitterly wrathful with her – full of resentment.

'I bet I s'll niver see you again,' he said, with a short, hard laugh. She put her arms round him, pressed him to her bosom, while the tears rose to her eyes. He was reassured, but not satisfied.

'Shall you write to me tonight?'

'Yes, I will.'

'And can I write to you – who shall I write to?'

'Mrs Bredon.'

' "Bredon"!' he repeated bitterly.

He was exceedingly uneasy.

The dawn had grown quite wan. He saw the hedges drooping wet down the grey mist. Then he told her about Maurice.

'Oh, you *shouldn't*!' she said. 'You should ha' put the ladder up for them, you *should*.'

'Well – I don't care.'

'Go and do it now – and I'll go.'

'No, don't you. Stop an' see our Maurice; go on, stop an' see him – then I'll be able to tell him.'

She consented in silence. He had her promise she would not go before he returned. She adjusted her dress, found her way to the trough, where she performed her toilet.

Geoffrey wandered round to the upper field. The stacks looked wet in the mist, the hedge was drenched. Mist rose like steam from the grass, and the near hills were veiled almost to a shadow. In the valley, some peaks of black poplar showed fairly definite, jutting up. He shivered with chill.

There was no sound from the stacks, and he could see nothing. After all, he wondered, were they up there? But he reared the ladder to the place whence it had been swept, then went down the hedge to gather dry sticks. He was breaking off thin dead twigs under a holly tree when he heard, on the perfectly still air: 'Well, I'm dashed!'

He listened intently. Maurice was awake.

'Sithee here!' the lad's voice exclaimed. Then, after a while, the foreign sound of the girl: 'What – oh, thair!'

'Aye, th' ladder's there, right enough.'

'You said it had fall down.'

'Well, I heard it drop – an' I couldna feel it nor see it.'

'You said it had fall down – you lie, you liar.'

'Nay, as true as I'm here – '

'You tell me lies – make me stay here – you tell me lies – ' She was passionately indignant.

'As true as I'm standing here – ' he began.

'Lies! – lies! – lies!' she cried. 'I don't believe you, never. You *mean*, you *mean, mean, mean*!'

'A' raïght, then!' He was now incensed, in his turn.

'You are bad, mean, mean, mean.'

'Are ter commin' down?' asked Maurice coldly.

'No – I will not come with you – mean, to tell me lies.'

'Are ter commin' down?'

'No, I don't want you.'

'A' raïght, then!'

Geoffrey, peering through the holly tree, saw Maurice negotiating the ladder. The top rung was below the brim of the stack, and rested on the cloth, so it was dangerous to approach. The Fräulein watched him from the end of the stack, where the cloth thrown back showed the light, dry hay. He slipped slightly, she screamed. When he had got on to the ladder, he pulled the cloth away, throwing it back, making it easy for her to descend.

'Now are ter commin'?' he asked.

'No!' She shook her head violently, in a pet.

Geoffrey felt slightly contemptuous of her. But Maurice waited.

'Are ter commin'?' he called again.

'No,' she flashed, like a wild cat.

'All right, then I'm going.'

He descended. At the bottom, he stood holding the ladder.

'Come on, while I hold it steady,' he said.

There was no reply. For some minutes he stood patiently with his foot on the bottom rung of the ladder. He was pale, rather washed-out in his appearance, and he drew himself together with cold.

'Are ter commin', or aren't ter?' he asked at length. Still there was no reply.

'Then stop up till tha'rt ready,' he muttered, and he went away. Round the other side of the stacks he met Geoffrey.

'What, are thaïgh here?' he exclaimed.

'Bin here a' naïght,' replied Geoffrey. 'I come to help thee wi' th' cloth, but I found it on, an' th' ladder down, so I thowt tha'd gone.'

'Did ter put th' ladder up?'

'I did a bit sin'.'

Maurice brooded over this, Geoffrey struggled with himself to get out his own news. At last he blurted: 'Tha knows that woman as wor here yis'day dinner – 'er come back, an' stopped i' th' shed a' night, out o' th' rain.'

'Oh – ah!' said Maurice, his eye kindling, and a smile crossing his pallor.

'An' I s'll gi'e her some breakfast.'

'Oh – ah!' repeated Maurice.

'It's th' man as is good-for-nowt, not her,' protested Geoffrey. Maurice did not feel in a position to cast stones.

'Tha pleases thysen,' he said, 'what ter does.' He was very quiet, unlike himself. He seemed bothered and anxious, as Geoffrey had not seen him before.

'What's up wi' thee?' asked the elder brother, who in his own heart was glad, and relieved.

'Nowt,' was the reply.

They went together to the hut. The woman was folding the blanket. She was fresh from washing, and looked very pretty. Her hair, instead of being screwed tightly back, was coiled in a knot low down, partly covering her ears. Before she had deliberately made herself plain-looking: now she was neat and pretty, with a sweet, womanly gravity.

'Hello. I didn't think to find you here,' said Maurice, very awkwardly, smiling. She watched him gravely without reply. 'But it was better in shelter than outside last night,' he added.

'Yes,' she replied.

'Shall you get a few more sticks?' Geoffrey asked him. It was a new thing for Geoffrey to be leader. Maurice obeyed. He wandered forth into the damp, raw morning. He did not go to the stack, as he shrank from meeting Paula.

At the mouth of the hut, Geoffrey was making the fire. The woman got out coffee from the box: Geoffrey set the tin to boil. They were arranging breakfast when Paula appeared. She was hatless. Bits of hay stuck in her hair, and she was white-faced – altogether, she did not show to advantage.

'Ah – you!' she exclaimed, seeing Geoffrey.

'Hello!' he answered. 'You're out early.'

'Where's Maurice?'

'I dunno, he should be back directly.'

Paula was silent.

'When have you come?' she asked.

'I come last night, but I could see nobody about. I got up half an hour sin', an' put th' ladder up ready to take the stack-cloth up.'

Paula understood, and was silent. When Maurice returned with the faggots, she was crouched warming her hands. She looked up at him, but he kept his eyes averted from her. Geoffrey met the eyes of Lydia, and smiled. Maurice put his hands to the fire.

'You cold?' asked Paula tenderly.

'A bit,' he answered, quite friendly, but reserved. And all the while the four sat round the fire, drinking their smoked coffee, eating each a small piece of toasted bacon, Paula watched eagerly for the eyes of Maurice, and he avoided her. He was gentle, but would not give his eyes to her looks. And Geoffrey smiled constantly to Lydia, who watched gravely.

The German girl succeeded in getting safely into the vicarage, her escapade unknown to anyone save the housemaid. Before a week was out, she was openly engaged to Maurice, and when her month's notice expired, she went to live at the farm.

Geoffrey and Lydia kept faith one with the other.

The Lovely Lady

AT SEVENTY-TWO, Pauline Attenborough could still sometimes be mistaken, in the half-light, for thirty. She really was a wonderfully preserved woman, of perfect *chic*. Of course, it helps a great deal to have the right frame. She would be an exquisite skeleton, and her skull would be an exquisite skull, like that of some Etruscan woman,[19] with feminine charm still in the swerve of the bone and the pretty naïve teeth.

Mrs Attenborough's face was of the perfect oval, and slightly flat type that wears best. There is no flesh to sag. Her nose rode serenely, in its finely bridged curve. Only her big grey eyes were a tiny bit prominent on the surface of her face, and they gave her away most. The bluish lids were heavy, as if they ached sometimes with the strain of keeping the eyes beneath them arch and bright; and at the corners of the eyes were fine little wrinkles which would slacken with haggardness, then be pulled up tense again, to that bright, gay look like a Leonardo woman[20] who really could laugh outright.

Her niece Cecilia was perhaps the only person in the world who was aware of the invisible little wire which connected Pauline's eye-wrinkles with Pauline's will-power. Only Cecilia *consciously* watched the eyes go haggard and old and tired, and remain so, for hours; until Robert came home. Then ping! – the mysterious little wire that worked between Pauline's will and her face went taut, the weary, haggard, prominent eyes suddenly began to gleam, the eyelids arched, the queer curved eyebrows which floated in such frail arches on Pauline's forehead began to gather a mocking significance, and you had the *real* lovely lady, in all her charm.

She really had the secret of everlasting youth; that is to say, she could don her youth again like an eagle. But she was sparing of it. She was wise enough not to try being young for too many people. Her son Robert, in the evenings, and Sir Wilfred Knipe sometimes in the afternoon to tea: then occasional visitors on Sunday, when Robert was home: for these she was her lovely and changeless self, that age could not wither, nor custom stale: so bright and kindly and yet subtly mocking, like Mona Lisa,[21] who knew a thing or two. But

Pauline knew more, so she needn't be smug at all, she could laugh that lovely mocking Bacchante[22] laugh of hers, which was at the same time never malicious, always good-naturedly tolerant, both of virtues and vices. The former, of course, taking much more tolerating. So she suggested, roguishly.

Only with her niece Cecilia she did not trouble to keep up the glamour. Ciss was not very observant, anyhow: and more than that, she was plain: more still, she was in love with Robert: and most of all, she was thirty, and dependent on her Aunt Pauline. Oh, Cecilia! Why make music for her!

Cecilia, called by her aunt and by her cousin Robert just Ciss, like a cat spitting, was a big dark-complexioned, pug-faced young woman who very rarely spoke, and when she did, couldn't get it out. She was the daughter of a poor Congregational minister who had been, while he lived, brother to Ronald, Aunt Pauline's husband. Ronald and the Congregational minister were both well dead, and Aunt Pauline had had charge of Ciss for the last five years.

They lived all together in a quite exquisite though rather small Queen Anne house[23] some twenty-five miles out of town, secluded in a little dale, and surrounded by small but very quaint and pleasant grounds. It was an ideal place and an ideal life for Aunt Pauline, at the age of seventy-two. When the kingfishers flashed up the little stream in the garden, going under the alders, something still flashed in her heart. She was that kind of woman.

Robert, who was two years older than Ciss, went every day to town, to his chambers in one of the Inns.[24] He was a barrister, and, to his secret but very deep mortification, he earned about a hundred pounds a year. He simply couldn't get above that figure, though it was rather easy to get below it. Of course, it didn't matter. Pauline had money. But then what was Pauline's was Pauline's, and though she could give almost lavishly, still, one was always aware of having a *lovely* and *undeserved* present made to one: presents are so much nicer when they are undeserved, Aunt Pauline would say.

Robert too was plain, and almost speechless. He was medium-sized, rather broad and stout, though not fat. Only his creamy, clean-shaven face was rather fat, and sometimes suggestive of an Italian priest, in its silence and its secrecy. But he had grey eyes like his mother, but very shy and uneasy, not bold like hers. Perhaps Ciss was the only person who fathomed his awful shyness and *malaise*, his habitual feeling that he was in the wrong place: almost like a soul that has got into the wrong body. But he never did anything about it. He went up to his chambers and read law. It was, however, all the weird old processes that interested him. He had, unknown to everybody but his mother, a quite extraordinary collection of old Mexican legal documents, reports of processes and trials, pleas, accusations, the weird and awful mixture of ecclesiastical law and common law in seventeenth-century Mexico. He had started a study in this direction through coming across a report of a trial of two English sailors, for murder, in Mexico in 1620, and he had gone on, when the next document was an accusation against a Don Miguel Estrada for seducing one of the nuns of the Sacred Heart Convent in Oaxaca in 1680.

Pauline and her son Robert had wonderful evenings with these old papers. The lovely lady knew a little Spanish. She even looked a trifle Spanish herself, with a high comb and a marvellous dark brown shawl embroidered in thick silvery silk embroidery. So she would sit at the perfect old table, soft as velvet in its deep brown surface, a high comb in her hair, earrings with dropping pendants in her ears, her arms bare and still beautiful, a few strings of pearls round her throat, a puce velvet dress on and this or another beautiful shawl, and by candle-light she looked, yes, a Spanish high-bred beauty of thirty-two or three. She set the candles to give her face just the chiaroscuro she knew suited her; her high chair that rose behind her face was done in old green brocade, against which her face emerged like a Christmas rose. They were always three at table; and they always drank a bottle of champagne: Pauline two glasses, Ciss two glasses, Robert the rest. The lovely lady sparkled and was radiant. Ciss, her black hair bobbed, her broad shoulders in a very nice and becoming dress that Aunt Pauline had helped her to make, stared from her aunt to her cousin and back again, with rather confused, mute, hazel eyes, and played the part of an audience suitably impressed. She *was* impressed, somewhere, all the time. And even rendered speechless by Pauline's brilliancy, even after five years. But at the bottom of her consciousness were the data of as weird a document as Robert ever studied: all the things she knew about her aunt and cousin.

Robert was always a gentleman, with an old-fashioned punctilious courtesy that covered his shyness quite completely. He was, and Ciss knew it, more confused than shy. He was worse than she was. Cecilia's own confusion dated from only five years back – Robert's must have started before he was born. In the lovely lady's womb he must have felt *very* confused.

He paid all his attention to his mother, drawn to her as a humble flower to the sun. And yet, priest-like, he was all the time aware, with the tail of his consciousness, that Ciss was there, and that she was a bit shut out of it, and that something wasn't right. He was aware of the third consciousness in the room. Whereas to Pauline, her niece Cecilia was an appropriate part of her own setting, rather than a distinct consciousness.

Robert took coffee with his mother and Ciss in the warm drawing-room, where all the furniture was so lovely, all collectors' pieces – Mrs Attenborough had made her own money, dealing privately in pictures and furniture and rare things from barbaric countries – and the three talked desultorily till about eight or half past. It was very pleasant, very cosy, very homely even: Pauline made a real home cosiness out of so much elegant material. The chat was simple, and nearly always bright. Pauline was her real self, emanating a friendly mockery and an odd, ironic gaiety. Till there came a little pause.

At which Ciss always rose and said goodnight and carried out the coffee-tray, to prevent Burnett from intruding any more.

And then! Oh, then, the lovely glowing intimacy of the evening, between mother and son, when they deciphered manuscripts and discussed points, Pauline with that eagerness of a girl, for which she was famous. And it was quite genuine. In some mysterious way she had *saved up* her power for being thrilled, in connection with a man. Robert, solid, rather quiet and subdued, seemed like the elder of the two: almost like a priest with a young girl pupil. And that was rather how he felt.

Ciss had a flat for herself just across the courtyard, over the old coach-house and stables. There were no horses. Robert kept his car in the coach-house. Ciss had three very nice rooms up there, stretching along in a row one after another, and she had got used to the ticking of the stable clock.

But sometimes she did not go up to her rooms. In the summer she would sit on the lawn, and from the open window of the drawing-room upstairs she would hear Pauline's wonderful heart-searching laugh. And in the winter the young woman would put on a thick coat and walk slowly to the little balustraded bridge over the stream, and then look back at the three lighted windows of that drawing-room where mother and son were so happy together.

Ciss loved Robert, and she believed that Pauline intended the two of them to marry: when she was dead. But poor Robert, he was so convulsed with shyness already, with man or woman. What would he be when his mother was dead in a dozen more years? He would be just a shell, the shell of a man who had never lived.

The strange unspoken sympathy of the young with one another, when they are overshadowed by the old, was one of the bonds between Robert and Ciss. But another bond, which Ciss did not know how to draw tight, was the bond of passion. Poor Robert was by nature a passionate man. His silence and his agonised, though hidden, shyness were both the result of a secret physical passionateness. And how Pauline could play on this! Ah, Ciss was not blind to the eyes which he fixed on his mother, eyes fascinated yet humiliated, full of shame. He was ashamed that he was not a man. And he did not love his mother. He was fascinated by her. Completely fascinated. And for the rest, paralysed in a lifelong confusion.

Ciss stayed in the garden till the lights leapt up in Pauline's bedroom – about ten o'clock. The lovely lady had retired. Robert would now stay another hour or so, alone. Then he too would retire. Ciss, in the dark outside, sometimes wished she could creep up to him and say: 'Oh, Robert! It's all wrong!' But Aunt Pauline would hear. And, anyhow, Ciss couldn't do it. She went off to her own rooms once more, and so for ever.

In the morning coffee was brought up on a tray to each of the three relatives. Ciss had to be at Sir Wilfred Knipe's at nine o'clock, to give two hours' lessons to his little granddaughter. It was her sole serious occupation, except that she played the piano for the love of it. Robert set off to town about nine. And, as a rule, Aunt Pauline appeared at lunch, though sometimes not until tea-time. When she appeared, she looked fresh and young. But she was inclined to fade rather quickly, like a flower without water, in the day-time. Her hour was the candle hour.

So she always rested in the afternoon. When the sun shone, if possible she took a sun-bath. This was one of her secrets. Her lunch was very light, she could take her sun-and-air-bath before noon or after, as it pleased her. Often it was in the afternoon, when the sun shone very warmly into a queer little yew-walled square just behind the stables. Here Ciss stretched out the lying-chair and rugs, and put the light parasol in the silent little enclosure of thick dark yew hedges beyond the red walls of the unused stables. And hither came the lovely lady with her book. Ciss then had to be on guard in one of her own rooms, should her aunt, who was very keen-eared, hear a footstep.

One afternoon it occurred to Cecilia that she herself might while away this rather long afternoon by taking a sun-bath. She was growing restive. The thought of the flat roof of the stable buildings, to which she could climb from a loft at the end, started her on a new adventure. She often went on to the roof: she had to, to wind up the stable clock, which was a job she had assumed to herself. Now she took a rug, climbed out under the heavens, looked at the sky and the great elm-tops, looked at the sun, then took off her things and lay down perfectly serenely, in a corner of the roof under the parapet, full in the sun.

It was rather lovely, to bask all one's length like this in warm sun and air. Yes, it was very lovely! It even seemed to melt some of the hard bitterness of her heart, some of that core of unspoken resentment which never dissolved. Luxuriously, she spread herself, so that the sun should touch her limbs fully, fully. If she had no other lover, she should have the sun! She rolled voluptuously. And suddenly her heart stood still in her body, and her hair almost rose on end as a voice said very softly, musingly in her ear: 'No, Henry dear! It was not my fault you died instead of marrying that Claudia. No, darling. I was quite, quite willing for you to marry her, unsuitable though she was.'

Cecilia sank down on her rug powerless and perspiring with dread. That awful voice, so soft, so musing, yet so unnatural. Not a human voice at all. Yet there must, there must be someone on the roof! Oh! how unspeakably awful!

She lifted her weak head and peeped across the sloping leads. Nobody! The chimneys were far too narrow to shelter anybody. There was nobody on the roof. Then it must be someone in the trees, in the elms. Either that, or terror unspeakable, a bodiless voice! She reared her head a little higher.

And as she did so, came the voice again: 'No, darling! I told you you would tire of her in six months. And you see, it was true, dear. It was true, true, true! I wanted to spare you that. So it wasn't I who made you feel weak and disabled, wanting that very silly Claudia; poor thing, she looked so woebegone afterwards! Wanting her and not wanting her, you got *yourself* into that perplexity, my dear. I only warned you. What else could I do? And you lost your spirit and died without ever knowing me again. It was bitter, bitter – '

The voice faded away. Cecilia subsided weakly on to her rug, after the anguished tension of listening. Oh, it was awful. The sun shone, the sky was blue, all seemed so lovely and afternoony and summery. And yet, oh, horror! – she was going to be forced to believe in the supernatural! And she loathed the supernatural, ghosts and voices and rappings and all the rest.

But that awful creepy bodiless voice, with its rusty sort of whisper of an overtone! It had something so fearfully familiar in it too! and yet was so utterly uncanny. Poor Cecilia could only lie there unclothed, and so all the more agonisingly helpless, inert, collapsed in sheer dread.

And then she heard the thing sigh! A deep sigh that seemed weirdly

familiar, yet was not human. 'Ah, well; ah, well, the heart must bleed!
Better it should bleed than break. It is grief, grief! But it wasn't my
fault, dear. And Robert could marry our poor dull Ciss tomorrow, if
he wanted her. But he doesn't care about it, so why force him into
anything!' The sounds were very uneven, sometimes only a husky
sort of whisper. Listen! Listen!

Cecilia was about to give vent to loud and piercing screams of
hysteria, when the last two sentences arrested her. All her caution
and her cunning sprang alert. It was Aunt Pauline! It must be Aunt
Pauline, practising ventriloquism or something like that! What a
devil she was!

Where was she? She must be lying down there, right below where
Cecilia herself was lying. And it was either some fiend's trick of
ventriloquism, or else thought transference that conveyed itself like
sound. The sounds were very uneven. Sometimes quite inaudible,
sometimes only a brushing sort of noise. Ciss listened intently. No, it
could not be ventriloquism. It was worse, some form of thought
transference. Some horror of that sort. Cecilia still lay weak and
inert, terrified to move, but she was growing calmer with suspicion.
It was some diabolic trick of that unnatural woman.

But *what a devil* of a woman! She even knew that she, Cecilia, had
mentally accused her of killing her son Henry. Poor Henry was
Robert's elder brother, twelve years older than Robert. He had died
suddenly when he was twenty-two, after an awful struggle with
himself, because he was passionately in love with a young and very
good-looking actress, and his mother had humorously despised him
for the attachment. So he had caught some sudden ordinary disease,
but the poison had gone to his brain and killed him before he ever
regained consciousness. Ciss knew the few facts from her own father.
And lately she had been thinking that Pauline was going to kill Robert
as she had killed Henry. It was clear murder: a mother murdering her
sensitive sons, who were fascinated by her: the Circe![25]

'I suppose I may as well get up,' murmured the dim, unbreaking
voice. 'Too much sun is as bad as too little. Enough sun, enough love
thrill, enough proper food, and not too much of any of them, and a
woman might live for ever. I verily believe for ever. If she absorbs as
much vitality as she expends! Or perhaps a trifle more!'

It was certainly Aunt Pauline! How, how horrible! She, Ciss, was
hearing Aunt Pauline's thoughts. Oh, how ghastly! Aunt Pauline was
sending out her thoughts in a sort of radio, and she, Ciss, had to *hear*
what her aunt was thinking. How ghastly! How insufferable! One of
them would surely have to die.

She twisted and she lay inert and crumpled, staring vacantly in front of her. Vacantly! Vacantly! And her eyes were staring almost into a hole. She was staring into it unseeing, a hole going down in the corner from the lead gutter. It meant nothing to her. Only it frightened her a little more.

When suddenly out of the hole came a sigh and a last whisper. 'Ah, well! Pauline! Get up, it's enough for today!' Good God! Out of the hole of the rain-pipe! The rain-pipe was acting as a speaking-tube! Impossible! No, quite possible. She had read of it even in some book. And Aunt Pauline, like the old and guilty woman she was, talked aloud to herself. That was it!

A sullen exultance sprang into Ciss's breast. *That* was why she would never have anybody, not even Robert, in her bedroom. That was why she never dozed in a chair, never sat absent-minded anywhere, but went to her room, and kept to her room, except when she roused herself to be alert. When she slackened off, she talked to herself! She talked in a soft little crazy voice to herself. But she was not crazy. It was only her thoughts murmuring themselves aloud.

So she had qualms about poor Henry! Well she might have! Ciss believed that Aunt Pauline had loved her big, handsome, brilliant first-born much more than she loved Robert, and that his death had been a terrible blow and a chagrin to her. Poor Robert had been only ten years old when Henry died. Since then he had been the substitute.

Ah, how awful!

But Aunt Pauline was a strange woman. She had left her husband when Henry was a small child, some years even before Robert was born. There was no quarrel. Sometimes she saw her husband again, quite amicably, but a little mockingly. And she even gave him money.

For Pauline earned all her own. Her father had been a consul in the East and in Naples: and a devoted collector of beautiful and exotic things. When he died, soon after his grandson Henry was born, he left his collection of treasures to his daughter. And Pauline, who had really a passion and a genius for loveliness, whether in texture or form or colour, had laid the basis of her fortune on her father's collection. She had gone on collecting, buying where she could, and selling to collectors and to museums. She was one of the first to sell old, weird African wooden figures to the museums, and ivory carvings from New Guinea. She bought Renoir as soon as she saw his pictures. But not Rousseau.[26] And all by herself she made a fortune.

After her husband died, she had not married again. She was not even *known* to have had lovers. If she did have lovers, it was not among the men who admired her most and paid her devout and open attendance. To these she was a 'friend'.

Cecilia slipped on her clothes and caught up her rug, hastened carefully down the ladder to the loft. As she descended she heard the ringing musical call: 'All right, Ciss!' which meant that the lovely lady was finished, and returning to the house. Even her voice was marvellously young and sonorous, beautifully balanced and self-possessed. So different from the little voice in which she talked to herself. *That* was much more the voice of an old woman.

Ciss hastened round to the yew enclosure, where lay the comfortable chaise-longue with the various delicate rugs. Everything Pauline had was choice, to the fine straw mat on the floor. The great yew walls were beginning to cast long shadows. Only in the corner, where the rugs tumbled their delicate colours, was there hot, still sunshine.

The rugs folded up, the chair lifted away, Cecilia stooped to look at the mouth of the rain-pipe. There it was, in the corner, under a little hood of masonry and just projecting from the thick leaves of the creeper on the wall. If Pauline, lying there, turned her face towards the wall, she would speak into the very mouth of the hole. Cecilia was reassured. She had heard her aunt's thoughts indeed, but by no uncanny agency.

That evening, as if aware of something, Pauline was a little quicker than usual, though she looked her own serene, rather mysterious self. And after coffee she said to Robert and Ciss: 'I'm so sleepy. The sun has made me so sleepy. I feel full of sunshine like a bee. I shall go to bed, if you don't mind. You two sit and have a talk.'

Cecilia looked quickly at her cousin.

'Perhaps you would rather be alone,' she said to him.

'No, no,' he replied. 'Do keep me company for a while, if it doesn't bore you.'

The windows were open, the scent of the honeysuckle wafted in with the sound of an owl. Robert smoked in silence. There was a sort of despair in the motionless, rather squat body. He looked like a caryatid bearing a weight. 'Do you remember Cousin Henry?' Cecilia asked him suddenly.

He looked up in surprise.

'Yes, very well,' he said.

'What did he look like?' she said, glancing into her cousin's big, secret-troubled eyes, in which there was so much frustration.

'Oh, he was handsome: tall and fresh-coloured, with mother's soft brown hair.' As a matter of fact, Pauline's hair was grey. 'The ladies admired him very much; he was at all the dances.'

'And what kind of character had he?'

'Oh, very good-natured and jolly. He liked to be amused. He was rather quick and clever, like mother, and very good company.'

'And did he love your mother?'

'Very much. She loved him too – better than she does me, as a matter of fact. He was so much more nearly her idea of a man.'

'Why was he more her idea of a man?'

'Tall – handsome – attractive, and very good company and would, I believe, have been very successful at law. I'm afraid I am merely negative in all those respects.'

Ciss looked at him attentively, with her slow-thinking hazel eyes. Under his impassive mask, she knew he suffered.

'Do you think you are so much more negative than he?' she said.

He did not lift his face. But after a few moments he replied: 'My life, certainly, is a negative affair.'

She hesitated before she dared ask him: 'And do you mind?'

He did not answer her at all. Her heart sank.

'You see, I am afraid my life is as negative as yours is,' she said. 'And I'm beginning to mind bitterly. I'm thirsty.'

She saw his creamy, well-bred hand tremble.

'I suppose,' he said, without looking at her, 'one will rebel when it is too late.'

That was queer, from him.

'Robert,' she said, 'do you like me at all?'

She saw his dusky, creamy face, so changeless in its folds, go pale. 'I am very fond of you,' he murmured.

'Won't you kiss me? Nobody ever kisses me,' she said pathetically.

He looked at her, his eyes strange with fear and a certain haughtiness. Then he rose and came softly over to her and kissed her gently on the cheek.

'It's an awful shame, Ciss!' he said softly.

She caught his hand and pressed it to her breast.

'And sit with me some time in the garden,' she said, murmuring with difficulty. 'Won't you?'

He looked at her anxiously and searchingly.

'What about mother?' he said.

Ciss smiled a funny little smile, and looked into his eyes. He suddenly flushed crimson, turning aside his face. It was a painful sight.

'I know,' he said, 'I am no lover of women.'

He spoke with sarcastic stoicism against himself, but even she did not know the shame it was to him.

'You never try to be!' she said.

Again his eyes changed uncannily.

'Does one have to try?' he said.

'Why, yes! One never does anything if one doesn't try.'

He went pale again.

'Perhaps you are right,' he said.

In a few minutes she left him and went to her room. At least, she had tried to take off the everlasting lid from things.

The weather continued sunny, Pauline continued her sun-baths, and Ciss lay on the roof eavesdropping in the literal sense of the word. But Pauline was not to be heard. No sound came up the pipe. She must be lying with her face away into the open. Ciss listened with all her might. She could just detect the faintest, faintest murmur away below, but no audible syllable.

And at night, under the stars, Cecilia sat and waited in silence, on the seat which kept in view the drawing-room windows and the side door into the garden. She saw the light go up in her aunt's room. She saw the lights at last go out in the drawing-room. And she waited. But he did not come. She stayed on in the darkness half the night, while the owl hooted. But she stayed alone.

Two days she heard nothing, her aunt's thoughts were not revealed and at evening nothing happened. Then the second night, as she sat with heavy, helpless persistence in the garden, suddenly she started. He had come out. She rose and went softly over the grass to him.

'Don't speak,' he murmured.

And in silence, in the dark, they walked down the garden and over the little bridge to the paddock, where the hay, cut very late, was in cock.[27] There they stood disconsolate under the stars.

'You see,' he said, 'how can I ask for love, if I don't feel any love in myself. You know I have a real regard for you – '

'How can you feel any love, when you never feel anything?' she said.

'That is true,' he replied.

And she waited for what next.

'And how can I marry?' he said. 'I am a failure even at making money. I can't ask my mother for money.'

She sighed deeply.

'Then don't bother yet about marrying,' she said. 'Only love me a little. Won't you?'

He gave a short laugh.

'It sounds so atrocious, to say it is hard to begin,' he said.

She sighed again. He was so stiff to move.

'Shall we sit down a minute,' she said. And then as they sat on the hay, she added: 'May I touch you? Do you mind?'

'Yes, I mind! But do as you wish,' he replied, with that mixture of shyness and queer candour which made him a little ridiculous, as he knew quite well. But in his heart there was almost murder.

She touched his black, always tidy hair with her fingers.

'I suppose I shall rebel one day,' he said again, suddenly.

They sat some time, till it grew chilly. And he held her hand fast, but he never put his arms round her. At last she rose and went indoors, saying goodnight.

The next day, as Cecilia lay stunned and angry on the roof, taking her sun-bath, and becoming hot and fierce with sunshine, suddenly she started. A terror seized her in spite of herself. It was the voice.

'*Caro, caro, tu non l'hai visto!*'[28] it was murmuring away, in a language Cecilia did not understand. She lay and writhed her limbs in the sun, listening intently to words she could not follow. Softly, whisperingly, with infinite caressiveness and yet with that subtle, insidious arrogance under its velvet, came the voice, murmuring in Italian: '*Bravo, sì molto bravo, poverino, ma uomo come te non lo sarà mai, mai, mai!*'![29] Oh especially in Italian Cecilia heard the poisonous charm of the voice, so caressive, so soft and flexible, yet so utterly egoistic. She hated it with intensity as it sighed and whispered out of nowhere. Why, why should it be so delicate, so subtle and flexible and beautifully controlled, while she herself was so clumsy! Oh, poor Cecilia, she writhed in the afternoon sun, knowing her own clownish clumsiness and lack of suavity, in comparison.

'No, Robert dear, you will never be the man your father was, though you have some of his looks. He was a marvellous lover, soft as a flower, yet piercing as a humming-bird. No, Robert dear, you will never know how to serve a woman as Monsignor Mauro did. *Cara, cara mia bellissima, ti ho aspettato come l'agonizzante aspetta la morte, morte deliziosa, quasi quasi troppo deliziosa per un'anima umana*[30] – Soft as a flower, yet probing like a humming-bird. He gave himself to a woman as he gave himself to God. Mauro! Mauro! How you loved me!'

The voice ceased in reverie, and Cecilia knew what she had guessed before, that Robert was not the son of her Uncle Ronald, but of some Italian.

'I am disappointed in you, Robert. There is no poignancy in you. Your father was a Jesuit,[31] but he was the most perfect and poignant lover in the world. You are a Jesuit like a fish in a tank. And that Ciss of yours is the cat fishing for you. It is less edifying even than poor Henry.'

Cecilia suddenly bent her mouth down to the tube, and said in a deep voice: 'Leave Robert alone! Don't kill him as well.'

There was a dead silence, in the hot July afternoon that was lowering for thunder. Cecilia lay prostrate, her heart beating in great thumps. She was listening as if her whole soul were an ear. At last she caught the whisper: 'Did someone speak?'

She leaned again to the mouth of the tube.

'Don't kill Robert as you killed me,' she said with slow enunciation, and a deep but small voice.

'Ah!' came the sharp little cry. 'Who is that speaking?'

'Henry!' said the deep voice.

There was a dead silence. Poor Cecilia lay with all the use gone out of her. And there was dead silence. Till at last came the whisper: 'I didn't kill Henry. No, No! Henry, surely you can't blame me! I loved you, dearest. I only wanted to help you.'

'You killed me!' came the deep, artificial, accusing voice. 'Now, let Robert live. Let him go! Let him marry!'

There was a pause.

'How very, very awful!' mused the whispering voice. 'Is it possible, Henry, you are a spirit, and you condemn me?'

'Yes! I condemn you!'

Cecilia felt all her pent-up rage going down that rain-pipe. At the same time, she almost laughed. It was awful.

She lay and listened and listened. No sound! As if time had ceased, she lay inert in the weakening sun. The sky was yellowing. Quickly she dressed herself, went down, and out to the corner of the stables.

'Aunt Pauline!' she called discreetly. 'Did you hear thunder?'

'Yes! I am going in. Don't wait,' came a feeble voice.

Cecilia retired, and from the loft watched, spying, as the figure of the lovely lady, wrapped in a lovely wrap of old blue silk, went rather totteringly to the house.

The sky gradually darkened, Cecilia hastened in with the rugs. Then the storm broke. Aunt Pauline did not appear to tea. She found the thunder trying. Robert also did not arrive till after tea, in the pouring rain. Cecilia went down the covered passage to her own house, and dressed carefully for dinner, putting some white columbines at her breast.

The drawing-room was lit with a softly-shaded lamp. Robert, dressed, was waiting, listening to the rain. He too seemed strangely cracking and on edge. Cecilia came in with the white flowers nodding at her breast. Robert was watching her curiously, a new look on his face. Cecilia went to the bookshelves near the door, and was peering for something, listening acutely. She heard a rustle, then the door softly opening. And as it opened, Ciss suddenly switched on the strong electric light by the door.

Her aunt, in a dress of black lace over ivory colour, stood in the doorway. Her face was made up, but haggard with a look of unspeakable irritability, as if years of suppressed exasperation and dislike of her fellow-men had suddenly crumpled her into an old witch.

'Oh, aunt!' cried Cecilia.

'Why, mother, you're a little old lady!' came the astounded voice of Robert: like an astonished boy: as if it were a joke.

'Have you only just found it out?' snapped the old woman venomously.

'Yes! Why, I thought – ' his voice tailed out in misgiving.

The haggard, old Pauline, in a frenzy of exasperation, said: 'Aren't we going down?'

She had never even noticed the excess of light, a thing she shunned. And she went downstairs almost tottering.

At table she sat with her face like a crumpled mask of unspeakable irritability. She looked old, very old, and like a witch. Robert and Cecilia fetched furtive glances at her. And Ciss, watching Robert, saw that he was so astonished and repelled by his mother's looks, that he was another man.

'What kind of a drive home did you have?' snapped Pauline, with an almost gibbering irritability.

'It rained, of course,' he said.

'How clever of you to have found that out!' said his mother, with the grisly grin of malice that had succeeded her arch smirk.

'I don't understand,' he said with quiet suavity.

'It's apparent,' said his mother, rapidly and sloppily eating her food.

She rushed through the meal like a crazy dog, to the utter consternation of the servant. And the moment it was over, she darted in a queer, crab-like way upstairs. Robert and Cecilia followed her, thunderstruck, like two conspirators.

'You pour the coffee. I loathe it! I'm going! Goodnight!' said the old woman, in a succession of sharp shots. And she scrambled out of the room.

There was a dead silence. At last he said: 'I'm afraid mother isn't well. I must persuade her to see a doctor.'

'Yes!' said Cecilia.

The evening passed in silence. Robert and Ciss stayed on in the drawing-room, having lit a fire. Outside was cold rain. Each pretended to read. They did not want to separate. The evening passed with ominous mysteriousness, yet quickly.

At about ten o'clock, the door suddenly opened, and Pauline appeared in a blue wrap. She shut the door behind her, and came to the fire. Then she looked at the two young people in hate, real hate.

'You two had better get married quickly,' she said in an ugly voice. 'It would look more decent; such a passionate pair of lovers!'

Robert looked up at her quietly.

'I thought you believed that cousins should not marry, mother,' he said.

'I do! But you're not cousins. Your father was an Italian priest.' Pauline held her daintily-slippered foot to the fire, in an old coquettish gesture. Her body tried to repeat all the old graceful gestures. But the nerve had snapped, so it was a rather dreadful caricature.

'Is that really true, mother?' he asked.

'True! What do you think? He was a distinguished man, or he wouldn't have been my lover. He was far too distinguished a man to have had you for a son. But that joy fell to me.'

'How unfortunate all round,' he said slowly.

'Unfortunate for you? You were lucky. It was *my* misfortune,' she said acidly to him.

She was really a dreadful sight, like a piece of lovely Venetian glass that has been dropped, and gathered up again in horrible, sharp-edged fragments.

Suddenly she left the room again.

For a week it went on. She did not recover. It was as if every nerve in her body had suddenly started screaming in an insanity of discordance. The doctor came, and gave her sedatives, for she never slept. Without drugs, she never slept at all, only paced back and forth in her room, looking hideous and evil, reeking with malevolence. She could not bear to see either her son or her niece. Only when either of them came, she asked in pure malice: 'Well! When's the wedding! Have you celebrated the nuptials yet?'

At first Cecilia was stunned by what she had done. She realised vaguely that her aunt, once a definite thrust of condemnation had penetrated her beautiful armour, had just collapsed squirming inside her shell. It was too terrible. Ciss was almost terrified into repentance. Then she thought: This is what she always was. Now let her live the rest of her days in her true colours.

But Pauline would not live long. She was literally shrivelling away. She kept to her room, and saw no one. She had her mirrors taken away.

Robert and Cecilia sat a good deal together. The jeering of the mad Pauline had not driven them apart, as she had hoped. But Cecilia dared not confess to him what she had done.

'Do you think your mother ever loved anybody?' Ciss asked him tentatively, rather wistfully, one evening.

He looked at her fixedly.

'Herself!' he said at last.

'She didn't even *love* herself,' said Ciss. 'It was something else – what was it?' She lifted a troubled, utterly puzzled face to him.

'Power!' he said curtly.

'But what power?' she asked. 'I don't understand.'

'Power to feed on other lives,' he said bitterly. 'She was beautiful, and she fed on life. She has fed on me as she fed on Henry. She put a sucker into one's soul and sucked up one's essential life.'

'And don't you forgive her?'

'No.'

'Poor Aunt Pauline!'

But even Ciss did not mean it. She was only aghast.

'I *know* I've got a heart,' he said, passionately striking his breast. 'But it's almost sucked dry. I *know* people who want power over others.'

Ciss was silent; what was there to say?

And two days later, Pauline was found dead in her bed, having taken too much veronal, for her heart was weakened. From the grave even she hit back at her son and her niece. She left Robert the noble sum of one thousand pounds; and Ciss one hundred. All the rest, with the nucleus of her valuable antiques, went to form the 'Pauline Attenborough Museum'.

Rawdon's Roof

RAWDON was the sort of man who said, privately, to his men friends, over a glass of wine after dinner: 'No woman shall sleep again under my roof!'

He said it with pride, rather vaunting, pursing his lips. 'Even my housekeeper goes home to sleep.'

But the housekeeper was a gentle old thing of about sixty, so it seemed a little fantastic. Moreover, the man had a wife, of whom he was secretly rather proud, as a piece of fine property, and with whom he kept up a very witty correspondence, epistolary, and whom he treated with humorous gallantry when they occasionally met for half an hour. Also he had a love affair going on. At least, if it wasn't a affair, what was it? However!

'No. I've come to the determination that no woman ever sleep under my roof again – not even a female cat!'

One looked at the roof, and wondered what it had done amiss. Besides, it wasn't his roof. He only rented the house. What does a man mean, anyhow, when he says 'my roof'? *My* roof! The only roof I am conscious of having, myself, is the top of my head. However, he hardly can have meant that no woman should sleep under the elegant dome of his skull. Though there's no telling. You see the top of a sleek head through a window, and you say: 'By Jove, what a pretty girl's head!' And after all, when the individual comes out, it's in trousers.

The point, however, is that Rawdon said so emphatically – no, not emphatically, succinctly: 'No woman shall ever again sleep under my roof.' It was a case of futurity. No doubt he had had his ceilings whitewashed, and their memories put out. Or rather, repainted, for it was a handsome wooden ceiling. Anyhow, if ceilings have eyes, as walls have ears, then Rawdon had given his ceilings a new outlook, with a new coat of paint, and all memory of any woman's having slept under them – for after all, in decent circumstances we sleep under ceilings, not under roofs – was wiped out for ever.

'And will you neither sleep under any woman's roof?'

That pulled him up rather short. He was not prepared to sauce his gander as he had sauced his goose. Even I could see the thought flitting through his mind, that some of his pleasantest holidays depended on the charm of his hostess. Even some of the nicest hotels were run by women.

'Ah! Well! That's not quite the same thing, you know. When one leaves one's own house one gives up the keys of circumstance, so to speak. But, as far as possible, I make it a rule not to sleep under a roof that is openly, and obviously, and obtrusively a woman's roof!'

'Quite!' said I with a shudder. 'So do I!'

Now I understood his mysterious love affair less than ever. He was never known to speak of this love affair: he did not even write about it to his wife. The lady – for she was a lady – lived only five minutes' walk from Rawdon. She had a husband, but he was in diplomatic service or something like that, which kept him occupied in the sufficiently-far distance. Yes, far enough. And, as a husband, he was a complete diplomat. A balance of power. If he was entitled to occupy the wide field of the world, she, the other and contrasting power, might concentrate and consolidate her position at home.

She was a charming woman, too, and even a beautiful woman. She had two charming children, long-legged, stalky, clove-pink-half-opened sort of children. But really charming. And she was a woman with a certain mystery. She never talked. She never said anything about herself. Perhaps she suffered; perhaps she was frightfully happy, and made that her cause for silence. Perhaps she was wise enough even to be beautifully silent about her happiness. Certainly she never mentioned her sufferings, or even her trials: and certainly she must have a fair handful of the latter, for Alec Drummond sometimes fled home in the teeth of a gale of debts. He simply got through his own money and through hers, and, third and fatal stride, through other people's as well. Then something had to be done about it. And Janet, dear soul, had to put her hat on and take journeys. But she never said anything of it. At least, she did just hint that Alec didn't *quite* make enough money to meet expenses. But after all, we don't go about with our eyes shut, and Alec Drummond, whatever else he did, didn't hide his prowess under a bushel.

Rawdon and he were quite friendly, but really! None of them ever talked. Drummond didn't talk, he just went off and behaved in his own way. And though Rawdon would chat away till the small hours, *he* never 'talked'. Not to his nearest male friend did he ever mention Janet save as a very pleasant woman and his neighbour: he admitted he adored her children. They often came to see him.

And one felt about Rawdon, he was making a mystery of something. And that was rather irritating. He went every day to see Janet, and of course we saw him going: going or coming. How can one help but see? But he always went in the morning, at about eleven, and did not stay for lunch: or he went in the afternoon, and came home to dinner. Apparently he was never there in the evening. Poor Janet, she lived like a widow.

Very well, if Rawdon wanted to make it so blatantly obvious that it was only platonic, purely platonic, why wasn't he natural? Why didn't he say simply: 'I'm very fond of Janet Drummond, she is my very dear friend?' Why did he sort of curl up at the very mention of her name, and curdle into silence: or else say rather forcedly: 'Yes, she is a charming woman. I see a good deal of her, but chiefly for the children's sake. I'm devoted to the children!' Then he would look at one in such a curious way, as if he were hiding something. And after all, what was there to hide? If he was the woman's friend, why not? It could be a charming friendship. And if he were her lover, why, heaven bless me, he ought to have been proud of it, and showed just a glint, just an honest man's glint.

But no, never a glint of pride or pleasure in the relation either way. Instead of that, this rather theatrical reserve. Janet, it is true, was just as reserved. If she could, she avoided mentioning his name. Yet one knew, sure as houses, she felt something. One suspected her of being more in love with Rawdon than ever she had been with Alec. And one felt that there was a hush upon it all. She had had a hush put upon her. By whom? By both the men? Or by Rawdon only? Or by Drummond? Was it for her husband's sake? Impossible! For the children's? But why! Her children were devoted to Rawdon.

It now had become the custom for them to go to him three times a week, for music. I don't mean he taught them the piano. Rawdon was a very refined musical amateur. He had them sing, in their delicate girlish voices, delicate little songs, and really he succeeded wonderfully with them; he made them so true, which children rarely are, musically, and so pure and effortless, like little flamelets of sound. It really was rather beautiful, and sweet of him. And he taught them *music*, the delicacy of the feel of it. They had a regular teacher for the practice.

Even the little girls, in their young little ways, were in love with Rawdon! So if their mother were in love too, in her ripened woman-hood, why not?

Poor Janet! She was so still, and so elusive: the hush upon her! She was rather like a half-opened rose that somebody had tied a string round, so that it couldn't open any more. But why? Why? In her there was a real touch of mystery. One could never *ask* her, because one knew her heart was too keenly involved: or her pride.

Whereas there was, really, no mystery about Rawdon, refined and handsome and subtle as he was. He had no mystery: at least, to a man. What *he* wrapped himself up in was a certain amount of mystification.

Who wouldn't be irritated to hear a fellow saying, when for months and months he has been paying a daily visit to a lonely and very attractive woman – nay, lately even a twice-daily visit, even if always before sundown – to hear him say, pursing his lips after a sip of his own very moderate port: 'I've taken a vow that no women shall sleep under my roof again!'

I almost snapped out: 'Oh, what the hell! And what about your Janet?' But I remembered in time, it was not *my* affair, and if he wanted to have his mystifications, let him have them.

If he meant he wouldn't have his wife sleep under his roof again, that one could understand. They were really very witty with one another, he and she, but fatally and damnably married.

Yet neither wanted a divorce. And neither put the slightest claim to any control over the other's behaviour. He said: 'Women live on the moon, men on the earth.' And she said: 'I don't mind in the least if he loves Janet Drummond, poor thing. It would be a change for him, from loving himself. And a change for her, if somebody loved her – '

Poor Janet! But he wouldn't have her sleep under his roof, no, not for any money. And apparently he never slept under hers – if she could be said to have one. So what the deuce?

Of course, if they were friends, just friends, all right! But then in that case, why start talking about not having a woman sleep under your roof? Pure mystification!

The cat never came out of the bag. But one evening I distinctly heard it mewing inside its sack, and I even believe I saw a claw through the canvas.

It was in November – everything much as usual – myself pricking my ears to hear if the rain had stopped, and I could go home, because I was just a little bored about 'cornemuse'[32] music. I had been having dinner with Rawdon, and listening to him ever since on his favourite topic: not, of course, women, and why they shouldn't sleep under his roof, but fourteenth-century melody and windbag accompaniment.

It was not late – not yet ten o'clock – but I was restless, and wanted to go home. There was no longer any sound of rain. And Rawdon was perhaps going to make a pause in his monologue.

Suddenly there was a tap at the door, and Rawdon's man, Hawken, edged in. Rawdon, who had been a major in some fantastic capacity during the war, had brought Hawken back with him. This fresh-faced man of about thirty-five appeared in the doorway with an intensely blank and bewildered look on his face. He was really an extraordinarily good actor.

'A lady, sir!' he said, with a look of utter blankness.

'A what?' snapped Rawdon.

'A lady!' – then with a most discreet drop in his voice: 'Mrs Drummond, sir!' He looked modestly down at his feet.

Rawdon went deathly white, and his lips quivered.

'Mrs Drummond! Where?'

Hawken lifted his eyes to his master in a fleeting glance.

'I showed her into the dining-room, there being no fire in the drawing-room.'

Rawdon got to his feet and took two or three agitated strides. He could not make up his mind. At last he said, his lips working with agitation: 'Bring her in here.'

Then he turned with a theatrical gesture to me.

'What this is all about, I *don't* know,' he said.

'Let me clear out,' said I, making for the door.

He caught me by the arm.

'No, for God's sake! For God's sake, stop and see me through!'

He gripped my arm till it really hurt, and his eyes were quite wild. I did not know my Olympic Rawdon.

Hastily I backed away to the side of the fire – we were in Rawdon's room, where the books and piano were – and Mrs Drummond appeared in the doorway. She was much paler than usual, being a rather warm-coloured woman, and she glanced at me with big reproachful eyes, as much as to say: You intruder! You interloper! For my part, I could do nothing but stare. She wore a black wrap, which I knew quite well, over her black dinner-dress.

'Rawdon!' she said, turning to him and blotting out my existence from her consciousness. Hawken softly closed the door, and I could *feel* him standing on the threshold outside, listening keen as a hawk.

'Sit down, Janet,' said Rawdon, with a grimace of a sour smile, which he could not get rid of once he had started it, so that his face looked very odd indeed, like a mask which he was unable either to fit on or take off. He had several conflicting expressions all at once, and they had all stuck.

She let her wrap slip back on her shoulders, and knitted her white fingers against her skirt, pressing down her arms, and gazing at him with a terrible gaze. I began to creep to the door.

Rawdon started after me.

'No, don't go! Don't go! I specially want you not to go,' he said in extreme agitation.

I looked at her. She was looking at him with a heavy, sombre kind of stare. Me she absolutely ignored. Not for a second could she forgive me for existing on the earth. I slunk back to my post behind the leather armchair, as if hiding.

'Do sit down, Janet,' he said to her again. 'And have a smoke. What will you drink?'

'No, thanks!' she said, as if it were one word slurred out. 'No, thanks.'

And she proceeded again to fix him with that heavy, portentous stare.

He offered her a cigarette, his hand trembling as he held out the silver box.

'No thanks!' she slurred out again, not even looking at the box, but keeping him fixed with that dark and heavy stare.

He turned away, making a great delay lighting a cigarette, with his back to her, to get out of the stream of that stare. He carefully went for an ashtray, and put it carefully within reach – all the time trying not to be swept away on that stare. And she stood with her fingers locked, her straight, plump, handsome arms pressed downwards against her skirt, and she gazed at him.

He leaned his elbow on the mantelpiece abstractedly for a moment – then he started suddenly, and rang the bell. She turned her eyes from him for a moment, to watch his middle finger pressing the bell-button. Then there was a tension of waiting, an interruption in the previous tension. We waited. Nobody came. Rawdon rang again.

'That's very curious!' he murmured to himself. Hawken was usually so prompt. Hawken, not being a woman, slept under the roof, so there was no excuse for his not answering the bell. The tension in the room had now changed quality, owing to this new suspense. Poor Janet's sombre stare became gradually loosened, so to speak. Attention was divided. Where was Hawken? Rawdon rang the bell a third time, a long peal. And now Janet was no longer the centre of suspense. Where was Hawken? The question loomed large over every other.

'I'll just look in the kitchen,' said I, making for the door.

'No, no. I'll go,' said Rawdon.

But I was in the passage – and Rawdon was on my heels.

The kitchen was very tidy and cheerful, but empty; only a bottle of beer and two glasses stood on the table. To Rawdon the kitchen was as strange a world as to me – he never entered the servants' quarters. But to me it was curious that the bottle of beer was empty, and both the glasses had been used. I knew Rawdon wouldn't notice.

'That's very curious!' said Rawdon: meaning the absence of his man.

At that moment we heard a step on the servants' stairs, and Rawdon opened the door, to reveal Hawken descending with an armful of sheets and things.

'What are you doing?'

'Why! – ' and a pause. 'I was airing the clean laundry, like not to waste the fire last thing.'

Hawken descended into the kitchen with a very flushed face and very bright eyes and rather ruffled hair, and proceeded to spread the linen on chairs before the fire.

'I hope I've not done wrong, sir,' he said in his most winning manner. 'Was you ringing?'

'Three times! Leave that linen and bring a bottle of the fizz.'

'I'm sorry, sir. You can't hear the bell from the front, sir.'

It was perfectly true. The house was small, but it had been built for a very nervous author, and the servants' quarters were shut off, padded off from the rest of the house.

Rawdon said no more about the sheets and things, but he looked more peaked than ever.

We went back to the music-room. Janet had gone to the hearth, and stood with her hand on the mantel. She looked round at us, baffled.

'We're having a bottle of fizz,' said Rawdon. 'Do let me take your wrap.'

'And where was Hawken?' she asked satirically.

'Oh, busy somewhere upstairs.'

'He's a busy young man, that!' she said sardonically. And she sat uncomfortably on the edge of the chair where I had been sitting.

When Hawken came with the tray, she said: 'I'm not going to drink.'

Rawdon appealed to me, so I took a glass. She looked enquiringly at the flushed and bright-eyed Hawken, as if she understood something.

The manservant left the room. We drank our wine, and the awkwardness returned.

'Rawdon!' she said suddenly, as if she were firing a revolver at him. 'Alec came home tonight in a bigger mess than ever, and wanted to make love to me to get it off his mind. I can't stand it any more. I'm in love with you, and I simply can't stand Alec getting too near to me. He's dangerous when he's crossed – and when he's worked up. So I just came here. I didn't see what else I could do.'

She left off as suddenly as a machine-gun leaves off firing. We were just dazed.

'You are quite right,' Rawdon began, in a vague and neutral tone . . .

'I am, am I not?' she said eagerly.

'I'll tell you what I'll do,' he said. 'I'll go round to the hotel tonight, and you can stay here.'

'Under the kindly protection of Hawken, you mean!' she said, with quiet sarcasm.

'Why! – I could send Mrs Betts, I suppose,' he said.

Mrs Betts was his housekeeper.

'You couldn't stay and protect me yourself?' she said quietly.

'I! I! Why, I've made a vow – haven't I, Joe?' – he turned to me – 'not to have any women sleep under my roof again.' He got the mixed sour smile on his face.

She looked up at the ceiling for a moment, then lapsed into silence. Then she said: 'Sort of monastery, so to speak!'

And she rose and reached for her wrap, adding:'I'd better go, then.'

'Joe will see you home,' he said.

She faced round on me.

'Do you mind *not* seeing me home, Mr Bradley?' she said, gazing at me.

'Not if you don't want me,' said I.

'Hawken will drive you,' said Rawdon.

'Oh, no, he won't!' she said. 'I'll walk. Goodnight.'

'I'll get my hat,' stammered Rawdon, in an agony. 'Wait! Wait! The gate will be locked.'

'It was open when I came,' she said.

He rang for Hawken to unlock the iron doors at the end of the short drive, whilst he himself huddled into a greatcoat and scarf, fumbling for a flashlight.

'You won't go till I come back, will you?' he pleaded to me. 'I'd be awfully glad if you'd stay the night. The sheets will be aired.'

I had to promise – and he set off with an umbrella, in the rain, at the same time asking Hawken to take a flashlight and go in front. So that was how they went, in single file along the path over the fields to Mrs Drummond's house, Hawken in front, with flashlight and umbrella, curving round to light up in front of Mrs Drummond, who, with umbrella only, walked isolated between two lights, Rawdon shining his flashlight on her from the rear from under his umbrella. I turned indoors.

So that was over! At least, for the moment!

I thought I would go upstairs and see how damp the bed in the guest-chamber was before I actually stayed the night with Rawdon. He never had guests – preferred to go away himself.

The guest-chamber was a good room across a passage and round a corner from Rawdon's room – its door just opposite the padded service-door. This latter service-door stood open, and a light shone through. I went into the spare bedroom, switching on the light.

To my surprise, the bed looked as if it had just been left – the sheets tumbled, the pillows pressed. I put in my hands under the bedclothes, and it was warm. Very curious!

As I stood looking round in mild wonder, I heard a voice call softly: 'Joe!'

'Yes!' said I instinctively, and, though startled, strode at once out of the room and through the servants' door, towards the voice. Light shone from the open doorway of one of the servants' rooms.

There was a muffled little shriek, and I was standing looking into what was probably Hawken's bedroom, and seeing a soft and pretty white leg and a very pretty feminine posterior very thinly dimmed in a rather short nightdress, just in the act of climbing into a narrow little bed, and, then arrested, the owner of the pretty posterior burying her face in the bedclothes, to be invisible, like the ostrich in the sand.

I discreetly withdrew, went downstairs and poured myself a glass of wine. And very shortly Rawdon returned looking like Hamlet in the last act.

He said nothing, neither did I. We sat and merely smoked. Only as he was seeing me upstairs to bed, in the now immaculate bedroom, he said pathetically: 'Why aren't women content to be what a man wants them to be?'

'Why aren't they!' said I wearily.

'I thought I had made everything clear,' he said.

'You start at the wrong end,' said I.

And as I said it, the picture came into my mind of the pretty feminine butt-end in Hawken's bedroom. Yes, Hawken made better starts, wherever he ended.

When he brought me my cup of tea in the morning, he was very soft and cat-like. I asked him what sort of day it was and he asked me if I'd had a good night, and was I comfortable?

'Very comfortable!' said I. 'But I turned you out, I'm afraid.'

'Me, sir?' He turned on me a face of utter bewilderment.

But I looked him in the eye.

'Is your name Joe?' I asked him.

'You're right, sir.'

'So is mine,' said I. 'However, I didn't see her face, so it's all right. I suppose you *were* a bit tight, in that little bed!'

'Well, sir!' and he flashed me a smile of amazing impudence, and lowered his tone to utter confidence. 'This is the best bed in the house, this is.' And he touched it softly.

'You've not tried them all, surely?'

A look of indignant horror on his face!

'No, sir, indeed I haven't.'

That day, Rawdon left for London, on his way to Tunis, and Hawken was to follow him. The roof of his house looked just the same.

The Drummonds moved too – went away somewhere, and left a lot of unsatisfied tradespeople behind.

The Rocking-Horse Winner

THERE WAS A WOMAN who was beautiful, who started with all the advantages, yet she had no luck. She married for love, and the love turned to dust. She had bonny children, yet she felt they had been thrust upon her, and she could not love them. They looked at her coldly, as if they were finding fault with her. And hurriedly she felt she must cover up some fault in herself. Yet what it was that she must cover up she never knew. Nevertheless, when her children were present, she always felt the centre of her heart go hard. This troubled her, and in her manner she was all the more gentle and anxious for her children, as if she loved them very much. Only she herself knew that at the centre of her heart was a hard little place that could not feel love, no, not for anybody. Everybody else said of her: 'She is such a good mother. She adores her children.' Only she herself, and her children themselves, know it was not so. They read it in each other's eyes.

There were a boy and two little girls. They lived in a pleasant house, with a garden, and they had discreet servants, and felt themselves superior to anyone in the neighbourhood.

Although they lived in style, they felt always an anxiety in the house. There was never enough money. The mother had a small income, and the father had a small income, but not nearly enough for the social position which they had to keep up. The father went into town to some office. But though he had good prospects, these prospects never materialised. There was always the grinding sense of the shortage of money, though the style was always kept up.

At last the mother said: 'I will see if *I* can't make something.' But she did not know where to begin. She racked her brains, and tried this thing and the other, but could not find anything successful. The failure made deep lines come into her face. Her children were growing up, they would have to go to school. There must be more money, there must be more money. The father, who was always very handsome and expensive in his tastes, seemed as if he never *would* be able to do anything worth doing. And the mother, who had a great belief in herself, did not succeed any better, and her tastes were just as expensive.

And so the house came to be haunted by the unspoken phrase: *There must be more money! There must be more money!* The children could hear it all the time, though nobody said it aloud. They heard it at Christmas, when the expensive and splendid toys filled the nursery. Behind the shining modern rocking-horse, behind the smart doll's house, a voice would start whispering: 'There *must* be more money! There *must* be more money!' And the children would stop playing, to listen for a moment. They would look into each other's eyes, to see if they had all heard. And each one saw in the eyes of the other two that they too had heard. 'There *must* be more money! There *must* be more money!'

It came whispering from the springs of the still-swaying rocking-horse, and even the horse, bending his wooden, champing head, heard it. The big doll, sitting so pink and smirking in her new pram¡ could hear it quite plainly, and seemed to be smirking all the more self-consciously because of it. The foolish puppy, too, that took the place of the teddy-bear, he was looking so extraordinarily foolish for no other reason but that he heard the secret whisper all over the house: 'There *must* be more money!'

Yet nobody ever said it aloud. The whisper was everywhere, and therefore no one spoke it. Just as no one ever says: 'We are breathing!' in spite of the fact that breath is coming and going all the time.

'Mother,' said the boy Paul one day, 'why don't we keep a car of our own? Why do we always use uncle's, or else a taxi?'

'Because we're the poor members of the family,' said the mother.

'But why *are* we, mother?'

'Well – I suppose,' she said slowly and bitterly, 'it's because your father had no luck.'

The boy was silent for some time.

'Is luck money, mother?' he asked, rather timidly.

'No, Paul. Not quite. It's what causes you to have money.'

'Oh!' said Paul vaguely. 'I thought when Uncle Oscar said *filthy lucker*, it meant money.'

'*Filthy lucre* does mean money,' said the mother. 'But it's lucre, not luck.'

'Oh!' said the boy. 'Then what *is* luck, mother?'

'It's what causes you to have money. If you're lucky you have money. That's why it's better to be born lucky than rich. If you're rich, you may lose your money. But if you're lucky, you will always get more money.'

'Oh! Will you? And is father not lucky?'

'Very unlucky, I should say,' she said bitterly.

The boy watched her with unsure eyes.

'Why?' he asked.

'I don't know. Nobody ever knows why one person is lucky and another unlucky.'

'Don't they? Nobody at all? Does *nobody* know?'

'Perhaps God. But He never tells.'

'He ought to, then. And aren't you lucky either, mother?'

'I can't be, if I married an unlucky husband.'

'But by yourself, aren't you?'

'I used to think I was, before I married. Now I think I am very unlucky indeed.'

'Why?'

'Well – never mind! Perhaps I'm not really,' she said.

The child looked at her to see if she meant it. But he saw, by the lines of her mouth, that she was only trying to hide something from him.

'Well, anyhow,' he said stoutly, 'I'm a lucky person.'

'Why?' said his mother, with a sudden laugh.

He stared at her. He didn't even know why he had said it. 'God told me,' he asserted, brazening it out.

'I hope He did, dear!' she said, again with a laugh, but rather bitter.

'He did, mother!'

'Excellent!' said the mother, using one of her husband's exclamations.

The boy saw she did not believe him; or rather, that she paid no attention to his assertion. This angered him somewhere, and made him want to compel her attention.

He went off by himself, vaguely, in a childish way, seeking for the clue to 'luck'. Absorbed, taking no heed of other people, he went about with a sort of stealth, seeking inwardly for luck. He wanted luck, he wanted it, he wanted it. When the two girls were playing dolls in the nursery, he would sit on his big rocking-horse, charging madly into space, with a frenzy that made the little girls peer at him uneasily. Wildly the horse careered, the waving dark hair of the boy tossed, his eyes had a strange glare in them. The little girls dared not speak to him.

When he had ridden to the end of his mad little journey, he climbed down and stood in front of his rocking-horse, staring fixedly into its lowered face. Its red mouth was slightly open, its big eye was wide and glassy-bright.

'Now!' he would silently command the snorting steed. 'Now, take me to where there is luck! Now take me!'

And he would slash the horse on the neck with the little whip he had asked Uncle Oscar for. He *knew* the horse could take him to where there was luck, if only he forced it. So he would mount again and start on his furious ride, hoping at last to get there. He knew he could get there.

'You'll break your horse, Paul!' said the nurse.

'He's always riding like that! I wish he'd leave off!' said his elder sister Joan.

But he only glared down on them in silence. Nurse gave him up. She could make nothing of him. Anyhow, he was growing beyond her.

One day his mother and his Uncle Oscar came in when he was on one of his furious rides. He did not speak to them.

'Hallo, you young jockey! Riding a winner?' said his uncle.

'Aren't you growing too big for a rocking-horse? You're not a very little boy any longer, you know,' said his mother.

But Paul only gave a blue glare from his big, rather close-set eyes. He would speak to nobody when he was in full tilt. His mother watched him with an anxious expression on her face.

At last he suddenly stopped forcing his horse into the mechanical gallop and slid down.

'Well, I got there!' he announced fiercely, his blue eyes still flaring, and his sturdy long legs straddling apart.

'Where did you get to?' asked his mother.

'Where I wanted to go,' he flared back at her.

'That's right, son!' said Uncle Oscar. 'Don't you stop till you get there. What's the horse's name?'

'He doesn't have a name,' said the boy.

'Gets on without all right?' asked the uncle.

'Well, he has different names. He was called Sansovino[33] last week.'

'Sansovino, eh? Won the Ascot. How did you know this name?'

'He always talks about horse-races with Bassett,' said Joan.

The uncle was delighted to find that his small nephew was posted with all the racing news. Bassett, the young gardener, who had been wounded in the left foot in the war and had got his present job through Oscar Cresswell, whose batman he had been, was a perfect blade of the 'turf'. He lived in the racing events, and the small boy lived with him.

Oscar Cresswell got it all from Bassett.

'Master Paul comes and asks me, so I can't do more than tell him, sir,' said Bassett, his face terribly serious, as if he were speaking of religious matters.

'And does he ever put anything on a horse he fancies?'

'Well – I don't want to give him away – he's a young sport a fine sport, sir. Would you mind asking him himself? He sort of takes a pleasure in it, and perhaps he'd feel I was giving him away, sir, if you don't mind.'

Bassett was serious as a church.

The uncle went back to his nephew and took him off for a ride in the car.

'Say, Paul, old man, do you ever put anything on a horse?' the uncle asked.

The boy watched the handsome man closely.

'Why, do you think I oughtn't to?' he parried.

'Not a bit of it! I thought perhaps you might give me a tip for the Lincoln.'

The car sped on into the country, going down to Uncle Oscar's place in Hampshire.

'Honour bright?' said the nephew.

'Honour bright, son!' said the uncle.

'Well, then, Daffodil.'

'Daffodil! I doubt it, sonny. What about Mirza?'

'I only know the winner,' said the boy. 'That's Daffodil.'

'Daffodil, eh?'

There was a pause. Daffodil was an obscure horse comparatively.

'Uncle!'

'Yes, son?'

'You won't let it go any further, will you? I promised Bassett.'

'Bassett be damned, old man! What's he got to do with it?'

'We're partners. We've been partners from the first. Uncle, he lent me my first five shillings, which I lost. I promised him, honour bright, it was only between me and him; only you gave me that ten-shilling note I started winning with, so I thought you were lucky. You won't let it go any further, will you?'

The boy gazed at his uncle from those big, hot, blue eyes, set rather close together. The uncle stirred and laughed uneasily.

'Right you are, son! I'll keep your tip private. Daffodil, eh? How much are you putting on him?'

'All except twenty pounds,' said the boy. 'I keep that in reserve.'

The uncle thought it a good joke.

'You keep twenty pounds in reserve, do you, you young romancer? What are you betting, then?'

'I'm betting three hundred,' said the boy gravely. 'But it's between you and me, Uncle Oscar! Honour bright?'

The uncle burst into a roar of laughter.

'It's between you and me all right, you young Nat Gould,'[34] he said, laughing. 'But where's your three hundred?'

'Bassett keeps it for me. We're partners.'

'You are, are you! And what is Bassett putting on Daffodil?'

'He won't go quite as high as I do, I expect. Perhaps he'll go a hundred and fifty.'

'What, pennies?' laughed the uncle.

'Pounds,' said the child, with a surprised look at his uncle. 'Bassett keeps a bigger reserve than I do.'

Between wonder and amusement Uncle Oscar was silent. He pursued the matter no further, but he determined to take his nephew with him to the Lincoln races.

'Now, son,' he said, 'I'm putting twenty on Mirza, and I'll put five on for you on any horse you fancy. What's your pick?'

'Daffodil, uncle.'

'No, not the fiver on Daffodil!'

'I should if it was my own fiver,' said the child.

'Good! Good! Right you are! A fiver for me and a fiver for you on Daffodil.'

The child had never been to a race-meeting before, and his eyes were blue fire. He pursed his mouth tight and watched. A Frenchman just in front had put his money on Lancelot. Wild with excitement, he flayed his arms up and down, yelling '*Lancelot! Lancelot!*' in his French accent.

Daffodil came in first, Lancelot second, Mirza third. The child, flushed and with eyes blazing, was curiously serene. His uncle brought him four five-pound notes, four to one.

'What am I to do with these?' he cried, waving them before the boy's eyes.

'I suppose we'll talk to Bassett,' said the boy. 'I expect I have fifteen hundred now; and twenty in reserve; and this twenty.'

His uncle studied him for some moments.

'Look here, son!' he said. 'You're not serious about Bassett and that fifteen hundred, are you?'

'Yes, I am. But it's between you and me, uncle. Honour bright?'

'Honour bright all right, son! But I must talk to Bassett.'

'If you'd like to be a partner, uncle, with Bassett and me, we could all be partners. Only, you'd have to promise, honour bright, uncle, not to let it go beyond us three. Bassett and I are lucky, and you must be lucky, because it was your ten shillings I started winning with . . . '

Uncle Oscar took both Bassett and Paul into Richmond Park for an afternoon, and there they talked.

'It's like this, you see, sir,' Bassett said. 'Master Paul would get me talking about racing events, spinning yarns, you know, sir. And he was always keen on knowing if I'd made or if I'd lost. It's about a year since, now, that I put five shillings on Blush of Dawn for him: and we lost. Then the luck turned, with that ten shillings he had from you: that we put on Singhalese. And since that time, it's been pretty steady, all things considering. What do you say, Master Paul?'

'We're all right when we're sure,' said Paul. 'It's when we're not quite sure that we go down.'

'Oh, but we're careful then,' said Bassett.

'But when are you *sure*?' smiled Uncle Oscar.

'It's Master Paul, sir,' said Bassett in a secret, religious voice. 'It's as if he had it from heaven. Like Daffodil, now, for the Lincoln. That was as sure as eggs.'

'Did you put anything on Daffodil?' asked Oscar Cresswell.

'Yes, sir. I made my bit.'

'And my nephew?'

Bassett was obstinately silent, looking at Paul.

'I made twelve hundred, didn't I, Bassett? I told uncle I was putting three hundred on Daffodil.'

'That's right,' said Bassett, nodding.

'But where's the money?' asked the uncle.

'I keep it safe locked up, sir. Master Paul he can have it any minute he likes to ask for it.'

'What, fifteen hundred pounds?'

'And twenty! And *forty*, that is, with the twenty he made on the course.'

'It's amazing!' said the uncle.

'If Master Paul offers you to be partners, sir, I would, if I were you: if you'll excuse me,' said Bassett.

Oscar Cresswell thought about it.

'I'll see the money,' he said.

They drove home again, and, sure enough, Bassett came round to the garden-house with fifteen hundred pounds in notes. The twenty pounds reserve was left with Joe Glee, in the Turf Commission deposit.

'You see, it's all right, uncle, when I'm sure! Then we go strong, for all we're worth. Don't we, Bassett?'

'We do that, Master Paul.'

'And when are you sure?' said the uncle, laughing.

'Oh, well, sometimes I'm *absolutely* sure, like about Daffodil,' said the boy; 'and sometimes I have an idea; and sometimes I haven't even an idea, have I, Bassett? Then we're careful, because we mostly go down.'

'You do, do you! And when you're sure, like about Daffodil, what makes you sure, sonny?'

'Oh, well, I don't know,' said the boy uneasily. 'I'm sure, you know, uncle; that's all.'

'It's as if he had it from heaven, sir,' Bassett reiterated.

'I should say so!' said the uncle.

But he became a partner. And when the Leger was coming on Paul was 'sure' about Lively Spark, which was a quite inconsiderable horse. The boy insisted on putting a thousand on the horse, Bassett went for five hundred, and Oscar Cresswell two hundred. Lively Spark came in first, and the betting had been ten to one against him. Paul had made ten thousand.

'You see,' he said, 'I was absolutely sure of him.'

Even Oscar Cresswell had cleared two thousand.

'Look here, son,' he said, 'this sort of thing makes me nervous.'

'It needn't, uncle! Perhaps I shan't be sure again for a long time.'

'But what are you going to do with your money?' asked the uncle.

'Of course,' said the boy, 'I started it for mother. She said she had no luck, because father is unlucky, so I thought if *I* was lucky, it might stop whispering.'

'What might stop whispering?'

'Our house. I *hate* our house for whispering.'

'What does it whisper?'

'Why – why' – the boy fidgeted – 'why, I don't know. But it's always short of money, you know, uncle.'

'I know it, son, I know it.'

'You know people send mother writs, don't you, uncle?'

'I'm afraid I do,' said the uncle.

'And then the house whispers, like people laughing at you behind your back. It's awful, that is! I thought if I was lucky –'

'You might stop it,' added the uncle.

The boy watched him with big blue eyes, that had an uncanny cold fire in them, and he said never a word.

'Well, then!' said the uncle. 'What are we doing?'

'I shouldn't like mother to know I was lucky,' said the boy.

'Why not, son?'

'She'd stop me.'

'I don't think she would.'

'Oh!' – and the boy writhed in an odd way – 'I *don't* want her to know, uncle.'

'All right, son! We'll manage it without her knowing.'

They managed it very easily. Paul, at the other's suggestion, handed over five thousand pounds to his uncle, who deposited it with the family lawyer, who was then to inform Paul's mother that a relative had put five thousand pounds into his hands, which sum was to be paid out a thousand pounds at a time, on the mother's birthday, for the next five years.

'So she'll have a birthday present of a thousand pounds for five successive years,' said Uncle Oscar. 'I hope it won't make it all the harder for her later.'

Paul's mother had her birthday in November. The house had been 'whispering' worse than ever lately, and, even in spite of his luck, Paul could not bear up against it. He was very anxious to see the effect of the birthday letter, telling his mother about the thousand pounds.

When there were no visitors, Paul now took his meals with his parents, as he was beyond the nursery control. His mother went into town nearly every day. She had discovered that she had an odd knack of sketching furs and dress materials, so she worked secretly in the studio of a friend who was the chief 'artist' for the leading drapers. She drew the figures of ladies in furs and ladies in silk and sequins for the newspaper advertisements. This young woman artist earned several thousand pounds a year, but Paul's mother only made several hundreds, and she was again dissatisfied. She so wanted to be first in something, and she did not succeed, even in making sketches for drapery advertisements.

She was down to breakfast on the morning of her birthday. Paul watched her face as she read her letters. He knew the lawyer's letter. As his mother read it, her face hardened and became more expressionless. Then a cold, determined look came on her mouth. She hid the letter under the pile of others, and said not a word about it.

'Didn't you have anything nice in the post for your birthday, mother?' said Paul.

'Quite moderately nice,' she said, her voice cold and absent.

She went away to town without saying more.

But in the afternoon Uncle Oscar appeared. He said Paul's mother had had a long interview with the lawyer, asking if the whole five thousand could not be advanced at once, as she was in debt.

'What do you think, uncle?' said the boy.

'I leave it to you, son.'

'Oh, let her have it, then! We can get some more with the other,' said the boy.

'A bird in the hand is worth two in the bush, laddie!' said Uncle Oscar.

'But I'm sure to *know* for the Grand National; or the Lincolnshire; or else the Derby. I'm sure to know for *one* of them,' said Paul.

So Uncle Oscar signed the agreement, and Paul's mother touched the whole five thousand. Then something very curious happened. The voices in the house suddenly went mad, like a chorus of frogs on a spring evening. There were certain new furnishings, and Paul had a tutor. He was *really* going to Eton, his father's school, in the following autumn. There were flowers in the winter, and a blossoming of the luxury Paul's mother had been used to. And yet the voices in the house, behind the sprays of mimosa and almond-blossom, and from under the piles of iridescent cushions, simply trilled and screamed in a sort of ecstasy: 'There *must* be more money! Oh–h–h; there *must* be more money. Oh, now, now–w! Now–w–w – there *must* be more money! – more than ever!

'More than ever!'

It frightened Paul terribly. He studied away at his Latin and Greek with his tutor. But his intense hours were spent with Bassett. The Grand National had gone by; he had not 'known', and had lost a hundred pounds. Summer was at hand. He was in agony for the Lincoln. But even for the Lincoln he didn't 'know', and he lost fifty pounds. He became wild-eyed and strange, as if something were going to explode in him.

'Let it alone, son! Don't you bother about it!' urged Uncle Oscar. But it was as if the boy couldn't really hear what his uncle was saying.

'I've got to know for the Derby! I've got to know for the Derby!' the child reiterated, his big blue eyes blazing with a sort of madness.

His mother noticed how overwrought he was.

'You'd better go to the seaside. Wouldn't you like to go now to the seaside, instead of waiting? I think you'd better,' she said, looking down at him anxiously, her heart curiously heavy because of him.

But the child lifted his uncanny blue eyes.

'I couldn't possibly go before the Derby, mother!' he said. 'I couldn't possibly!'

'Why not?' she said, her voice becoming heavy when she was opposed. 'Why not? You can still go from the seaside to see the Derby with your Uncle Oscar, if that's what you wish. No need for you to wait here. Besides, I think you care too much about these races. It's a bad sign. My family has been a gambling family, and you won't know till you grow up how much damage it has done. But it has done damage. I shall have to send Bassett away, and ask Uncle Oscar not to talk racing to you, unless you promise to be reasonable about it: go away to the seaside and forget it. You're all nerves!'

'I'll do what you like, mother, so long as you don't send me away till after the Derby,' the boy said.

'Send you away from where? Just from this house?'

'Yes,' he said, gazing at her.

'Why, you curious child, what makes you care about this house so much, suddenly? I never knew you loved it.'

He gazed at her without speaking. He had a secret within a secret, something he had not divulged, even to Bassett or to his Uncle Oscar.

But his mother, after standing undecided and a little bit sullen for some moments, said: 'Very well, then! Don't go to the seaside till after the Derby, if you don't wish it. But promise me you won't let your nerves go to pieces. Promise you won't think so much about horse-racing, and *events*, as you call them!'

'Oh no,' said the boy casually. 'I won't think much about them, mother. You needn't worry. I wouldn't worry, mother, if I were you.'

'If you were me and I were you,' said his mother, 'I wonder what we *should* do!'

'But you know you needn't worry, mother, don't you?' the boy repeated.

'I should be awfully glad to know it,' she said wearily.

'Oh, well, you *can*, you know. I mean, you *ought* to know you needn't worry,' he insisted.

'Ought I? Then I'll see about it,' she said.

Paul's secret of secrets was his wooden horse, that which had no name. Since he was emancipated from a nurse and a nursery-governess, he had had his rocking-horse removed to his own bedroom at the top of the house.

'Surely you're too big for a rocking-horse!' his mother had remonstrated.

'Well, you see, mother, till I can have a *real* horse, I like to have *some* sort of animal about,' had been his quaint answer.

'Do you feel he keeps you company?' she laughed.

'Oh yes! He's very good, he always keeps me company when I'm there,' said Paul.

So the horse, rather shabby, stood in an arrested prance in the boy's bedroom.

The Derby was drawing near, and the boy grew more and more tense. He hardly heard what was spoken to him, he was very frail, and his eyes were really uncanny. His mother had sudden strange seizures of uneasiness about him. Sometimes, for half an hour, she would feel a sudden anxiety about him that was almost anguish. She wanted to rush to him at once, and know he was safe.

Two nights before the Derby, she was at a big party in town, when one of her rushes of anxiety about her boy, her first-born, gripped her heart till she could hardly speak. She fought with the feeling, might and main, for she believed in common sense. But it was too strong. She had to leave the dance and go downstairs to telephone to the country. The children's nursery-governess was terribly surprised and startled at being rung up in the night.

'Are the children all right, Miss Wilmot?'

'Oh yes, they are quite all right.'

'Master Paul? Is he all right?'

'He went to bed as right as a trivet. Shall I run up and look at him?'

'No,' said Paul's mother reluctantly. 'No! Don't trouble. It's all right. Don't sit up. We shall be home fairly soon.' She did not want her son's privacy intruded upon.

'Very good,' said the governess.

It was about one o'clock when Paul's mother and father drove up to their house. All was still. Paul's mother went to her room and slipped off her white fur cloak. She had told her maid not to wait up for her. She heard her husband downstairs, mixing a whisky and soda.

And then, because of the strange anxiety at her heart, she stole upstairs to her son's room. Noiselessly she went along the upper corridor. Was there a faint noise? What was it?

She stood, with arrested muscles, outside his door, listening. There was a strange, heavy, and yet not loud noise. Her hear stood still. It was a soundless noise, yet rushing and powerful. Something huge, in violent, hushed motion. What was it? What in God's name was it? She ought to know. She felt that she knew the noise. She knew what it was.

Yet she could not place it. She couldn't say it was. And on and on it went, like a madness.

Softly, frozen with anxiety and fear, she turned the door-handle.

The room was dark. Yet in the space near the window, she heard and saw something plunging to and fro. She gazed in fear and amazement.

Then suddenly she switched on the light, and saw her son in his green pyjamas, madly! surging on the rocking-horse. The blaze of light suddenly lit him up, as he urged the wooden horse, and lit her up, as she stood, blonde, in her dress of pale green and crystal, in the doorway.

'Paul!' she cried. 'Whatever are you doing?'

'It's Malabar!' he screamed in a powerful, strange voice. 'It's Malabar!'

His eyes blazed at her for one strange and senseless second, as he ceased urging his wooden horse. Then he fell with a crash to the ground, and she, all her tormented motherhood flooding upon her, rushed to gather him up.

But he was unconscious and unconscious he remained, with some brain-fever. He talked and tossed, and his mother sat stonily by his side.

'Malabar! It's Malabar! Bassett, Bassett, I *know*! It's Malabar!'

So the child cried, trying to get up and urge the rocking-horse that gave him his inspiration.

'What does he mean by Malabar?' asked the heart-frozen mother.

'I don't know,' said the father stonily.

'What does he mean by Malabar?' she asked her brother Oscar.

'It's one of the horses running for the Derby,' was the answer.

And, in spite of himself, Oscar Cresswell spoke to Bassett, and himself put a thousand on Malabar: a fourteen to one.

The third day of the illness was critical: they were waiting for a change. The boy, with his rather long, curly hair, was tossing ceaselessly on the pillow. He neither slept nor regained consciousness, and his eyes were like blue stones. His mother sat, feeling her heart had gone, turned actually into a stone.

In the evening, Oscar Cresswell did not come, but Bassett sent a message, saying could he come up for one moment, just one moment? Paul's mother was very angry at the intrusion, but on second thoughts she agreed. The boy was the same. Perhaps Bassett might bring him to consciousness.

The gardener, a shortish fellow with a little brown moustache and sharp little brown eyes, tiptoed into the room, touched his imaginary cap to Paul's mother, and stole to the bedside, staring with glittering, smallish eyes at the tossing, dying child.

'Master Paul!' he whispered. 'Master Paul! Malabar came in first all right, a clean win. I did as you told me. You've made over seventy thousand pounds, you have; you've got over eighty thousand. Malabar came in all right, Master Paul.'

'Malabar! Malabar! Did I say Malabar, mother? Did I say Malabar? Do you think I'm lucky, mother? I knew Malabar, didn't I? Over eighty thousand pounds! I call that lucky, don't you, mother? Over eighty thousand pounds! I knew, didn't I know I knew? Malabar came in all right. If I ride my horse till I'm sure, then I tell you, Bassett, you can go as high as you like. Did you go for all you were worth, Bassett?'

'I went a thousand on it, Master Paul.'

'I never told you, mother, that if I can ride my horse, and *get there*, then I'm absolutely sure – oh, absolutely! Mother, did I ever tell you? I *am* lucky!'

'No, you never did,' said his mother.

But the boy died in the night.

And even as he lay dead, his mother heard her brother's voice saying to her: 'My God, Hester, you're eighty-odd thousand to the good, and a poor devil of a son to the bad. But, poor devil, poor devil, he's best gone out of a life where he rides his rocking-horse to find a winner.'

The Man Who Loved Islands

CHAPTER ONE

THERE WAS A MAN who loved islands. He was born on one, but it didn't suit him, as there were too many other people on it, besides himself. He wanted an island all of his own: not necessarily to be alone on it, but to make it a world of his own.

An island, if it is big enough, is no better than a continent. It has to be really quite small, before it feels like an island; and this story will show how tiny it has to be, before you can presume to fill it with your own personality.

Now circumstances so worked out that this lover of islands, by the time he was thirty-five, actually acquired an island of his own. He didn't own it as freehold property, but he had a ninety-nine years' lease of it, which, as far as a man and an island are concerned, is as good as everlasting. Since, if you are like Abraham,[35] and want your offspring to be numberless as the sands of the sea-shore, you don't choose an island to start breeding on. Too soon there would be over-population, overcrowding, and slum conditions. Which is a horrid thought, for one who loves an island for its insulation. No, an island is a nest which holds one egg, and one only. This egg is the islander himself.

The island acquired by our potential islander was not in the remote oceans. It was quite near at home, no palm trees nor boom of surf on the reef, nor any of that kind of thing; but a good solid dwelling-house, rather gloomy, above the landing-place, and beyond, a small farmhouse with sheds, and a few outlying fields. Down on the little landing-bay were three cottages in a row, like coastguards' cottages, all neat and whitewashed.

What could be more cosy and home-like? It was four miles if you walked all round your island, through the gorse and the blackthorn bushes, above the steep rocks of the sea and down in the little glades where the primroses grew. If you walked straight over the two humps of hills, the length of it, through the rocky fields where the cows lay chewing, and through the rather sparse oats, on into the gorse again, and so to the low cliffs' edge, it took you only twenty minutes. And when you came to the edge, you could see another, bigger island lying beyond. But the sea was between you and it. And as you returned over the turf where the short, downland cowslips nodded, you saw to the east still another island, a tiny one this time, like the calf of the cow. This tiny island also belonged to the islander.

Thus it seems that even islands like to keep each other company.

Our islander loved his island very much. In early spring, the little ways and glades were a snow of blackthorn, a vivid white among the Celtic stillness of close green and grey rock, blackbirds calling out in the whiteness their first long, triumphant calls. After the blackthorn and the nestling primroses came the blue apparition of hyacinths, like elfin lakes and slipping sheets of blue, among the bushes and under the glade of trees. And many birds with nests you could peep into, on the island all your own. Wonderful what a great world it was!

Followed summer, and the cowslips gone, the wild roses faintly fragrant through the haze. There was a field of hay, the foxgloves stood looking down. In a little cove, the sun was on the pale granite where you bathed, and the shadow was in the rocks. Before the mist came stealing, you went home through the ripening oats, the glare of the sea fading from the high air as the fog-horn started to moo on the other island. And then the sea-fog went, it was autumn, the oat-sheaves lying prone, the great moon, another island, rose golden out of the sea, and rising higher, the world of the sea was white.

So autumn ended with rain, and winter came, dark skies and dampness and rain, but rarely frost. The island, your island, cowered dark, holding away from you. You could feel, down in the wet, sombre hollows, the resentful spirit coiled upon itself, like a wet dog coiled in gloom, or a snake that is neither asleep nor awake. Then in the night, when the wind left off blowing in great gusts and volleys, as at sea, you felt that your island was a universe, infinite and old as the darkness; not an island at all, but an infinite dark world where all the souls from all the other bygone nights lived on, and the infinite distance was near.

Strangely, from your little island in space, you were gone forth into the dark, great realms of time, where all the souls that never die veer and swoop on their vast, strange errands. The little earthly island has dwindled, like a jumping-off place, into nothingness, for you have jumped off, you know not how, into the dark wide mystery of time, where the past is vastly alive, and the future is not separated off.

This is the danger of becoming an islander. When, in the city, you wear your white spats and dodge the traffic with the fear of death down your spine, then you are quite safe from the terrors of infinite time. The moment is your little islet in time, it is the spatial universe that careers round you.

But once isolate yourself on a little island in the sea of space, and the moment begins to heave and expand in great circles, the solid earth is gone, and your slippery, naked dark soul finds herself out in the timeless world, where the chariots of the so-called dead dash down the old streets of centuries, and souls crowd on the footways that we, in the moment, call bygone years. The souls of all the dead are alive again, and pulsating actively around you. You are out in the other infinity.

Something of this happened to our islander. Mysterious 'feelings' came upon him that he wasn't used to; strange awarenesses of old, far-gone men, and other influences; men of Gaul,[36] with big moustaches, who had been on his island, and had vanished from the face of it, but not out of the air of night. They were there still, hurtling their big, violent, unseen bodies through the night. And there were priests, with golden knives and mistletoe; then other priests with a crucifix; then pirates with murder on the sea.

Our islander was uneasy. He didn't believe, in the day-time, in any of this nonsense. But at night it just was so. He had reduced himself to a single point in space, and, a point being that which has neither length nor breadth, he had to step off it into somewhere else. Just as you must step into the sea, if the waters wash your foothold away, so he had, at night, to step off into the other worlds of undying time.

He was uncannily aware, as he lay in the dark, that the blackthorn grove that seemed a bit uncanny even in the realm of space and day, at night was crying with old men of an invisible race, around the altar stone. What was a ruin under the hornbeam trees by day, was a moaning of blood-stained priests with crucifixes, on the ineffable night. What was a cave and a hidden beach between coarse rocks, became in the invisible dark the purple-lipped imprecation of pirates.

To escape any more of this sort of awareness, our islander daily concentrated upon his material island. Why should it not be the Happy Isle at last? Why not the last small isle of the Hesperides,[37] the perfect place, all filled with his own gracious, blossom-like spirit? A minute world of pure perfection, made by man himself.

He began, as we begin all our attempts to regain Paradise, by spending money. The old, semi-feudal dwelling-house he restored, let in more light, put clear lovely carpets on the floor, clear, flower-petal curtains at the sullen windows, and wines in the cellars of rock.

He brought over a buxom housekeeper from the world, and a soft-spoken, much-experienced butler. These two were to be islanders.

In the farmhouse he put a bailiff, with two farmhands. There were Jersey cows, tinkling a slow bell, among the gorse. There was a call to meals at midday, and the peaceful smoking of chimneys at evening, when rest descended.

A jaunty sailing-boat with a motor accessory rode in the shelter in the bay, just below the row of three white cottages. There was also a little yawl, and two row-boats drawn up on the sand. A fishing-net was drying on its supports, a boatload of new white planks stood criss-cross, a woman was going to the well with a bucket.

In the end cottage lived the skipper of the yacht, and his wife and son. He was a man from the other, large island, at home on this sea. Every fine day he went out fishing, with his son, every fair day there was fresh fish in the island.

In the middle cottage lived an old man and wife, a very faithful couple. The old man was a carpenter, and man of many jobs. He was always working, always the sound of his plane or his saw; lost in his work, he was another kind of islander.

In the third cottage was a mason, a widower with a son and two daughters. With the help of his boy, this man dug ditches and built fences, raised buttresses and erected a new out-building, and hewed stone from the little quarry. One daughter worked at the big house.

It was a quiet, busy little world. When the islander brought you over as his guest, you met first the dark-bearded, thin, smiling skipper, Arnold, then his boy Charles. At the house, the smooth-lipped butler who had lived all over the world valeted you, and created that curious creamy-smooth, disarming sense of luxury around you which only a perfect and rather untrustworthy servant can create. He disarmed you and had you at his mercy. The buxom housekeeper smiled and treated you with the subtly respectful familiarity that is only dealt out to the true gentry. And the rosy maid threw a glance at you, as if you were very wonderful, coming from the greater outer world. Then you met the smiling but watchful bailiff, who came from Cornwall, and the shy farmhand from Berkshire, with his clean wife and two little children: then the rather sulky farmhand from Suffolk. The mason, a Kent man, would talk to you by the yard if you let him. Only the old carpenter was gruff and elsewhere absorbed.

Well then, it was a little world to itself, and everybody feeling very safe, and being very nice to you, as if you were really something special. But it was the islander's world, not yours. He was the Master.

The special smile, the special attention was to the Master. They all knew how well off they were. So the islander was no longer Mr So-and-So. To everyone on the island, even to you yourself, he was 'the Master'.

Well, it was ideal. The Master was no tyrant. Ah, no! He was a delicate, sensitive, handsome Master, who wanted everything perfect and everybody happy. Himself, of course, to be the fount of this happiness and perfection.

But in his way, he was a poet. He treated his guests royally, his servants liberally. Yet he was shrewd, and very wise. He never came the boss over his people. Yet he kept his eye on everything, like a shrewd, blue-eyed young Hermes.[38] And it was amazing what a lot of knowledge he had at hand. Amazing what he knew about Jersey cows, and cheese-making, ditching and fencing, flowers and gardening, ships and the sailing of ships. He was a fount of knowledge about everything, and this knowledge he imparted to his people in an odd, half-ironical, half-portentous fashion, as if he really belonged to the quaint, half-real world of the gods.

They listened to him with their hats in their hands. He loved white clothes; or creamy white; and cloaks, and broad hats. So, in fine weather, the bailiff would see the elegant tall figure in creamy-white serge coming like some bird over the fallow, to look at the weeding of the turnips. Then there would be a doffing of hats, and a few minutes of whimsical, shrewd, wise talk, to which the bailiff answered admiringly, and the farmhands listened in silent wonder, leaning on their hoes. The bailiff was almost tender, to the Master.

Or, on a windy morning, he would stand with his cloak blowing in the sticky sea-wind, on the edge of the ditch that was being dug to drain a little swamp, talking in the teeth of the wind to the man below, who looked up at him with steady and inscrutable eyes.

Or at evening in the rain he would be seen hurrying across the yard, the broad hat turned against the rain. And the farm-wife would hurriedly exclaim: 'The Master! Get up, John, and clear him a place on the sofa.' And then the door opened, and it was a cry of: 'Why, of all things, if it isn't the Master! Why, have ye turned out then, of a night like this, to come across to the like of we?' And the bailiff took his cloak, and the farm-wife his hat, the two farmhands drew their chairs to the back, he sat on the sofa and took a child up near him. He was wonderful with children, talked to them simply wonderful, made you think of Our Saviour Himself, said the woman.

He was always greeted with smiles, and the same peculiar deference, as if he were a higher, but also frailer being. They handled him almost tenderly, and almost with adulation. But when he left, or when they spoke of him, they had often a subtle, mocking smile on their faces. There was no need to be afraid of 'the Master'. Just let him have his own way. Only the old carpenter was sometimes sincerely rude to him; so he didn't care for the old man.

It is doubtful whether any of them really liked him, man to man, or even woman to man. But then it is doubtful if he really liked any of them, as man to man, or man to woman. He wanted them to be happy, and the little world to be perfect. But anyone who wants the world to be perfect must be careful not to have real likes or dislikes. A general goodwill is all you can afford.

The sad fact is, alas, that general goodwill is always felt as something of an insult, by the mere object of it; and so it breeds a quite special brand of malice. Surely general goodwill is a form of egoism, that it should have such a result!

Our islander, however, had his own resources. He spent long hours in his library, for he was compiling a book of references to all the flowers mentioned in the Greek and Latin authors. He was not a great classical scholar, the usual public-school equipment. But there are such excellent translations nowadays. And it was so lovely, tracing flower after flower as it blossomed in the ancient world.

So the first year on the island passed by. A great deal had been done. Now the bills flooded in, and the Master, conscientious in all things, began to study them. The study left him pale and breathless. He was not a rich man. He knew he had been making a hole in his capital to get the island into running order. When he came to look, however, there was hardly anything left but hole. Thousands and thousands of pounds had the island swallowed into nothingness.

But surely the bulk of the spending was over! Surely the island would now begin to be self-supporting, even if it made no profit! Surely he was safe. He paid a good many of the bills, and took a little heart. But he had had a shock, and the next year, the coming year, there must be economy, frugality. He told his people so in simple and touching language. And they said: 'Why, surely! Surely!'

So, while the wind blew and the rain lashed outside, he would sit in his library with the bailiff over a pipe and pot of beer, discussing farm projects. He lifted his narrow, handsome face, and his blue eyes became dreamy. '*What* a wind!' It blew like cannon-shots. He thought of his island, lashed with foam, and inaccessible, and he exulted . . . No, he must not lose it. He turned back to the farm projects with the zest of genius, and his hands flicked white emphasis, while the bailiff intoned: 'Yes, sir! Yes, sir! You're right, Master!'

But the man was hardly listening. He was looking at the Master's blue lawn shirt and curious pink tie with the fiery red stone, at the enamel sleeve-links, and at the ring with the peculiar scarab.[39] The brown searching eyes of the man of the soil glanced repeatedly over the fine, immaculate figure of the Master, with a sort of slow, calculating wonder. But if he happened to catch the Master's bright, exalted glance, his own eye lit up with a careful cordiality and deference, as he bowed his head slightly.

Thus between them they decided what crops should be sown, what fertilisers should be used in different places, which breed of pigs should be imported, and which line of turkeys. That is to say, the bailiff, by continually cautiously agreeing with the Master, kept out of it, and let the young man have his own way.

The Master knew what he was talking about. He was brilliant at grasping the gist of a book, and knowing how to apply his knowledge. On the whole, his ideas were sound. The bailiff even knew it. But in the man of the soil there was no answering enthusiasm. The brown eyes smiled their cordial deference, but the thin lips never changed. The Master pursed his own flexible mouth in a boyish versatility, as he cleverly sketched in his ideas to the other man, and the bailiff made eyes of admiration, but in his heart he was not attending, he was only watching the Master as he would have watched a queer, caged animal, quite without sympathy, not implicated.

So, it was settled, and the Master rang for Elvery, the butler, to bring a sandwich. He, the Master, was pleased. The butler saw it, and came back with anchovy and ham sandwiches, and a newly opened bottle of vermouth. There was always a newly opened bottle of something.

It was the same with the mason. The Master and he discussed the drainage of a bit of land, and more pipes were ordered, more special bricks, more this, more that.

Fine weather came at last; there was a little lull in the hard work on the island. The Master went for a short cruise in his yacht. It was not really a yacht, just a little bit of a thing. They sailed along the coast of the mainland, and put in at the ports. At every port some friend turned up, the butler made elegant little meals in the cabin. Then the Master was invited to villas and hotels, his people disembarked him as if he were a prince.

And oh, how expensive it turned out! He had to telegraph to the bank for money. And he went home again to economise.

The marsh-marigolds were blazing in the little swamp where the ditches were being dug for drainage. He almost regretted, now, the work in hand. The yellow beauties would not blaze again.

Harvest came, and a bumper crop. There must be a harvest-home supper. The long barn was now completely restored and added to. The carpenter had made long tables. Lanterns hung from the beams of the high-pitched roof. All the people of the island were assembled. The bailiff presided. It was a gay scene.

Towards the end of the supper the Master, in a velvet jacket, appeared with his guests. Then the bailiff rose and proposed 'The Master! Long life and health to the Master!' All the people drank the health with great enthusiasm and cheering. The Master replied with a little speech: They were on an island in a little world of their own. It depended on them all to make this world a world of true happiness and content. Each must do his part. He hoped he himself did what he could, for his heart was in his island, and with the people of his island.

The butler responded: As long as the island had such a Master, it could not help but be a little heaven for all the people on it. This was seconded with virile warmth by the bailiff and the mason, the skipper was beside himself. Then there was dancing, the old carpenter was fiddler.

But under all this, things were not well. The very next morning came the farmboy to say that a cow had fallen over the cliff. The Master went to look. He peered over the not very high declivity, and saw her lying dead on a green ledge under a bit of late-flowering broom. A beautiful, expensive creature, already looking swollen. But what a fool, to fall so unnecessarily!

It was a question of getting several men to haul her up the bank, and then of skinning and burying her. No one would eat the meat. How repulsive it all was!

This was symbolic of the island. As sure as the spirits rose in the human breast, with a movement of joy, an invisible hand struck malevolently out of the silence. There must not be any joy, nor even any quiet peace. A man broke a leg, another was crippled with rheumatic fever. The pigs had some strange disease. A storm drove the yacht on a rock. The mason hated the butler, and refused to let his daughter serve at the house.

Out of the very air came a stony, heavy malevolence. The island itself seemed malicious. It would go on being hurtful and evil for weeks at a time. Then suddenly again one morning it would be fair, lovely as a morning in Paradise, everything beautiful and flowing. And everybody would begin to feel a great relief, and a hope for happiness.

Then as soon as the Master was opened out in spirit like an open flower, some ugly blow would fall. Somebody would send him an anonymous note, accusing some other person on the island. Somebody else would come hinting things against one of his servants.

'Some folks think they've got an easy job out here, with all the pickings they make!' the mason's daughter screamed at the suave butler, in the Master's hearing. He pretended not to hear.

'My man says this island is surely one of the lean kine of Egypt,[40] it would swallow a sight of money, and you'd never get anything back out of it,' confided the farmhand's wife to one of the Master's visitors.

The people were not contented. They were not islanders. 'We feel we're not doing right by the children,' said those who had children. 'We feel we're not doing right by ourselves,' said those who had no children. And the various families fairly came to hate one another.

Yet the island was so lovely. When there was a scent of honeysuckle and the moon brightly flickering down on the sea, then even the grumblers felt a strange nostalgia for it. It set you yearning, with a wild yearning; perhaps for the past, to be far back in the mysterious past of the island, when the blood had a different throb. Strange floods of passion came over you, strange violent lusts and imaginations of cruelty. The blood and the passion and the lust which the island had known. Uncanny dreams, half-dreams, half-evocated yearnings.

The Master himself began to be a little afraid of his island. He felt here strange, violent feelings he had never felt before, and lustful desires that he had been quite free from. He knew quite well now that his people didn't love him at all. He knew that their spirits were secretly against him, malicious, jeering, envious, and lurking to down him. He became just as wary and secretive with regard to them.

But it was too much. At the end of the second year, several departures took place. The housekeeper went. The Master always blamed self-important women most. The mason said he wasn't going to be monkeyed about any more, so he took his departure, with his family. The rheumatic farmhand left.

And then the year's bills came in, the Master made up his accounts. In spite of good crops, the assets were ridiculous, against the spending. The island had again lost, not hundreds but thousands of pounds. It was incredible. But you simply couldn't believe it! Where had it all gone?

The Master spent gloomy nights and days going through accounts in the library. He was thorough. It became evident, now the housekeeper had gone, that she had swindled him. Probably everybody was swindling him. But he hated to think it, so he put the thought away.

He emerged, however, pale and hollow-eyed from his balancing of unbalanceable accounts, looking as if something had kicked him in the stomach. It was pitiable. But the money had gone, and there was an end of it. Another great hole in his capital. How could people be so heartless?

It couldn't go on, that was evident. He would soon be bankrupt. He had to give regretful notice to his butler. He was afraid to find out how much his butler had swindled him. Because the man was such a wonderful butler, after all. And the farm bailiff had to go. The Master had no regrets in that quarter. The losses on the farm had almost embittered him.

The third year was spent in rigid cutting down of expenses. The island was still mysterious and fascinating. But it was also treacherous and cruel, secretly, fathomlessly malevolent. In spite of all its fair show of white blossom and bluebells, and the lovely dignity of foxgloves bending their rose-red bells, it was your implacable enemy.

With reduced staff, reduced wages, reduced splendour, the third year went by. But it was fighting against hope. The farm still lost a good deal. And once more there was a hole in that remnant of capital. Another hole in that which was already a mere remnant round the old holes. The island was mysterious in this also: it seemed to pick the very money out of your pocket, as if it were an octopus with invisible arms stealing from you in every direction.

Yet the Master still loved it. But with a touch of rancour now.

He spent, however, the second half of the fourth year intensely working on the mainland, to be rid of it. And it was amazing how difficult he found it, to dispose of an island.

He had thought that everybody was pining for such an island as his; but not at all. Nobody would pay any price for it. And he wanted now to get rid of it, as a man who wants a divorce at any cost.

It was not till the middle of the fifth year that he transferred it, at a considerable loss to himself, to a hotel company who were willing to speculate in it. They were to turn it into a handy honeymoon-and-golf island.

There, take that, island which didn't know when it was well off. Now be a honeymoon-and-golf island!

CHAPTER TWO

The Second Island

THE ISLANDER had to move. But he was not going to the mainland. Oh, no! He moved to the smaller island, which still belonged to him. And he took with him the faithful old carpenter and wife, the couple he never really cared for; also a widow and daughter, who had kept house for him the last year; also an orphan lad, to help the old man.

The small island was very small; but being a hump of rock in the sea, it was bigger than it looked. There was a little track among the rocks and bushes, winding and scrambling up and down around the islet, so that it took you twenty minutes to do the circuit. It was more than you would have expected.

Still, it was an island. The islander moved himself, with all his books, into the commonplace six-roomed house up to which you had to scramble from the rocky landing-place. There were also two joined-together cottages. The old carpenter lived in one, with his wife and the lad, the widow and daughter lived in the other.

At last all was in order. The Master's books filled two rooms. It was already autumn, Orion[41] lifting out of the sea. And in the dark nights, the Master could see the lights on his late island, where the hotel company were entertaining guests who would advertise the new resort for honeymoon-golfers.

On his lump of rock, however, the Master was still master. He explored the crannies, the odd hand-breadths of grassy level, the steep little cliffs where the last harebells hung and the seeds of summer were brown above the sea, lonely and untouched. He peered down the old well. He examined the stone pen where the pig had been kept. Himself, he had a goat.

Yes, it was an island. Always, always underneath among the rocks the Celtic sea sucked and washed and smote its feathery greyness. How many different noises of the sea! Deep explosions, rumblings, strange long sighs and whistling noises; then voices, real voices of people clamouring as if they were in a market, under the waters: and again, the far-off ringing of a bell, surely an actual bell! Then a tremendous trilling noise, very long and alarming, and an undertone of hoarse gasping.

On this island there were no human ghosts, no ghosts of any

ancient race. The sea, and the spume and the weather, had washed them all out, washed them out so there was only the sound of the sea itself, its own ghost, myriad-voiced, communing and plotting and shouting all winter long. And only the smell of the sea, with a few bristly bushes of gorse and coarse tufts of heather, among the grey, pellucid rocks, in the grey, more-pellucid air. The coldness, the greyness, even the soft, creeping fog of the sea, and the islet of rock humped up in it all, like the last point in space.

Green star Sirius[42] stood over the sea's rim. The island was a shadow. Out at sea a ship showed small lights. Below, in the rocky cove, the row-boat and the motor-boat were safe. A light shone in the carpenter's kitchen. That was all.

Save, of course, that the lamp was lit in the house, where the widow was preparing supper, her daughter helping. The islander went in to his meal. Here he was no longer the Master, he was an islander again and he had peace. The old carpenter, the widow and daughter were all faithfulness itself. The old man worked while ever there was light to see, because he had a passion for work. The widow and her quiet, rather delicate daughter of thirty-three worked for the Master, because they loved looking after him, and they were infinitely grateful for the haven he provided them. But they didn't call him 'the Master'. They gave him his name: 'Mr Cathcart, sir!' softly and reverently. And he spoke back to them also softly, gently, like people far from the world, afraid to make a noise.

The island was no longer a 'world'. It was a sort of refuge. The islander no longer struggled for anything. He had no need. It was as if he and his few dependents were a small flock of sea-birds alighted on this rock, as they travelled through space, and keeping together without a word. The silent mystery of travelling birds.

He spent most of his day in his study. His book was coming along. The widow's daughter could type out his manuscript for him, she was not uneducated. It was the one strange sound on the island, the typewriter. But soon even its spattering fitted in with the sea's noises, and the wind's.

The months went by. The islander worked away in his study, the people of the island went quietly about their concerns. The goat had a little black kid with yellow eyes. There were mackerel in the sea. The old man went fishing in the row-boat with the lad, when the weather was calm enough; they went off in the motor-boat to the biggest island for the post. And they brought supplies, never a penny wasted. And the days went by, and the nights, without desire, without ennui.[43]

The strange stillness from all desire was a kind of wonder to the islander. He didn't want anything. His soul at last was still in him, his spirit was like a dim-lit cave under water, where strange sea-foliage expands upon the watery atmosphere, and scarcely sways, and a mute fish shadowily slips in and slips away again. All still and soft and uncrying, yet alive as rooted seaweed is alive.

The islander said to himself: 'Is this happiness?' He said to himself: 'I am turned into a dream. I feel nothing, or I don't know what I feel. Yet it seems to me I am happy.'

Only he had to have something upon which his mental activity could work. So he spent long, silent hours in his study, working not very fast, nor very importantly, letting the writing spin softly from him as if it were drowsy gossamer. He no longer fretted whether it were good or not, what he produced. He slowly, softly spun it like gossamer, and if it were to melt away as gossamer in autumn melts, he would not mind. It was only the soft evanescence of gossamy things which now seemed to him permanent. The very mist of eternity was in them. Whereas stone buildings, cathedrals for example, seemed to him to howl with temporary resistance, knowing they must fall at last; the tension of their long endurance seemed to howl forth from them all the time.

Sometimes he went to the mainland and to the city. Then he went elegantly, dressed in the latest style, to his club. He sat in a stall at the theatre, he shopped in Bond Street. He discussed terms for publishing his book. But over his face was that gossamy look of having dropped out of the race of progress, which made the vulgar city people feel they had won it over him, and made him glad to go back to his island.

He didn't mind if he never published his book. The years were blending into a soft mist, from which nothing obtruded. Spring came. There was never a primrose on his island, but he found a winter-aconite. There were two little sprayed bushes of blackthorn, and some wind-flowers. He began to make a list of the flowers of his islet, and that was absorbing. He noted a wild currant bush and watched for the elder flowers on a stunted little tree, then for the first yellow rags of the broom, and wild roses. Bladder campion, orchids, stitchwort, celandine, he was prouder of them than if they had been people on his island. When he came across the golden saxifrage, so inconspicuous in a damp corner, he crouched over it in a trance, he knew not for how long, looking at it. Yet it was nothing to look at. As the widow's daughter found, when he showed it her.

He had said to her in real triumph: 'I found the golden saxifrage this morning.'

The name sounded splendid. She looked at him with fascinated brown eyes, in which was a hollow ache that frightened him a little.

'Did you, sir? Is it a nice flower?'

He pursed his lips and tilted his brows.

'Well – not showy exactly. I'll show it you if you like.'

'I should like to see it.'

She was so quiet, so wistful. But he sensed in her a persistency which made him uneasy. She said she was so happy: really happy. She followed him quietly, like a shadow, on the rocky track where there was never room for two people to walk side by side. He went first, and could feel her there, immediately behind him, following so submissively, gloating on him from behind.

It was a kind of pity for her which made him become her lover: though he never realised the extent of the power she had gained over him, and how *she* willed it. But the moment he had fallen, a jangling feeling came upon him, that it was all wrong. He felt a nervous dislike of her. He had not wanted it. And it seemed to him, as far as her physical self went, she had not wanted it either. It was just her will. He went away, and climbed at the risk of his neck down to a ledge near the sea. There he sat for hours, gazing all jangled at the sea, and saying miserably to himself: 'We didn't want it. We didn't really want it.'

It was the automatism of sex that had caught him again. Not that he hated sex. He deemed it, as the Chinese do, one of the great life-mysteries. But it had become mechanical, automatic, and he wanted to escape that. Automatic sex shattered him, and filled him with a sort of death. He thought he had come through, to a new stillness of desirelessness. Perhaps beyond that there was a new fresh delicacy of desire, an unentered frail communion of two people meeting on untrodden ground.

Be that as it might, this was not it. This was nothing new or fresh. It was automatic, and driven from the will. Even she, in her true self, hadn't wanted it. It was automatic in her.

When he came home, very late, and saw her face white with fear and apprehension of his feeling against her, he pitied her, and spoke to her delicately, reassuringly. But he kept himself remote from her.

She gave no sign. She served him with the same silence, the same hidden hunger to serve him, to be near where he was. He felt her love following him with strange, awful persistency. She claimed nothing. Yet now, when he met her bright, brown, curiously vacant eyes, he saw in them the mute question. The question came direct at him, with a force and a power of will he never realised.

So he succumbed, and asked her again.

'Not,' she said, 'if it will make you hate me.'

'Why should it?' he replied, nettled. 'Of course not.'

'You know I would do anything on earth for you.'

It was only afterwards, in his exasperation, he remembered what she said, and was more exasperated. Why should she pretend to do this *for him*? Why not herself? But in his exasperation, he drove himself deeper in. In order to achieve some sort of satisfaction, which he never did achieve, he abandoned himself to her. Everybody on the island knew. But he did not care.

Then even what desire he had left him, and he felt only shattered. He felt that only with her will had she wanted him. Now he was shattered and full of self-contempt. His island was smirched and spoiled. He had lost his place in the rare, desireless levels of Time to which he had at last arrived, and he had fallen right back. If only it had been true, delicate desire between them, and a delicate meeting on the third rare place where a man might meet a woman, when they were both true to the frail, sensitive, crocus-flame of desire in them. But it had been no such thing: automatic, an act of will, not of true desire, it left him feeling humiliated.

He went away from the islet, in spite of her mute reproach. And he wandered about the continent, vainly seeking a place where he could stay. He was out of key; he did not fit in the world any more.

There came a letter from Flora – her name was Flora – to say she was afraid she was going to have a child. He sat down as if he were shot, and he remained sitting. But he replied to her: 'Why be afraid? If it is so, it is so, and we should rather be pleased than afraid.'

At this very moment, it happened there was an auction of islands. He got the maps, and studied them. And at the auction he bought, for very little money, another island. It was just a few acres of rock away in the north, on the outer fringe of the isles. It was low, it rose low out of the great ocean. There was not a building, not even a tree on it. Only northern sea-turf, a pool of rain-water, a bit of sedge, rock, and sea-birds. Nothing else. Under the weeping wet western sky.

He made a trip to visit his new possession. For several days, owing to the seas, he could not approach it. Then, in a light sea-mist, he landed, and saw it hazy, low, stretching apparently a long way. But it was illusion. He walked over the wet, springy turf, and dark-grey sheep tossed away from him, spectral, bleating hoarsely. And he came to the dark pool, with the sedge. Then on in the dampness, to the grey sea sucking angrily among the rocks.

This was indeed an island.

So he went home to Flora. She looked at him with guilty fear, but also with a triumphant brightness in her uncanny eyes. And again he was gentle, he reassured her, even he wanted her again, with that curious desire that was almost like toothache. So he took her to the mainland, and they were married, since she was going to have his child.

They returned to the island. She still brought in his meals, her own along with them. She sat and ate with him. He would have it so. The widowed mother preferred to stay in the kitchen. And Flora slept in the guest-room of his house, mistress of his house.

His desire, whatever it was, died in him with nauseous finality. The child would still be months coming. His island was hateful to him, vulgar, a suburb. He himself had lost all his finer distinction. The weeks passed in a sort of prison, in humiliation. Yet he stuck it out, till the child was born. But he was meditating escape. Flora did not even know.

A nurse appeared, and ate at table with them. The doctor came sometimes, and, if the sea were rough, he too had to stay. He was cheery over his whisky.

They might have been a young couple in Golders Green.

The daughter was born at last. The father looked at the baby, and felt depressed, almost more than he could bear. The millstone was tied round his neck. But he tried not to show what he felt. And Flora did not know. She still smiled with a kind of half-witted triumph in her joy, as she got well again. Then she began again to look at him with those aching, suggestive, somehow impudent eyes. She adored him so.

This he could not stand. He told her that he had to go away for a time. She wept, but she thought she had got him. He told her he had settled the best part of his property on her, and wrote down for her what income it would produce. She hardly listened, only looked at him with those heavy, adoring, impudent eyes. He gave her a cheque-book, with the amount of her credit duly entered. This did arouse her interest. And he told her, if she got tired of the island, she could choose her home wherever she wished.

She followed him with those aching, persistent brown eyes, when he left, and he never even saw her weep.

He went straight north, to prepare his third island.

CHAPTER THREE

The Third Island

THE THIRD ISLAND was soon made habitable. With cement and the big pebbles from the shingle beach, two men built him a hut, and roofed it with corrugated iron. A boat brought over a bed and table, and three chairs, with a good cupboard, and a few books. He laid in a supply of coal and paraffin and food he wanted so little.

The house stood near the flat shingle bay where he landed, and where he pulled up his light boat. On a sunny day in August the men sailed away and left him. The sea was still and pale blue. On the horizon he saw the small mail-steamer slowly passing northwards, as if she were walking. She served the outer isles twice a week. He could row out to her if need be, in calm weather, and he could signal her from a flagstaff behind his cottage.

Half a dozen sheep still remained on the island, as company; and he had a cat to rub against his legs. While the sweet, sunny days of the northern autumn lasted, he would walk among the rocks, and over the springy turf of his small domain, always coming to the ceaseless, restless sea. He looked at every leaf, that might be different from another, and he watched the endless expansion and contraction of the water-tossed seaweed. He had never a tree, not even a bit of heather to guard. Only the turf, and tiny turf-plants, and the sedge by the pool, the seaweed in the ocean. He was glad. He didn't want trees or bushes. They stood up like people, too assertive. His bare, low-pitched island in the pale blue sea was all he wanted.

He no longer worked at his book. The interest had gone. He liked to sit on the low elevation of his island, and see the sea; nothing but the pale, quiet sea. And to feel his mind turn soft and hazy, like the hazy ocean. Sometimes, like a mirage, he would see the shadow of land rise hovering to northwards. It was a big island beyond. But quite without substance.

He was soon almost startled when he perceived the steamer on the near horizon, and his heart contracted with fear, lest it were going to pause and molest him. Anxiously he watched it go, and not till it was out of sight did he feel truly relieved, himself again. The tension of waiting for human approach was cruel. He did not want to be approached. He did not want to hear voices. He was shocked by the sound of his own voice, if he inadvertently spoke to his cat. He rebuked himself for having broken the great silence. And he was irritated when his cat would look up at him and mew faintly, plaintively. He frowned at her. And she knew. She was becoming wild, lurking in the rocks, perhaps fishing.

But what he disliked most was when one of the lumps of sheep opened its mouth and baa–ed its hoarse, raucous baa. He watched it, and it looked to him hideous and gross. He came to dislike the sheep very much.

He wanted only to hear the whispering sound of the sea, and the sharp cries of the gulls, cries that came out of another world to him. And best of all, the great silence.

He decided to get rid of the sheep when the boat came. They were accustomed to him now, and stood and stared at him with yellow or colourless eyes, in an insolence that was almost cold ridicule. There was a suggestion of cold indecency about them. He disliked them very much. And when they jumped with staccato jumps off the rocks, and their hoofs made the dry, sharp hit, and the fleece flopped on their square backs, he found them repulsive, degrading.

The fine weather passed, and it rained all day. He lay a great deal on his bed, listening to the water trickling from his roof into the zinc water-butt, looking through the open door at the rain, the dark rocks, the hidden sea. Many gulls were on the island now: many sea-birds of all sorts. It was another world of life. Many of the birds he had never seen before. His old impulse came over him, to send for a book, to know their names. In a flicker of the old passion, to know the name of everything he saw, he even decided to row out to the steamer. The names of these birds! He must know their names, otherwise he had not got them, they were not quite alive to him.

But the desire left him, and he merely watched the birds as they wheeled or walked around him, watched them vaguely without discrimination. All interest had left him. Only there was one gull, a big, handsome fellow, who would walk back and forth, back and forth in front of the open door of the cabin, as if he had some mission there. He was big, and pearl-grey, and his roundnesses were as smooth and lovely as a pearl. Only the folded wings had shut black pinions, and on the closed black feathers were three distinct white dots, making a pattern. The islander wondered very much, why this bit of trimming on the bird out of the far, cold seas. And as the gull walked back and forth, back and forth in front of the cabin, strutting on pale-dusky gold feet, holding up his pale yellow beak, that was curved at the tip, with curious alien importance, the man wondered over him. He was portentous, he had a meaning.

Then the bird came no more. The island, which had been full of sea-birds, the flash of wings, the sound and cut of wings and sharp eerie cries in the air, began to be deserted again. No longer they sat like living eggs on the rocks and turf, moving their heads, but scarcely rising into flight round his feet. No longer they ran across the turf among the sheep, and lifted themselves upon low wings. The host had gone. But some remained, always.

The days shortened, and the world grew eerie. One day the boat came: as if suddenly, swooping down. The islander found it a violation. It was torture to talk to those two men, in their homely clumsy clothes. The air of familiarity around them was very repugnant to him. Himself, he was neatly dressed, his cabin was neat and tidy. He resented any intrusion, the clumsy homeliness, the heavy-footedness of the two fishermen was really repulsive to him.

The letters they had brought he left lying unopened in a little box. In one of them was his money. But he could not bear to open even that one. Any kind of contact was repulsive to him. Even to read his name on an envelope. He hid the letters away.

And the hustle and horror of getting the sheep caught and tied and put in the ship made him loathe with profound repulsion the whole of the animal creation. What repulsive god invented animals and evil-smelling men? To his nostrils, the fishermen and the sheep alike smelled foul: an uncleanness on the fresh earth.

He was still nerve-racked and tortured when the ship at last lifted sail and was drawing away, over the still sea. And sometimes, days after, he would start with repulsion, thinking he heard the munching of sheep.

The dark days of winter drew on. Sometimes there was no real day at all. He felt ill, as if he were dissolving, as if dissolution had already set in inside him. Everything was twilight, outside, and in his mind and soul. Once, when he went to the door, he saw black heads of men swimming in his bay. For some moments he swooned unconscious. It was the shock, the horror of unexpected human approach. The horror in the twilight! And not till the shock had undermined him and left him disembodied, did he realise that the black heads were the heads of seals swimming in. A sick relief came over him. But he was barely conscious, after the shock. Later on, he sat and wept with gratitude, because they were not men. But he never realised that he wept. He was too dim. Like some strange, ethereal animal, he no longer realised what he was doing.

Only he still derived his single satisfaction from being alone, absolutely alone, with the space soaking into him. The grey sea alone, and the footing of his sea-washed island. No other contact. Nothing human to bring its horror into contact with him. Only space, damp, twilit, sea-washed space! This was the bread of his soul.

For this reason, he was most glad when there was a storm, or when the sea was high. Then nothing could get at him. Nothing could come through to him from the outer world. True, the terrific violence of the wind made him suffer badly. At the same time, it swept the world utterly out of existence for him. He always liked the sea to be heavily rolling and tearing. Then no boat could get at him. It was like eternal ramparts round his island.

He kept no track of time, and no longer thought of opening a book. The print, the printed letters, so like the depravity of speech, looked obscene. He tore the brass label from his paraffin stove. He obliterated any bit of lettering in his cabin.

His cat had disappeared. He was rather glad. He shivered at her thin, obtrusive call. She had lived in the coalshed. And each morning he had put her a dish of porridge, the same as he ate. He washed her saucer with repulsion. He did not like her writhing about. But he fed her scrupulously. Then one day she did not come for her porridge; she always mewed for it. She did not come again.

He prowled about his island in the rain, in a big oilskin coat, not knowing what he was looking at, nor what he went out to see. Time had ceased to pass. He stood for long spaces, gazing from a white, sharp face, with those keen, far-off blue eyes of his, gazing fiercely and almost cruelly at the dark sea under the dark sky. And if he saw the labouring sail of a fishing-boat away on the cold waters, a strange malevolent anger passed over his features.

Sometimes he was ill. He knew he was ill, because he staggered as he walked, and easily fell down. Then he paused to think what it was. And he went to his stores and took out dried milk and malt, and ate that. Then he forgot again. He ceased to register his own feelings.

The days were beginning to lengthen. All winter the weather had been comparatively mild, but with much rain, much rain. He had forgotten the sun. Suddenly, however, the air was very cold, and he began to shiver. A fear came over him. The sky was level and grey, and never a star appeared at night. It was very cold. More birds began to arrive. The island was freezing. With trembling hands he made a fire in his grate. The cold frightened him.

And now it continued, day after day, a dull, deathly cold. Occasional crumblings of snow were in the air. The days were greyly longer, but no change in the cold. Frozen grey daylight. The birds passed away, flying away. Some he saw lying frozen. It was as if all life were drawing away, contracting away from the north, contracting southwards. 'Soon,' he said to himself, 'it will all be gone, and in all these regions nothing will be alive.' He felt a cruel satisfaction in the thought.

Then one night there seemed to be a relief; he slept better, did not tremble half-awake, and writhe so much, half-conscious. He had become so used to the quaking and writhing of his body, he hardly noticed it. But when for once it slept deep, he noticed that.

He woke in the morning to a curious whiteness. His window was muffled. It had snowed. He got up and opened his door, and shuddered. Ugh! How cold! All white, with a dark leaden sea, and black rocks curiously speckled with white. The foam was no longer pure. It seemed dirty. And the sea ate at the whiteness of the corpse-like land. Crumbles of snow were silting down the dead air.

On the ground the snow was a foot deep, white and smooth and soft, windless. He took a shovel to clear round his house and shed. The pallor of morning darkened. There was a strange rumbling of far-off thunder in the frozen air, and through the newly-falling snow, a dim flash of lightning. Snow now fell steadily down in the motionless obscurity.

He went out for a few minutes. But it was difficult. He stumbled and fell in the snow, which burned his face. Weak, faint, he toiled home. And when he recovered, took the trouble to make hot milk.

It snowed all the time. In the afternoon again there was a muffled rumbling of thunder, and flashes of lightning blinking reddish through the falling snow. Uneasy, he went to bed and lay staring fixedly at nothingness.

Morning seemed never to come. An eternity long he lay and waited for one alleviating pallor on the night. And at last it seemed the air was paler. His house was a cell faintly illuminated with white light. He realised the snow was walled outside his window. He got up, in the dead cold. When he opened his door, the motionless snow stopped him in a wall as high as his breast. Looking over the top of it, he felt the dead wind slowly driving, saw the snow-powder lift and travel like a funeral train. The blackish sea churned and champed, seeming to bite at the snow, impotent. The sky was grey, but luminous.

He began to work in a frenzy, to get at his boat. If he was to be shut in, it must be by his own choice, not by the mechanical power of the elements. He must get to the sea. He must be able to get at his boat.

But he was weak, and at times the snow overcame him. It fell on him, and he lay buried and lifeless. Yet every time he struggled alive before it was too late, and fell upon the snow with the energy of fever. Exhausted, he would not give in. He crept indoors and made coffee and bacon. Long since he had cooked so much. Then he went at the snow once more. He must conquer the snow, this new, white brute force which had accumulated against him.

He worked in the awful, dead wind, pushing the snow aside, pressing it with his shovel. It was cold, freezing hard in the wind, even when the sun came out for a while, and showed him his white, lifeless surroundings, the black sea rolling sullen, flecked with dull spume, away to the horizons. Yet the sun had power on his face. It was March.

He reached the boat. He pushed the snow away, then sat down under the lee of the boat, looking at the sea, which swirled nearly to his feet, in the high tide. Curiously natural the pebbles looked, in a world gone all uncanny. The sun shone no more. Snow was falling in hard crumbs, that vanished as if by a miracle as they touched the hard blackness of the sea. Hoarse waves rang in the shingle, rushing up at the snow. The wet rocks were brutally black. And all the time the myriad swooping crumbs of snow, demonish, touched the dark sea and disappeared.

During the night there was a great storm. It seemed to him he could hear the vast mass of snow striking all the world with a ceaseless thud; and over it all, the wind roared in strange hollow volleys, in between which came a lump of blindfold lightning, then the low roll of thunder heavier than the wind. When at last the dawn faintly discoloured the dark, the storm had more or less subsided, but a steady wind drove on. The snow was up to the top of his door.

Sullenly, he worked to dig himself out. And he managed through sheer persistency to get out. He was in the tail of a great drift, many feet high. When he got through, the frozen snow was not more than two feet deep. But his island was gone. Its shape was all changed, great heaping white hills rose where no hills had been, inaccessible, and they fumed like volcanoes, but with snow powder. He was sickened and overcome.

His boat was in another, smaller drift. But he had not the strength to clear it. He looked at it helplessly. The shovel slipped from his hands, and he sank in the snow, to forget. In the snow itself, the sea resounded.

Something brought him to. He crept to his house. He was almost without feeling. Yet he managed to warm himself, just that part of him which leaned in snow-sleep over the coal fire. Then again he made hot milk. After which, carefully, he built up the fire.

The wind dropped. Was it night again? In the silence, it seemed he could hear the panther-like dropping of infinite snow. Thunder rumbled nearer, crackled quick after the bleared reddened lightning. He lay in bed in a kind of stupor. The elements! The elements! His mind repeated the word dumbly. You can't win against the elements.

How long it went on, he never knew. Once, like a wraith,[44] he got out and climbed to the top of a white hill on his unrecognisable island. The sun was hot. 'It is summer,' he said to himself, 'and the time of leaves.' He looked stupidly over the whiteness of his foreign island, over the waste of the lifeless sea. He pretended to imagine he saw the wink of a sail. Because he knew too well there would never again be a sail on that stark sea.

As he looked, the sky mysteriously darkened and chilled. From far off came the mutter of the unsatisfied thunder, and he knew it was the signal of the snow rolling over the sea. He turned, and felt its breath on him.

The Man Who Died[45]

CHAPTER ONE

THERE WAS A PEASANT near Jerusalem who acquired a young gamecock which looked a shabby little thing, but which put on brave feathers as spring advanced, and was resplendent with arched and orange neck by the time the fig trees were letting out leaves from their end-tips.

This peasant was poor, he lived in a cottage of mud-brick, and had only a dirty little inner courtyard with a tough fig tree for all his territory. He worked hard among the vines and olives and wheat of his master, then came home to sleep in the mud-brick cottage by the path. But he was proud of his young rooster. In the shut-in yard were three shabby hens which laid small eggs, shed the few feathers they had, and made a disproportionate amount of dirt. There was also, in a corner under a straw roof, a dull donkey that often went out with the peasant to work, but sometimes stayed at home. And there was the peasant's wife, a black-browed youngish woman who did not work too hard. She threw a little grain, or the remains of the porridge mess, to the fowls, and she cut green fodder with a sickle for the ass.

The young cock grew to a certain splendour. By some freak of destiny, he was a dandy rooster, in that dirty little yard with three patchy hens. He learned to crane his neck and give shrill answers to the crowing of other cocks, beyond the walls, in a world he knew nothing of. But there was a special fiery colour to his crow, and the distant calling of the other cocks roused him to unexpected outbursts.

'How he sings,' said the peasant, as he got up and pulled his day-shirt over his head.

'He is good for twenty hens,' said the wife.

The peasant went out and looked with pride at his young rooster. A saucy, flamboyant bird, that had already made the final acquaintance of the three tattered hens. But the cockerel was tipping his head, listening to the challenge of far-off unseen cocks, in the unknown world. Ghost voices, crowing at him mysteriously out of limbo. He answered with a ringing defiance, never to be daunted.

'He will surely fly away one of these days,' said the peasant's wife.

So they lured him with grain, caught him, though he fought with all his wings and feet, and they tied a cord round his shank, fastening it against the spur; and they tied the other end of the cord to the post that held up the donkey's straw pent-roof.

The young cock, freed, marched with a prancing stride of indignation away from the humans, came to the end of his string, gave a tug and a hitch of his tied leg, fell over for a moment, scuffled frantically on the unclean earthen floor, to the horror of the shabby hens, then with a sickening lurch, regained his feet, and stood to think. The peasant and the peasant's wife laughed heartily, and the young cock heard them. And he knew, with a gloomy, foreboding kind of knowledge that he was tied by the leg.

He no longer pranced and ruffled and forged his feathers. He walked within the limits of his tether sombrely. Still he gobbled up the best bits of food. Still, sometimes, he saved an extra-best bit for his favourite hen of the moment. Still he pranced with quivering, rocking fierceness upon such of his harem as came nonchalantly within range, and gave off the invisible lure. And still he crowed defiance to the cock-crows that showered up out of limbo, in the dawn.

But there was now a grim voracity in the way he gobbled his food, and a pinched triumph in the way he seized upon the shabby hens. His voice, above all, had lost the full gold of its clangour. He was tied by the leg, and he knew it. Body, soul, and spirit were tied by that string.

Underneath, however, the life in him was grimly unbroken. It was the cord that should break. So one morning, just before the light of dawn, rousing from his slumbers with a sudden wave of strength, he leaped forward on his wings, and the string snapped. He gave a wild, strange squawk, rose in one lift to the top of the wall, and there he crowed a loud and splitting crow. So loud, it woke the peasant.

At the same time, at the same hour before dawn, on the same morning, a man awoke from a long sleep in which he was tied up. He woke numb and cold, inside a carved hole in the rock. Through all the long sleep his body had been full of hurt, and it was still full of hurt. He did not open his eyes. Yet he knew that he was awake, and numb, and cold, and rigid, and full of hurt, and tied up. His face was banded with cold bands, his legs were bandaged together. Only his hands were loose.

He could move if he wanted: he knew that. But he had no want. Who would want to come back from the dead? A deep, deep nausea stirred in him, at the premonition of movement. He resented already the fact of the strange, incalculable moving that had already taken place in him: the moving back into consciousness. He had not wished it. He had wanted to stay outside, in the place where even memory is stone dead.

But now, something had returned to him, like a returned letter, and in that return he lay overcome with a sense of nausea. Yet suddenly his hands moved. They lifted up, cold, heavy and sore. Yet they lifted up, to drag away the cloth from his face, and push at the shoulder bands. Then they fell again, cold, heavy, numb, and sick with having moved even so much, unspeakably unwilling to move further.

With his face cleared and his shoulders free, he lapsed again, and lay dead, resting on the cold nullity of being dead. It was the most desirable. And almost, he had it complete: the utter cold nullity of being outside.

Yet when he was most nearly gone, suddenly, driven by an ache at the wrists, his hands rose and began pushing at the bandages of his knees, his feet began to stir, even while his breast lay cold and dead still.

And at last, the eyes opened. On to the dark. The same dark! Yet perhaps there was a pale chink, of the all-disturbing light, prising open the pure dark. He could not lift his head. The eyes closed. And again it was finished.

Then suddenly he leaned up, and the great world reeled. Bandages fell away. And narrow walls of rock closed upon him, and gave the new anguish of imprisonment. There were chinks of light. With a wave of strength that came from revulsion, he leaned forward, in that narrow well of rock, and leaned frail hands on the rock near the chinks of light.

Strength came from somewhere, from revulsion; there was a crash and a wave of light, and the dead man was crouching in his lair, facing the animal onrush of light. Yet it was hardly dawn. And the strange, piercing keenness of daybreak's sharp breath was on him. It meant full awakening.

Slowly, slowly he crept down from the cell of rock with the caution of the bitterly wounded. Bandages and linen and perfume fell away, and he crouched on the ground against the wall of rock, to recover oblivion. But he saw his hurt feet touching the earth again, with unspeakable pain, the earth they had meant to touch no more, and he saw his thin legs that had died, and pain unknowable, pain like utter bodily disillusion, filled him so full that he stood up, with one torn hand on the ledge of the tomb.

To be back! To be back again, after all that! He saw the linen swathing-bands fallen round his dead feet, and stooping, he picked them up, folded them, and laid them back in the rocky cavity from which he had emerged. Then he took the perfumed linen sheet, wrapped it round him as a mantle, and turned away, to the wanness of the chill dawn.

He was alone; and having died, was even beyond loneliness.

Filled still with the sickness of unspeakable disillusion, the man stepped with wincing feet down the rocky slope, past the sleeping soldiers, who lay wrapped in their woollen mantles under the wild laurels. Silent, on naked scarred feet, wrapped in a white linen shroud, he glanced down for a moment on the inert, heap-like bodies of the soldiers. They were repulsive, a slow squalor of limbs, yet he felt a certain compassion. He passed on towards the road, lest they should wake.

Having nowhere to go, he turned from the city that stood on her hills. He slowly followed the road away from the town, past the olives, under which purple anemones were drooping in the chill of dawn, and rich-green herbage was pressing thick. The world, the same as ever, the natural world, thronging with greenness, a nightingale winsomely, wistfully, coaxingly calling from the bushes beside a runnel of water, in the world, the natural world of morning and evening, for ever undying, from which he had died.

He went on, on scarred feet, neither of this world nor of the next. Neither here nor there, neither seeing nor yet sightless, he passed dimly on, away from the city and its precincts, wondering why he should be travelling, yet driven by a dim, deep nausea of disillusion, and a resolution of which he was not even aware.

Advancing in a kind of half-consciousness under the dry stone wall of the olive orchard, he was roused by the shrill, wild crowing of a cock just near him, a sound which made him shiver, as if electricity had touched him. He saw a black and orange cock on a bough above the road, then running through the olives of the upper level, a peasant in a grey woollen shirt-tunic. Leaping out of greenness, came the black and orange cock with the red comb, his tail-feathers streaming lustrous.

'Oh, stop him, master!' called the peasant. 'My escaped cock!'

The man addressed, with a sudden flicker of smile, opened his great white wings of a shroud in front of the leaping bird. The cock fell back with a squawk and a flutter, the peasant jumped forward, there was a terrific beating of wings and whirring of feathers, then the peasant had the escaped cock safely under his arm, its wings shut

down, its face crazily craning forward, its round eyes goggling from
its white chops.

'It's my escaped cock!' said the peasant, soothing the bird with his
left hand, as he looked perspiringly up into the face of the man
wrapped in white linen.

The peasant changed countenance, and stood transfixed, as he
looked into the dead-white face of the man who had died. That dead-
white face, so still, with the black beard growing on it as if in death;
and those wide-open, black, sombre eyes, that had died! and those
washed scars on the waxy forehead! The slow-blooded man of the
field let his jaw drop, in childish inability to meet the situation.

'Don't be afraid,' said the man in the shroud. 'I am not dead. They
took me down too soon. So I have risen up. Yet if they discover me,
they will do it all over again . . . '

He spoke in a voice of old disgust. Humanity! Especially humanity,
in authority! There was only one thing it could do! He looked with
black, indifferent eyes into the quick, shifty eyes of the peasant. The
peasant quailed, and was powerless under the look of deathly
indifference and strange, cold resoluteness. He could only say the
one thing he was afraid to say: 'Will you hide in my house, master?'

'I will rest there. But if you tell anyone, you know what will happen.
You will have to go before a judge.'

'Me! I shan't speak. Let us be quick!'

The peasant looked round in fear, wondering sulkily why he had
let himself in for this doom. The man with scarred feet climbed
painfully up to the level of the olive garden, and followed the sullen,
hurrying peasant across the green wheat among the olive trees. He
felt the cool silkiness of the young wheat under his feet that had been
dead, and the roughishness of its separate life was apparent to him. At
the edges of rocks, he saw the silky, silvery-haired buds of the scarlet
anemone bending downwards. And they, too, were in another world.
In his own world he was alone, utterly alone. These things around
him were in a world that had never died. But he himself had died, or
had been killed from out of it, and all that remained now was the
great void nausea of utter disillusion.

They came to a clay cottage, and the peasant waited dejectedly for
the other man to pass.

'Pass!' he said. 'Pass! We have not been seen.'

The man in white linen entered the earthen room, taking with him
the aroma of strange perfumes. The peasant closed the door, and
passed through the inner doorway into the yard, where the ass stood
within the high walls, safe from being stolen. There the peasant, in

great disquietude, tied up the cock. The man with the waxen face sat
down on a mat near the hearth, for he was spent and barely conscious.
Yet he heard outside the whispering of the peasant to his wife, for the
woman had been watching from the roof.

Presently they came in, and the woman hid her face. She poured
water, and put bread and dried figs on a wooden platter.

'Eat, master!' said the peasant. 'Eat! No one has seen.'

But the stranger had no desire for food. Yet he moistened a little
bread in the water, and ate it, since life must be. But desire was dead
in him, even for food and drink. He had risen without desire,
without even the desire to live, empty save for the all-overwhelming
disillusion that lay like nausea where his life had been. Yet perhaps,
deeper even than disillusion, was a desireless resoluteness, deeper
even than consciousness.

The peasant and his wife stood near the door, watching. They saw
with terror the livid wounds on the thin, waxy hands and the thin feet
of the stranger, and the small lacerations in the still dead forehead.
They smelled with terror the scent of rich perfumes that came from
him, from his body. And they looked at the fine, snowy, costly linen.
Perhaps really he was a dead king, from the region of terrors. And he
was still cold and remote in the region of death, with perfumes
coming from his transparent body as if from some strange flower.

Having with difficulty swallowed some of the moistened bread, he
lifted his eyes to them. He saw them as they were: limited, meagre in
their life, without any splendour of gesture and of courage. But they
were what they were, slow, inevitable parts of the natural world.
They had no nobility, but fear made them compassionate.

And the stranger had compassion on them again, for he knew
that they would respond best to gentleness, giving back a clumsy
gentleness again.

'Do not be afraid,' he said to them gently. 'Let me stay a little while
with you. I shall not stay long. And then I shall go away for ever. But
do not be afraid. No harm will come to you through me.'

They believed him at once, yet the fear did not leave them. And
they said: 'Stay, master, while ever you will. Rest! Rest quietly!'

But they were afraid.

So he let them be, and the peasant went away with the ass. The sun
had risen bright, and in the dark house with the door shut, the man
was again as if in the tomb. So he said to the woman: 'I would lie in
the yard.'

And she swept the yard for him, and laid him a mat, and he lay
down under the wall in the morning sun. There he saw the first green

leaves spurting like flames from the ends of the enclosed fig tree, out
of the bareness to the sky of spring above. But the man who had died
could not look, he only lay quite still in the sun, which was not yet too
hot, and had no desire in him, not even to move. But he lay with his
thin legs in the sun, his black, perfumed hair falling into the hollows
of his neck, and his thin, colourless arms utterly inert. As he lay there,
the hens clucked, and scratched, and the escaped cock, caught and
tied by the leg again, cowered in a corner.

The peasant woman was frightened. She came peeping, and, seeing
him never move, feared to have a dead man in the yard. But the sun
had grown stronger, he opened his eyes and looked at her. And now
she was frightened of the man who was alive but spoke nothing.

He opened his eyes, and saw the world again bright as glass. It was
life, in which he had no share any more. But it shone outside him,
blue sky, and a bare fig tree with little jets of green leaf. Bright as
glass, and he was not of it, for desire had failed.

Yet he was there, and not extinguished. The day passed in a kind of
coma, and at evening he went into the house. The peasant man came
home, but he was frightened, and had nothing to say. The stranger,
too, ate of the mess of beans, a little. Then he washed his hands and
turned to the wall, and was silent. The peasants were silent too. They
watched their guest sleep. Sleep was so near death he could still sleep.

Yet when the sun came up, he went again to lie in the yard. The sun
was the one thing that drew him and swayed him, and he still wanted
to feel the cool air of the morning in his nostrils, see the pale sky
overhead. He still hated to be shut up.

As he came out, the young cock crowed. It was a diminished,
pinched cry, but there was that in the voice of the bird stronger than
chagrin. It was the necessity to live, and even to cry out the triumph
of life. The man who had died stood and watched the cock who had
escaped and been caught, ruffling himself up, rising forward on his
toes, throwing up his head, and parting his beak in another challenge
from life to death. The brave sounds rang out, and though they were
diminished by the cord round the bird's leg, they were not cut off.
The man who had died looked naked on life, and saw a vast
resoluteness everywhere flinging itself up in stormy or subtle wave-
crests, foam-tips emerging out of the blue invisible, a black and
orange cock or the green flame-tongues out of the extremes of the
fig tree. They came forth, these things and creatures of spring,
glowing with desire and with assertion. They came like crests of
foam, out of the blue flood of the invisible desire, out of the vast
invisible sea of strength, and they came coloured and tangible,

evanescent, yet deathless in their coming. The man who had died looked on the great swing into existence of things that had not died, but he saw no longer their tremulous desire to exist and to be. He heard instead their ringing, ringing, defiant challenge to all other things existing.

The man lay still, with eyes that had died now wide open and darkly still, seeing the everlasting resoluteness of life. And the cock, with the flat, brilliant glance, glanced back at him, with a bird's half-seeing look. And always the man who had died saw not the bird alone, but the short, sharp wave of life of which the bird was the crest. He watched the queer, beaky motion of the creature as it gobbled into itself the scraps of food; its glancing of the eye of life, ever alert and watchful, over-weening and cautious, and the voice of its life, crowing triumph and assertion, yet strangled by a cord of circumstance. He seemed to hear the queer speech of very life, as the cock triumphantly imitated the clucking of the favourite hen, when she had laid an egg, a clucking which still had, in the male bird, the hollow chagrin of the cord round his leg. And when the man threw a bit of bread to the cock, it called with an extraordinary cooing tenderness, tousling and saving the morsel for the hens. The hens ran up greedily, and carried the morsel away beyond the reach of the string.

Then, walking complacently after them, suddenly the male bird's leg would hitch at the end of his tether, and he would yield with a kind of collapse. His flag fell, he seemed to diminish, he would huddle in the shade. And he was young, his tail-feathers, glossy as they were, were not fully grown. It was not till evening again that the tide of life in him made him forget. Then when his favourite hen came strolling unconcernedly near him, emitting the lure, he pounced on her with all his feathers vibrating. And the man who had died watched the unsteady, rocking vibration of the bent bird, and it was not the bird he saw, but one wave-tip of life overlapping for a minute another, in the tide of the swaying ocean of life. And the destiny of life seemed more fierce and compulsive to him even than the destiny of death. The doom of death was a shadow compared to the raging destiny of life, the determined surge of life.

At twilight the peasant came home with the ass, and he said: 'Master! It is said that the body was stolen from the garden, and the tomb is empty, and the soldiers are taken away, accursed Romans! And the women are there to weep.'

The man who had died looked at the man who had not died.

'It is well,' he said. 'Say nothing, and we are safe.'

And the peasant was relieved. He looked rather dirty and stupid, and even as much flaminess as that of the young cock, which he had tied by the leg, would never glow in him. He was without fire.

But the man who had died thought to himself: 'Why, then, should he be lifted up? Clods of earth are turned over for refreshment, they are not to be lifted up. Let the earth remain earthy, and hold its own again the sky. I was to seek to lift it up. I was wrong to try to interfere. The ploughshare of devastation will be set in the soil of Judea, and the life of this peasant will be overturned like the sods of the field. No man can save the earth from tillage. It is tillage, not salvation . . . '

So he saw the man, the peasant, with compassion; but the man who had died no longer wished to interfere in the soul of the man who had not died, and who could never die, save to return to earth. Let him return to earth in his own good hour, and let no one try to interfere when the earth claims her own.

So the man with scars let the peasant go from him, for the peasant had no rebirth in him. Yet the man who had died said to himself: 'He is my host.'

And at dawn, when he was better, the man who had died rose up, and on slow, sore feet retraced his way to the garden. For he had been betrayed in a garden, and buried in a garden. And as he turned round the screen of laurels, near the rock-face, he saw a woman hovering by the tomb, a woman in blue and yellow. She peeped again into the mouth of the hole, that was like a deep cupboard. But still there was nothing. And she wrung her hands and wept. And as she turned away, she saw the man in white, standing by the laurels, and she gave a cry, thinking it might be a spy, and she said: 'They have taken him away!'

So he said to her: 'Madeleine!'[46]

Then she reeled as if she would fall, for she knew him.

And he said to her: 'Madeleine! Do not be afraid. I am alive. They took me down too soon, so I came back to life. Then I was sheltered in a house.'

She did not know what to say, but fell at his feet to kiss them.

'Don't touch me, Madeleine,' he said. 'Not yet! I am not yet healed and in touch with men.'

So she wept because she did not know what to do. And he said: 'Let us go aside, among the bushes, where we can speak unseen.'

So in her blue mantle and her yellow robe, she followed him among the trees, and he sat down under a myrtle bush. And he said: 'I am not yet quite come to. Madeleine, what is to be done next?'

'Master!' she said. 'Oh, we have wept for you! And will you come back to us?'

'What is finished is finished, and for me the end is past,' he said. 'The stream will run till no more rains fill it, then it will dry up. For me, that life is over.'

'And will you give up your triumph?' she said sadly.

'My triumph,' he said, 'is that I am not dead. I have outlived my mission and know no more of it. It is my triumph. I have survived the day and the death of my interference, and am still a man. I am young still, Madeleine, not even come to middle-age. I am glad all that is over. It had to be. But now I am glad it is over, and the day of my interference is done. The teacher and the saviour are dead in me; now I can go about my business, into my own single life.'

She heard him, and did not fully understand. But what he said made her feel disappointed.

'But you will come back to us?' she said, insisting.

'I don't know what I shall do,' he said. 'When I am healed, I shall know better. But my mission is over, and my teaching is finished, and death has saved me from my own salvation. Oh, Madeleine, I want to take my single way in life, which is my portion. My public life is over, the life of my self-importance. Now I can wait on life, and say nothing, and have no one betray me. I wanted to be greater than the limits of my hands and feet, so I brought betrayal on myself. And I know I wronged Judas, my poor Judas. For I have died, and now I know my own limits. Now I can live without striving to sway others any more. For my reach ends in my fingertips, and my stride is no longer than the ends of my toes. Yet I would embrace multitudes, I who have never truly embraced even one. But Judas and the high priests saved me from my own salvation, and soon I can turn to my destiny like a bather in the sea at dawn, who had just come down to the shore alone.'

'Do you want to be alone henceforward?' she asked. 'And was your mission nothing? Was it all untrue?'

'Nay!' he said. 'Neither were your lovers in the past nothing. They were much to you, but you took more than you gave. Then you came to me for salvation from your own excess. And I, in my mission, I too ran to excess. I gave more than I took, and that also is woe and vanity. So Pilate and the high priests saved me from my own excessive salvation. Don't run to excess now in living, Madeleine. It only means another death.'

She pondered bitterly, for the need for excessive giving was in her, and she could not bear to be denied.

'And will you not come back to us?' she said. 'Have you risen for yourself alone?'

He heard the sarcasm in her voice, and looked at her beautiful face which still was dense with excessive need for salvation from the woman she had been, the female who had caught men at her will. The cloud of necessity was on her, to be saved from the old, wilful Eve, who had embraced many men and taken more than she gave. Now the other doom was on her. She wanted to give without taking. And that, too, is hard, and cruel to the warm body.

'I have not risen from the dead in order to seek death again,' he said.

She glanced up at him, and saw the weariness settling again on his waxy face, and the vast disillusion in his dark eyes, and the underlying indifference.

He felt her glance, and said to himself: 'Now my own followers will want to do me to death again, for having risen up different from their expectation.'

'But you will come to us, to see us, us who love you?' she said.

He laughed a little and said: 'Ah, yes.' Then he added: 'Have you a little money? Will you give me a little money? I owe it.'

She had not much, but it pleased her to give it to him.

'Do you think,' he said to her, 'that I might come and live with you in your house?'

She looked up at him with large blue eyes, that gleamed strangely.

'Now?' she said with peculiar triumph.

And he, who shrank now from triumph of any sort, his own or another's, said: 'Not now! Later, when I am healed, and . . . and I am in touch with the flesh.'

The words faltered in him. And in his heart he knew he would never go to live in her house. For the flicker of triumph had gleamed in her eyes; the greed of giving. But she murmured in a humming rapture: 'Ah, you know I would give up everything to you.'

'Nay!' he said. 'I didn't ask that.'

A revulsion from all the life he had known came over him again, the great nausea of disillusion, and the spear-thrust through his bowels. He crouched under the myrtle bushes, without strength. Yet his eyes were open. And she looked at him again, and she saw that it was not the Messiah. The Messiah had not risen. The enthusiasm and the burning purity were gone, and the rapt youth. His youth was dead. This man was middle-aged and disillusioned, with a certain terrible indifference, and a resoluteness which love would never conquer. This was not the Master she had so adored, the young, flamy, unphysical exalter of her soul. This was nearer to the lovers she had known of old, but with a greater indifference to the personal issue, and a lesser susceptibility.

She was thrown out of the balance of her rapturous, anguished adoration. This risen man was the death of her dream.

'You should go now,' he said to her. 'Do not touch me, I am in death. I shall come again here, on the third day. Come if you will, at dawn. And we will speak again.'

She went away, perturbed and shattered. Yet as she went, her mind discarded the bitterness of the reality, and she conjured up rapture and wonder, that the Master was risen and was not dead. He was risen, the Saviour, the exalter, the wonder-worker! He was risen, but not as man; as pure God, who should not be touched by flesh, and who should be rapt away into Heaven. It was the most glorious and most ghostly of the miracles.

Meanwhile the man who had died gathered himself together at last, and slowly made his way to the peasants' house. He was glad to go back to them, and away from Madeleine and his own associates. For the peasants had the inertia of earth and would let him rest, and as yet, would put no compulsion on him.

The woman was on the roof, looking for him. She was afraid that he had gone away. His presence in the house had become like gentle wine to her. She hastened to the door, to him.

'Where have you been?' she said. 'Why did you go away?'

'I have been to walk in a garden, and I have seen a friend, who gave me a little money. It is for you.'

He held out his thin hand, with the small amount of money, all that Madeleine could give him.

The peasant's wife's eyes glistened, for money was scarce, and she said: 'Oh, master! And is it truly mine?'

'Take it!' he said. 'It buys bread, and bread brings life.'

So he lay down in the yard again, sick with relief at being alone again. For with the peasants he could be alone, but his own friends would never let him be alone. And in the safety of the yard, the young cock was dear to him, as it shouted in the helpless zest of life, and finished in the helpless humiliation of being tied by the leg. This day the ass stood swishing her tail under the shed. The man who had died lay down and turned utterly away from life, in the sickness of death in life.

But the woman brought wine and water, and sweetened cakes, and roused him, so that he ate a little, to please her. The day was hot, and as she crouched to serve him, he saw her breasts sway from her humble body, under her smock. He knew she wished he would desire her, and she was youngish, and not unpleasant. And he, who had never known a woman, would have desired her if he could. But he could not want her, though he felt gently towards her soft, crouching, humble body. But it was her thoughts, her consciousness, he could not mingle with. She was pleased with the money, and now she wanted to take more from him. She wanted the embrace of his body. But her little soul was hard, and short-sighted, and grasping, her body had its little greed, and no gentle reverence of the return gift. So he spoke a quiet, pleasant word to her and turned away. He could not touch the little, personal body, the little, personal life of this woman, nor in any other. He turned away from it without hesitation.

Risen from the dead, he had realised at last that the body, too, has its little life, and beyond that, the greater life. He was virgin, in recoil from the little, greedy life of the body. But now he knew that virginity is a form of greed; and that the body rises again to give and to take, to take and to give, ungreedily. Now he knew that he had risen for the woman, or women, who knew the greater life of the body, not greedy to give, not greedy to take, and with whom he could mingle his body. But having died, he was patient, knowing there was time, an eternity of time. And he was driven by no greedy desire, either to give himself to others, or to grasp anything for himself. For he had died.

The peasant came home from work and said: 'Master, I thank you for the money. But we did not want it. And all I have is yours.'

But the man who had died was sad, because the peasant stood there in the little, personal body, and his eyes were cunning and sparkling with the hope of greater rewards in money later on. True, the peasant had taken him in free, and had risked getting no reward. But the hope was cunning in him. Yet even this was as men are made. So when the peasant would have helped him to rise, for night had fallen, the man who had died said: 'Don't touch me, brother. I am not yet risen to the Father.'

The sun burned with greater splendour, and burnished the young cock brighter. But the peasant kept the string renewed, and the bird was a prisoner. Yet the flame of life burned up to a sharp point in the cock, so that it eyed askance and haughtily the man who had died. And the man smiled and held the bird dear, and he said to it: 'Surely thou art risen to the Father, among birds.'

And the young cock, answering, crowed.

When at dawn on the third morning the man went to the garden, he was absorbed, thinking of the greater life of the body, beyond the little, narrow, personal life. So he came through the thick screen of laurel and myrtle bushes, near the rock, suddenly, and he saw three women near the tomb. One was Madeleine, and one was the woman who had been his mother, and the third was a woman he knew, called Joan. He looked up, and saw them all, and they saw him, and they were all afraid.

He stood arrested in the distance, knowing they were there to claim him back, bodily. But he would in no wise return to them. Pallid, in the shadow of a grey morning that was blowing to rain, he saw them, and turned away. But Madeleine hastened towards him.

'I did not bring them,' she said. 'They have come of themselves. See, I have brought you money! . . . Will you not speak to them?'

She offered him some gold pieces, and he took them, saying: 'May I have this money? I shall need it. I cannot speak to them, for I am not yet ascended to the Father. And I must leave you now.'

'Ah! Where will you go?' she cried.

He looked at her, and saw she was clutching for the man in him who had died and was dead, the man of his youth and his mission, of his chastity and his fear, of his little life, his giving without taking.

'I must go to my Father!' he said.

'And you will leave us? There is your mother!' she cried, turning round with the old anguish, which yet was sweet to her.

'But now I must ascend to my Father,' he said, and he drew back into the bushes, and so turned quickly, and went away, saying to himself: 'Now I belong to no one and have no connection, and mission or gospel is gone from me. Lo! I cannot make even my own life, and what have I to save? . . . I can learn to be alone.'

So he went back to the peasants' house, to the yard where the young cock was tied by the leg with a string. And he wanted no one, for it was best to be alone; for the presence of people made him lonely. The sun and the subtle salve of spring healed his wounds, even the gaping wound of disillusion through his bowels was closing up. And his need of men and women, his fever to have them and to be saved by them, this too was healing in him. Whatever came of touch between himself and the race of men, henceforth, should come without trespass or compulsion. For he said to himself: 'I tried to compel them to live, so they compelled me to die. It is always so, with compulsion. The recoil kills the advance. Now is my time to be alone.'

Therefore he went no more to the garden, but lay still and saw the sun, or walked at dusk across the olive slopes, among the green wheat, that rose a palm-breadth higher every sunny day. And always he thought to himself: 'How good it is to have fulfilled my mission, and to be beyond it. Now I can be alone, and leave all things to themselves, and the fig tree may be barren if it will, and the rich may be rich. My way is my own alone.'

So the green jets of leaves unspread on the fig tree, with the bright, translucent, green blood of the tree. And the young cock grew brighter, more lustrous with the sun's burnishing; yet always tied by the leg with a string. And the sun went down more and more in pomp, out of the gold and red-flushed air. The man who had died was aware of it all, and he thought: 'The Word is but the midge that bites at evening. Man is tormented with words like midges, and they follow him right into the tomb. But beyond the tomb they cannot go. Now I have passed the place where words can bite no more and the air is clear, and there is nothing to say, and I am alone within my own skin, which is the walls of all my domain.'

So he healed of his wounds, and enjoyed his immortality of being alive without fret. For in the tomb he had slipped that noose which we call care. For in the tomb he had left his striving self, which cares and asserts itself. Now his uncaring self healed and became whole within his skin, and he smiled to himself with pure aloneness, which is one sort of immortality.

Then he said to himself: 'I will wander the earth, and say nothing. For nothing is so marvellous as to be alone in the phenomenal world, which is raging, and yet apart. And I have not seen it, I was too much blinded by my confusion within it. Now I will wander among the stirring of the phenomenal world, for it is the stirring of all things among themselves which leaves me purely alone.'

So he communed with himself, and decided to be a physician. Because the power was still in him to heal any man or child who touched his compassion. Therefore he cut his hair and his beard after the right fashion, and smiled to himself. And he bought himself shoes, and the right mantle, and put the right cloth over his head, hiding all the little scars. And the peasant said: 'Master, will you go forth from us?'

'Yes, for the time is come for me to return to men.'

So he gave the peasant a piece of money, and said to him: 'Give me the cock that escaped and is now tied by the leg. For he shall go forth with me.'

So for a piece of money the peasant gave the cock to the man who had died, and at dawn the man who had died set out into the phenomenal world, to be fulfilled in his own loneliness in the midst of it. For previously he had been too much mixed up in it. Then he had died. Now he must come back, to be alone in the midst. Yet even now he did not go quite alone, for under his arm, as he went, he carried the cock, whose tail fluttered gaily behind, and who craned his head excitedly, for he too was adventuring out for the first time into the wider phenomenal world, which is the stirring of the body of cocks also. And the peasant woman shed a few tears, but then went indoors, being a peasant, to look again at the pieces of money. And it seemed to her, a gleam came out of the pieces of money, wonderful.

The man who had died wandered on, and it was a sunny day. He looked around as he went, and stood aside as the pack-train passed by, towards the city.

And he said to himself: 'Strange is the phenomenal world, dirty and clean together! And I am the same. Yet I am apart! And life bubbles variously. Why should I have wanted it to bubble all alike? What a pity I preached to them! A sermon is so much more likely to cake into mud, and to close the fountains, than is a psalm or a song. I made a mistake. I understand that they executed me for preaching to them. Yet they could not finally execute me, for now I am risen in my own aloneness, and inherit the earth, since I lay no claim on it. And I will be alone in the seethe of all things; first and foremost, for ever, I shall be alone. But I must toss this bird into the seethe of phenomena, for he must ride his wave. How hot he is with life! Soon, in some place, I shall leave him among the hens. And perhaps one evening I shall meet a woman who can lure my risen body, yet leave me my aloneness. For the body of my desire has died, and I am not in touch anywhere. Yet how do I know! All at least is life. And this cock gleams with bright aloneness, though he answers the lure of hens. And I shall hasten on to that village on the hill ahead of me; already I am tired and weak, and want to close my eyes to everything.'

Hastening a little with the desire to have finished going, he overtook two men going slowly, and talking. And being soft-footed, he heard they were speaking of himself. And he remembered them, for he had known them in his life, the life of his mission. So he greeted them, but did not disclose himself in the dusk, and they did not know him.

He said to them: 'What then of him who would be king, and was put to death for it?'

They answered, suspiciously: 'Why ask you of him?'

'I have known him, and thought much about him,' he said.

So they replied: 'He has risen.'

'Yea! And where is he, and how does he live?'

'We know not, for it is not revealed. Yet he is risen, and in a little while will ascend unto the Father.'

'Yea! And where then is his Father?'

'Know ye not? You are then of the Gentiles! The Father is in Heaven, above the cloud and the firmament.'

'Truly? Then how will he ascend?'

'As Elijah the Prophet, he shall go up in a glory.'[47]

'Even into the sky.'

'Into the sky.'

'Then is he not risen in the flesh?'

'He is risen in the flesh.'

'And will he take flesh up into the sky?'

'The Father in Heaven will take him up.'

The man who had died said no more, for his say was over, and words beget words, even as gnats.

But the man asked him: 'Why do you carry a cock?'

'I am a healer,' he said, 'and the bird hath virtue.'

'You are not a believer?'

'Yea! I believe the bird is full of life and virtue.'

They walked on in silence after this, and he felt they disliked his answer. So he smiled to himself, for a dangerous phenomenon in the world is a man of narrow belief, who denies the right of his neighbour to be alone.

And as they came to the outskirts of the village, the man who had died stood still in the gloaming and said in his old voice: 'Know ye me not?'

And they cried in fear: 'Master!'

'Yea!' he said, laughing softly. And he turned suddenly away, down a side lane, and was gone under the wall before they knew.

So he came to an inn where the asses stood in the yard. And he called for fritters, and they were made for him. So he slept under a shed. But in the morning he was wakened by a loud crowing, and his cock's voice ringing in his ears. So he saw the rooster of the inn walking forth to battle, with his hens, a goodly number, behind him. Then the cock of the man who had died sprang forth, and a battle began between the birds.

The man of the inn ran to save his rooster, but the man who had died said: 'If my bird wins I will give him thee. And if he lose, thou shalt eat him.'

So the birds fought savagely, and the cock of the man who had died killed the common cock of the yard. Then the man who had died said to his young cock: 'Thou at least hast found thy kingdom, and the females to thy body. Thy aloneness can take on splendour, polished by the lure of thy hens.'

And he left his bird there, and went on deeper into the phenomenal world, which is a vast complexity of entanglements and allurements. And he asked himself a last question: 'From what, and to what, could this infinite whirl be saved?'

So he went his way, and was alone. But the way of the world was past belief, as he saw the strange entanglement of passions and circumstance and compulsion everywhere, but always the dread insomnia of compulsion. It was fear, the ultimate fear of death, that made men mad. So always he must move on, for if he stayed, his neighbours wound the strangling of their fear and bullying round him. There was nothing he could touch, for all, in a mad assertion of the ego, wanted to put a compulsion on him, and violate his intrinsic solitude. It was the mania of cities and societies and hosts, to lay a compulsion upon a man, upon all men. For men and women alike were mad with the egoistic fear of their own nothingness. And he thought of his own mission, how he had tried to lay the compulsion of love on all men. And the old nausea came back on him. For there was no contact without a subtle attempt to inflict a compulsion. And already he had been compelled even into death. The nausea of the old wound broke out afresh, and he looked again on the world with repulsion, dreading its mean contacts.

CHAPTER TWO

THE WIND CAME cold and strong from inland, from the invisible snows of Lebanon. But the temple, facing south and west, towards Egypt, faced the splendid sun of winter as he curved down towards the sea, the warmth and radiance flooded in between the pillars of painted wood. But the sea was invisible, because of the trees, though its dashing sounded among the hum of pines. The air was turning golden to afternoon. The woman who served Isis[48] stood in her yellow robe, and looked up at the steep slopes coming down to the sea, where the olive trees silvered under the wind like water splashing. She was alone save for the goddess. And in the winter afternoon the light stood erect and magnificent off the invisible sea, filling the hills of the coast. She went towards the sun, through the grove of Mediterranean pine trees and evergreen oaks, in the midst of which the temple stood, on a little, tree-covered tongue of land between two bays.

It was only a very little way, and then she stood among the dry

trunks of the outermost pines, on the rocks under which the sea
smote and sucked, facing the open where the bright sun gloried in
winter. The sea was dark, almost indigo, running away from the land,
and crested with white. The hand of the wind brushed it strangely
with shadow, as it brushed the olives of the slopes with silver. And
there was no boat out.

The three boats were drawn high up on the steep shingle of the
little bay, by the small grey tower. Along the edge of the shingle ran
a high wall, inside which was a garden occupying the brief flat of the
bay, then rising in terraces up the steep slope of the coast. And there,
some little way up, within another wall, stood the low white villa,
white and alone as the coast, overlooking the sea. But higher, much
higher up, where the olives had given way to pine trees again, ran the
coast road, keeping to the height to be above the gullies that came
down to the bays.

Upon it all poured the royal sunshine of the January afternoon. Or
rather, all was part of the great sun, glow and substance and
immaculate loneliness of the sea, and pure brightness.

Crouching in the rocks above the dark water, which only swung up
and down, two slaves, half naked, were dressing pigeons for the
evening meal. They pierced the throat of a blue, live bird, and let the
drops of blood fall into the heaving sea, with curious concentration.
They were performing some sacrifice, or working some incantation.
The woman of the temple, yellow and white and alone like a winter
narcissus, stood between the pines of the small, humped peninsula
where the temple secretly hid, and watched.

A black-and-white pigeon, vividly white, like a ghost escaped
over the low dark sea, sped out, caught the wind, tilted, rode,
soared, and swept over the pine trees, and wheeled away, a speck,
inland. It had escaped. The priestess heard the cry of the boy
slave, a garden slave of about seventeen. He raised his arms to
heaven in anger as the pigeon wheeled away, naked and angry
and young he held out his arms. Then he turned and seized the
girl in an access of rage, and beat her with his fist that was stained
with pigeon's blood. And she lay down with her face hidden,
passive and quivering. The woman who owned them watched.
And as she watched, she saw another onlooker, a stranger, in a
low, broad hat, and a cloak of grey homespun, a dark bearded
man standing on the little causeway of a rock that was the neck of
her temple peninsula. By the blowing of his dark-grey cloak she
saw him. And he saw her, on the rocks like a white-and-yellow
narcissus, because of the flutter of her white linen tunic, below

the yellow mantle of wool. And both of them watched the two slaves.

The boy suddenly left off beating the girl. He crouched over her, touching her, trying to make her speak. But she lay quite inert, face down on the smoothed rock. And he put his arms round her and lifted her, but she slipped back to earth like one dead, yet far too quickly for anything dead. The boy, desperate, caught her by the hips and hugged her to him, turning her over there. There she seemed inert, all her fight was in her shoulders. He twisted her over, intent and unconscious, and pushed his hands between her thighs, to push them apart. And in an instant he was covering her in the blind, frightened frenzy of a boy's first passion. Quick and frenzied his young body quivered naked on hers, blind, for a minute. Then it lay quite still, as if dead.

And then, in terror, he peeped up. He peeped round, and drew slowly to his feet, adjusting his loin-rag. He saw the stranger, and then he saw, on the rocks beyond, the lady of Isis, his mistress. And as he saw her, his whole body shrank and cowed, and with a strange cringing motion he scuttled lamely towards the door in the wall.

The girl sat up and looked after him. When she had seen him disappear, she too looked round. And she saw the stranger and the priestess. Then with a sullen movement she turned away, as if she had seen nothing, to the four dead pigeons and the knife, which lay there on the rock. And she began to strip the small feathers, so that they rose on the wind like dust.

The priestess turned away. Slaves! Let the overseer watch them. She was not interested. She went slowly through the pines again, back to the temple, which stood in the sun in a small clearing at the centre of the tongue of land. It was a small temple of wood, painted all pink and white and blue, having at the front four wooden pillars rising like stems to the swollen lotus-bud of Egypt at the top, supporting the roof and open, spiky lotus-flowers of the outer frieze, which went round under the eaves. Two low steps of stone led up to the platform before the pillars, and the chamber behind the pillars was open. There a low stone altar stood, with a few embers in its hollow, and the dark stain of blood in its end groove.

She knew her temple so well, for she had built it at her own expense, and tended it for seven years. There it stood, pink and white, like a flower in the little clearing, backed by blackish evergreen oaks; and the shadow of afternoon was already washing over its pillar bases.

She entered slowly, passing through to the dark inner chamber, lighted by a perfumed oil-flame. And once more she pushed shut the door, and once more she threw a few grains of incense on a brazier before the goddess, and once more she sat down before her goddess, in the almost-darkness, to muse, to go away into the dreams of the goddess.

It was Isis; but not Isis, Mother of Horus. It was Isis Bereaved, Isis in Search.[49] The goddess, in painted marble, lifted her face and strode, one thigh forward, through the frail fluting of her robe, in the anguish of bereavement and of search. She was looking for the fragments of the dead Osiris, dead and scattered asunder, dead, torn apart, and thrown in fragments over the wide world. And she must find his hands and his feet, his heart, his thighs, his head, his belly, she must gather him together and fold her arms round the re-assembled body till it became warm again, and roused to life, and could embrace her, and could fecundate her womb. And the strange rapture and anguish of search went on through the years, as she lifted her throat and her hollowed eyes looked inward, in the tormented ecstasy of seeking, and the delicate navel of her bud-like belly showed through the frail, girdled robe with the eternal asking, asking, of her search. And through the years she found him bit by bit, heart and head and limbs and body. And yet she had not found the last reality, the final clue to him, that alone could bring him really back to her. For she was Isis of the subtle lotus, the womb which waits submerged and in bud, waits for the touch of that other inward sun that streams its rays from the loins of the male Osiris.

This was the mystery the woman had served alone for seven years, since she was twenty, till now she was twenty-seven. Before, when she was young, she had lived in the world, in Rome, in Ephesus, in Egypt. For her father had been one of Antony's captains and comrades, had fought with Antony[50] and had stood with him when Caesar was murdered, and through to the days of shame. Then he had come again across to Asia, out of favour with Rome, and had been killed in the mountains beyond Lebanon. The widow, having no favour to hope for from Octavius, had retired to her small property on the coast under Lebanon, taking her daughter from the world, a girl of nineteen, beautiful but unmarried.

When she was young the girl had known Caesar, and had shrunk from his eagle-like rapacity. The golden Antony had sat with her many a half-hour, in the splendour of his great limbs and glowing manhood, and talked with her of the philosophies and the gods. For he was fascinated as a child by the gods, though he mocked at them, and forgot them in his own vanity. But he said to her: 'I have sacrificed two doves for you, to Venus,[51] for I am afraid you make no offering to the sweet goddess. Beware you will offend her. Come, why is the flower of you so cool within? Does never a ray nor a glance find its way through? Ah, come, a maid should open to the sun, when the sun leans towards her to caress her.'

And the big, bright eyes of Antony laughed down on her, bathing her in his glow. And she felt the lovely glow of his male beauty and his amorousness bathe all her limbs and her body. But it was as he said: the very flower of her womb was cool, was almost cold, like a bud in shadow of frost, for all the flooding of his sunshine. So Antony, respecting her father, who loved her, had left her.

And it had always been the same. She saw many men, young and old. And on the whole, she liked the old ones best, for they talked to her still and sincere, and did not expect her to open like a flower to the sun of their maleness.

Once she asked a philosopher: 'Are all women born to be given to men?' To which the old man answered slowly: 'Rare women wait for the reborn man. For the lotus, as you know, will not answer to all the bright heat of the sun. But she curves her dark, hidden head in the depths, and stirs not. Till, in the night, one of these rare, invisible suns that have been killed and shine no more, rises among the stars in unseen purple, and like the violet, sends its rare purple rays out into the night. To these the lotus stirs as to a caress, and rises upwards through the flood, and lifts up her bent head, and opens with an expansion such as no other flower knows, and spreads her sharp rays of bliss, and offers her soft, gold depths such as no other flower possesses, to the penetration of the flooding, violet-dark sun that has died and risen and makes no show. But for the golden brief day-suns of show, such as Antony, and for the hard winter suns of power, such as Caesar, the lotus stirs not, nor will ever stir. Those will only tear open the bud. Ah, I tell you, wait for the reborn and wait for the bud to stir.'

So she had waited. For all the men were soldiers or politicians in the Roman spell, assertive, manly, splendid apparently but of an inward meanness, an inadequacy. And Rome and Egypt alike had left her alone, unroused. And she was a woman to herself, she would not give herself for a surface glow, nor marry for reasons. She would wait for the lotus to stir.

And then, in Egypt, she had found Isis, in whom she spelled her mystery. She had brought Isis to the shores of Sidon, and lived with her in the mystery of search; whilst her mother, who loved affairs, controlled the small estate and the slaves with a free hand.

When the woman had roused from her muse and risen to perform the last brief ritual to Isis, she replenished the lamp and left the sanctuary, locking the door. In the outer world, the sun had already set, and twilight was chill among the humming trees, which hummed still, though the wind was abating.

A stranger in a dark, broad hat rose from the corner of the temple steps, holding his hat in the wind. He was dark-faced, with a black pointed beard. 'Oh, madam, whose shelter may I implore?' he said to the woman, who stood in her yellow mantle on a step above him, beside a pink-and-white painted pillar. Her face was rather long and pale, her dusky blonde hair was held under a thin gold net. She looked down on the vagabond with indifference. It was the same she had seen watching the slaves.

'Why come you down from the road?' she asked.

'I saw the temple like a pale flower on the coast, and would rest among the trees of the precincts, if the lady of the goddess permits.'

'It is Isis in Search,' she said, answering his first question.

'The goddess is great,' he replied.

She looked at him still with mistrust. There was a faint, remote smile in the dark eyes lifted to her, though the face was hollow with suffering. The vagabond divined her hesitation, and was mocking her.

'Stay here upon the steps,' she said. 'A slave will show you the shelter.'

'The lady of Egypt is gracious.'

She went down the rocky path of the humped peninsula in her gilded sandals. Beautiful were her ivory feet, beneath the white tunic, and above the saffron mantle her dusky-blonde head bent as with endless musings. A woman entangled in her own dream. The man smiled a little, half bitterly, and sat again on the step to wait, drawing his mantle round him, in the cold twilight.

At length a slave appeared, also in hodden[52] grey.

'Seek ye the shelter of our lady?' he said insolently.

'Even so.'

'Then come.'

With the brusque insolence of a slave waiting on a vagabond, the young fellow led through the trees and down into a little gully in the rock, where, almost in darkness, was a small cave, with a litter of the tall heaths that grew on the waste places of the coast, under the stone-pines. The place was dark, but absolutely silent from the wind. There was still a faint odour of goats.

'Here sleep!' said the slave. 'For the goats come no more on this half-island. And there is water!' He pointed to a little basin of rock where the maidenhair fern fringed a dripping mouthful of water.

Having scornfully bestowed his patronage, the slave departed. The man who had died climbed out to the tip of the peninsula, where the wave thrashed. It was rapidly getting dark, and the stars were coming out. The wind was abating for the night. Inland, the steep grooved up-slope was dark to the long wavering outline of the crest against the translucent sky. Only now and then a lantern flickered towards the villa.

The man who had died went back to the shelter. There he took bread from his leather pouch, dipped it in the water of the tiny spring, and slowly ate. Having eaten and washed his mouth, he looked once more at the bright stars in the pure windy sky, then settled the heath for his bed. Having laid his hat and his sandals aside, and put his pouch under his cheek for a pillow, he slept, for he was very tired. Yet during the night the cold woke him pinching wearily through his weariness. Outside was brilliantly starry, and still windy. He sat and hugged himself in a sort of coma, and towards dawn went to sleep again.

In the morning the coast was still chill in shadow, though the sun was up behind the hills, when the woman came down from the villa towards the goddess. The sea was fair and pale blue, lovely in newness, and at last the wind was still. Yet the waves broke white in the many rocks, and tore in the shingle of the little bay. The woman came slowly towards her dream. Yet she was aware of an interruption.

As she followed the little neck of rock on to her peninsula, and climbed the slope between the trees to the temple, a slave came down and stood, making his obeisance. There was a faint insolence in his humility. 'Speak!' she said.

'Lady, the man is there, he still sleeps. Lady, may I speak?'

'Speak!' she said, repelled by the fellow.

'Lady, the man is an escaped malefactor.'

The slave seemed to triumph in imparting the unpleasant news.

'By what sign?'

'Behold his hands and feet! Will the lady look on him?'

'Lead on!'

The slave led quickly over the mound of the hill down to the tiny ravine. There he stood aside, and the woman went into the crack towards the cave. Her heart beat a little. Above all, she must preserve her temple inviolate.

The vagabond was asleep with his cheek on his scrip,[53] his mantle wrapped round him, but his bare, soiled feet curling side by side, to keep each other warm, and his hand lying clenched in sleep. And in the pale skin of his feet usually covered by sandal-straps, she saw the scars, and in the palm of the loose hand.

She had no interest in men, particularly in the servile class. Yet she looked at the sleeping face. It was worn, hollow, and rather ugly. But, a true priestess, she saw the other kind of beauty in it, the sheer stillness of the deeper life. There was even a sort of majesty in the dark brows, over the still, hollow cheeks. She saw that his black hair, left long, in contrast to the Roman fashion, was touched with grey at the temples, and the black pointed beard had threads of grey. But that must be suffering or misfortune, for the man was young. His dusky skin had the silvery glisten of youth still.

There was a beauty of much suffering, and the strange calm candour of finer life in the whole delicate ugliness of the face. For the first time, she was touched on the quick at the sight of a man, as if the tip of a fine flame of living had touched her. It was the first time. Men had roused all kinds of feeling in her, but never had touched her with the flame-tip of life.

She went back under the rock to where the slave waited.

'Know!' she said. 'This is no malefactor, but a free citizen of the east. Do not disturb him. But when he comes forth, bring him to me; tell him I would speak with him.'

She spoke coldly, for she found slaves invariably repellent, a little repulsive. They were so embedded in the lesser life, and their appetites and their small consciousness were a little disgusting. So she wrapped her dream round her and went to the temple, where a slave girl brought winter roses and jasmine for the altar. But today, even in her ministrations, she was disturbed.

The sun rose over the hill, sparkling, the light fell triumphantly on the little pine-covered peninsula of the coast, and on the pink temple, in the pristine newness. The man who had died woke up, and put on his sandals. He put on his hat too, slung his scrip under his mantle, and went out, to see the morning in all its blue and its new gold. He glanced at the little yellow-and-white narcissus sparkling gaily in the rocks. And he saw the slave waiting for him like a menace.

'Master!' said the slave. 'Our lady would speak with you at the house of Isis.'

'It is well,' said the wanderer.

He went slowly, staying to look at the pale blue sea like a flower in unruffled bloom, and the white fringes among the rocks, like white rock-flowers, the hollow slopes sheering up high from the shore, grey with olive trees and green with bright young wheat, and set with the white, small villa. All fair and pure in the January morning.

The sun fell on the corner of the temple, he sat down on the step in the sunshine, in the infinite patience of waiting. He had come back to life, but not the same life that he had left, the life of little people and the little day. Reborn, he was in the other life, the greater day of the human consciousness. And he was alone and apart from the little day, and out of contact with the daily people. Not yet had he accepted the irrevocable *noli me tangere* which separates the reborn from the vulgar. The separation was absolute, as yet here at the temple he felt peace, the hard, bright pagan peace with hostility of slaves beneath.

The woman came into the dark inner doorway of the temple from the shrine, and stood there, hesitating. She could see the dark figure of the man, sitting in that terrible stillness that was portentous to her, had something almost menacing in its patience.

She advanced across the outer chamber of the temple, and the man, becoming aware of her, stood up. She addressed him in Greek, but he said: 'Madam, my Greek is limited. Allow me to speak vulgar Syrian.'

'Whence come you? Whither go you?' she asked, with a hurried preoccupation of a priestess.

'From the east beyond Damascus – and I go west as the road goes,' he replied slowly.

She glanced at him with sudden anxiety and shyness.

'But why do you have the marks of a malefactor?' she asked abruptly.

'Did the Lady of Isis spy upon me in my sleep?' he asked, with a grey weariness.

'The slave warned me – your hands and feet – ' she said.

He looked at her. Then he said: 'Will the Lady of Isis allow me to bid her farewell, and go up to the road?'

The wind came in a sudden puff, lifting his mantle and his hat. He put up his hand to hold the brim, and she saw again the thin brown hand with its scar.

'See! The scar!' she said, pointing.

'Even so!' he said. 'But farewell, and to Isis my homage and my thanks for sleep.'

He was going. But she looked up at him with her wondering blue eyes.

'Will you not look at Isis?' she said, with sudden impulse. And something stirred in him, like pain.

'Where then?' he said.

'Come!'

He followed her into the inner shrine, into the almost-darkness. When his eyes got used to the faint glow of the lamp, he saw the goddess striding like a ship, eager in the swirl of her gown, and he made his obeisance.

'Great is Isis!' he said. 'In her search she is greater than death. Wonderful is such walking in a woman, wonderful the goal. All men praise thee, Isis, thou greater than the mother unto man.'

The woman of Isis heard, and threw incense on the brazier. Then she looked at the man.

'Is it well with thee here?' she asked him. 'Has Isis brought thee home to herself?'

He looked at the priestess in wonder and trouble.

'I know not,' he said.

But the woman was pondering that this was the lost Osiris. She felt in the quick of her soul. And her agitation was intense.

He would not stay in the close, dark, perfumed shrine. He went out again to the morning, to the cold air. He felt something approaching to touch him, and all his flesh was still woven with pain and the wild commandment: *Noli me tangere!* Touch me not! Oh, don't touch me!

The woman followed into the open with timid eagerness. He was moving away.

'Oh, stranger, do not go! Oh, stay a while with Isis!'

He looked at her, at her face open like a flower, as if a sun had risen in her soul. And again his loins stirred.

'Would you detain me, girl of Isis?' he said.

'Stay! I am sure you are Osiris!' she said.

He laughed suddenly. 'Not yet!' he said. Then he looked at her wistful face. 'But I will sleep another night in the cave of the goats, if Isis wills it,' he added.

She put her hands together with a priestess's childish happiness.

'Ah! Isis will be glad!' she said.

So he went down to the shore in great trouble, saying to himself: 'Shall I give myself into this touch? Shall I give myself into this touch? Men have tortured me to death with their touch. Yet this girl of Isis is a tender flame of healing. I am a physician, yet I have no healing like the flame of this tender girl. The flame of this tender girl! Like the first pale crocus of the spring. How could I have been blind to the healing and the bliss in the crocus-like body of a tender woman! Ah, tenderness! More terrible and lovely than the death I died – '

He pried small shellfish from the rocks, and ate them with relish and wonder for the simple taste of the sea. And inwardly he was tremulous, thinking: 'Dare I come into touch? For this is farther than death. I have dared to let them lay hands on me and put me to death. But dare I come into this tender touch of life? Oh, this is harder – '

But the woman went into the shrine again, and sat rapt in pure muse, through the long hours, watching the swirling stride of the yearning goddess, and the navel of the bud-like belly, like a seal on the virgin urge of the search. And she gave herself to the woman-flow and to the urge of Isis in Search.

Towards sundown she went on the peninsula to look for him. And she found him gone towards the sun, as she had gone the day before, and sitting on the pine-needles at the foot of the tree, where she had stood when first she saw him. Now she approached tremulously and slowly, afraid lest he did not want her. She stood near him unseen, till suddenly he glanced up at her from under his broad hat, and saw the westering sun on her netted hair. He was startled, yet he expected her.

'Is that your home?' he said, pointing to the white, low villa on the slope of olives.

'It is my mother's house. She is a widow, and I am her only child.'

'And are these all her slaves?'

'Except those that are mine.'

Their eyes met for a moment.

'Will you too sit to see the sun go down?' he said.

He had not risen to speak to her. He had known too much pain. So she sat on the dry brown pine-needles, gathering her saffron mantle round her knees. A boat was coming in, out of the open glow into the shadow of the bay, and slaves were lifting small nets, their babble coming off the surface of the water.

'And this is home to you,' he said.

'But I serve Isis in Search,' she replied.

He looked at her. She was like a soft, musing cloud, somehow remote. His soul smote him with passion and compassion.

'Mayst thou find thy desire, maiden,' he said, with sudden earnestness.

'And art thou not Osiris?' she asked.

He flushed suddenly.

'Yes, if thou wilt heal me!' he said. 'For the death aloofness is still upon me, and I cannot escape it.'

She looked at him for a moment in fear from the soft blue sun of her eyes. Then she lowered her head, and they sat in silence in the warmth and glow of the western sun: the man who had died, and the woman of the pure search.

The sun was curving down to the sea, in grand winter splendour. It fell on the twinkling, naked bodies of the slaves, with their ruddy

broad hams and their small black heads, as they ran spreading the
nets on the pebble beach. The all-tolerant Pan[54] watched over them.
All-tolerant Pan should be their god for ever.

The woman rose as the sun's rim dipped, saying: 'If you will stay, I
shall send down victual and covering.'

'The lady your mother, what will she say?'

The woman of Isis looked at him strangely, but with a tinge of
misgiving.

'It is my own,' she said.

'It is good,' he said, smiling faintly and foreseeing difficulties.

He watched her go, with her absorbed, strange motion of the self-
dedicate. Her dun head was a little bent, the white linen swung about
her ivory ankles. And he saw the naked slaves stand to look at her,
with a certain wonder, and even a certain mischief. But she passed
intent through the door in the wall, on the bay.

The man who had died sat on at the foot of the tree overlooking
the strand, for on the little shore everything happened. At the small
stream which ran in round the corner of the property wall, women
slaves were still washing linen, and now and again came the hollow
chock! chock! chock! as they beat it against the smooth stones in the
dark little hollow of the pool. There was a smell of olive refuse on the
air; and sometimes still the faint rumble of the grindstone that was
milling the olives, inside the garden, and the sound of the slave
calling to the ass at the mill. Then through the doorway a woman
stepped, a grey-haired woman in a mantle of whitish wool, and there
followed her a bare-headed man in a toga, a Roman: probably her
steward or overseer. They stood on the high shingle above the sea,
and cast round a rapid glance. The broad-hammed, ruddy-bodied
slaves bent absorbed and abject over the nets, picking them clean, the
women washing linen thrust their palms with energy down on the
wash, the old slave bent absorbed at the water's edge, washing the
fish and the polyps of the catch. And the woman and the overseer saw
it all in one glance. They also saw, seated at the foot of the tree on the
rocks of the peninsula, the strange man silent and alone. And the man
who had died saw that they spoke of him. Out of the little sacred
world of the peninsula he looked on the common world, and saw it
still hostile.

The sun was touching the sea, across the tiny bay stretched the
shadow of the opposite humped headland. Over the shingle, now
blue and cold in shadow, the elderly woman trod heavily, in
shadow too, to look at the fish spread in the flat basket of the old
man crouching at the water's edge: a naked old slave with fat hips

and shoulders, on whose soft, fairish-orange body the last sun twinkled, then died. The old slave continued cleaning the fish absorbedly, not looking up: as if the lady were the shadow of twilight falling on him.

Then from the gateway stepped two slave-girls with flat baskets on their heads, and from one basket the terracotta wine-jar and the oil-jar poked up, leaning slightly. Over the massive shingle, under the wall, came the girls, and the woman of Isis in her saffron mantle stepped in twilight after them. Out at sea, the sun still shone. Here was shadow. The mother with grey head stood at the sea's edge and watched the daughter, all yellow and white, with dun blonde head, swinging unseeing and unheeding after the slave-girls, towards the neck of rock of the peninsula; the daughter, travelling in her absorbed other-world. And not moving from her place, the elderly mother watched that procession of three file up the rise of the headland, between the trees, and disappear, shut in by trees. No slave had lifted a head to look. The grey-haired woman still watched the trees where her daughter had disappeared. Then she glanced again at the foot of the tree, where the man who had died was still sitting, inconspicuous now, for the sun had left him; and only the far blade of the sea shone bright. It was evening. Patience! Let destiny move!

The mother plodded with a stamping stride up the shingle: not long and swinging and rapt, like the daughter, but short and determined. Then down the rocks opposite came two naked slaves trotting with huge bundles of dark green on their shoulders, so their broad, naked legs twinkled underneath like insects' legs, and their heads were hidden. They came trotting across the shingle, heedless and intent on their way, when suddenly the man, the Roman-looking overseer, addressed them, and they stopped dead. They stood invisible under their loads, as if they might disappear altogether, now they were arrested. Then a hand came out and pointed to the peninsula. Then the two green-heaped slaves trotted on, towards the temple precincts. The grey-haired woman joined the man, and slowly the two passed through the door again, from the shingle of the sea to the property of the villa. Then the old, fat-shouldered slave rose, pallid in the shadow, with his tray of fish from the sea, and the woman rose from the pool, dusky and alive, piling the wet linen in a heap on to the flat baskets, and the slaves who had cleaned the net gathered its whitish folds together. And the old slave with the fish-basket on his shoulder, and the women-slaves with the heaped baskets of wet linen on their heads, and the two slaves with the folded net, and the slave with oars on his shoulders, and the boy with the folded sail on his arm, gathered in a naked group near the door, and the man who had died heard the low buzz of their chatter. Then as the wind wafted cold, they began to pass through the door.

It was the life of the little day, the life of little people. And the man who had died said to himself: 'Unless we encompass it in the greater day, and set the little life in the circle of the greater life, all is disaster.'

Even the tops of the hills were in shadow. Only the sky was still upwardly radiant. The sea was a vast milky shadow. The man who had died rose a little stiffly and turned into the grove.

There was no one at the temple. He went on to his lair in the rock. There, the slave-men had carried out the old heath of the bedding, swept the rock floor, and were spreading with nice art the myrtle, then the rougher heath, then the soft, bushy heath-tips on top, for a bed. Over it all they put a well-tanned white ox-skin. The maids had laid folded woollen covers at the head of the cave, and the wine-jar, the oil-jar, a terracotta drinking-cup and a basket containing bread, salt, cheese, dried figs, and eggs stood neatly arranged. There was also a little brazier of charcoal. The cave was suddenly full, and a dwelling-place.

The woman of Isis stood in the hollow by the tiny spring.

Only one slave at a time could pass. The girl-slaves waited at the entrance to the narrow place. When the man who had died appeared, the woman sent the girls away. The men-slaves still arranged the bed, making the job as long as possible. But the woman of Isis dismissed them too. And the man who had died came to look at his house.

'Is it well?' the woman asked him.

'It is very well,' the man replied. 'But the lady, your mother, and he who is no doubt the steward, watched while the slaves brought the goods. Will they not oppose you?'

'I have my own portion! Can I not give of my own? Who is going to oppose me and the gods?' she said, with a certain soft fury, touched with exasperation. So that he knew that her mother would oppose her, and that the spirit of the little life would fight against the spirit of the greater. And he thought: 'Why did the woman of Isis relinquish her portion in the daily world? She should have kept her goods fiercely!'

'Will you eat and drink?' she said. 'On the ashes are warm eggs. And I will go up to the meal at the villa. But in the second hour of the night I shall come down to the temple. Oh, then, will you come too to Isis?' She looked at him, and a queer glow dilated her eyes. This was her dream, and it was greater than herself. He could not bear to thwart her or hurt her in the least thing now. She was in the full glow of her woman's mystery.

'Shall I wait at the temple?' he said.

'Oh, wait at the second hour and I shall come.' He heard the humming supplication in her voice and his fibres quivered.

'But the lady, your mother?' he said gently.

The woman looked at him, startled.

'She will not thwart me!' she said.

So he knew that the mother would thwart the daughter, for the daughter had left her goods in the hands of her mother, who would hold fast to this power.

But she went, and the man who had died lay reclining on his couch, and ate the eggs from the ashes, and dipped his bread in oil, and ate it, for his flesh was dry: and he mixed wine and water, and drank. And so he lay still, and the lamp made a small bud of light. He was absorbed and enmeshed in new sensations. The woman of Isis was lovely to him, not so much in form as in the wonderful womanly glow of her. Suns beyond suns had dipped her in mysterious fire, the mysterious fire of a potent woman, and to touch her was like touching the sun. Best of all was her tender desire for him, like sunshine, so soft and still.

'She is like sunshine upon me,' he said to himself, stretching his limbs. 'I have never before stretched my limbs in such sunshine, as her desire for me. The greatest of all gods granted me this.'

At the same time he was haunted by the fear of the outer world. 'If they can, they will kill us,' he said to himself. 'But there is a law of the sun which protects us.'

And again he said to himself: 'I have risen naked and branded. But if I am naked enough for this contact, I have not died in vain. Before I was clogged.'

He rose and went out. The night was chill and starry, and of a great wintry splendour. 'There are destinies of splendour,' he said to the night, 'after all our doom of littleness and meanness and pain.'

So he went up silently to the temple, and waited in darkness against the inner wall, looking out on a grey darkness, stars, and rims of trees. And he said again to himself: 'There are destinies of splendour, and there is a greater power.'

So at last he saw the light of her silk lanthorn swinging, coming intermittent between the trees, yet coming swiftly. She was alone, and near, the light softly swishing on her mantle-hem. And he trembled with fear and with joy, saying to himself: 'I am almost more afraid of this touch than I was of death. For I am more nakedly exposed to it.'

'I am here, Lady of Isis,' he said softly out of the dark.

'Ah!' she cried, in fear also, yet in rapture. For she was given to her dream.

She unlocked the door of the shrine, and he followed after her. Then she latched the door shut again. The air inside was warm and close and perfumed. The man who had died stood by the closed door and watched the woman. She had come first to the goddess. And dim-lit, the goddess-statue stood surging forward, a little fearsome like a great woman-presence urging.

The priestess did not look at him. She took off her saffron mantle and laid it on a low couch. In the dim light she was bare armed, in her girdled white tunic. But she was still hiding herself away from him. He stood back in shadow and watched her softly fan the brazier and fling on incense. Faint clouds of sweet aroma arose on the air. She turned to the statue in the ritual of approach, softly swaying forward with a slight lurch, like a moored boat, tipping towards the goddess.

He watched the strange rapt woman, and he said to himself: 'I must leave her alone in her rapture, her female mysteries.' So she tipped in her strange forward-swaying rhythm before the goddess. Then she broke into a murmur of Greek, which he could not understand. And, as she murmured, her swaying softly subsided, like a boat on a sea that grows still. And as he watched her, he saw her soul in its aloneness, and its female difference. He said to himself: 'How different she is from me, how strangely different! She is afraid of me, and my male difference. She is getting herself naked and clear of her fear. How sensitive and softly alive she is, with a life, so different from mine! How beautiful with a soft, strange courage, of life so different from my courage of death! What a beautiful thing like the heart of a rose, like the core of a flame. She is making herself completely penetrable. Ah! how terrible to fail her, or to trespass on her!'

She turned to him, her face glowing from the goddess.

'You are Osiris, aren't you?' she said naïvely.

'If you will,' he said.

'Will you let Isis discover you? Will you not take off your things?'

He looked at the woman, and lost his breath. And his wounds, and especially the death-wound through his belly, began to cry again.

'It has hurt so much!' he said. 'You must forgive me if I am still held back.'

But he took off his cloak and his tunic and went naked towards the idol, his breast panting with the sudden terror of overwhelming pain, memory of overwhelming pain, and grief too bitter.

'They did me to death!' he said in excuse of himself, turning his face to her for a moment.

And she saw the ghost of the death in him as he stood there thin and stark before her, and suddenly she was terrified, and she felt robbed. She felt the shadow of the grey, grisly wing of death triumphant.

'Ah, goddess,' he said to the idol in the vernacular. 'I would be so glad to live, if you would give me my clue again.'

For her again he felt desperate, faced by the demand of life, and burdened still by his death.

'Let me anoint you!' the woman said to him softly. 'Let me anoint the scars! Show me, and let me anoint them!'

He forgot his nakedness in this re-evoked old pain. He sat on the edge of the couch, and she poured a little ointment into the palm of his hand. And as she chafed his hand, it all came back, the nails, the holes, the cruelty, the unjust cruelty against him who had offered only kindness. The agony of injustice and cruelty came over him again, as in his death-hour. But she chafed the palm, murmuring: 'What was torn becomes a new flesh, what was a wound is full of fresh life; this scar is the eye of the violet.'

And he could not help smiling at her, in her naïve priestess's absorption. This was her dream, and he was only a dream-object to her. She would never know or understand what he was. Especially she would never know the death that was gone before in him. But what did it matter? She was different. She was woman: her life and her death were different from him. Only she was good to him.

When she chafed his feet with oil and tender, tender healing, he could not refrain from saying to her: 'Once a woman washed my feet with tears, and wiped them with her hair, and poured on precious ointment.'

The woman of Isis looked up at him from her earnest work, interrupted again.

'Were they hurt then?' she said. 'Your feet?'

'No, no! It was while they were whole.'

'And did you love her?'

'Love had passed in her. She only wanted to serve,' he replied. 'She had been a prostitute.'

'And did you let her serve you?' she asked.

'Yea.'

'Did you let her serve you with the corpse of her love?'

'Ay!'

Suddenly it dawned on him: I asked them all to serve me with the corpse of their love. And in the end I offered them only the corpse of my love. This is my body – take and eat my corpse –

A vivid shame went through him. 'After all,' he thought, 'I wanted them to love with dead bodies. If I had kissed Judas with live love, perhaps he would never have kissed me with death. Perhaps he loved me in the flesh, and I will that he should love me bodylessly, with the corpse of love – '

There dawned on him the reality of the soft, warm love which is in touch, and which is full of delight. 'And I told them, blessed are they that mourn,' he said to himself. 'Alas if I mourned even this woman here, now I am in death, I should have to remain dead, and I want so much to live. Life has brought me to this woman with warm hands. And her touch is more to me now than all my words. For I want to live – '

'Go then to the goddess!' she said softly, gently pushing him towards Isis. And as he stood there dazed and naked as an unborn thing, he heard the woman murmuring to the goddess, murmuring, murmuring with a plaintive appeal. She was stooping now, looking at the scar in the soft flesh of the socket of his side, a scar deep and like an eye sore with endless weeping, just in the soft socket above the hip. It was here that his blood had left him, and his essential seed. The woman was trembling softly and murmuring in Greek. And he in the recurring dismay of having died, and in the anguished perplexity of having tried to force life, felt his wounds crying aloud, and the deep places of the body howling again: 'I have been murdered, and I lent myself to murder. They murdered me, but I lent myself to murder – '

The woman, silent now, but quivering, laid oil in her hand and put her palm over the wound in his right side. He winced, and the wound absorbed his life again, as thousands of times before. And in the dark, wild pain and panic of his consciousness rang only one cry: 'Oh, how can she take this death out of me? She can never know! She can never understand! She can never equal it! . . . '

In silence, she softly rhythmically chafed the scar with oil. Absorbed now in her priestess's task, softly, softly gathering power, while the vitals of the man howled in panic. But as she gradually gathered power, and passed in a girdle round him to the opposite scar, gradually warmth began to take the place of the cold terror, and he felt: 'I am going to be warm again, and I am going to be whole! I shall be warm like the morning. I shall be a man. It doesn't need understanding. It needs newness. She brings me newness – '

And he listened to the faint, ceaseless wail of distress of his wounds, sounding as if for ever under the horizons of his consciousness. But the wail was growing dim, more dim.

He thought of the woman toiling over him: 'She does not know! She does not realise the death in me. But she has another consciousness. She comes to me from the opposite end of the night.'

Having chafed all his lower body with oil, having worked with her slow intensity of a priestess, so that the sound of his wounds grew dimmer and dimmer, suddenly she put her breast against the wound in his left side, and her arms round him, folding over the wound in his right side, and she pressed him to her, in a power of living warmth, like the folds of a river. And the wailing died out altogether, and there was a stillness, and darkness in his soul, unbroken, dark stillness, wholeness.

Then slowly, slowly, in the perfect darkness of his inner man, he felt the stir of something coming. A dawn, a new sun. A new sun was coming up in him, in the perfect inner darkness of himself. He waited for it breathless, quivering with a fearful hope . . . 'Now I am not myself. I am something new . . . '

And as it rose, he felt, with a cold breath of disappointment, the girdle of the living woman slip down from him, the warmth and the glow slipped from him, leaving him stark. She crouched, spent, at the feet of the goddess, hiding her face.

Stooping, he laid his hand softly on her warm, bright shoulder, and the shock of desire went through him, shock after shock, so that he wondered if it were another sort of death: but full of magnificence.

Now all his consciousness was there in the crouching, hidden woman. He stooped beside her and caressed her softly, blindly, murmuring inarticulate things. And his death and his passion of sacrifice were all as nothing to him now, he knew only the crouching fullness of the woman there, the soft white rock of life . . . 'On this rock I built my life.'[55] The deep-folded, penetrable rock of the living woman! The woman, hiding her face. Himself bending over, powerful and new like dawn.

He crouched to her, and he felt the blaze of his manhood and his power rise up in his loins, magnificent.

'I am risen!'

Magnificent, blazing indomitable in the depths of his loins, his own sun dawned, and sent its fire running along his limbs, so that his face shone unconsciously.

He untied the string on the linen tunic and slipped the garment down, till he saw the white glow of her white-gold breasts. And he touched them, and he felt his life go molten. 'Father!' he said, 'why did you hide this from me?' And he touched her with the poignancy of wonder, and the marvellous piercing transcendence of desire. 'Lo!' he said, 'this is beyond prayer.' It was the deep, interfolded warmth,

warmth living and penetrable, the woman, the heart of the rose! My mansion is the intricate warm rose, my joy is this blossom!

She looked up at him suddenly, her face like a lifted light, wistful, tender, her eyes like many wet flowers. And he drew her to his breast with a passion of tenderness and consuming desire, and the last thought: 'My hour is upon me, I am taken unawares – '

So he knew her, and was one with her.

Afterwards, with a dim wonder, she touched the great scars in his sides with her fingertips, and said: 'But they no longer hurt?'

'They are suns!' he said. 'They shine from your torch. They are my atonement with you.'

And when they left the temple, it was the coldness before dawn. As he closed the door, he looked again at the goddess, and he said: 'Lo, Isis is a kindly goddess; and full of tenderness. Great gods are warm-hearted, and have tender goddesses.'

The woman wrapped herself in her mantle and went home in silence, sightless, brooding like the lotus softly shutting again, with its gold core full of fresh life. She saw nothing, for her own petals were a sheath to her. Only she thought: 'I am full of Osiris. I am full of the risen Osiris! . . . '

But the man looked at the vivid stars before dawn, as they rained down to the sea, and the dog-star green towards the sea's rim. And he thought: 'How plastic it is, how full of curves and folds like an invisible rose of dark-petalled openness that shows where the dew touches its darkness! How full it is, and great beyond all gods. How it leans around me, and I am part of it, the great rose of Space. I am like a grain of its perfume, and the woman is a grain of its beauty. Now the world is one flower of many petalled darknesses, and I am in its perfume as in a touch.'

So, in the absolute stillness and fullness of touch, he slept in his cave while the dawn came. And after the dawn, the wind rose and brought a storm, with cold rain. So he stayed in his cave in the peace and the delight of being in touch, delighting to hear the sea, and the rain on the earth, and to see one white-and-gold narcissus bowing wet, and still wet. And he said: 'This is the great atonement, the being in touch. The grey sea and the rain, the wet narcissus and the woman I wait for, the invisible Isis and the unseen sun are all in touch, and at one.'

He waited at the temple for the woman, and she came in the rain. But she said to him: 'Let me sit awhile with Isis. And come to me, will you come to me, in the second hour of night?'

So he went back to the cave and lay in stillness and in the joy of being in touch, waiting for the woman who would come with the night, and consummate again the contact. Then when night came the woman came, and came gladly, for her great yearning, too, was upon her, to be in touch, to be in touch with him, nearer.

So the days came, and the nights came, and days came again, and the contact was perfected and fulfilled. And he said: 'I will ask her nothing, not even her name, for a name would set her apart.'

And she said to herself: 'He is Osiris. I wish to know no more.'

Plum blossom blew from the trees, the time of the narcissus was past, anemones lit up the ground and were gone, the perfume of bean-field was in the air. All changed, the blossom of the universe changed its petals and swung round to look another way. The spring was fulfilled, a contact was established, the man and the woman were fulfilled of one another, and departure was in the air.

One day he met her under the trees, when the morning sun was hot, and the pines smelled sweet, and on the hills the last pear blossom was scattering. She came slowly towards him and in her gentle lingering, her tender hanging back from him he knew a change in her.

'Hast thou conceived?' he asked her.

'Why?' she said.

'Thou art like a tree whose green leaves follow the blossom full of sap. And there is a withdrawing about thee.'

'It is so,' she said. 'I am with young by thee. Is it good?'

'Yes!' he said. 'How should it not be good? So the nightingale calls no more from the valley-bed. But where wilt thou bear the child, for I am naked of all but life?'

'We will stay here,' she said.

'But the lady, your mother?'

A shadow crossed her brow. She did not answer

'What when she knows?' he said.

'She begins to know.'

'And would she hurt you?'

'Ah, not me! What I have is all my own. And I shall be big with Osiris . . . But thou, do you watch her slaves.'

She looked at him, and the peace of her maternity was troubled by anxiety.

'Let not your heart be troubled!' he said. 'I have died the death once.'

So he knew the time was come again for him to depart. He would go alone, with his destiny. Yet not alone, for the touch would be upon him, even as he left his touch on her. And invisible suns would go with him.

Yet he must go. For here on the bay the little life of jealousy and property was resuming sway again, as the suns of passionate fecundity relaxed their sway. In the name of property, the widow and her slaves would seek to be revenged on him for the bread he had eaten, and the living touch he had established, the woman he had delighted in. But he said: 'Not twice. They shall not now profane the touch in me. My wits against theirs.'

So he watched. And he knew they plotted. So he moved from the little cave and found another shelter, a tiny cove of sand by the sea, dry and secret under the rocks.

He said to the woman: 'I must go now soon. Trouble is coming to me from the slaves. But I am a man, and the world is open. But what is between us is good, and is established. Be at peace. And when the nightingale calls again from your valley-bed, I shall come again, sure as spring.'

She said: 'Oh, don't go! Stay with me on half the island, and I will build a house for you and me under the pine trees by the temple, where we can live apart.'

Yet she knew that he would go. And even she wanted the coolness of her own air around her, and the release from anxiety.

'If I stay,' he said, 'they will betray me to the Romans and to their justice. But I will never be betrayed again. So when I am gone, live in peace with the growing child. And I shall come again: all is good between us, near or apart. The suns come back in their seasons: and I shall come again.'

'Do not go yet,' she said. 'I have set a slave to watch at the neck of the peninsula. Do not go yet, till the harm shows.'

But as he lay in his little cove, on a calm, still night, he heard the soft knock of oars, and the bump of a boat against the rock. So he crept out to listen. And he heard the Roman overseer say: 'Lead softly to the goat's den. And Lysippus shall throw the net over the malefactor while he sleeps, and we will bring him before justice, and the Lady of Isis shall know nothing of it . . . '

The man who had died caught a whiff of flesh from the oiled and naked slaves as they crept up, then the faint perfume of the Roman. He crept nearer to the sea. The slave who sat in the boat sat motionless, holding the oars, for the sea was quite still. And the man who had died knew him.

So out of the deep cleft of a rock he said, in a clear voice: 'Art thou not that slave who possessed the maiden under the eyes of Isis? Art thou not the youth? Speak!'

The youth stood up in the boat in terror. His movement sent the boat bumping against the rock. The slave sprang out in wild fear, and fled up the rocks. The man who had died quickly seized the boat and stepped in, and pushed off. The oars were yet warm with the unpleasant warmth of the hands of the slaves. But the man pulled slowly out, to get into the current, which set down the coast and would carry him in silence. The high coast was utterly dark against the starry night. There was no glimmer from the peninsula: the priestess came no more at night. The man who had died rowed slowly on, with the current, and laughed to himself: 'I have sowed the seed of my life and my resurrection, and put m   middle of my being. But the gold and flowing serpent is coiling up again, to sleep at the root of my tree.

'So let the boat carry me. Tomorrow is another day.'

NOTES

These notes are informative rather than interpretative; they focus on classical, biblical, cultural and historical references, and on non-English vocabulary. For more detailed annotation and editorial histories of the stories in this volume, see the following Cambridge University Press editions of Lawrence's works: *Love Among the Haystacks and Other Stories*, ed. John Worthen, Cambridge University Press, Cambridge 1987; *The Woman Who Rode Away and Other Stories*, eds Dieter Mehl and Christa Jansohn, Cambridge University Press, Cambridge 1995.

1 (p. 3) *éclat*   flash, minor explosion (French)

2 (p. 4) *in perpetuum*   eternally (Latin)

3 (p. 13) *King Charles' Head*   Charles 1, King of England, beheaded by Cromwell's army in 1649; to understand this reference, see Charles Dickens, *David Copperfield* (1850), where Mr Dick is obsessed by 'King Charles the First's Head'

4 (p. 17) *'And see the coloured counties'*   from the poem 'A Shropshire Lad' (1896), xxi, by A. E Housman (1859–1936)

5 (p. 32) *Tant de bruit pour une omelette*   literally, so much noise over an omelette; a fuss about nothing (French)

6 (p. 33) *Lady of Shalott*   poem (1832) by Alfred, Lord Tennyson (1809–92)

7 (p. 36) *dégagé*   free and easy, untrammelled (French)

8 (p. 47) *Arras*   town in Northern France, north-east of Paris; the site of a major First World War battle, 9 April–5 May 1917, during which the Allied Forces sustained severe losses but gained some strategic advantage

9 (p. 49) *rococo*   A phase of decorative and ornamentative art originating *c.* 1700 in France during the reign of Louis XV, emphasising lightness, elegance and delicacy

10 (p. 49) *old Saxe and Capo di Monte figurines*   Old Saxe: a region of Germany, where rococo was later and more hybrid in style than the above. Capo di Monte: a village north of Naples, first producing porcelain in the reign of King Charles III of Naples, *c.* 1740 (white artefacts painted with colourful folk figures, landscapes or flowers)

11   (p. 51) *like Peter when the cock crew*   Matthew 26:33–75; Luke 22: 34–62

12   (p. 55) *conservative anarchist*   Anarchism is the political belief that society should be a free association of all its members, without established government, law, police or other forms of authority.

13   (p. 56) *maquereau*   pimp (French)

14   (p. 62) *Philistine . . . temple down*   The Philistines were enemies of the Hebrews and reviled as intellectually and artistically uncivilised. In the Old Testament, Samson pushes down the pillars of the temple, destroying them and himself: Judges 13–16.

15   (p. 75) *winrows*   lines of drying hay

16   (p. 77) *Ich bin . . . Christ allein*   childhood prayer: 'I am small, my heart is pure / There is no one in it but Christ alone' (German)

17   (p. 86) *Nation*   a quality weekly paper, price sixpence in 1911, which Lawrence read, and which printed some of his early work

18   (p. 102) *câline*   soft, sweet, caressible (French)

19   (p. 109) *some Etruscan woman*   Etruscan civilisation appeared in central Italy in the eighth century BC and endured until the first century BC, when it was absorbed into the Roman Empire. D. H. Lawrence's *Etruscan Places* was published in 1932.

20   (p. 109) *a Leonardo woman*   Leonardo da Vinci (1452–1519), most renowned artist and polymath of the Italian Renaissance

21   (p. 109) *like Mona Lisa*   famously enigmatic painting by Leonardo da Vinci, early sixteenth century, hanging in the Louvre (Paris)

22   (p. 110) *Bacchante*   female priest or votaress of the wine god Bacchus (Dionysos), partaking in orgiastic / bloody ceremonies and celebrations

23   (p. 110) *Queen Anne house*   term applied (loosely, given that Anne's reign was 1702–14) to red-brick houses and their decoration between *c.*1660 and *c.*1720

24   (p.110) *one of the Inns*   Inns of Court, London

25   (p. 115) *the Circe!*   Greek sorceress who, in Homer's *Odyssey* (Book X), turns Odysseus and his companions into swine

26   (p. 116) *Renoir . . . But not Rousseau*   Pierre Auguste Renoir (1841–1919), French Impressionist painter; Henri (or Le Douanier) Rousseau (1844–1910), modern Primitivist painter

27   (p. 119) *in cock*   as in haycock, a conical heap of hay

28   (p. 120) *Caro . . . l'hai visto!*   My dear, my dear, you did not see him! (Italian)

29 (p. 120) *Bravo . . . mai, mai!* Well done, yes, very well done, poor little thing, but he will never, ever, ever be a man like you! (Italian)

30 (p. 120) *Cara . . . un'anima umana* My dear, my most beautiful dear, I have waited for you as one in agony waits for death, delicious death, almost too delicious for a human soul (Italian)

31 (p. 120) *Jesuit* Roman Catholic order, The Society of Jesus, founded by Ignatius Loyola in 1534

32 (p. 128) *'cornemuse'* a horn-pipe, early form of the bagpipe

33 (p. 138) *Sansovino* horse which won the Derby and the Prince of Wales' Stakes at Ascot in 1924

34 (p. 140) *Nat Gould* Nathaniel Gould (1857–1919), popular journalist, novelist and racing pundit

35 (p. 149) *Abraham* God's promises to Abraham (Genesis 17:16) and to his grandson Jacob: 'I will surely do thee good, and make thy seed as the sand of the sea, which cannot be numbered for multitude' (Genesis 32:12)

36 (p. 151) *Gaul* Brittany, North-Western France

37 (p. 151) *Hesperides* the Isles of the Blessed, where the three daughters of Hesperus guarded the golden apples given as a wedding present to the goddess Hera (Greek mythology)

38 (p. 153) *Hermes* messenger and herald of the gods, and patron of travellers (Greek mythology)

39 (p. 155) *scarab* ancient Egyptian images of the scarab or dungbeetle were held in reverence as types of the sun-god

40 (p. 157) *one of the lean kine of Egypt* Pharoah's dream, interpreted by Joseph, in which the seven thin cows denote seven years of famine to come (Genesis 41: 1–32)

41 (p. 159) *Orion* a clear constellation of the northern winter sky, named after the great hunter slain by Diana and metamorphosed into a group of stars (Greek mythology)

42 (p. 160) *Sirius* the dog-star, after the Greek *seirios*, 'hot and scorching'

43 (p. 160) *ennui* boredom, particularly that associated with the modern condition

44 (p. 171) *wraith* spectral appearance of someone still living, presaging their imminent death

45 (p. 173) *The Man Who Died* Chapter One is an extended allusion to the story of Christ's resurrection and journey on the

road to Emmaus, as told in the Gospels of the New Testament. The story's original title was 'The Escaped Cock'.

46 (p. 181) *'Don't touch me, Madeleine'* 'Noli me tangere' (see Chapter Two of the story), the words of Christ to Mary Magdalene after his resurrection (John 20:17)

47 (p. 189) *'As Elijah the Prophet, he shall go up in a glory'* Elijah, the Old Testament prophet who preaches against wickedness, and is taken into heaven in a chariot of fire at his death (I Kings 17–19 and II Kings 2:11, and II Chronicles 21:12–15)

48 (p. 190) *Isis* principal goddess of ancient Egypt, sister and wife of Osiris, associated with the discovery and cultivation of wheat and barley and therefore seen by J. G. Frazer (*The Golden Bough*) as a 'corn-goddess'. Isis was worshipped in Roman culture as a more spiritual figure, a 'queen' of nature representing purity and sanctity, the loyal wife and the tender mother.

49 (p. 193) *Isis Bereaved, Isis in Search* When Osiris, ancient Egyptian god of fertility, offspring of sky and earth, suffered a violent death at the hands of his brother and companions, Isis set out to find his dismembered body and, through ritual, to resurrect him to become King of the Underworld.

50 (p. 193) *Antony* Mark Antony, triumvir of the Roman Empire who fought with Octavius Caesar for control of the empire around 40BC. Antony's downfall was said to be caused by his fatal attraction to Cleopatra, Queen of Egypt.

51 (p. 194) *to Venus* Roman goddess of beauty and sensual love

52 (p. 195) *hodden* coarse, undyed homespun woollen cloth

53 (p. 197) *scrip* a small bag, wallet or satchel, especially one carried by a pilgrim or beggar

54 (p. 201) *all-tolerant Pan* the universal pagan deity of the Greeks, and the woodland god of the Romans

55 (p. 208) *'On this rock I built my life'* an allusion to Matthew 16:18 – 'Thou art Peter, and upon this rock I will build my church . . .'